# JAZZ MOON

## JOE OKONKWO

KENSINGTON BOOKS
www.kensingtonbooks.com

KENSINGTON BOOKS are published by

Kensington Publishing Corp.
119 West 40th Street
New York, NY 10018

All Kensington titles, imprints, and distributed lines are available at special quantity discounts for bulk purchases for sales promotion, premiums, fund-raising, educational, or institutional use.

Special book excerpts or customized printings can also be created to fit specific needs. For details, write or phone the office of the Kensington Sales Manager: Kensington Publishing Corp., 119 West 40th Street, New York, NY 10018. Attn. Sales Department. Phone: 1-800-221-2647.

Kensington and the K logo Reg. U.S. Pat. & TM Off.

eISBN-13: 978-1-4967-0117-6
eISBN-10: 1-4967-0117-8
First Kensington Electronic Edition: June 2016

ISBN-13: 978-1-4967-0116-9
ISBN-10: 1-4967-0116-X
First Kensington Trade Paperback Printing: June 2016

10 9 8 7 6 5 4 3 2 1

Printed in the United States of America

## Advance praise for Joe Okonkwo

"Joe Okonkwo is an incredibly unique new voice and a very familiar one at the same time. His haunting style is reminiscent of Richard Wright, James Baldwin, and Gabriel García Márquez. *Jazz Moon* is an elegantly written gift and a stunning literary debut. The characters are so vibrant and precise! The delicate plot about race, jazz, betrayal, and sex in early Harlem and Paris snatched me and held me hostage until the very last sentence."

—Mary Monroe, *New York Times* bestselling author

"Okonkwo's sweeping debut novel combines the rich history of jazz's golden age with the emotional turmoil of an African American male coming to terms with his sexuality."

—*Library Journal*

"*Jazz Moon* has it all: drama, intrigue, sex and romance, crime, drugs, alcohol, poetry, blues, love and betrayal, ecstatic joy, lost dreams, regrets, and redemption. It is a richly human and poignant story about all of us. With commitment and compassion, the author deposits the reader back in time as he takes us on a roller-coaster ride of human experiences and emotions. He conjures an alluring, nostalgic, sentimental, but also tragic atmosphere of black gay Harlem and Paris during the heyday of the Jazz Age. Through its emotionally and psychologically complicated protagonist, an aspiring poet named Ben Charles, the narrative dramatizes what we already know, or more precisely, what we think we know about Harlem and Paris during the 1920s."

—James Smalls, PhD, author of *Gay Art* and *The Homoerotic Photography of Carl Van Vechten: Public Face, Private Thoughts*

"*Jazz Moon* is an unexpected and original grand romance: sweeping, evocative, and colorful. Okonkwo is an author to enjoy now and watch in the future."

—Felice Picano

*To Howard*

Love hath the voice of the storm at night.

—*Paul Laurence Dunbar*

A man shalt not lie with a man, as with a woman.
It is an abomination: They shall surely be put to death.

—*Leviticus 18:22*

I ain't never heard of such shit!

—*Bessie Smith*

# this thing
## 1925

Harlem had been hit by a hurricane: It was raining cats and jazz. White folks called it *race music*. Old colored folks branded it the *devil's music* because its saucy beats made men pump their hips in slow pirouettes and women lift their skirts above the knee with a sweltering look that said *come and get it, papa.* But, whatever you called it, it was everywhere. Gliding out of glossy nightclubs; smoking lush and torrid out of basement speakeasies; in the streets, louder than a growling subway train. And if you ventured down Lenox Avenue or 125th Street, you wouldn't be surprised to pass a first-floor apartment, window open, and glimpse a couple dancing as jazz crackled out of a phonograph. You'd stand on that sidewalk—right outside their window—and watch them for a while, but they wouldn't even notice you.

In 1925 the devil did his best work in Jungle Alley—a stretch of 133rd Street between Lenox and Seventh Avenues splattered with glittering clubs where Duke Ellington brushstroked his jazz canvas, café au lait chorus cuties high-kicked it, and a hoofing Bojangles took and shook center stage. Clubs gorged themselves on white swells from downtown drawn to the *sensual,* the *primitive,* the *exotic;* who, after seeing a Cole Porter musical on Broadway or a Verdi opera at The Met, cabbed it to Harlem in droves to slum to the tune of "Sweet Georgia Brown" and romp in the jungle of their uptown backyard.

The swells paid good money to see Negroes sing and dance in supper clubs, but drew the line at sharing supper, which is why Ben and Angeline, arm in arm, half walking, half prancing up Seventh Avenue, didn't bother with the clubs in Jungle Alley. They bypassed 133rd Street altogether and shot onto 136th instead, laughing like fools the whole time.

"You have a good time, Angel?" Ben asked.

"Ooh, baby," Angeline said between giggles. "That party was jumping. Hot, hot, hot."

"Yeah. Donny Boy know how to swing it."

"Where'd he learn to cook? Them pig's feet and black-eyed peas reminded me of back home," Angeline said.

They rollicked down 136th. The street was besieged with people leaving rent parties, clubs, picture shows, most laughing like Ben and Angeline, some downright drunk, and you could smell reefer everywhere. An eternal line of brownstones rose above them on either side of the street, high flights of steps with black wrought-iron railings ascending to stoops where people talked and drank. Folks hung out of windows or sat on fire escapes and shouted down to the people on the stoops or to passersby on the sidewalk as taxis streaked by.

And it was *hot*. Two a.m. and the July air was so humid and thick, Ben felt he was wading through it. He was tempted to loosen his tie for some relief, but on Saturday night he wanted to shine.

"Ben, you remember where we going? What's this lap joint called?" Angeline asked.

"Teddy's. All the hepcats go there. Reggie told me about it. Says the band's a killer-diller."

"That's great, baby, but maybe we should go on home and kill some dill in private." They walked side by side, but she managed to nudge her breasts against him. "If you know what I mean."

"Girl, you a mess."

They heard the music before they even descended the short flight of steps to the basement bar. The rough, concrete floor held two dozen rickety tables crushed in close together and filled with boisterous men in tight suits and chicks in beaded dresses and pearl-studded headbands. The air was steeped in smoke from cigars, cigarettes, and reefer. The July heat made it steam. Teddy's vibrated with the clinking of glasses and rousing conversations and torrents of laughter. At the rear of the club, a band: piano, drums, banjo, and trombone beating it out and how. A bit of light hit the stage with the rest of Teddy's smothered in shadows.

"Hello, suckers!" the hostess greeted them, voice thundering, her abundant frame housed in a loose-fitting black dress decked with an ocean of multicolored beads and sequins. The low-cut number showed off her big breasts. A horsehair wig decorated with a red rose sat atop her head, and she carried a fluffy, red feather boa around her ample shoulders.

"Welcome to Teddy's," she said, "where the jazz is hot and the liquor's bootleggin' cold! Just y'all two tonight? Ooh, girl, where'd you find this cat? If I was you, I wouldn't come in here. I'd take him home and blow his . . . top."

"Honey, I'ma do just that!" Angeline said. "A couple of drinks and we out of here."

Ben slung her an admonishing look. She knew he didn't favor such graphic talk in public.

The hostess laughed. A big, robust guffaw. "Girl, I heard that! Y'all come with me."

She got between them, hooked her arms in theirs, and guided them to a table. A woman appeared onstage just as they sat down, singing in a raspy, down-home voice, the kind that made you think she *was* the blues.

> *"My man sho ain't lazy,*
> *He goes all day and works downtown.*
> *My man sho ain't lazy,*
> *He goes all day and works downtown.*
> *When he comes home at night,*
> *I make him turn my damper down."*

A waitress arrived at the table. In her sleeveless satin dress with its thigh-high hem, she looked like a chorus girl in one of those all-colored musical revues. She carried a tray with two teacups, which

she placed before Ben and Angeline. They each took a big gulp of
*tea*. It sent a shudder from their eyebrows to their toes.

Ben recovered first. "This some good damn tea." His voice was
hoarse.

"Righteous," Angeline said. "Benny?" She tickled her knee against
his under the table. "Benny," she said again, her voice a cross between
an innocent coo and a seductive purr. "Can't wait to get you home."

The spot where she rubbed his knee burned. Without warning,
she leaned over and kissed him, rough, her tongue flicking over his
lips. Ben didn't like doing this in front of people, but had no choice
but to respond in kind.

"Yeah, man!" someone behind them yelled. "You go on and
kiss that chick!"

Others chimed in, cheering them on as they kissed.

"Mmm-hmm. That's his main queen. I can see that!"

"She sure is! And she a good piece of barbecue!"

"That chick sure is some fine dinner!"

The crowd whooped and applauded as if Ben and Angeline
were the opening act of a floor show. He jerked away from her,
leaving her reeling from the sudden stop. He was embarrassed, but
intoxicated, too. The gin. The crowd. The salty funk of sweat and
the odor of reefer wafting through the place. And now the real
show began as the hostess mounted the stage, big breasts leading
the way, dress rustling as she climbed the steps.

"Hey, suckers! How y'all doing tonight? Everybody got enough
*tea*? Glad to hear it 'cause at Teddy's it's always teatime. But you
know what, honey? I need me a man to pour my tea—right out of a
nice, long *spout*. You know that's right! If you know a man got a
good spout, you send him right on over. And if he ain't got a good
spout, tell him to keep his ass home with his wife! And if anyone
here tonight got a good spout, you come see me in the back room!
Mmm-hmm. Well, suckers, we got a good show for y'all tonight, so
let's get started. Ladies and gentlemens, Teddy's is proud to present
to y'all The Blackberry Jam featuring Sweeeeeeet Baby Back Johnston!"

The light dimmed more. The audience clapped. Ben watched as
a cat with a trumpet came up onstage and began to play.

Mellow. That was the only word Ben could think of to describe Baby Back Johnston. No fanfare like Armstrong. Just a sound that was blue and smooth. One moment it floated up with the reefer smoke, the next it was low down. Baby Back took that horn through a swirling maze of rhythm as the band underscored his every lick. He caressed those flats and sharps, fondled those swinging eighth notes, fingered that melody till it cried. Yeah. Baby Back broke it *up*. The crowd fell out. Ben was hypnotized. Hypnotized by Baby Back's horn. A horn attached to a face coffee-colored and soft as polish. A tall man, his broad shoulders flared down to a trim waist accentuated by his tight suit. His eyes were shut, lightly, as he blew. As he blew. That. Horn.

The lights brightened a little when Baby Back's set ended.

*"Ben. Benny."*

Someone called out to him from far away, from the edge of someplace.

"Benny!"

Ben bounced back to consciousness.

"What's the matter, baby?" Angeline asked. "You clocked out for a minute. You OK?"

"Sure, Angel. Just knocked out by this band. This trumpeter is . . . something."

Then the trumpeter appeared, glad-handing from table to table. "Hey, how y'all doing? Baby Back Johnston. Y'all enjoying the show? Thank you. Nice to meet you. Y'all come back to Teddy's, hear?"

He schmoozed and joked and flirted his way through the club with a devilish smile and brilliant eyes that muted just a shade when they fell on Ben.

"Baby Back Johnston. How y'all doing?" His voice reverberated, a plush baritone.

"We're pretty solid," Ben said as the trumpeter clasped his hand. When Ben tried to retrieve it, Baby Back held on a second longer than he should have. "You sure can play."

"All in a night's work."

"Ben Charles. My wife, Angeline."

"My husband's right," Angeline said. "You can play."

Baby Back's eyes found Ben and clung to him. "What do you folks do?"

"Angeline does hair."

"And sells cosmetics," she said. "Little side business."

"I work in a hotel. Downtown. Waiting tables," Ben said, then lowered his head. "But I'm really a writer. Poetry."

The devilish smile stretched Baby Back's face till it was as broad as his shoulders. "Killer. Anything published?"

"One thing in *The Crisis*. And I just sent something to a new magazine called *Fire* that's starting up."

From the corner of his eye, Ben saw Angeline's bottom lip quiver. A subtle twitch nobody but himself would notice, especially in the speakeasy's murky light.

"Benny," Angeline said. She scooted her chair closer and draped her arms around him. "Mr. Johnston's a busy cat. He don't want to hear about your poetry, even though I know he'd love it. He needs to get back to work." She relaxed her head on Ben's shoulder, then trained her eyes on Baby Back. "Ain't that right, Mr. Johnston?"

Baby Back looked down at her. "Please. It's Baby Back. And I'd love to hear about Ben's poetry. Next time you come, recite one for me."

All three got quiet. Angeline pulled herself closer to her husband till she was almost in his lap. Ben's eyes alternated between Baby Back's face and the teacup in front of him, but he knew the musician's eyes kept steady on him.

"My next set's about to start," Baby Back said. "Sure was nice meeting you folks. Hope to see you again soon."

He got back onstage. The lights dimmed again and the band flung itself into a raucous dance number, the notes from Baby Back's trumpet ricocheting off the walls. The hostess shimmied out in front of the stage holding a tea kettle.

"All right, suckers! Party time!"

The patrons unleashed a holler and, as if on cue, stood up and let loose, kicking up the Charleston, the Mess Around, the Black Bottom, while the hostess ambled deftly through the ruckus filling teacups, her big hips swerving in rhythm like a metronome. More folks piled into Teddy's, clowning, smoking reefer, and chugging out of teacups faster than the hostess could replenish them. Men bumped and grinded against women whose breasts were thrust forward, arms hoisted above their heads, heat sparkling in their eyes.

Ben and Angeline did not dance. Her head still snuggled against him. And his eyes stayed glued to the stage, to the trumpeter whose licks whizzed out of his horn like fireworks.

# 2

Three a.m. when they cut out of Teddy's. She had been set on getting home, but once outside the smoky speakeasy, Angeline allowed them to take their time. Warmed by the tea-kettle gin, jazz still chiming in their ears, they strolled hand in hand down Seventh Avenue, stopping every so often to giggle or talk or so Angeline could smooth down the lapels of Ben's jacket and straighten his tie so the knot didn't veer to the side as the knots of all his ties tended to.

"You know, Benny," she said, "it's been a long time since we . . ." She gave his tie a final nudge, then her lips drifted to his cheek and lingered there.

It was his fault they hadn't been intimate in so long. He'd make it up to her tonight. Try to.

By three thirty they had turned onto 128th Street and moments later scaled the stone steps to their four-story brownstone. As Ben fumbled in his pocket for the keys, Angeline took him from behind, turned him around, and kissed him as if they had already made it to their bedroom.

"Angeline," Ben said, withdrawing from her for the second time that evening. "The neighbors gonna see us."

"No they ain't, neither. That no-good super still ain't fixed this porch light. Remind me to thank him."

She resumed kissing him.

"Humph. You need to be thankful for not getting struck down with lightning."

Ben and Angeline froze mid-kiss.

"I've never seen such behavior in all my life. Practically having relations right on the front stoop. And at almost four in the morning, to boot."

With the porch light out and their heads swimming in bootleg gin, Ben and Angeline had been unaware of anyone else's presence. But the person sharpened into focus now: an old colored woman with white hair done up in plaits. Their next-door neighbor: Mrs. Evelyn Harrisburg. She sat in a wicker chair, hand hooked onto the head of her walking stick, facing straight ahead onto 128th Street. Upright, stolid. In the darkness, her silhouette resembled the statue of a goddess sitting in judgment.

Ben squirmed away from Angeline. "Mrs. Harrisburg, what you doing out here at this hour?"

"Snooping," Angeline said. "As usual. What you think she doing?"

"I'm not snooping," Evelyn Harrisburg said, without facing them. Her voice was scratchy. "I'm sitting here, minding my own business."

Angeline stepped toward the old lady. "You never mind your own business."

Though feeble, Mrs. Harrisburg was everywhere and heard everything. Terrified that she would abruptly materialize, folks kept conversations in the hallways short and scandal-free. Even *good morning* or *doin' fine, child* were sometimes whispered.

She gave Angeline a once-over. "In my day, proper young ladies didn't go gallivanting out in public wearing dresses that showed off their bare legs and arms. We called that type of women *jezebels.*"

Angeline balled her hands into fists, fixed them to her hips, and started toward the old woman. Ben intercepted her and then crouched by Evelyn Harrisburg's chair.

"Tell you what, Mrs. Harrisburg. Let me help you upstairs," he said, offering his hand.

She slapped it away. "I can't go inside. I can't. I won't! I won't! I won't! They're playing that devil's music. The folks right above me. Been playing it and partying all night. Hollering and stomping like they don't have a bit of sense. Inconsiderate. If my late husband was here, he'd go up there and tell them a thing or two." She paused. "God bless his dear soul."

Angeline rolled her eyes. "That's it. This jezebel's going in. Ben, if I was you, I'd leave her ass there." From the front door, she looked back. "Don't take too long, Benny, you hear?" She pursed her lips in a kiss, then disappeared into the building, slim hips bumping.

"Tell you what," Ben said to Mrs. Harrisburg. "I'll ask the folks to turn the music down. Let's go inside."

She nodded and took his arm. During the slow tramp up the stairs, he pondered how someone who moved with such difficulty could be everywhere hearing people's gossip. From above, he heard a phonograph, full-throated laughter, and the pounding of dancing feet. Mrs. Harrisburg stopped and sniffed the air.

"They're still cooking up that stinky, Southern food."

Ben inhaled the scent of collard greens and chitterlings, and was famished. They continued their haul up the stairs. "You know what?" Ben said. "You ain't lived till you had a good plate of chitterlings."

"That mess is for ignorant, backwoods niggers from down South, not civilized folks."

Angeline was right: He should have left her on the stoop.

"They come up here by the trainload," Mrs. Harrisburg said, "with their Uncle Tom ways and their bad English and their stinky food. They make respectable colored folks look bad."

She became stoic again and her pace waned as she took the stairs like a soon-to-be martyr ascending a scaffold. They finally reached the second floor and arrived at the old lady's door. The party sounds from up above were clearer, the smell of collard greens potent.

She held on to his arm. "You go up there and tell them to stop that noise."

"I'll go up there now and ask them."

"No. You *tell* them."

Then she stepped into her apartment and slammed the door.

Ben walked up to the third floor and to the door of the offending neighbors. With all their cackling, singing, and shouting, Ben didn't know how his request would be received. He raised his hand to knock and stopped cold. A record played behind the door: a sweet ballad, a trumpet soloing through it, the notes dipping and diving and weaving in and out. Suddenly that trumpeter—the one from earlier—*Baby Back*—suddenly Baby Back's face flooded Ben's eyes and he couldn't bring himself to knock. He descended the stairs to his apartment. *Angeline's waiting.*

He drew a few breaths—to brace himself—and went inside.

# 3

Ben climbed out of the subway at East Twentieth-eighth Street and headed west towards Madison Avenue. He was downtown, well outside the safe zone of Harlem. For a Negro, and especially a Negro *man,* that required that he carry himself differently. Not with his head held too high since the last thing whites wanted to see was an uppity Negro, too haughty to realize his place. But not with his head down, an Uncle Tom. So he kept his chin level, his eyes straight ahead, his pace moderate.

He turned onto Madison and then onto Twenty-ninth, a street booming with skyscrapers that housed insurance companies, banks, law firms. Luxury hotels—the swankiest in Manhattan—peppered the area. As Ben continued on Twenty-ninth, one of them—all twenty-five stories of it—soared into view. The Pavilion Hotel. Consummate luxury. From its marble-floored lobby to its cavernous and voluptuously decorated suites, all catering to the preposterously wealthy. Gentlemen strolled the banquet halls in top hats and tails, jeweled cuff links gleaming on their sleeves. Women draped themselves in mink or ermine or fox and drenched their necks and limbs in their gem of choice: diamond, emerald, sapphire—whatever complemented the color scheme of their outfit or their mood.

The Pavilion's enormous dining hall buzzed. The smell of breakfast swam through the room: airy smells of fruit and pastry, the hearty aroma of bacon. But sound dominated. Silverware clinked against custom-made china; gurgling beverages from crystal pitchers and silver coffee urns vied with the Haydn sonatas gamboling out of the grand piano. The genteel babble of the patrons' voices lilted on the air, voices constrained and controlled. A lady held a gloved hand to her mouth when she laughed. A gentleman made his point by arching his eyebrows rather than his volume.

Ben moved about the dining hall delivering food and filling and refilling beverages, his service tight and efficient. But a sprint invigorated his step and carried him to a table near the center of the dining hall where his favorite customer waited.

"Morning, Mr. Kittredge." He poured tea. "How you doing?"

The man looked up from a leather-bound book. His serious eyes lightened; a smile sprawled across his face.

"Benjamin! My dear boy, the question, really, is how are *you?* Last we spoke, you and your wife were going to be—how did you phrase it?—painting the town red." Mr. Kittredge plopped two sugar cubes into his tea and stirred. "So. Is the town any redder than it was prior to last Saturday evening?"

His English accent was aristocratic, but less pretentious than many of the Brits Ben had served. He sounded like a real person, not a stuff-shirt. As one of the hotel's more elite patrons, he maintained long-term quarters there.

"Sir, I'm happy to report that it *is* a little bit redder," Ben said.

"I take it you've recovered sufficiently. Or did you have too much . . . ?" Mr. Kittredge pantomimed drinking from a bottle.

"Mr. Kittredge," Ben said, in a mock-offended tone, "that's illegal. I'm much too charming and innocent to be doing something like that."

"Dear boy, you are indeed charming, but I have the very distinct impression that you are far from innocent."

Mr. Kittredge's smile exposed lines around his eyes and mouth that suggested his age as fifty or so. His brown hair and mustache—precisely cut, meticulously styled—were stippled with crumbs of gray. He was handsome. For a white guy.

He ordered a bowl of grapefruit and half an English muffin. Ben brought the meal and then refilled his Earl Grey tea.

"Anything else, sir?"

"No. That will be all."

Ben nodded and made to go.

"Oh, Benjamin. I almost forgot." Kittredge reached inside his coat pocket and drew out a small vial of perfume. An intricate pattern of vines and flowers encrusted the glass. The stopper was in the shape of a golden rosebud. "I bought it to take back to my wife in England, but I doubt if she'll approve of it. She never seems to approve of the fragrances I choose." He handed the vial to Ben. "Take it. Give it to your wife. Angeline, isn't it?"

"Yes. Angeline. But, Mr. Kittredge, I—" He stopped himself, then accepted the perfume. He had never held anything so classy. "Thank you. Thank you very much, sir."

"You're welcome, dear boy."

The Englishman went back to his book and his grapefruit. Ben pocketed the perfume, the most extravagant thing he'd ever been given. He resumed his duties, feeling like a rich man.

The quiet and cool of the staff dressing room welcomed him after the long day submitting to rich, exacting whites. He sat in a prehistoric wingback chair, a remnant from the hotel's past, that used to occupy a suite. Still in his uniform, Ben reeked of food and cigar smoke. He couldn't wait to get home and wash.

After bathing, he would present the perfume to Angeline. He closed his eyes and concentrated on what he'd do after they'd undressed, after she'd dribbled the perfume on her breasts, neck, between her legs. He would have to let her take control. He envisioned her tumbling him onto his back, easing herself down, onto him. *Concentrate.* But he would fatigue rapidly. He always did. He never had enough momentum to fully please her. But since he had begun concentrating *now,* a couple of hours early, then maybe by the time he saw her . . .

The dressing room door swung open.

"Ben! Hey, jack! What do you say?"

Reggie the bellhop. A rumbling spark of restless energy. Twenty, hip, handsome, and proud to death of all three. He stood in the doorway, eyes scintillating with mischief. A short man rendered clownish in his big bellhop uniform with all of its military-style epaulets and regal gold braid.

He inspected Ben. "You look sadder than a map, jack."

Ben laughed. "Boy, get in here and close that door."

Reggie jumped up onto a haggard chair with a missing arm. "Why you look so ragged?"

"I'm tired."

"Tired? Listen, you don't know the least bit of nothing about tired till you've been toting white folks' suitcases all day."

"I know about running back and forth and all around fetching food for them. Try that. That'll tire you out."

Reggie jumped down. "Now that's some off-time jive. You can't tell me carrying a tray of food's harder than carrying a damn trunk."

"Reggie, I started here as a bellhop. I know how it is."

Reggie removed his high-collared jacket and revealed a blemish that seared his skin just below the neckline. Even with his dark complexion, it flashed red and angry.

"Boy, what is that on your neck?" Ben said.

"What can I say? The girl the other night got a little wild on me."

"Jadine?"

"Oh, hell no. I nixed that chick."

"Leslie?"

"Nixed her, too."

"Sandra?"

The bellhop grabbed his chest as if he'd been bashed by a heart attack. "No, jack! You're killing me! I'm talking about Lila. She's my main queen now." He removed his shirt. Muscle padded the shoulders, arms, and pectorals of his slim, trim body. "Met Lila at Teddy's." He whipped his trousers down, stepped out of them, and tossed them into his locker, all in one fleet move. "You know—that joint I told you about."

Ben's face heated as he watched him. "Went there Saturday."

"Does that joint jump or what? And they got this new trumpeter. Man, he is solid murder with his horn! Was he there?"

Reggie stood directly in front of Ben in only his undershorts. A hoard of sweat gathered on Ben's chin.

"Yeah. Baby Back Johnston. He was there," he said.

The love bite snagged Ben's eye again. Reggie's body odor breezed off him, strong, but not unpleasant. Back at his locker, Reggie stripped off his shorts. His ass—small and buoyant—defied gravity. It jiggled a little as he rummaged in his locker. Ben looked away and busied himself with the removal of his own uniform.

But his eyes kept lurking back, watching as Reggie spread powder on his underarms, then doused himself with fragrance—something harsh and alcohol-smelling. Reggie dressed himself as methodically as a valet would a rich man. First a clean pair of shorts followed by socks, which he clipped to garters halfway up his calves. Then a fresh undershirt that he tucked into his shorts. A crisp white shirt followed, the sleeves creased sharp enough to slice. On went his pinstriped pants: black, pleated, and cuffed. Next up: a tie, midnight-blue, knotted with such exactitude, you'd need a map to undo it. Cuff links— imitation gold, Ben could tell, but nice enough. Two-toned shoes—black and white—burnished to a fierce shine. The double-breasted suit jacket created a svelte contour. Reggie topped off his ensemble with a fedora, the brim angling down in debonair *fash*. He spent minutes styling it, then several more preening.

"Where you off to in these fine threads on a Monday?" Ben said. "Seeing Lila?"

"No, jack. She's my weekend chick."

"I thought you said she was your main queen."

"She is. But I branch out Monday to Friday. Well, Ben, as usual, it's been a pleasure. I'll plant you now and dig you later."

Reggie strutted out the door like a bouncy peacock.

And Ben exhaled, relieved. He removed the perfume from his pants pocket and shut his eyes tight. "Come on. Concentrate, damn it."

He tried to excite himself by imagining the places Angeline would dab the fragrance.

*Breasts. Neck. Between her legs.*

4

*I got love runnin' through me,*
*Like a river,*
*Like wine,*
*Like sweet jazz in an uptown dive.*
*Runs through me, and through me, and through me.*

*May I kiss your pretty cheek?*
*May I kiss your pretty lips?*
*Your pretty hips?*
*Be my beauty,*
*'Cause I got love runnin' through me.*

The poem was Angeline's anniversary gift, although not a surprise:
He always composed a poem for their anniversary. It started when
he told her about Shakespeare's mysterious Dark Lady—the inspiration for many of his sonnets.

"Well," Angeline had told him, "I'm a dark lady. And I'm mysterious. So you can start writing poems for me."

She now bragged to the ladies at the beauty shop that her husband immortalized her in verse, declared to her friends that she
was the muse of a great *artiste.*

"I don't hear that typewriter!" she hollered from their bedroom. "I know you ain't finished writing my poem yet."

"Just taking a break, Angel. Can't rush great art."

Angeline swept into the living room, pivoting around and modeling her new dress: a creamy white, sleeveless number made entirely of long strands of fringe. Her straightened hair was styled into the undulating curves of a marcel wave. She twirled into a statuesque pose: chin in the air, chest up, arms outstretched like a stage star at curtain call.

"How do you like it?" Her best temptress voice.

"It looks all right," Ben said, then began typing as he suppressed a laugh and waited for the explosion.

He didn't wait long.

The stage star pose disintegrated. Her hands sprang to her hips. "*All right?* Benjamin Marcus Charles, you did *not* tell me this dress—which took me six months to save up for—just looks *all right*. You better be writing some poems about this dress, 'cause it looks beautiful on me! Do you hear? Beautiful!"

Ben kept his head buried in his typewriter.

"Ben? You listening to me? BEN!"

He looked up. "You say something, Angel?"

He tried to keep his face straight, but it cracked wide open and a snicker bounded out as Angeline hurled herself at him.

"I'm gonna kill you! I'm gonna make a widow out of myself right now!"

Ben imprisoned her on his lap as she swiped at him and laughed at the same time. They sat quietly when their fun subsided. Her perfume smelled of vanilla with a dash of rose—Mr. Kittredge's gift. A gold heart-shaped locket hung at her breast. She wore it every day. Angeline gazed at him, unblinking. He sensed desire swirling in her. He avoided her eyes, traced a random pattern on her thigh with his finger. He could feel her willing him to look at her. He didn't. Couldn't.

With a terse outtake of breath, she shifted to the typewriter and began to study the poem.

"Hey! Not yet," Ben said. "Not till next Saturday."

"Hush." She kept on reading.

He recalled the first time he sent a poem to a magazine. He had worked so hard, had been so sure it would be published. When it wasn't, he said he would give up writing. Angeline wouldn't let him.

"Shut up with that nonsense," she had said. "Work harder. Try again. And again. And again."

He did. Four months later, he had his first published poem.

Angeline smiled bigger with each verse of her anniversary poem. "I love it, Benny." She kissed him. "I love *you*."

She said it with a firmness that verged on a proclamation. Or a challenge he had to rise to. She awaited his response. Her tiny weight on his lap felt heavier, more intrusive than it should have. *I love you, too, Angeline.* The words should have come, and easily; she was his best friend after all. He wanted to be able to say the words, force them out if necessary, but they were thwarted by the tiny weight that threatened to crush him. He opened his mouth, then closed it, then went back to tracing the pattern on her thigh.

A battalion of chorines—all with café au lait complexions and *good* hair that fell about their shoulders like silk waterfalls—high-kicked a Tin Pan Alley number in front of the closed curtain. After their exit, the audience sat forward in their red velvet seats. A tall man in the balcony leaned over the gilded railing until threatened back into his chair by the woman behind him. Everyone awaited the main draw of the evening, what they'd endured the endless rounds of comedians and tap dancers and novelty acts to see.

People mumbled and fidgeted. The tension tingled. When the curtain rose revealing Florence Mills, the audience went senseless. Small as a schoolgirl, delicious as a pixie, she was costumed as a hobo against the painted backdrop of an open road. Hitchhiking Florence stuck her thumb out and sang "I'm a Little Blackbird Looking for a Bluebird," her voice as sweet as a cello. Later, she did "I'm Craving for *That* Kind of Love," starting mid stage, then vamping to the footlights in a slinky dress with a slit all the way up the waist. The crowd almost rioted.

Show over, the doors of the Lincoln Theater burst open and Ben, Angeline, and legions of folks splashed onto 132nd Street. Lights everywhere. Automobile headlights. Porch lights. Lights in store and restaurant windows and muted lights behind apartment drapes. Clara Bow's name lit up a movie theater marquee. JELLY ROLL MORTON AND HIS RED HOT PEPPERS gleamed above a nightclub. The street glowed. Even the sidewalk seemed to glimmer. And people were everywhere, ready for the next phase of their Saturday night. Ben and Angeline walked to Seventh Avenue, he in his best suit, she in her brand-new dress and hanging on her husband's arm. A flotilla of taxis streamed toward Jungle Alley, ferrying well-dressed whites from downtown, faces glued to the cab windows as they pointed and gawked at everything.

Angeline laughed quietly, almost to herself.

"What?" Ben said.

"Thinking about your poem:

> *I got love runnin' through me,*
> *Like a river,*
> *Like wine,*
> *Like sweet jazz in an uptown dive.*
> *Runs through me, and through me, and through me.*

It's the best poem you ever wrote, Benny."

She made to kiss him, but he evaded her, deftly, took her hand and continued walking, swinging her hand playfully as if to repent for the evaded kiss.

They meandered along 135th Street, undecided about where to go.

"Teddy's?" Ben said.

"I don't know. It's all right, but—"

"Angel, that hostess was a mess. And that band . . ." *That trumpet player. Baby Back.* "Come on, Angel. Teddy's? Please? For *me?*"

Packed beyond capacity, beyond reason, Teddy's convulsed with hepcat pandemonium. Guys shouted entire conversations to one another from opposite ends of the club. Waitresses scampered with trays overloaded with teacups. The hostess hustled and bustled her fat hips through the crowd, chatting up patrons and laughing garishly at everyone's jokes, especially her own. The band blasted with an intensity that was almost violent.

The hostess said they'd have to wait for a table, but someone yelled, "Ben! Ben! Angeline! Over here!"

Reggie sat at a table in back with a skinny tree limb of a woman wearing long ropes of fake pearls and a slew of bangles.

"Want y'all to meet my main queen," he said when they were seated.

Ben cut in. "You must be Lila. Reggie told me about you."

Reggie grimaced and, through gritted teeth, said, "No, jack. This is *Vivian*. You know, my *main* queen."

"Oh. Uh...I'm sorry. Lila is my *other* friend's...uh...girl-friend."

Angeline sped to his rescue. "He's terrible with names. Can't even remember mine half the time. I'm Angeline. How are you?"

"I'm gangbusters! How are you?" Vivian said, high-pitched and squeaky as a piccolo. The girl seesawed in her seat. Ben detected gin on her breath, and a hiccup confirmed that Reggie's main queen was drunk.

"Where y'all coming from?" Reggie asked.

Ben fluffed up. "The Lincoln. Just saw Florence Mills."

"Florence Mills? I bet the audience blew their wigs over her. Copasetic, jack!"

Vivian hiccupped. "Copasetic."

The club was busy, the waitresses harried, but within moments they had a round of teacups. The people in front of them blocked his view of the stage, but Ben could hear a trumpet capering through a song.

Reggie and Vivian sat close, his arm ringing her.

"You live in the neighborhood?" Angeline asked her.

"She sure do," Reggie said. "On 123rd. Ain't that right, baby girl?"

"That's right, papa."

"She calls me *papa*. Ain't that cute?"

Reggie and Vivian kissed, tongues lapping and overlapping. One of Reggie's hands sneaked under the table. Soon after, Vivian's eyes rolled back in her head.

"Ooh. Ooh. Papa," she tooted.

While Reggie toyed with his main queen, the band's violence segued into a blues. Sorrowful. Beguiling. The crowd had thinned a little, but Ben still couldn't see the band. The place had gotten quieter, the noise submersing into a drone. Ben heard the trumpet, at times sliding through the blues, other times driving it. And he could just make out the head of a girl singer.

> *"You better listen careful,*
> *You ain't treatin' me the way you should,*
> *You better listen careful,*
> *You ain't treatin' me the way you should.*
> *If you don't watch it, mister,*
> *I'll get my daddy's gun and shoot you good.*
>
> *You a low-down cheater,*
> *I ain't gonna take your stuff no more,*
> *You a low-down cheater,*
> *I ain't gonna take your stuff no more.*
> *I catch you with some floozy,*
> *I'll bash that bitch's head into the floor."*

The trumpet furnished an intricate obbligato that riffed off the singer's vocal. It punctuated it, added flavor and a bit of play.

"Hey, Ben," Reggie said. "Bought a new record. It's called—"

Vivian hunched over the table. "Papa? I don't feel good."

Angeline lurched her chair back. "Girl, don't you throw up on this table."

Reggie popped straight up. "Ha! That means it's time to take my baby girl home." He lifted Vivian from her seat, propped her up on wavering legs. "There, there, baby girl," he said. He petted her backside, his face set in a dark pout. "Let's go home." Turning to Ben and Angeline, he brightened like lightning. "It's been gang-busters! I'll plant y'all now and dig you later!"

As Reggie hauled Vivian out of Teddy's, the band dispensed with the inferno of dance music, ceased the vengeful no-good-man blues, and began something new. Something misty and whimsical, cloaked in a downy thread of blues, but not quite blues. The poet in Ben peeled back the bluesy threads and discovered a love song. The table in front of them had emptied, the crowd had dissipated, and he relished an unobstructed view of the band.

Baby Back's trumpet stepped lightly, carrying the melody, improvising and re-creating it as he went along, twisting and bending it to his will. Ben watched the trumpeter's face. There was nothing going on in Baby Back's world except that horn and that song as he manifested himself through his instrument.

Beautiful. So beautiful, Ben wanted to cry.

"Ben? Benny?" Angeline whispered in his ear, her voice edgy.

He had to strain his eyes away from Baby Back. He hoped she wouldn't see the tears in them. "Hey. How's my Angel?"

She glanced up. Something had caught her attention. A veil dropped over her face. Ben looked. Baby Back was approaching.

"Mr. Poet. Good to see you again."

Ben hung his head, bashful. "Nice playing. The band's outrageous."

"Thank you, sir." Baby Back nodded to Angeline. "Mrs. Poet."

"Mrs. *Charles,*" she said. She fingered the locket around her neck.

"Come again?"

"I'm Mrs. Charles. Ben's wife."

Angeline and Baby Back faced each other. She didn't blink.

"I apologize. Mrs. Charles."

"Oh, I forgive you. Just call me Angeline."

"I think I'll stick with Mrs. Charles."

Angeline affixed herself to Ben's arm. "Suit yourself."

The trumpeter stood thinking, as if strategizing a crucial move. He grabbed a chair from a nearby table, plunked it down, seated himself. "Mind if I join you?"

Ben smirked against his will. "Looks like you just did."

"We was just about to cut out," Angeline said.

Baby Back ignored her. He surveyed Ben with a grin, as if he adored what he saw. Made Ben warm with embarrassment. Made him giggle. He turned away, covered his mouth the way the fancy ladies at The Pavilion did when they laughed.

"You're shy," Baby Back said. "You're a shy guy."

Ben flushed even more, but not so much that he couldn't take in Baby Back's powerful body, his face that scored looks from all the chicks in the room. This Negro Adonis. This African Hercules.

"You married, Mr. Johnston?" Angeline said, startling Ben. Even though she cleaved to his arm, he had almost forgotten her.

Baby Back shook his head *no.*

"You mean to tell me a good-looking man like you ain't married?" She sounded a little desperate when she said, "Girlfriend?"

Baby Back's eyes stuck to Ben like printed words to a page. "No."

They sat in silence, Ben sweating, Angeline clinging, Baby Back cool and confident. His eyes never left Ben even as he yelled out, "Hey, Fanny!"

A waitress sashayed to the table as everyone in Teddy's took inventory of her hourglass shape: big and pushed up on top, slim through the torso, copious hips. She placed one hand on Baby Back's shoulder, the other on her hip, beaming.

"Yeah, honey?" Fanny said. "What can I do you out of?"

"Bring these folks a round of whiskey. On me."

Angeline piped in, her words rushing out. "We appreciate that. We really do, Mr. Johnston, but—"

Baby Back cut her off with a lordly wave of his hand. He nodded to Fanny, who left the table. Ben sensed Angeline's breathing quicken. The palms of her hands were so warm, the place on his arm where she gripped him was damp. Baby Back kept grinning and his eyes kept pawing him. Ben kept turning away, but couldn't resist turning back.

"How'd you get the name 'Baby Back'?" he asked, just to fill the silence.

"When I was a little kid, about three or four, I wandered off. My whole family searched for me. Finally found me in a cotton field crying my eyes out 'cause I thought I was lost forever. When they carried me home, my ma hugged me and kept saying over and over, 'I sho is glad I got my baby back.' Then she whipped my ass raw for running off. But 'Baby Back' stuck."

"What's your real name?"

Baby Back reached over, straightened the knot in Ben's tie. "I'll tell you when you know me better."

He took a long time with the knot. Prodding it, tinkering with it, pressing it just so. Ben felt the warmth from his hands, smelled his sweat. A finger strayed onto his neck, scalding him.

"How old are you, Mr. Poet?"

"Twenty-one. You?"

"Thirty-one. How long y'all been married? Got any kids?"

"Six years next week." Ben was whispering, didn't know why. "And no."

Baby Back finished with the tie. He sat back in his chair. His gaze shifted to Angeline, then back to Ben. "Married six years. And no kids. Now, what kind of folks is married six years and ain't got no kids?"

Angeline shut her eyes, turned away.

"We can't have them," Ben said.

Fanny reappeared with fresh teacups, placed them in front of Ben and Angeline, punched Baby Back playfully on the back, and sashayed away. Ben dove into his drink, grateful for the distraction from Baby Back's gaze. He drank half the whiskey in one gulp.

"You like playing Teddy's?"

"It's all right. Ain't really where I want to be."

"Where you really want to be?"

"Paris."

"Paris, France?" Ben said.

"Sure as hell don't mean Paris, Mississippi."

The men laughed. Angeline strangled Ben's arm so tight, it went limp. He wanted to unfasten her. He took another gulp of whiskey.

"When do you think you'll be leaving? For Paris?" Angeline said.

Baby Back laughed harder. "Looks like Mrs. Charles wants to get rid of me. She's hurting my feelings!"

Ben laughed, too. It billowed up and out before he could stop it. And once up and out, it multiplied. Soon they were laughing like silly schoolboys at a dirty joke. Angeline loosened her clutch on Ben's arm, enabling blood to flow again. She still held on to him, but her touch was a shadow of what it had been.

The schoolboys recovered.

"A lot going on for colored musicians in Paris," Baby Back said. "I'm saving money to go, but I'm hoping I get discovered by a promoter who'll take me there first."

Ben didn't know Baby Back at all, but the thought of his leaving devastated him. He finished off his whiskey and looked at Angeline's. She hadn't touched it. "You gonna drink this?" He didn't wait for a reply, but grabbed her teacup and threw back a long swallow. Then another. The whiskey galvanized him. He spoke and laughed and yelled out loud; invoked the coarse humor he normally spurned; shouted across the room when he spotted someone he thought he knew. He drank two more teacups that Baby Back ordered for him even as Angeline begged him not to.

"Now, when you was here last week," Baby Back said, "we decided you'd recite one of your poems next time you came. Well?"

"It's late," Angeline said in not even a voice, but a breath. "Ben. We need to go. Please."

"It ain't that late, Mrs. Charles," Baby Back bellowed. "Hell, it's Saturday night. You a square or something?" He barked out a volcanic laugh that made the table vibrate.

"My wife's a square!" Ben yelled through sputtering laughter. "Ain't that something? Angeline's a square!" He drank more whiskey.

Angeline rose from her seat and grabbed her purse.

"You leaving us, Mrs. Charles?" Baby Back said. "Good! That'll give me and Mr. Poet a chance to talk. All. By. Our. Selves."

Baby Back's velvet baritone resounded. The devilish smile smeared his face. Ben drained his drink. Angeline hesitated, then threw her purse on the table and reseated herself.

"Ben don't recite his poems for strangers. And besides—"

Baby Back talked over her. "I want my poem!"

*My poem.* Ben felt himself sink. A drop of sweat made a harrowing descent down his face. His knee burned. He felt a slight pressure as the burn swelled. Then a grazing as Baby Back pressed his knee with his own, scraping it up and down under the table. He gazed at Baby Back's full lips, his gorgeous brown eyes, the touch of scruff on his cheeks.

"Mr. Poet. Ben. Recite me a poem."

Ben finished off his whiskey, then recited the best poem he had ever written.

> *"I got love runnin' through me,*
> *Like a river,*
> *Like wine,*
> *Like sweet jazz in an uptown dive.*
> *Runs through me, and through me, and through me.*
>
> *May I kiss your pretty cheek?*
> *May I kiss your pretty lips?*
> *Your pretty hips?*
> *Be my beauty,*
> *'Cause I got love runnin' through me."*

His head whirled from alcohol and secondhand reefer smoke. Baby Back still pressed his knee. The heat had abated, but the seductive pressure remained. Angeline cupped her face in her hands. Her body quaked. She pushed her chair back from the table and ran out.

The club had gotten quieter and half as full, but it simmered. The hostess sat on the edge of the stage, talking to patrons at a table up front. Some waitresses clustered at the bar, joking with the bartender. Voices boomed as patrons laughed and gossiped and talked mess.

Ben leaned forward, head hanging. "What'd you think, Mr. Johnston? What'd you think of *your* poem?"

The pressure vanished from Ben's knee. It cooled instantly.

Baby Back rose. "I think . . . I think you better go after your woman. Before you and me get in trouble."

He walked away, stepped back onto the stage, grabbed his horn, began to play. It was seamless, the way he fit right back in with the band. As if he'd never left that stage.

# 5

The liquor weighed him down. He had to fight to get up from the chair. As he left Teddy's, the band roared behind him and then dissipated as he gained more distance from the place. He stumbled home and found Evelyn Harrisburg on the stoop, facing the street, her hand gnarled around her walking stick.

"Your wife got in a while ago. She was crying. And you're drunk. Must be quite a story behind that."

"I'm sure you'll make one, Mrs. Harrisburg."

"Those country niggers are up there playing that devil's music again."

"I'm sorry to hear that, ma'am."

The apartment was dark and quiet and soothing after a night of shows and speakeasies. He approached the bedroom. A crevice of moonlight slipped through the window. Angeline had defected to one side of the bed, facing away from him. He undressed and got in. He sensed she was awake. He lay on his back so she could bundle up against his chest, pour her legs over his if she wanted. He wished she would cry, gift him with an excuse to comfort her, because he couldn't reach for her on his own. He neither touched her nor spooned himself into the curves of her tight, still body.

He couldn't believe *this thing* was back. He had fought it for so long, had spent these last years in Harlem fending off each and every temptation that vexed him morning, noon, and night. He thought he had subdued *this thing,* tamped it down into the littlest pocket so that it took up no more room than a speck. But it had slithered up again and rooted itself inside him.

The sounds of late-night Harlem wandered into the apartment: a barking dog; someone, probably homeless, ransacking a garbage can; a wino howling a popular song off-key; the *devil's music* upstairs. Ben couldn't sleep, but not because of the noise. A memory accosted him. A memory of the first time he had grappled with *this thing.*

His fourteenth birthday arrived on a summer morning in June without fanfare. Ben knew he wouldn't receive presents, but he expected, hoped for, some sort of acknowledgment: an extra treat at breakfast; a kiss from his ma or a handshake from his pa; a *happy birthday, son* from both or either of them.

At breakfast he sat on the wooden bench on his side of the table while his pa demolished grits and coffee and his ma added yeast to some dough at the stove. His eyes bounded from one parent to the other, waiting. The wait became vain hope. His appetite dwindled. He picked at his food.

Her bread yeasted, his ma turned from the stove, wiped her hands on the front of her dress, and noticed her sullen son. "Boy, what you doin'? We ain't got time for you to be dawdlin'. Hurry up and eat and get out there and feed them animals! Go on now. What you waitin' for? They ain't gone feed themselves."

"Yes'm."

He finished his grits, now cold, and left to begin his chores.

While watering the mule, his parents announced they were leaving for errands. His ma assigned him a catalog of work: "Chop the firewood. Clear the weeds out the cabbage patch. Spread fresh hay in the barn."

His pa didn't say anything. He rarely did now.

His ma's list grew. "Kill a chicken for supper and skin it, too. The fat one. Pick some blackberries so I can make that pie I promised the Reverend Ledger's wife. Make sure they ripe."

"Yes'm."

His ma shouldered her way up the dirt path with long strides, a big cloth bag hanging in the crook of her arm. His pa followed.

They hadn't remembered his birthday. Or hadn't cared enough to acknowledge it. That hurt. Losing four children—two in childbirth, one in infancy, and another after an illness at eleven years old—had made his ma and pa vacant inside. Their bodies still functioned, but their hearts had evaporated. It seemed all of their love had been buried with their four dear babies. So what that one had survived? Why waste affection on him when there were so many ways he could be taken from them? Sickness. Farm accident. White folks.

Anything could happen in Dogwood, Georgia. Ensconced in the central part of the state, the white folks claimed the town was named for the fragrant, leafy dogwood trees that flourished in the region. But colored folks grumbled that it was really named in honor of the hounds that hunted down their fugitive ancestors back in slavery days.

Ben watched his ma and pa. As soon as they rounded a bend and were out of sight, he dashed into the chicken coop, lifted up a squawking, protesting hen—the fat one his ma had instructed him to butcher—and removed a book hidden under a loose board beneath her. *Lyrics of Lowly Life* by Paul Laurence Dunbar.

It had been a gift from the teacher, Miss Percy, a pretty, young colored woman all the boys were sweet on. She traveled through Georgia, teaching a month here, a semester there. One day Miss Percy read them Dunbar. The verses put some of his classmates to sleep, but captivated Ben, who shyly asked the teacher if she had an extra copy to loan him. She didn't, but gave him her own prized volume at the end of the semester and told him to use it well and often. She must have used it well and often herself because the cover was worn and the corners of many a page had been turned down as bookmarks. Penciled notes were scrawled throughout. Proud Ben ran home to show his folks.

"What you need poetry for? That's for white folks," his ma said. She was boiling laundry in a giant pot, stirring it with a wooden pole. She chewed tobacco while she worked.

"But Paul Laurence Dunbar's colored, Ma. And these poems is pretty."

She spat a straight line of tobacco out of the corner of her mouth. It pierced the dirt like an arrow. "Pretty? You don't need pretty. You need to learn how to plough that field. Will that book teach you that? Give it back to that high-falutin' teacher. Or throw it away. I don't want to see it. I catch you reading it, I'ma whip you good."

"Yes'm."

She hadn't allowed him to attend school after that semester ended.

Now, with his ma and pa off the farm for a few hours, Ben had a minute window of time. He grabbed the Dunbar book and sallied through the groves of dogwood trees to Sugarfish Pond. If he budgeted his time wisely, he could swim, enjoy a few poems, and get back before his parents did. His ma would yell about his incomplete work, but he had to do something to celebrate his birthday.

When he broke through the trees and onto the bank of the pond, he saw that another boy had beaten him there: Willful Hutchison, son of the "Widow" Hutchison, and brother of those five raggedy Hutchison girls.

Eighteen years old and the handsomest colored boy in Dogwood.

Silly, chattering girls went silent when he walked by. In church, women—unmarried and married alike—peeked over prayer books and murmured, "Have mercy." Christened "William" and nicknamed "Willie," he was so hardheaded and disobedient, folks took to calling him *Willful*. Hardly anybody even remembered his given name.

Willful was knee-deep in the pond, facing the opposite direction, naked. Ben was presented with his muscled back; his full, round buttocks; his skin the color of dark, varnished wood. His weight was shifted onto one leg, causing one of his buttocks to lift into the air while the other sloped provocatively. Willful stood idly. Serene as sculpture. He was beautiful. Ben tried, but could not take his eyes away. In his fourteen years, he had often been mesmerized by the beauty of a poem or a sunrise. Years later, exquisite jazz would send him. But right now, it was Willful Hutchison holding him spellbound.

"Jesus," Ben said. It escaped his mouth like an agitated bird from a cage.

Willful heard it. He turned around, surprised but by no means scared, and saw Ben. He neither sprang for his pile of clothes that lay in a heap near a sapling, nor attempted to hide his nakedness. He appraised Ben with the same curiosity with which Ben appraised him.

And now that Willful faced him, Ben saw the rest of his body: the chest with its two mounds of muscle; the stomach with a thin line of fuzz extending down the middle before culminating in a thicket of hair; the penis that dangled between his legs.

"Jesus."

Why couldn't he look away? Ben feared every second he took in Willful's body plunged him further into a realm he would neither understand, nor escape.

They didn't move. Ben was confused, riveted, but Willful exuded supreme calm, as if it was perfectly natural to stand naked in a pond with a dumbstruck boy staring at him. He radiated a monster confidence that bewitched Ben and made him understand why the women in church muttered, "Have mercy," between hymns and sometimes during them.

Willful shifted in the water. The movement broke the spell. Ben looked around, desperate to regain his bearings. Like waking from a rattling dream and needing assurance that you're in the same place in which you went to sleep. But Ben sensed he wasn't in the same place. And when his eyes rambled back and found Willful touching himself, that sense received a jolt. Willful's eyes zeroed in on Ben. The spell transfixed him again.

"Jesus." No agitated bird this time, but a plea for help. Because he couldn't stop looking. He had heard other boys boast about touching themselves while looking at dirty pictures. And now the handsomest boy in town touched himself while looking at Ben. The thought puffed up his pride one moment, shamed him the next. *Why can't I stop looking?*

Willful inhaled and exhaled, his chest fully expanding then fully deflating. His face, so placid before, now contorted. He clamped his eyes shut. His entire body heaved.

Ben felt something sticky in his pants. Moisture stained the front of his pants, rapidly expanded into a near-perfect sphere. He looked at Willful again. The handsomest boy in Dogwood had turned his big, muscled back on him, leaving Ben with the same picture he had encountered when he arrived.

He panicked, then raced through the woods. Once home, he assaulted his chores. By the time his ma and pa returned, the blackberries had been picked, the barn smelled of fresh hay, and the fat hen was a skinned corpse.

That night, as Ben lay on his pallet waiting for sleep that barely came, Willful Hutchison planted himself inside him. And Ben kept whispering, "Jesus."

Angeline still faced away, crying softly now. He knew she commandeered every ounce of strength to cry just softly.

"You promised." Her words were breathy, almost inaudible. "You promised me you wouldn't go back to that. You promised you'd never go back to being that way."

"I've kept my promise," Ben said. "Ever since we've been married. I swear. I've kept it. So far."

Breakfast was a war zone. Waiters soldiered from the kitchen to the trenches of the dining hall, servicing abrasive guests irritated that their Sunday agendas—church at St. Patrick's, breakfast at Delmonico's—had been scuttled by an exuberant downpour. Ben capitulated to the hard work, partly to garner the plump cache of tips, but mostly to keep moving. If he achieved a certain physical velocity, perhaps *this thing* would shrink away.

The war relented when the rain let up. Without work to do, Ben's energy waned and with it, his ability to keep *this thing* at bay. Then Mr. Kittredge arrived and seated himself at his usual table. He didn't wait for the host. He never did.

"Hello, sir. How are you this morning?"

"Benjamin! Here on a Sunday? What's the special occasion?"

"Have to make sure my favorite guest is taken care of."

He poured Earl Grey tea, then tipped his head to see the title of the book in Mr. Kittredge's hands: *John Keats: Selected Poems.*

"I commend your taste in literature, sir," Ben said.

"*You* know Keats?"

"Yes, sir. Is 'Endymion' in that volume?"

The Englishman eyed him with skepticism, suspicion. "Why,

yes. I'm reading it for the thousandth time. It's sublime. *You* know 'Endymion'?"

> *"A thing of beauty is a joy for ever:*
> *Its loveliness increases; it will never*
> *Pass into nothingness; but still will keep*
> *A bower quiet for us, and a sleep*
> *Full of sweet dreams, and health, and quiet breathing."*

"What can I get you this morning? Grapefruit?"

"No," Kittredge said, mystified. "Toast." He arched his eyebrows. "Dry, and not too crisp."

Mr. Kittredge always ate lightly. Ben fancied that his physique was lithe, supple. He had only seen Kittredge in his jacket and vest and could only ruminate on what dwelled beneath. A lean, compact stomach? Muscled chest? The few times he'd seen a white man shirtless, he'd marveled at the hair—sometimes wiry straight, sometimes curly—that fleeced their chests. Or perhaps Mr. Kittredge's chest was smooth and warm to the touch. Or cool. Or—

*No. Stop it! Stop. Please.*

He breathed to regain his balance. Flustered, he placed Mr. Kittredge's order with the kitchen, then returned to the table—with a wedge of grapefruit. He was shaking as he approached the table. "Here you are, sir. Anything else?"

Mr. Kittredge eyed him. A mix of irritation and reproach. Ben realized his error and whisked the grapefruit away. He had never made a mistake with Mr. Kittredge's orders, and rarely with anyone else's.

"I'm sorry about that, sir," Ben said when he returned with the correct food.

"Are you all right, Benjamin? You seem rather out of sorts."

Ben looked away.

"There *is* something wrong," Mr. Kittredge said. "Well, sit down, dear boy. I'm happy to listen."

"Sir, thank you. But I'm not allowed to do that."

Kittredge's face reddened. "No, of course not. I wasn't thinking."

Ben started to leave the table. Kittredge stopped him.

"Oh, Benjamin."

The Englishman handed him the Keats book. His hands were smooth, his fingernails buffed and manicured. "Please have it. We can't sit and talk together here, but I'd like to do something for you. Perhaps this will cheer you a little."

Ben accepted the book. "Thank you, sir. I'll use it well and often."

In a dream world he would have sat at that table and confided in Mr. Kittredge about *this thing.* But in a dream world *this thing* wouldn't have existed. It wouldn't have poisoned his anniversary the previous evening.

A week had elapsed since that night at Teddy's, its shade hanging large and chilly. Silence consumed the apartment. Angeline hadn't once sat on his lap while he labored at the typewriter. The shade towered largest and chilliest in their bedroom. But they went to dinner for their anniversary and Ben unveiled a new poem, reciting it between the main course and dessert.

> *"If you'll love me, I'll pick all*
> *The fruit in the garden,*
> *Serve it to you*
> *On a golden platter,*
> *Then fall asleep*
> *In your arms,*
> *Enthroned on a pedestal*
> *Of light while a rainbow*
> *Snuggles between us . . .*
>
> *But only if you'll*
> *Fall in love with me."*

"It's . . . beautiful, Benny. Thank you," she said. But her bloodless smile and tepid kiss she tapped on his lips betrayed that this consolation prize insulted her.

Back home, they undressed on opposite sides of the bedroom,

eyes evading each other. Ben battled the discomfort. He set her down on the bed.

*Concentrate.*

She twitched and writhed as he strove into the familiar regions of her body. But he couldn't get aroused. He concentrated. He groped himself. He prayed. But he stayed soft as cotton.

"Shit!" he said, dismounting, leaving Angeline disoriented and still aroused.

Her eyes shot down to his groin and her expression degraded from concern to horror. She crouched over him to take him in her mouth, but he threw up a hand in refusal. She retreated to her side of the bed. She began to cry. He closed his eyes and he clenched his dick and he concentrated again. When lukewarm fantasies of wifely intimacy failed to ignite him, he did the unthinkable: He summoned a vision of Willful Hutchison.

Sugarfish Pond; Willful naked in the water; his luminous brown body. It worked. He mounted Angeline again and began to drill, the image of Willful the engine that powered him as he thrusted as hard as he could, his face buried so deep and rough in her neck, the next morning a bruise would show.

Angeline groaned her satisfaction as a pinprick of lightning struck somewhere at the base of his dick. He concentrated to keep Willful firmly in his mind's eye, but the image blurred to a smudge and reemerged as Baby Back. The pinprick bloated. Ben ruptured. He lay collapsed on top of her. A heaving, sweating mess.

"That's my Benny. You ain't going back to being *that way*," she said with the relief of a woman who has rescued the paradise of her marriage. "No, sir. My Benny keeps his promises."

In the morning Ben lay awake. Angeline lay blanketed across his body, motionless, at peace. As if the tumult of the previous week was an inconvenient memory.

Sunday morning.

Ben remembered Sunday mornings in Dogwood. A day for church and, supposedly, for rest, but chickens still had to be fed and cows milked. A farm never put itself on hold. Ben hadn't crossed the threshold of any church since he left Georgia. He wondered if his ma and pa still went. When he was a kid, they attended service like dutiful Christian soldiers. God's Valley Baptist Church was a derelict building with crumbling brick stilts and white paint that had sickened to a flaking gray. Weeds gashed through the gaps in the steps. With Sugarfish Pond so close, some days a damp, muddy scent invaded the air. Inside, parts of the floor caved steeply. But fresh, white linen always arrayed the altar, and twice a month a squad of volunteer ladies deserted their sharecropping and farming to scrub the wood pews.

A week after the pond incident Ben saw the Hutchison family at Sunday services, occupying the same bench they always did—the one set against the wall beside the altar. It was originally intended to accommodate additional worshippers on Easter and Christmas, but the Hutchisons had colonized it like squatters and made it their own private pew.

What a sight. Mrs. Hutchison, Willful, and five pitiful-looking girls. A husbandless, fatherless clan. Two versions of how that transpired had infiltrated the folklore of colored Dogwood—one official, the other scandalous. The official version decreed that Neale Hutchison had journeyed out of town to purchase farm supplies, and died. His body was never brought back and no funeral was ever held, which lent credence to the scandalous version: that he ran off with "Loose" Louise, a harlot in a shanty out on Ol' Cane Road with a door painted red, the same as the brazen coloring on her lips.

Most of Dogwood scorned the official version.

"That woman lyin'."

"How your husband gone die and you don't hold no funeral?"

"*Widow,* my foot. She made it up. Don't wanna sully her reputation."

But regardless of what folks thought of the "Widow" Hutchison, she and her brood were destitute, subsisting on the kindness of their neighbors, costumed in other families' hand-me-downs.

Mrs. Hutchison sat spine-straight on the bench in an ancient dress and a white bonnet that had sallowed to a pale yellow. Her five girls sat next to her in rags that had been cleaned up just enough and shoes that hung off their feet in shreds. They had sunken cheeks and ashy skin. Seated next to the girls: Willful. Slumped back, bored, like he couldn't be bothered. Oddly, he didn't wear tatters like his sisters. He was almost dapper in his fresh shirt, suspenders, and woolen pants. Even fully clothed Ben could see how muscular he was: stalwart thighs, prominent chest, hulky forearms revealed by his rolled-up shirtsleeves (a no-no in church). Ben's heart flipped and flopped at the sight of Willful's long legs spread wide into the shape of an inverted capital *V*.

Ben became aroused. It appalled him that his body would go rogue in the house of God. He couldn't stop looking between those legs. He wasn't alone. Young girls caught gaping at Willful's wide-open legs got their heads lurched back into place by fathers or slapped by mothers.

Because the handsomest boy in Dogwood was also its biggest scoundrel. Everyone knew he frequented that brothel over in Robertville, though where he got the money was a mystery. And when Ned Raymond's fast daughter got pregnant, Willful had topped the list of suspects.

When Mrs. Hutchison saw the gaping and slapping, her eyes automatically went to her son. She whispered in the ear of the daughter next to her and that daughter whispered to the next daughter and the message traveled down the bench to Willful. He rolled his eyes, lengthened his shirtsleeves, sat up straight. He made a scene of closing his capital *V,* so lazily, so dramatically, that it magnified the tension in the little church.

He turned his head randomly, caught Ben staring, and stared right back.

Services started. The Reverend Ledger began lecturing his congregation on the Beatitudes. Willful switched his attention to the reverend. Ben felt forsaken. *Why won't he stop looking?* became *Why did he stop looking?*

After church, Ben stood outside with his ma and pa as they spoke to a neighbor. Mrs. Hutchison led her offspring in a line as they clattered down the church steps, Willful at the back. As he passed Ben, he whispered, "Meet me at Sugarfish Pond. Two o'clock," his mouth so close, it almost brushed Ben's face.

Angeline wanted to fuck. She bowled him onto his back and attempted to ram herself down onto him. He clinched his eyes shut and conjured up Willful. Then Baby Back. Then Reggie.

Nothing.

He couldn't do his job as a husband. Couldn't do his job as a man. Hadn't done anything in weeks.

Next day, he rose before dawn, as he always did these days. Summer had evolved into September and mornings were cool. Angeline had covered herself with the blanket. She slept on her side of the bed. *Her side of the bed.* A new phenomenon. He shut the door softly as he left the bedroom, then sat at his desk and began writing. He'd write for hours until it was time to go to work. Or until Angeline woke. At work his boss lauded him as his "best colored worker." But he was really an obsessed man who had to keep occupied to prevent perverse desires from crawling up and strangling him.

> You want a love
> I cannot give.
> No matter how I pray.

*And I regret,*
*Sweet angel dear,*
*Desire has gone away.*

He was about to start the next stanza, but the bedroom door opened.

"Good morning," Angeline said, more yawn than words.

He didn't look up. "Morning."

She contemplated him from the doorway, waiting for something from him. "I'll get your breakfast."

He brushed by her en route to the bathroom. "I don't want none. Thank you."

Half an hour later, he found Angeline at his desk reading the poem he had neglected to remove from the typewriter. He ran and tore the page out so hard, the paper ripped.

"Don't!" he yelled. "It ain't none of your business!"

" '*I regret, sweet angel dear, desire has gone away.*' That ain't my business? That ain't my fucking business?"

She rose and advanced on him. He instinctively backed up.

"I didn't mean for you to see that," he said.

She trapped him at the front door. "Have you . . . Have you been—" She ran away. "No! I don't want to know. I don't *ever* want to know."

"Angeline—"

"Get out of here, Ben. Go to work. Go. Now!"

On the subway, streaking toward downtown, he realized he still carried the ripped poem.

He worked an extra shift and dreaded the thought of home. So he got off the subway at 125th Street and kept walking. Even on a weeknight Harlem throbbed. The same verve as Saturday night at the clubs, but filtered into workaday tasks. Ben passed a store on 126th where two old ladies ganged up on a helpless grocer, complaining he was charging "too damn much" for vegetables they considered less than fresh. An ice man walked toward him carrying on one shoulder a wood bucket with a single, bulky slab of ice. He wore overalls over a sweat-soaked union suit snug enough to high-light his stevedore's build. His hair was gray, but his haggard face hovered between young and old. People scurried into drugstores and delicatessens, then scurried out with items wrapped in brown paper. Old men sat on crates and smoked pipes outside a barber shop while those inside leaned back in the chairs for a cut and a shave and a helping of timeless barber wisdom. A man waiting his turn joked around with the barber, told him to take his time with the customer in the chair. "Don't slice his ear off, like you did mine last time." The barber replied, "What you complaining about? It grew back."

Outside a beauty parlor on 129th, a street preacher evangelized. Nearly seven feet tall, his huge hair and beard were wild explosions of solid white, flying in every direction. He preached barefoot and rattled a tambourine for emphasis. "My children, God never sad-dles a man with a burden larger than he is capable of bearing. So accept your burden humbly and bow down before The Lamb who bore a cross and a crown of thorns so that you might be redeemed and one day walk with Him in the kingdom of heaven." The ladies in the parlor got their hair straightened and marceled and paid the barefoot sermonizer no mind.

At 130th, a painter displayed canvasses smoldering with Negro life. One depicted a pastoral scene of weary cotton pickers, the sun seething down on them. In another, musicians jammed in a dark speakeasy. Magnificent African women clothed in a sunset of col-ors emblazoned a third.

Ben reached 131st Street and Seventh Avenue. A crowd assem-bled near the corner. Some musicians—trombonist, a couple of trumpeters, sax player, a violinist—were blowing up an improv ses-sion. These cats didn't know each other. They just showed up and played, driving off of one another, coaxing chords and melodies out of each other, each musician challenging himself and the others to scale that next plain, and creating an impromptu jazz symphony right there on the street.

He listened a while, but when the notes roiling out of the trum-pets recalled Baby Back, Ben fled, pushed up the avenue, and turned east onto 135th Street. Before he could think about it, he had marched through the doors of the Harlem branch of the New York Public Library. A sign inside read POETRY READING TONIGHT. DOWNSTAIRS. Ben walked down to the basement, and seated himself amidst a small audience.

"Good evening, ladies and gentlemen," a lovely colored woman said from the podium. "I'm Regina Anderson, assistant librarian here at the Harlem Library. Thank you so much for being here. At this time I'd like to introduce our featured poet. He recently published work in the March edition of *Survey Graphic* and in the anthology *The New Negro*. His poems have also appeared in *Opportunity* and he was a recipient of that magazine's 1925 literary awards. He'll read tonight from his first poetry collection, *Heart of Pearl,* which will be published this fall by Alfred A. Knopf. Please join me in welcoming Mr. Marcellus S. Gibson."

He was a pretty young man with beige skin and a small frame. He held his manuscript in delicate hands. He wore a cravat instead of a tie. As he read his first selection, Ben became alarmed at his girlish voice.

> *"By light of the sumptuous moon,*
> *Our two fair souls unite.*
> *Oh love, please blossom soon,*
> *Give day to oppressive night.*

> *Anon comes morning, fleet and fair,*
> *To spread fresh dew on grass.*
> *I dry my tears upon your hair*
> *As we depart, sweet lass."*

Ben despised it. It was nothing but entanglements of silly rhymes and embarrassing clichés. But a group of men in the front row applauded stupidly at the conclusion of each piece. Apparently Mr. Gibson's friends, they were as mincing and effeminate as he. Squealing laughter. Limp wrists. Ben envisioned them jostling around in bed together, touching one another, squealing the whole time. Fairies, not men. They were the essence of everything he struggled so hard against with *this thing,* but he wasn't like them. He—

*He wasn't like them.*

He leapt out of the room in the middle of the poet's next piece as people scowled at his rude exit. The crisis had ended. He swaggered up Seventh Avenue, feeling strong enough to test himself. Because he wasn't like *them*.

Teddy's couldn't sizzle on a Tuesday like it did on a Saturday. No brusque conversations shouted from opposite ends of the room. Only a light smell of reefer in the quarter-full room. The absence of the riotous hostess made the place a cave. Fanny—the hourglass-shaped waitress—worked the room solo. But the band was there. Baby Back was there. They played a popular tune, something hummable, not as untamed or low-down as their Saturday night fare.

Ben sat right up front so Baby Back couldn't miss him. He ordered bourbon and watched the band, antsy for the break between sets when the trumpeter would step down to schmooze. He thought about the effeminate men at the poetry reading. If he wasn't like them, then he couldn't have the desires they did. He would test himself when the trumpeter approached.

But he couldn't suppress the memory of another time when he tried—and failed—to prove that *this thing* was gone.

One morning, Ben's ma came into the barn and shoved a crate at him.

"Take this over to Miz Hutchison," she said, her eyes swollen and wet and red.

The thought of seeing Willful petrified Ben.

"What you waiting for, boy? Get yonder and get on back here. There's a lot of work to do."

Wildflowers—white shooting stars, orange butterfly weeds, and purple ironweeds—poked out of the grass bordering the dirt road. The grooves of wagon wheels and the indentations of horses' hooves pockmarked the path along with the occasional impression of an automobile's tire treads. On his way up the path, he peeked inside the crate. It was full of little girl's clothes: bonnets and shoes; a pretty white Easter dress with pink lace hand-stitched around the collar and sleeves. Emma Jane's clothes. His sister who died of pneumonia a year earlier. Ol' Doc Cullen never left her side, but he hadn't had enough medicine and there had been no point in beseeching the town's white doctor.

Emma Jane. His baby sister whom he had loved and, sometimes, loathed. Loved because she was pretty and she was dear and she was bubbly and she was blood. She'd giggle and he couldn't help but giggle, too. She'd hold his hand and something protective flitted up inside him. But Emma Jane was their ma's precious baby, Pa's too, and she'd monopolized their attention and their love, leaving Ben with scraps.

He continued up the path, intentionally taking his time. Another hot day. Summer never let up. It got under your skin so that you felt hot from the inside out and from top to bottom. He needed a swim. It was the only relief: to take off all his clothes and dive into cool water. Just the vision brought a semblance of relief. But he kept it at bay. Because every vision of Sugarfish Pond also contained Willful Hutchison. He couldn't control it. What would happen when he saw him? In a town as tiny as Dogwood, permanently eluding another person wasn't an option. This afternoon would be a useful test.

The Hutchisons' deserted yard and fields surprised him. "Anyone home?"

The only answer was the high-pitched, insect-like call of a grasshopper sparrow.

The barn walls were pimpled with holes. Fences foundered. A laundry line hosted a few bedraggled dresses that flapped in the wind. But the fields mostly thrived with leafy stalks. A small garden abounded with tomatoes, carrots, corn. Inside the barn were a gaunt mule, an ancient horse, and Willful asleep in a chair. Head furled back. Mouth open. Legs spread into his signature capital V. Ben lowered the crate to the floor noiselessly, then tiptoed back to the door.

"Please don't go yet."

Not the bullish voice you'd expect from a strapping male. Not childlike, but not quite adult. A half voice. "Don't go."

Ben stopped and turned, then wished he hadn't. Willful's legs were still amply spread and his eyes were aimed at him.

"You ain't meet me at the pond like I told you," he said, part disappointment, part rebuke.

"My ma gave me a whole mess of chores," Ben said.

Willful chuckled. "My ma gives me chores all the time. If I don't feel like it, I don't do 'em."

Ben already knew that. Tales of Willful's laziness were legion. The Hutchison women ploughed, planted, and harvested while Willful did little or nothing. "I would'a kicked his freeloadin' ass out the house a long time ago and not thought twice," Ben's ma once said. But six colored women alone—five of them budding young girls—needed a man's presence to avert catastrophe.

Willful kept chuckling, as if obeying a parent was the dumbest thing he'd ever heard. Ben retaliated with the best defense he could think of.

"The Bible say you gotta mind your ma and pa."

"The Bible say a lot of things. Don't mean you gotta believe any of 'em. What's in that crate?"

The blasphemy sauntered off Willful's tongue as casually as spit. Horrified, it took Ben a moment to remember why he'd come.

"Clothes for your sisters. My ma sent 'em over. Miz Hutchison around?"

Willful eased toward him. "She and them gals is over to the church, helpin' Reverend Ledger with . . . something. Anything in there for me?"

"No."

He was in front of Ben now. He punched him softly, playfully, on the arm. "Why not?"

"I don't know."

Willful punched him again. "You don't know?" *Punch.* "You don't know?" *Punch.* "Why don't you know?" *Punch-punch-punch.*

"I don't know."

A giggle spurted out of Ben and once he started, he couldn't stop.

"That's what I thought," Willful said. "Got me a boy in here don't know *nothin'*. That's what I'm gone call you: Know-nothin'. 'Cause you don't know nothin'!"

The punching transitioned to tickling. It felt good to be teased, touched, paid attention to. Willful smiled like a prankish adult savoring his fun with a delighted child. The tickling stopped, but the smile remained. He touched Ben's cheek, skimmed his thumb along his neck, under his chin, along his Adam's apple.

"I'm glad you here. I don't got nobody to talk to most times," Willful said.

"You got your ma. Your sisters."

Willful snorted. "A bunch of jibber-jabbering women. Please. It's hard when you ain't got nobody to talk to."

Ben understood loneliness. He had no one to tease or coddle him. All he had were a ma who snarled orders, a pa who said nothing, and four dead siblings.

Willful placed both his hands on Ben's shoulders. "You a good boy. That's nice."

Ben looked up into the older boy's eyes. The sin at the pond wasted away. He just wanted Willful to keep touching him.

But Willful stepped away. "You best be gettin' back home. Your ma and pa be waitin' for you, wonderin' what's takin' you so long. Don't want you gettin' in no trouble. Go on home now."

Ben hesitated, then went to the door, stopped. He didn't want to leave. The desire to hug Willful, to *be* hugged, crushed him. He turned around. And when Willful spread his arms, Ben ran straight into them. Willful hugged him tight, tight, tight, grasping his head to his chest as Ben wept.

"Shh," Willful whispered, and kissed his forehead. "Shh."

He didn't know how long they stayed locked in that hug. He didn't care. This was the first affection he could remember in a long time and he basked in it. It felt so good, losing himself in Willful's chest, those arms secured around him. He had started to flit into something like unconsciousness when Willful pulled away, gently.

"You best be gettin' home, Know-nothin'. We'll see each other again. I promise."

"Refill? Sir? Hello?"

He'd been too rapt by the memory to see Fanny standing there. "Yes. Please. A double."

"You got it, swinger."

Though several years and a thousand miles from Dogwood, he could still feel the muscle and bone and flesh that was Willful's chest as he huddled close against it that day. It warmed him. He consciously tensed his body—his neck, shoulders, arms, fingers, jaw—to expel the warmth, restrict any more of it from entering, festering. But it was too late.

By the time Fanny brought the drink, the band had finished its set. Ben readied himself. The trumpeter stepped off the stage, saw him, nodded a brief, formal acknowledgment, and then toured the room, traipsing from table to table, shaking hands and laughing it up. The inattention shocked Ben. That cursory nod wasn't enough. Envy needled him when Baby Back sat with a nice-looking guy. Ben wondered what was happening under that table as the two chatted and the trumpeter commanded Fanny to bring a round of drinks.

Ben needed to go home. But *this thing* would just go with him.

Baby Back ended his conversation, rose from the table, and saw Ben. He nodded again. This time his eyes spoke delight. Ben exhaled in relief, despite himself. A long look ensued between them; it was a bridge, a bridge meant to be crossed, the distance minimal, not miles, merely steps. And when Baby Back pressed his lips to his hand and blew a kiss, it wasn't even steps anymore. Ben sat unmoving, but felt himself plunging. He couldn't fight *this thing*. Couldn't run from it. Couldn't resist—

"Got a light?"

*What?*

"Hey. Hey, mister. Psst! Got a light?"

Ben looked to his right. A woman was sitting at his table, gouging through her purse. An unlit cigarette sagged from the corner of her mouth.

"Ain't that just like me? Got a damn cigarette, but no fuckin' light. Oh, here's a match." She lit up. "I found one. Don't worry about it, mister."

"Um . . . I won't."

The woman smoked and smiled at the perplexed Ben.

"What's the name of this place? Psst! Hey, mister? You know the name of this joint?"

"Teddy's," Ben said.

"Teddy's. Ain't never been in here. I'm usually at Edmond's. Over at 132nd and Fifth? You been in there, mister? You'd remember it. Joint's a mess. People be gamblin'. All kind of shit be goin' down. Turn your back for a minute and you might find a knife stuck in it. But the bartender makes the drinks plenty strong—'specially if you a regular—and the music's killer. I ain't feel like walking all the way over there tonight. My feet be *hurtin'* in these heels, child. And I gets tired of goin' to the same damn place all the time. I need me some variety. You know what I'm sayin', mister?"

She stopped talking, but only briefly and only to puff her cigarette.

"You sure is quiet," she said. "You all right? By the way, I'm Honey. As in: sweeter than." She threw her head back, slapped the table, and hooted out loud at her own joke.

Honey's green charmeuse dress frazzled at the seams. The beaded embroidery was missing a few. Dark bags drooped under her eyes. Fine lines sprouted when she smiled. Strings of gray hair were tucked in among the black. She had made herself at home at Ben's table, puffing on her cigarette, content as a cat on a lap.

"Honey, can I help you with something?" Ben asked.

"Maybe. I don't live far. Don't charge much either."

He stammered, "I don't think ... I really ..." then remembered Baby Back, still standing there, waiting for him to cross the bridge. But Ben wanted to exterminate *this thing*.

He rose, looked down at Honey. "Let's go."

"Well, all right, mister. For a minute, I thought you was a square or something."

He helped her push back her chair and offered his arm.

"And you a gentleman, too? Guess I got lucky tonight." She appraised Teddy's. "Gotta make sure I come back to this place."

As they exited, they passed by one confused and furious-looking trumpeter.

\* \* \*

The room stank of grime and too much perfume. Honey lay on the lump of covered stuffing that served as a mattress. The sheet covered only her ankles. Her careworn face had deceived him. He had assumed her body would match and was surprised by its beauty. Taut, polished skin dressing her opulent curves. Places that bred shadows and intrigue—the cleft between her breasts, her deep and perfectly round valley of a navel, the florid valley between her legs.

And still he'd been unable to do it. He had tried. But *this thing* had succeeded.

"You still gotta pay, mister," Honey said.

The sounds of sex from the room next door—headboard banging against the wall, a man's throaty moaning—mocked him. Ben got out of bed, began to dress. He looked around. Water spots blotched the ceiling. Wallpaper flaked off the walls. The bed's metal headboard was awash in rust. A bedbug trawled across the sheets.

"Two dollars, mister. Put 'em on the bureau," Honey said. "And come back anytime." She winked. "You gentleman."

He left.

*Why can't I make this end?* he thought. *Make this end, please.*

He walked toward home. He could smell Honey's sweat and perfume on him. How many other men had she fucked? How many, like himself, had used her to reestablish their manhood, their normalcy, as if she was a sexual proving ground?

He turned onto his street. Except for a few lit windows, the street slept. Not a soul. Not a sound. Ben stopped, closed his eyes, imbibed the stillness, cherished the quiet on the street, the quiet inside his head. His head, that colony of noise. The barked orders of The Pavilion's guests. The untamed voices of nascent poems. *This thing*'s merciless nagging. It was too much. This quiet was a pearl.

Then he heard something. A dapple of voices coming from nearby. Ben opened his eyes. Two men, standing in front of a brownstone a little ways down. One quite tall, the other short enough that his head only reached the taller man's chest. Both young, Ben's age. They talked and laughed in a restrained manner, as if eager to preserve the stillness. Something uncomfortably intimate tinted the scene. They stood too close to each other. Looked in each other's eyes with too much joy, too much need.

The short one said something. The tall one bent down, leaned his ear close to his friend's mouth, then straightened once again. He cupped his hand on the back of the short guy's neck, and left it there. It seemed they would stay that way forever if they had their preference. On that dark street. Gauzy light in a couple of windows. The crush of stillness.

Ben began to walk in their direction. He had to, to get home. But his intent was stabbed with vindictiveness, too.

"Good evening," he bellowed, as he strutted toward them.

The two men scrambled apart, their erstwhile intimacy skewered and replaced with fear.

Ben kept walking. "How you guys doing? Nice night, huh?"

Each man mumbled something unintelligible. The tall one crossed the street and took off at a clip in the opposite direction. The short one almost tripped as he ran up the steps and into the building and slammed the door shut.

When Ben arrived home, he saw Evelyn Harrisburg's door ajar about an inch. Surprised at her carelessness, he moved to close it, but it did so, seemingly on its own, with a soft *click*.

He went into the bedroom after a thorough sponge bath. Angeline rounded on him before he could slip into bed.

"It's late."

He didn't respond.

"Ben. I said, it's late."

"Is it really? Thanks. I couldn't have figured that out without you."

"What's your problem?"

"You are. Now shut the fuck up!"

He had never spoken to her like that. Ever. It took her a moment to reorient herself. But only a moment.

"Get out! Get out of here! Go sleep on the sofa. Go!"

She pushed and socked and kicked him until he was running for his life into the living room. Then she slammed the door shut, splitting their life in two.

# 8

Mornings he rose early to write, vigilant about escaping the apartment before Angeline awoke. At The Pavilion, he'd work so many hours, his boss had to order him out. Then he'd retreat to Harlem and walk its length and breadth. From 110th Street straight up to the northernmost fringe of Sugar Hill. From the Hudson River on the west side to the Harlem River on the northeast. He walked and composed poems in his head.

> *Stride through the African metropolis*
> *Teeming on the margin of America.*
> *That sepia mayhem that sweats*
> *To the dirge of spirituals*
> *And struts with a horn in its heels.*
>
> *Stride the toiling days and fervent nights,*
> *Through the cacophony of*
> *Savory tans and virile browns,*
> *Through the majestic strivers*
> *And the have-nots,*
> *All dreaming amongst the asphalt*
> *And flying on the lips of poems.*
>
> *Stride.*

* * *

Life became a pattern to be duplicated each day, like the day itself with its rote predictability: dawn, sunrise, dusk, nightfall, moonrise, dawn again. *Rise. Write. Work. Walk. Sleep.* He adhered to the pattern, perfected it. It didn't make him happy, but it kept him sane.

He was too slow one morning and didn't slip out before Angeline awoke. She came into the room, her step businesslike, eyes not so much as straying in his direction. She began fixing her breakfast while Ben lowered his head and pecked the typewriter's keys quietly, as if that would hide him.

"The rent's due," she said. "Leave your share on the table tonight or tomorrow morning and I'll take care of it. And the grocery bill. You ain't been eating much, so just leave a few dollars on the table."

"Sure, Angel," he said, then wondered if he was still allowed to use her pet name.

"I'll be home late tonight. Me and Ruby going to a picture show."

"Ruby. Hmm."

She looked at him for the first time. "What's the *hmm* for?"

"You know I don't like that woman. She thinks she knows everything. Loves to tell people what's best for them. Likes to gossip, too. Ruby could give Mrs. Harrisburg a run for her money." He rose from the typewriter, panicked. "What have you told her about us?"

"I think you really want to know what I've told her about *you.*"

Was that glee in her voice? Malice spoiling on her lips, flexing her mouth into a dark grin? He'd never seen this ugly side of Angeline before. It stunned him. He wondered if it had always been there, prowling in some secret, dirty corner of their marriage, now prompted out of hiding because of *this thing.* For the first time, he was afraid of her.

Ben watched her closely, saw the ugly side recede, saw his wife return to a semblance of the woman he'd lived with for six years.

"Don't worry," Angeline said. "I ain't going to expose you. What good would that do?"

A breeze of relief, but he hated that word: *expose.* A harsh word

that signaled danger and betrayal. A word—and an action—that
endowed the world with a blank check to judge.

He attended more readings at the Harlem Library. He didn't
see the effeminate poet again, but the more he wandered Harlem,
the more cravats he saw adorning the necks of men whose hips
flopped from side to side; the more male voices he heard embossed
with feminine textures. Ben couldn't comprehend why any man
would adopt such behavior, especially with Harlem's abundance of
masculinity. There were men who moved firmly and with purpose,
big arms swinging and big, brute backs casting shadows on the sidewalk, their broad, solid backsides taking command of the space.
Men with virile faces, engraved with hard, flinty edges. Dapper
men, godly with confidence, who grandstanded their way up and
down the avenues, brandishing slick suits and two-toned shoes.
Working men, tired and tireless, the veins in their arms and necks
as thick as pipes. Dark-chocolate men. Café au lait men. Blue-black
men. Men the color of caramel or red earth or tea. Ben would
dream about the eclectic variety and wake up aroused. Exiled to
the living room sofa and unobstructed by a wife's objections, he relieved himself in private, guilty pleasure.

*Rise. Write. Work. Walk. Sleep.*

The poems poured out and the rejections from publishers piled
up. He persevered because writing was all he had. That and his ex-
peditions through Harlem, which led him one night to 142nd
Street and Lenox Avenue: The Cotton Club. The marquee—so
ablaze it lit the entire block—proclaimed that Fletcher Henderson
and his orchestra were starring. A doorman stood curbside as taxis
and Daimlers and Stutzes cruised to the curb, dropping off merry
whites in tuxes, flapper dresses, gowns, even furs, though it was
only October. Jazz bopped out of the club and into the street. Ben
watched the parade from across the street. Out of one taxi stepped
a figure he recognized. Mr. Kittredge dazzled with his self-assured
flair. He appraised the surroundings, smiling his approval, impart-
ing faultless elegance in his top hat, tails, and spats. A much younger
man also stepped out of the cab. Mr. Kittredge touched, just briefly,
the small of the younger man's back as he ushered him into the club.

Next day, the same young man joined Mr. Kittredge at breakfast. Ben watched as they talked and laughed, hands brushing a
moment here, a second or two there. Their cheeks nearly grazed as
they leaned in to each other and the young man confided something
in Kittredge's ear with an intimacy that Ben would never share with
him. He looked Ben's age with oil-black hair, skin as smooth as
cream and almost as white.

"Good morning, Benjamin. Allow me to introduce my friend,
David-Nicholas." Mr. Kittredge's eyes never left the young man.

Ben nodded. "Pleased to meet you. You from England?"

David-Nicholas glanced at Kittredge, amused. "No," he said.
"The Upper East Side. You?"

"Harlem."

"We were there just last night, weren't we, Geoffrey?"

Kittredge gave the young man's arm a pat that looked as though
it aspired to a caress. "That we were. The Cotton Club."

"It was swell!" David-Nicholas said. "The waiters danced as
they delivered the food! You must go there all the time, since you
live in Harlem."

Mr. Kittredge fidgeted.

"Cotton Club don't allow colored," Ben said. He debated with
himself, then added, "Except to work onstage or wait tables. What
can I get you gentlemen this morning?"

Later, Mr. Kittredge said, "I've been meaning to ask you: How
are you enjoying the Keats?"

"Very much, sir. Thank you."

He lied. He had buried the book in the depths of his desk
drawer. But that night he dug it out from beneath an old, heavy dictionary, took it to Pigfoot Mary's Restaurant on the corner of 135th
and Lenox, and asked for the most isolated table they had. After a
meal of ham hocks, collard greens, and black-eyed peas, he opened
the Keats.

> *A thing of beauty is a joy for ever:*
> *Its loveliness increases; it will never*
> *Pass into nothingness; but still will keep*

*A bower quiet for us, and a sleep*
*Full of sweet dreams, and health, and quiet breathing.*

He hadn't read those words in years, but they were evergreen.

Ben had sat against a dogwood tree, Willful's head in his lap, the last time he read that poem. That was how they whiled away their time together. After they'd tired from splashing in Sugarfish Pond and had kissed themselves numb, Ben read to Willful. They started with the Paul Laurence Dunbar—the only book Ben owned—reading the difficult and beautiful poems worn cover to worn cover over the course of weeks, always while trifling in the groves of dogwoods as yellow-head blackbirds and laughing gulls chirped and clucked overhead.

Willful couldn't read or write. Ben wanted to teach him, begged to, but Willful always deferred with, "Maybe someday."

When they finished the Dunbar, Willful pulled a new book out of his pocket with what seemed like sleight of hand. "For you, Know-nothin'. I don't know what it is, but it's so pretty."

It *was* pretty. Leather-bound. Gold gilting the pages' edges, the title, *Poems of John Keats,* spelled out in ornate lettering. They started it right away. Ben bumbled and fumbled the verses at first and Willful constantly asked, "What does that mean?" The language was so strange, it might as well have been foreign. They recognized individual words, but the phrases they created were a mystery. The two boys had to train themselves to submit to the language. When they did, they lost themselves in its beauty, although they never got through more than the first few pages.

It was an open secret between them that Willful had stolen the book from the store in the white part of town. That and all of the gifts he had given him: candies, sweet apples, a pocketknife with a mother-of-pearl handle. After the Keats poems, more contraband books came. So many that they no longer fit in secret compartments under fussy chickens and Ben had to invent creative ways to stash them. Meanwhile, in the grove of sweet-scented dogwoods, Ben and Willful lamented their lack of books by colored writers, but gorged themselves on what they did have.

Spinning in a whirlpool of *I'll die if don't see him soon,* Ben didn't comprehend what consumed him. But when Willful got lost in the beauty of words and faraway places—so immersed that a look of peace illuminated him—he wasn't just the handsomest boy in Dogwood or a thief or a lazy, good-for-nothing son and brother. Willful was the love of Ben's life. The whirlpool spun and spun. Out of the dizziness he wrote his first poem:

> *Underneath the dogwood trees us lie,*
> *Sweet delights get took on borrowed time.*
> *You is sunnier than day.*
> *I got your love, you got mine.*

Their afternoons in the dogwood groves exceeded poems and pilfered gifts. Willful loved to sit against a tree, Ben kneeling in front of him.

"Undo my pants."

Ben obeyed, was happy to obey, happy to make Willful happy. Even if Willful didn't reciprocate. At least not that way. But he would work Ben until the cream spewed down his big, dark-brown hand in white stripes.

"When you gone let me inside you?" Willful asked, numerous times, during the year they'd been together. That act could complete the circle of their intimacy, he said, but it was the one desire of Willful's that Ben wouldn't obey. Because one day, Willful had played with him, back there, with an intrusive finger. The deeper he prodded, the worse it hurt.

More gifts: chocolates in boxes wrapped in tissue paper; a razor for shaving; a bottle of Scotch (it made them sick); a set of suspenders, which he couldn't wear without provoking suspicion. Things he couldn't possibly use: a lady's jewelry box; a parasol.

He loved the books, but the gold heart-shaped locket was his favorite gift.

"I know it's for a gal," Willful said, "but it made me think of our favorite poem. *A thing of beauty is a joy forever.*"

The thievery benefited Ben, but not Willful's own impoverished family. Nevertheless, he anticipated each gift, even as he worried about the consequences if the white folks caught them.

But always, his most vicious worry was *When will I see him again?* Days—sometimes few, sometimes many—divided their meetings. The separation gnawed, so Ben employed himself in disciplined work to alleviate it. He drove himself like a soldier, fulfilled each job his ma assigned, and voluntarily took on more. He worked so hard, so efficiently that, for once, she couldn't invent a reason to complain at him.

The day after he received the locket, the Reverend Ledger's wife paid a call on his ma. She munched sweet potato pie and drank sassafras tea while he sat in a corner shucking corn. Mrs. Ledger was a proper colored lady and a proper preacher's wife. She was tall and mostly trim except for a mildly protruding belly that Ben figured to be the consequence of eating desserts in the homes of her husband's congregants.

"My Trina gettin' to be quite the young lady," she said of her eldest daughter. "She practically engaged to the Reverend Glover. You know, the pastor over in Weldon Grove?"

Ben's ma frowned. "He gotta be over thirty. Trina how old? Sixteen? He even proposed yet?"

Mrs. Ledger cut her pie to polite pieces with a knife. Ben had never seen anyone treat dessert so formally. "Not yet. But he will. I ain't worried."

"In this family, we don't count our chickens till they's hatched." Ben's ma called to him. "Ain't that right, boy?"

"Yes'm."

He went back to the corn and paid no attention to the women, until he heard Willful's name.

"That sorry Hutchison boy," Mrs. Ledger said, "is up to no good. Again. He takes what little money the family got and gambles it away or spends it on whores and corn liquor. Just like his no-good pa. Now Miz Hutchison and those girls almost starvin'."

"Boy," Ben's ma called, "take a basket of eggs over to the Hutchison place." She turned back to her guest. "Them hens been workin' overtime. We got extra. If that fool woman rations 'em right, they'll have food for a few mornings at least." Back to Ben: "Give the eggs to Miz Hutchison or one of the girls, *not* Willful."

"Oh, Miz Hutchison and the girls ain't home," Mrs. Ledger said. "They at the church."

"Doin' what," Ben's ma said. "Prayin' for food?"

"It's their turn to clean it."

"They need to be workin' them fields."

Mrs. Ledger put her fork down, firmly. "Sister Charles, starvin' or not, the Lord's work still got to be done."

The locket jangled in one pocket and the Keats poems filled the other as Ben sprinted up the road, anxious for the look on Willful's face when he arrived. He laughed out loud at their unexpected luck. They might not have time for reading. Didn't matter. As long as they could kiss for a while. He hoped the church was plenty dirty and that the Hutchison women took their time.

He headed straight to the barn, swung through the door, and saw Trina Ledger, on her back in the hay, Willful on top of her, his backside pumping up and down, his thrusts accompanied by a slapping sound while Trina moaned.

That morning's breakfast sludged up Ben's throat. A bitter ooze. He felt faint.

The muscles in Willful's back constricted as he worked that bitch, the preacher's daughter who was supposed to marry another preacher and whose mother had stuffed her face on his ma's pie as she boasted about her young lady of a daughter.

They didn't realize anybody had come in. Willful kept pumping. Sweat cascaded off him. His dark skin glistened. Rage displaced Ben's urge to faint. He remembered he still held the basket of eggs. He pounced onto the hay and began pelting Trina at close range.

"Bitch! You bitch! You whore!"

Willful pulled out clumsily and yanked Ben away from Trina who now sat up, screaming, as egg yolk and shells slimed her hair, face, and bare chest.

"Know-nothin'! Calm down!" Willful said.

He locked Ben's arms behind him. But Ben's rage detonated. He wrenched free and bashed Willful in the stomach. Willful toppled and floundered in the hay, naked and sweaty, as Ben kicked him and kicked him and kicked him until Willful crunched in on himself like a fetus.

"Stop! Stop it!" Trina screamed.

Willful tried to hoist himself up from the hay, one hand pushing against the ground, the other cradling his stomach.

"Whore!" Ben screamed, so shrill he felt the scratch in his throat. He started toward her. She shrieked and scrambled to her feet.

"Ben. No," Willful said, still grappling on the ground, the flesh where Ben had kicked him already starting to bruise.

"Get away from me!" Trina yelled. "Willful! Do somethin'!" She shot desperate glances around the barn, whether for her clothes or for some weapon to fend him off, Ben didn't know.

He was about to leap at her when the barn door busted open. There stood Mrs. Hutchison, her daughters peeking around her. She stepped inside, looked from her naked son to the preacher's naked daughter to Ben, the only clothed member of the trio.

She moved immediately to Trina. "Let's get you into your clothes. Where's your dress, chile?"

She located Trina's dress, helped her into it, and called to her eldest daughter. "Nella! Take Trina to the pump, get her cleaned up. Then take her in the house."

Nella and her sisters faltered in the doorway, too scared to inject themselves into the sordid scene.

"Come on, gal!" Mrs. Hutchison snapped. "Don't be standin' there gawkin'. Believe me, we ain't got all day!"

Nella still hesitated. Mrs. Hutchison's hands were small, but she slammed them together in a single deafening clap and roared, "Move!"

Nella tripped into the barn. She glanced at her brother, then lowered her head and took the sobbing Trina by the hand. The other girls followed as she led her out. Willful had wriggled into a squat, still flailing from the impact of Ben's shoes in his gut. His ma ignored him and approached Ben, keeping at arm's length. She spoke with caution. As if trying to appease a vicious animal.

"We gone get Trina cleaned up. Then we gone get her home safe. She gone be all right. Ben. You always been a good boy. Your family been generous to us. I know it ain't right to ask another favor. But

I'ma ask anyhow: Don't say nothin' about this. Please. I'm beggin' you. For my family's sake, please don't say nothin' about what happened here."

Willful had made it to a standing position. He masked his privates with his hands. His head hung down. The handsomest boy in Dogwood had been man enough to fuck the preacher's daughter in the barn, but couldn't look Ben in the eye. Ben ran out, rampaged up the dirt road, so addled he didn't know if he ran toward his house or away from it. He just kept running until he heard "Know-nothin'!" He stopped, turned. Willful hobbled up the path, half dressed. Shoes untied. Shirt mostly unbuttoned. Pants trailing down because his suspenders weren't done up. He was gasping.

"What you saw—it ain't mean nothin'," he said.

"The way y'all was moanin' and groanin', looked like it *did* mean somethin'."

"Please tell me nothin's changed with us. Tell me everything's all right."

Ben kept seeing Trina Ledger's open legs, Willful between them as he rode her.

"Why?" Ben asked. "Why? Why'd you do this?"

Willful's face blanked. Its features dissolved and then worked to reassemble themselves. "I . . . I ain't know you was comin' over."

He said it with the innocence of a little child seasoned at eluding punishment by exerting charm, looking up at you in that adorable way that he hopes will wilt your anger.

Ben retrieved the Keats book from his pocket and smashed it into Willful's face. He heard a crunch, saw blood on Willful's nose and forehead. He hurled the book onto the grass and took off as Willful howled after him like a tortured dog.

He closed the Keats.

He looked around. Pigfoot Mary's bustled with mostly former Southerners, Ben guessed; folks who, like him and Angeline, didn't give a damn about the South except for the food.

"Everyone down there can go to hell," Angeline once said, "long as they leave the pigs' feet and cornbread."

It was their favorite restaurant. They had heard that Pigfoot

Mary got rich off her cooking, then went into real estate and got richer. The story went that if a tenant was late with the rent, she'd send a note saying, *Send it, and send it damn quick.* They used to laugh every time they heard it. Sometimes Angeline would retell the story to cheer Ben up, or he'd use it to amuse her.

He wondered how she was doing, then almost laughed aloud at the outlandish thought that he didn't know how his own wife was doing.

He threw money on the table and left, then lingered on the sidewalk. He watched Harlemites cram into restaurants that scattered the sweet and tart aromas of barbecue out into the street and pack into clubs with pining horns and plinking piano keys. Some gathered on the sidewalk outside the clubs, smoking and ostensibly gossiping or catching up, but really trying to catch the remnants of jazz coming from inside.

What to do? Catch a reading at the library? Kill some hours walking up to Sugar Hill and back? Or go home and pray that Angeline was already asleep and the bedroom door shut? He opted for Sugar Hill, but saw a familiar face coming toward him.

"Hey. Baby Back," he said when the trumpeter was a couple of feet away.

Baby Back didn't stop, respond, or look.

"It's me. Ben. Ben Charles. Mr. Poet. How you doing?"

Baby Back brushed on by. Ben trailed him.

"Hey. Hey! Baby Back. Mr. Johnston? I know you ain't ignoring me when I'm talking to you. *Trying* to talk to you."

Baby Back neither sped up nor slowed down as Ben tagged after him like an unwanted puppy too dumb to accept that it's being left behind. "I'm talking to you! Damn it, turn around and talk to me!"

But Baby Back continued apace.

"You think because you're a big-time musician on his way to Paris one day, you can ignore me? Well, you ain't that big. If you're so big, why you working in a basement dive? Huh? Why ain't you at one of the *good* clubs? You ain't no King Oliver, that's why. And never will be. You ain't nothing! You hear me, Mr. Baby Back Johnston? You ain't nothing, so fuck you!"

Baby Back kept going as though Ben's shouting was nothing but normal Harlem street noise. He rounded a corner, disappeared. The puppy didn't pursue. Ben propped himself against a building. When he was calm, he saw he'd attracted a small crowd that kept its distance, staring at him. Like he was crazy.

# 9

*I ride the moon*
*To the dark place,*
*Traveling swiftly.*

*The moon is a slave ship.*
*I am trapped, shriveling.*

*I want to leap overboard.*
*Chains bind me.*

*I want to ditch the moon,*
*Dance to the true beat of my heart,*
*Sip nectar from the stem of a rose.*

His work ethic betrayed him. He couldn't concentrate. He bungled orders, grabbed the wrong food from the kitchen, delivered it to the wrong tables. Even Mr. Kittredge scolded him. "No, no, no, Benjamin. I ordered grapefruit, not toast," he said one morning, his English accent crisper than usual, as David-Nicholas kept his head and eyes down. "This is the third time this week you've botched my order!"

Other patrons complained, too. His boss berated him. He needed a drink.

Licks from a certain trumpet seeped through Teddy's closed door, almost luring Ben out from under the streetlamp across the street. But he pinched his coat snug against the frigid November air, found another bar, and drank double whiskeys until he could pretend he'd blotted out Willful, Baby Back, *this thing*. Alcohol became his refuge. Every night he drank for hours, spent too much, tipped the bartenders more than they deserved, then wobbled home, always bracing to encounter Evelyn Harrisburg. More than once had her door been open an inch. It always clinked closed as he ventured toward it.

His poor service at work yielded less in tips. Less in tips and sizeable spending on liquor spawned money problems. Money problems inflated the tension at home.

"You can't pay your share of the rent this month," Angeline said. "*I* gotta make up the difference. I shouldn't have to bear the brunt of running this house. It ain't fair."

"What the hell you complaining about? You're making plenty of money."

Angeline's pocketbook ballooned from double shifts at the beauty shop, doing hair on her own in people's homes, and her door-to-door cosmetics sales.

"I shouldn't be paying everything," she said.

"Then don't. Just . . . don't."

He left, went to a bar, and shambled home drunk. Next morning, he overslept and Angeline had to shake him awake. He arrived at work late and his boss suspended him for two weeks.

Ben left, shuffling up Twenty-ninth Street, and saw Mr. Kittredge approaching. He wanted to run to him. Until he saw David-Nicholas. They walked so close to each other, they may as well have held hands. David-Nicholas carried a suitcase.

"Why, Benjamin," Kittredge said, frowning, "it's rather early for your shift to have ended."

"I was suspended, sir." He shocked himself with his directness, his non-embarrassment. His eyes went to David-Nicholas's suitcase.

"Ah, yes," Kittredge said. "David-Nicholas is bringing some things to store in my suite. He has so little space in his rooms and I have so much in mine. Nicky, go on. I'm going to talk to Benjamin a moment." He touched the small of the young man's back.

"Certainly, Geoffrey," David-Nicholas said. He nodded to Ben as he left.

Mr. Kittredge produced his billfold. A rich scent floated off the leather. He handed Ben a ten-dollar bill. "Don't bother saying you can't accept it because you can and you will."

Ben's sense of good manners demanded that he refuse, but he was too tired. "That's too kind of you. Thank you, sir."

"I do hope you can resolve what's troubling you. Whatever it may be." He touched Ben's chin. His hand stayed a shade longer than it should have. "Dear, dear boy."

As he walked away, Ben wished that Mr. Kittredge would touch the small of his back.

"Suspended?" Angeline said. "What's happened to you?" More accusation than question.

"As if you don't know."

Her hands flew to her ears to shield them. "I don't want to hear about that. You still going to church?"

Hoping church could buffer against *this thing*, he had attended a few services at Abyssinian Baptist where he swayed to the gospel music, but couldn't stop leering at the black, brown, and beige men bedecked in their Sunday best.

"No. Not no more," he said.

"Why not? It would help. I know it would. We'll go together."

"You ain't never been no churchgoer, Angeline."

"I'll start. I'll do it for you."

He moped on the sofa, his face in his hands. Angeline played with the keys on the typewriter. Delicately, the way you would a newborn baby's toes.

"Remember when we moved in to this place?" she said, as if baiting him to join her in a memory. He saw her tinkering with the typewriter keys and knew exactly which memory. He stayed silent, but reprised the scene in his head.

They had been living in the Bowery in a tenement flat that they shared with three other families. The bathroom was in the hall. The whole floor used it. It stank so bad, they got good at going in, doing their business, and getting out fast. Ben used to play a game with himself: He'd take a big breath before going in, then try to finish before his lungs burst.

They worked hard, saved every penny, and rented this new place on 128th. They owned no furniture when they moved in, not even a bed, and Mrs. Harrisburg sneered that their presence in the building was disgraceful. She gossiped that they were ignorant Southern trash. It was six months before the women in the building would even say "Good morning" to Angeline.

Their first day in the apartment, a small crate sat up against the wall in the living room. He assumed it had been left by mistake, but then saw Angeline laughing into her hand. He fiddled with it, opened it, and found a typewriter. The white circular keys were rimmed with metal. The black letters had faded a bit, but stood out in bold, formal strokes. The typewriter's black casing bore a few scratches, but had been buffed to a shine.

"You got this . . . you bought this? For me?" he said. "How?"

"Smart saving," she said. "And a couple of odd jobs. Stash away a penny here, a nickel there: Takes a while, but it adds up. Got it secondhand, so it wasn't too much. You like it?"

"Hell, yeah, I like it. Thank you, Angel."

"Now you can take all them poems you been writing longhand and type 'em up."

"Well, not right away," he said.

"Why not?"

"Gotta learn how to type first!"

He led her into their new bedless bedroom, spread a blanket on the floor, and had no trouble doing his duty.

The memory decayed. Ben removed his face from his hands. Angeline stood before him with a look of pity. *For me? For herself?* She touched him and he hopped up from the sofa, fled to his desk, quickly typed out a poem that had vexed him all day.

*A single wavering jazz phrase,*
*Dipping and cresting, dipping and cresting,*
*Carving out melody as it sways*
*The room with an ebony haze.*

Angeline loitered in the Neutral Territory: the doorway between the bedroom and living room. "Ben. This ain't right. What's happening with us—with *you*—it ain't right."

She spoke like she couldn't go on like this. More fearful to Ben, she spoke like she *wouldn't*. If she left him, he was lost. She was the only thing standing between him and *this thing*.

"You gonna leave me, Angel? You gonna divorce me?"

She said nothing for a long time. When she did at last, it was with the resignation of someone who had dissected all of her options and found them all lacking.

"Ruby's youngest sister got divorced. Said it was the worst mistake of her life. She thought it'd set her free. Please. People avoid her. Women at church won't talk to her. Nobody trusts a divorced woman. She wants to get married again, but no man wants some other man's used goods, especially if she can't . . . if she can't bear children."

She turned to enter the bedroom, then stopped. She spoke with her back to Ben. "If you decide to go back to church, I'll go with you."

She stepped into the bedroom. She left the door open.

# 10

Willful. Too reckless to survive in Dogwood. He cracked at the seams of that nothing town. He needed more. But in church, the Sunday following the Trina incident, what Willful Hutchison needed was medical attention. The congregation speculated about his bandaged nose, the scar lighting up his forehead.

"Looks like some gal's pappy done gone upside his head," an old woman said.

"Or maybe it was the *gal*," her companion replied.

Trina sat with her new fiancé. Her ma beamed as if her daughter was marrying the prince of Ethiopia. The Reverend Glover was, in fact, the most eligible colored bachelor within twenty miles, and Trina should have been the giddiest girl in that church. But she looked bereft.

Mrs. Hutchison must have warned Willful to behave. He restrained his legs from their preferred capital *V* and kept his hands folded in his lap. During service, he looked over at Ben, his eyes begging forgiveness, Ben unwilling to bestow it.

He submerged himself in chores, but the vision of Willful embedded between Trina's legs boiled up again and again. It persecuted him. He tripped and dropped the bucket after milking the cow; let the grits burn when his ma told him to watch the stove;

dropped a basket of eggs, breaking them all before wasting into tears. He thought his ma would yell, but he sensed from her something new—concern.

His pa spoke to him one day as they labored in the field, first time he'd said a thing to his son in forever.

"We's worried about you, boy. We's prayin' for you."

For the first time in a long time, Ben knew his parents loved him.

In church several Sundays later, Willful and Trina remained numb. The bruises on his face had scabbed over and Trina held her fiancé's hand, but her eyes kept roaming across the church to Willful.

Services ended and in the mayhem of exiting the church, Willful closed in on Ben.

"Meet me at the swimmin' hole at four o'clock."

"I don't want to."

"Don't lie."

Misery and love and desire. They played with Ben, flopped him back and forth. Misery produced pride and pride insisted he hold on to Willful's betrayal. But desire, addictive and unwieldy, reduced him to the brink of forgiveness. Ben began to understand the pitfalls of love, how it lured you, spoiled you with bliss, made you so dependent that you couldn't combat its pull.

He arrived at the pond, found Willful sitting on a large rock on the bank, staring out at the water as a couple of long-tailed ducks skated across.

"I'm dyin' without you," Willful said.

Ben dropped his head onto his lover's shoulder. Willful's arm coiled around him, but only momentarily before he removed it. He looked around. He seemed nervous.

"The thing with Trina, it ain't gone happen again," he said.

"Better not. She gettin' married."

"Yeah. To that prissy preacher."

They laughed, then looked out at the water, quiet, trying to feel comfortable with each other again. During the interval, Ben made his decision.

"Will? What you did with Trina . . . do that to me. I want you inside me."

Willful smiled. "We ain't got no place we can go."

"We got the woods."

The flesh on Willful's neck and throat tightened. The veins swelled. "The woods ain't safe for us. Not no more."

"What you mean, 'not no more'?"

Willful took a handkerchief from his pocket and wiped his face and the back of his neck. "The woods ain't private enough. We gotta be careful, Know-nothin'."

"Did something happen? What—"

"I know a place we can go. You know that house on Ol' Cane Road? The one with the red door? Meet me there. Not tomorrow night, but the next. And be careful. Make sure don't nobody see you."

Ben knew peace again. The blank space of the last few weeks was now refilled with his Willful. The next two days on the farm saw the return of his restless work ethic and he sensed relief from his folks as he executed his chores without spilling or breaking anything.

Willful inside him. He wouldn't need Trina Ledger or whores ever again. But they couldn't sneak around like this forever. If the groves of dogwood trees couldn't safeguard them, maybe the house with the red door could be *their* place. They could fix it up, plant a garden, live there together. And there was enough land there to start a farm. Ben would have to purge Willful of his lazy ways, but he could see them working their fields by day and spending their nights with their books, reading *to each other,* because Willful would finally let Ben teach him.

But this was fantasy. Two men couldn't live together like a husband and a wife.

The day he was to meet Willful, Mrs. Ledger called on his ma with a new parcel of gossip.

"Julius and Paula Sue Thurman's twin boys swear they seen Willful in the woods, kissin' and huggin' on a boy."

Ben sat in his corner shelling peas. He started to sweat.

"The twins say they seen Willful and this boy touchin' each other," Mrs. Ledger said. "Intimate-like."

Ben's ma frowned. "Who the boy?"

"The twins never got close enough to see clear."

"When this happen?"

"Paula Sue say the twins just told her and Julius. But they seen Willful and the boy a few times over the last few months."

Ben's ma cut another piece of pie for her guest. "Few months. Hmm."

"The Bible say, 'A man shalt not lie with a man, as with a woman. It is an abomination: They shall surely be put to death.' "

Those words raked through him as he languished under the streetlamp across from Teddy's. They had cursed him often, and always in Mrs. Ledger's pious voice.

Rain fell. The music behind Teddy's door competed with shouts and laughter and records from the second floor of an apartment half a block down. A dim lamp lit the apartment. The silhouettes of partiers darted across the window.

*It is an abomination. They shall surely be put to death.*

But he was dying *now*. And he hadn't touched a man since Willful.

The rain continued, a little heavier, a little colder. Ben's least favorite weather: cold, wet, and windy. He scrunched his hands down into his coat pockets for the journey home or maybe to a bar. Then Teddy's door opened and out stepped Baby Back. Surprised and annoyed by the rain, he crumpled his hat down on his head before walking toward Seventh Avenue with the same undaunted gait as the night he ignored Ben.

It was only midnight on a Friday. He wondered where Baby Back was headed. The trumpeter would normally be jamming till all hours. Before he had a chance to argue himself out of it, curiosity angled Ben's feet toward Seventh Avenue, and he followed Mr. Baby Back Johnston.

## 11

Baby Back carried his trumpet case. *Means he left Teddy's for the night,* Ben thought. He stayed far enough back so Baby Back wouldn't see him, but close enough that he wouldn't lose him. Rain fell steadily, but not enough to deter Harlemites on a Friday night. Ben had to wind through crowds bundled up in coats and huddling under umbrellas. He kept his eyes on the trumpeter as he tailed him. His height and his big, broad back stood out like a beacon. The rain poured harder now. Ben wished he had an umbrella.

It had rained the night he went to meet Willful at the house with the red door. What started as a pitter-pat of drops soon toughened into a downpour with thunder and lightning thrown in for good measure. By the time he reached the place, he was sopped.

The house was more of a hut. Small. Dirty. Gloomy. The wood was aged, the red paint on the door fading and chipping off. From outside it looked uninviting, but there was a glow in the window and Ben went inside to a hearty blaze in the fireplace.

And then he saw Willful, on the bed, naked. He came to Ben.

"How's my Know-nothin'?"

"Wet."

"Come here."

Willful undressed him, wrapped him in a blanket, held him as they stood in front of the fire. Then he took him by the hand and led him to the bed. Ben's heart trounced as Willful unwrapped the blanket and laid him on his back on the thin, linen-less mattress. It gave off an odor, stale and musty.

Willful touched him all over, finessed him to a sense of safety. He spread Ben's legs apart with his knees, released a stream of saliva onto his penis, then penetrated him.

It was like being split open from the inside. Ben cried out as his body resisted the intrusion.

"Know-nothin', relax."

Ben hadn't known it would hurt this bad. Willful jabbed in and out with excruciating speed. Ben wanted to stop, but also wanted to be strong for Willful. It hadn't hurt Trina Ledger—she couldn't seem to get enough. He shut his eyes to block the tears and grinded his teeth together so hard, he thought they'd break. Finally he screamed, "Stop! Willful! Will! Stop!"

But Willful pummeled him. He didn't let up. Drops of his sweat pelted Ben's face and chest. Ben opened his mouth to scream again just as Willful growled—a feral, uncurbed sound—and fell on top of him, sweaty and spent. It was minutes before he regained his strength and withdrew. He used the blanket to wipe himself off.

Ben's tears ballooned. His body shook.

"Shh. Shh," Willful said, rocking him.

Ben got up, started to dress. Willful sat on the edge of the bed, watching. He opened his mouth, then shut it. He opened it again and said, "It ain't gone hurt that bad next time. I promise."

Ben slipped into his clothes. They were heavy from all the rain they had absorbed. Cold, too. His shoes were soaked and muddy. It would probably take days for them to dry out. They would never be clean again.

"Know-nothin'?" Willful said. "Ben? You hearin' me? Next time'll be all right."

"Next time."

"See you soon?"

Ben left the house, left Willful sitting there on the bed, naked.

The storm was mostly over; only a few vagrant drops sloshed onto the ground now. The air smelled damp and muddy. Dazed, he inhaled deeply to clear his head so he could get home, sneak back in the house undetected.

He was sore, back there.

*A man shalt not lie with a man, as with a woman. It is an abomination.*

The verse stabbed at him again the following morning when he realized he had bled back there. Had Trina bled?

The next Sunday in church, when Willful looked over, Ben aimed his sight straight ahead, refusing him a crumb of hope. In his periphery were Trina Ledger and her fiancé, set to be married within weeks. Her eyes were fixed on Willful.

Life returned to its mundane, pre-Willful regularity. Ben worked himself to death, to purge the sins of the past year. The soreness from that night was gone. Shame blossomed in its place.

The next three Sundays, Mrs. Hutchison and the daughters attended church without Willful. Ben hoped he had gone to the brothel in Robertville and would stay there. On that third Sunday, Julius and Paula Sue Thurman's twin boys tugged at their ma and pa and pointed at something on the other side of the church. The Thurmans followed the line of their sons' pointing fingers. It led to Ben.

*The twins say they seen Willful and this boy touchin' each other. Intimate-like.*

The gossip spread like an epidemic. On a trip to town with his pa two days later, men poked each other, cocking their heads in his direction. When his ma dispatched him on errands, neighbors received him cordially as they stashed their children indoors. The rumors reached his folks. One night at supper, they confronted him.

"There's a ugly story goin' around 'bout you and that Hutchison boy," his ma said. "You heard it?"

"Yes'm."

"It true?"

"No'm," he said, careful to sound decisive, but not overdo it.

His folks exchanged glances, then went back to their supper.

Next evening, they went to church for a revival meeting to be presided over by the Reverend Glover, Trina Ledger's fiancé. As they waited for the service to begin, the couple dozen congregants watched Ben like he was new in town. The allegations revolted and titillated them. The Thurmans were there, wallowing in their status as the originators of the story.

But Reverend Glover hadn't arrived for his own revival. Trina and her folks hadn't either. Folks grew impatient. A few had gone home, resigned to finding the Holy Spirit some other time, when the Reverend Ledger vaulted into the church with a shotgun.

"She's dead!" he shouted. "My Trina's dead! Willful Hutchison—he as good as killed her. She was with child. By Willful. She died trying to get rid of it. It's Willful's fault. Him and that mother of his. She knew about them."

Nobody moved. Nobody talked. The only sound was the reverend's wild panting. And with that shotgun in his hands, the people didn't know whether to console their beloved preacher or take cover.

"I need some good men. I'ma run that whole Hutchison family out this town. Who'll come with me?"

An ensemble of men trooped forward, Ben's pa among them.

"I'll come."

"Count me in."

"We gone rid ourselves and our womenfolk of that Hutchison boy once and for all!"

The reverend held the shotgun in quaking hands. "Lord Jesus, keep me from killing that boy, though I know you wouldn't count it a sin."

It hit Ben: These men intended to tear the Hutchisons from their home, banish them to the open road with no money, no food. But that wouldn't appease the Reverend Ledger. He wanted blood for blood. The injustice sent Ben spiraling at him.

"No!" he screamed. He tried to wrest the shotgun from the preacher's hands. "Don't kill him! Don't kill Willful!"

The gun swung here, there, and everywhere as they battled over it. The women screamed and flung themselves into the pews, joined by most of the men. The reverend, powered by hysteria and aided by sheer bodily size, clobbered Ben to the ground where he cried and writhed like someone hit with the Holy Spirit on a threshing floor. The tussle for the shotgun over, people left the pews. They circled Ben as he blubbered on. His screams devolved to sobs.

"Please don't hurt Willful. Please."

By the time his ma lugged him out of the church, the Reverend Ledger and his posse had gone.

They didn't kill Willful. But they did expel the Hutchison family from Dogwood with just the tattered clothes on their backs. Ben never knew what became of them. He never saw Willful again.

Trina's death shattered colored Dogwood. Different versions of the events circulated—some plausible, some preposterous—but when all the various and varying stories were distilled down to their essences, the facts added up to this:

Trina Ledger, a preacher's daughter and a preacher's betrothed, had been three months' pregnant. Facing disgrace at best, exile at worst, Trina settled on a third option: her ma's knitting needles. On her deathbed, she admitted that Willful was the only man she'd ever been with. Then she implicated his ma and sisters in the hiding of the affair. She did not implicate Ben. Why would remain a mystery. The tragedy was compounded when the Reverend Glover said he would have taken the blame for the pregnancy and married her anyway. He loved her that much.

"They touched each other the way a man and woman touch each other."

"Willful's older. He must'a been the one instigated it."

"They was doin' it in the dogwood groves."

"Willful sodomized Ben."

Dogwood shunned the Charles family. Visitors no longer called. His ma was ousted from the roster of church-cleaning women. Folks who'd known his pa for decades walked by without a word or a nod. At church no one spoke to them or even sat in the same pew.

He heard his folks murmuring behind the barn and in their room, conspiring. At supper a week after Trina's funeral, they disclosed their plan.

"Ol' man Zachary's plantation need cotton pickers," his ma said. "We sending you there for the season. You'll bring your wages home. Maybe by the time you get back, folks'll forget this mess. Or at least forgive a little."

The Zachary plantation sat twenty miles east of town. A contingent of colored folks from Dogwood was heading there to seek work, traveling in a caravan of wagons. Ben's ma packed him some salt pork and a canteen of sassafras tea for the trip. Sitting in the back of the flatbed wagon, some of his neighbors stared at him or whispered to one another or laughed. Others turned eyes, heads, whole bodies away in disgust. Trina Ledger had sinned, but her sin had been natural. Ben's marked him a degenerate.

Picking cotton was hard, hard, hard work. A picker needed quick, agile hands and flinty skin on his fingers to repel the burrs from the cotton stalks. A strong back was a blessing since the stalks were low and you had to bend down to pick. Ben's first few days were wretched. His fingers bled and his lower back ached so bad, he had to stagger on his knees to pick in the damning heat. The plantation paid forty cents for each hundred pounds picked. In his first week, he couldn't even get to a hundred pounds a day.

But blockheaded determination prevailed. His hands became impervious to the burrs. He heeded the advice of veteran pickers who advised him to stretch his back in the morning and at night to fend off the soreness. He soon upped his totals to three hundred pounds a day and more.

The workers hailed from a medley of nearby towns. Ben barely spoke to any of them, afraid that Dogwood tongues had wagged about him. At night, he slept under the spreading branches of the laurel oak trees, like most of the workers. He could have rented floor space in someone's shack, but that would cost. He didn't want to spend any more than necessary.

He had a plan. One that required money.

One night after a particularly brutal day of picking, he lay motionless under the trees, trying to catch what there was of a breeze. The night was cave-black except for a quarter slice of moon, the stars strewn across the sky. Snores and whispers of the other workers thrummed around him, while only vague outlines of bodies were visible. He listened in on two men's conversation.

"Where *you* wanna go?"

"Philly."

"Where's that?"

"I don't know."

"How you gone go someplace and you don't even know where it's at?"

"It's up north. All I gotta know."

They talked Boston, Newark, Pittsburgh. Aside from being Up North, neither man knew the particulars of any of these utopias, with one exception.

"They say New York City ain't nothin' but pretty lights, pretty girls, and some pretty loose women!"

"Is it big?"

"Ten thousand of people live there."

*Ten thousand people. I could get lost among ten thousand, be anonymous, start over.*

"And they got lots of jazz music."

"What's jazz music?"

"What? Boy, you ain't never heard jazz?"

"Is it like church hymns?"

"No, it ain't like no church hymns!"

"What's it like?"

The man considered. "Fire. Magic. Dancin'. You ever read poetry?"

"You know I can't read."

"Pretend you can. Then take fire, magic, dancing, and poetry, mix 'em all together, throw in ragtime and a banjo, and that's what jazz sounds like. And they got plenty of it in New York City."

Ten thousand people and a music that sounded like poetry.

Cotton-picking season ended and the folks from Dogwood boarded the wagons to go home. Ben didn't join them. He made his way on foot to the nearest train station. He bought a ticket on a northbound train. He didn't send word to his ma and pa that he was never coming home.

# 12

<u>Shall I?</u>

By Benjamin Marcus Charles

The door looms shut.
It drips red,
Like the bruised
Insides of my thighs.

*Try the window.*
It is sealed.
Through it the moon
Hangs far and lazy
In some other sky,
Cowering from the
Sting of ancient verses
That revel in the
Mirth of condemnation.

*Open the door.*
No. The red will singe my hands,
Make them unfit for love
And me unworthy.

*But you got love running through you!*
*It runs through you, and through you,*
    *and through you.*
*Kiss his pretty lips,*
*His pretty hips.*

Shall I open the door?
Taste the moon?
It shines like an epiphany,
Writes over the red
With ink that sings peace.

The melody sways me,
Slays me,
Persuades me.

Drink the wine.
Taste the moon.
Open the door.
Sing, peace.

# 13

It was still raining. He had followed Baby Back to a brownstone on 140th Street. People drifted in and out while jazz thudded through its windows. Baby Back had gone inside ten minutes before. Something festive was transpiring. *A rent party,* Ben thought.

"Well, hello."

A young man sat behind a small folding table in the vestibule. He wore a chic suit with a green carnation in the buttonhole. His slicked-back hair gleamed. Makeup glazed his lips, cheeks, and above his eyes.

"What can we do for you tonight?" he said in a voice part girlish alto, part gritty baritone.

"Just want to go in."

"Two meters, jack."

Ben handed over the two quarters. "This a rent party, right?"

The young man laughed. "You ain't hip to this jive, is you?"

"What jive is that?"

"Go on in and you'll see. But don't touch the displays."

"Displays?"

"Yeah. They bite."

The stink of reefer ambushed Ben. The rumble of conversation and jazz commingled. There were sofas packed with guys and chicks consuming liquor. Dusky light. A side table stacked with fried fish, fried chicken, cornbread, chitterlings, collard greens, pigs' feet. A small band. A bar in the corner crammed with bottles of bootleg and a stockpile of teacups. And Ben understood what that *displays* business was all about when he saw, in the center of the room, a man and woman fucking on a small raised stage.

This was no rent party. It was a *buffet flat*. A house featuring a cafeteria-style variety of naughty offerings from which guests could take their pick.

People loitered and drank and carried on and devoured the action on the stage. Ben couldn't pull his eyes away. He liked the woman's pretty face. She had a big, shiny spit curl plastered to her forehead like that Josephine Baker girl who had just made a splash over in Paris. But he fell in love with the man's dark brown, sweat-slicked body.

"You better step to the bar if you plan on staying."

A woman's voice, but he turned to see a burly man in a suit. A short crop of hair flowered above a mean face.

"Only gonna be here a few minutes," Ben said. "I'm looking for someone."

"Don't matter. Step to the bar now or get the fuck out."

Something didn't gibe. Woman's voice. Big man's body. Then Ben realized: It was a manly woman who liked women. A *bulldagger*. She coerced him to the bar. He bought a whiskey.

"Hey, like I said, I'm looking for someone. You see a tall cat carrying a trumpet case?"

"What I look like? The fucking Bureau of Missing Persons?" She marched away, then turned back. "And don't touch the displays!" She headed to the door to bulldoze newly arrived customers to the bar.

Ben set his sights on the stage. He wasn't aroused at all—until he tuned the woman out and zeroed in on the man. He made himself look away. He eyed the stairs, went up to the second floor to search for Baby Back.

Another bar. Another table cluttered with food. More people on sofas. And another stage: one guy and *two* chicks this time.

"Go on, get your hambone boiled, jack!" someone yelled out.

"Yeah! Look at him knockin' that pad!"

There wasn't enough room on the sofas. A woman in a full-length beaver coat roosted on the arm of a chair. A man in overalls stood and ate while watching the action. Serious cats played cards at a table in a corner. The game ended, money changed hands, and Ben saw a sinister flash of metal as one of the losers opened his suit jacket. Across the room, a guy handed some dollar bills to a chick in a white dress. She jammed them down her brassiere, piloted him to a room, shut the door. Other prostitutes worked the crowd, some allowing men to fondle them right there, others escorting their quarry into private rooms. Reefer cigarettes were being passed around and a bunch of folks knelt over a coffee table sniffing up cocaine as Ethel Waters's "Shake That Thing" bumped out of a phonograph.

But no Baby Back.

Ben went to the third floor. The display: two women getting snug. One with big breasts with dark aureoles, the other with perky breasts as small and pretty as figs. They fondled each other, each sticking fingers and tongues in places that made the other growl. Several guys flanked the stage, drooling. Every now and then men in suits patrolled the room to keep the droolers in check.

But the main audience on this floor was women. Some in flapper dresses and makeup, others in men's suits and sporting short hair. A few in dresses reclined on the laps of those in suits. The woman in white from the second floor was there, chatting up a suit who took her by the hand and steered her into a private room.

A second stage on the other side of the floor housed a three-piece, all-female gutbucket band with a dark black girl singer in a blond wig.

> *"Don't send me no men,*
> *I don't need the hassle.*
> *Got me a woman*
> *Cleanin' my castle.*
>
> *She cleans it real thorough,*
> *I never complain.*

*She mops it so good,*
*It drives me insane."*

Where was Baby Back? And what would Ben do when he found him?

One last floor awaited exploration.

A guy in a seersucker suit and red necktie sat on the floor of the basement, next to a door, long legs spread wide, his feet shoeless and sockless. He smoked a reefer cigarette and smiled like the cat who had swallowed the canary, the eggs, the nest, *and* the tree.

"Heyyyyyy, mon. What you looking for?" he asked in a singsong West Indian accent.

"Uh . . . a guy. I think he—"

"A guy? Ain't we all? You let me know when you find one, mon, and if he got a cute friend, you tell him I'm available. Oh, you mean a specific guy? You think he might be down *here?* It's one meter to come in here, mon."

"I already paid at the door," Ben said.

"That was general admission. This here is a special exhibition."

"And don't touch the displays, right?"

"I didn't say that, mon."

It was darker than the other rooms. A saxophone whined. A bar sat at the back. The display: two guys—one black, one tan. The black one on all fours, the tan one topping him. Ben paid heightened attention to the one on all fours. He didn't seem to be in pain.

Small tables along the walls took the place of sofas. Only men in this room. They sat in twos or an occasional three, talking quietly and drinking. Only a few single guys and they scrutinized each new man who entered. Candles lit each table. Couples slow-danced in the empty space in the center of the floor. Cheek against cheek. Lips bruising lips. All to the moan of the sax and the clinking of teacups filled with bootleg liquor.

Ben didn't know if he'd discovered Sodom and Gomorrah or paradise, but he watched these men and felt like he'd come home. He bought a drink, found a table, and hadn't been sitting two minutes when he saw him: Baby Back, at a table along the opposite wall with two guys. He faced Ben's direction, but was too consumed in his conversation to notice him. Ben willed him to look over. It took ten minutes, but he did. Baby Back eyed him, frowned, then resumed his conversation. He looked over again, said something to his friends, then crossed the floor, weaving in and out through the dancing couples.

"Mr. Poet," he said. "You ain't sitting with a whore this time."

"And you ain't ignoring me this time." Silence, then, "That hurt my feelings."

"You hurt mine. When you walked out with that three-dollar whore."

"Two," Ben said.

"Come again?"

"She was a *two*-dollar whore. And I'm sorry."

Baby Back analyzed Ben. A judge sizing up a defendant. "What's your story? I don't understand you. You don't make sense. You let me flirt with you right in front of your wife. You recite a love poem for me. And then you flaunt that whore in my face. What the fuck is wrong with you? You need to go to one of them head doctors."

He nearly capsized two dancers as he clomped back across the floor to rejoin his friends.

Ben sedated himself with more alcohol to keep from crying.

It got late. The place began to clear out. He finished his whiskey, wanted another, but had run out of money. Baby Back and company headed to the door, laughing. He slapped one of his friends on his backside. And now Ben regretted his poverty because he needed more alcohol to buffer his pain.

He felt a hand squeeze his shoulder. It was warm, its weight good.

"I shouldn't have said that, about the head doctor," Baby Back said.

"But it's true."

Baby Back sat. "Mrs. Charles know you're here?"

Ben shook his head *no*.

"You think she'd believe it if she knew?" Baby Back said.

"I don't think *I* believe it. This place is a mess."

They laughed.

"Looks like you've had a lot to drink tonight," Baby Back said.

"I have a lot to drink *every* night. Trying to flush *this thing* out of me."

"What thing?"

"Look around you."

Baby Back did. Something caught his eye; Ben followed his gaze to the dance floor. Only two couples dancing now. One couple dipped each other and threw back their heads, laughing. But Baby Back watched the quieter, slower pair. You couldn't even call what they were doing *dancing*. They just held each other and swayed a little to the sax.

"They're sweet, ain't they?" Baby Back said.

"They look like . . . like they love each other."

"They do." Baby Back reached across the table, touched Ben's hand, pressed it. "Now why would you want to flush that out of you?"

Ben slid his hand away. "Where you from, Baby Back?"

His abruptness made the trumpeter wince. "South Carolina. You?"

"Georgia. How long you been up here?"

"Nine years. Had to get away from them goddamn crackers. South Carolina ain't no place for a colored boy. 'Specially one who . . ." He looked over at the sweet couple on the dance floor. The shorter man pressed his head against his tall partner's chest. His partner's hand cupped the back of his head. Both held their eyes shut. "Well. I had to go. Can I tell you something? Please?"

Ben lifted his eyes out of his empty glass.

"You're the handsomest, most charming man I've ever met," Baby Back said.

"I don't believe you."

"I'm really, really sorry to hear that."

He took Ben's hand again, and kissed it. It felt so good, Ben shuddered. Baby Back kissed it again. And again. Then he pulled Ben up from the table and onto the dance floor. Now they, too, slow danced, Ben's head against Baby Back's shoulder, his forehead just touching the trumpeter's neck where the skin was warm, a little stubbly. He let Baby Back lead, let himself flow and float.

The sax player started a new tune and they returned to the table.

They pressed hands again, their fingers skating across each other's palms.

"Recite me your best poem," Baby Back said.

"You always ask guys to recite poems for you?"

"Just the guys I like. Now do like I said: Recite me your best poem."

He wasn't smiling. There was no humor about him. He had issued a command and expected to be obeyed. His aggressiveness aroused Ben.

He took a breath.

> *"A single wavering jazz phrase,*
> *dipping and cresting, dipping and cresting,*
> *carving out melody as it sways*
>
> *the room with an ebony haze.*
> *But the horn player maintains, 'I'm just testing*
> *a single wavering jazz phrase.'*
>
> *The blues in his sound enchants all my days.*
> *Is he worth my blue soul's investing?*
> *Carving out melody as he sways,*
>
> *his desert-brown face captures my gaze.*
> *I'm blinded. Inside my heart he's nesting.*
> *Carving out melody as he sways,*
>
> *the horn player drawls me into a daze.*
> *He burns my knees with his rhythmic ways."*

The room was mostly empty now, only the sweet couple left dancing. A few people still drank at the tables. The black man and the tan man on the stage had gone. The sax whispered. Baby Back's knees pressed Ben's under the table.

"You can have that poem. If you want it," Ben said.

Baby Back looked at him, shrewd, suspicious. "Yeah?"

Ben considered a moment. But only a moment. "Yeah. Take it. Please."

# 14

The West Indian in the seersucker suit was still on the floor outside the basement room, but more prostrate than before. He lay back, supporting himself on his elbows, his half-smoked reefer cigarette pinched between the thumb and forefinger of one hand.

"Ahh, looks like you found him, mon," he said to Ben. "I didn't know this was the cat you was looking for. You cuties get out of here now before you make me jealous. And if you two decide you want a third tonight, you let me know."

They left the buffet flat and walked randomly around Harlem. They counted the cabs en route to Jungle Alley. Made jokes about the white swells. Passed a theater where Bessie Smith was singing. Came close to entering a club featuring an up-and-coming trumpeter Baby Back was suspicious of. As they walked, Ben saw attractive men and, for the first time, looked at them—let himself look at them—and felt no shame. Not an ounce.

"Recite me a poem," Baby Back said.

"Again? Right now?"

"Yeah."

> *"A thing of beauty is a joy for ever:*
> *Its loveliness increases; it will never*

Pass into nothingness; but still will keep
A bower quiet for us, and a sleep
Full of sweet dreams, and health, and quiet breathing."

"You wrote that?"

"No."

"Cheater!"

They hit the 131st Street corner. As always, musicians were riffing an improv session. Baby Back looked at his trumpet case. Looked at Ben. Looked at the trumpet case. Grinned at Ben.

"Go on," Ben said.

Baby Back jumped in and transformed a low-key improv into a world-class jam, vanquishing the other musicians like the genius trumpeter he was. The corner attracted a gigantic crowd. Snobs who would never have paid attention to lowly street musicians pressed in to get a look at the cat who was killing it with his horn. Ben had never seen Baby Back perform outside of Teddy's. Had never seen him perform *outside*. The street venue energized him. The bigger, booze-less audience. No walls to constrict his sound, which rocketed up and over and across Harlem.

Watching Baby Back, it planted something in Ben. Something fresh, a little bouncy. A little possessive, too. The trumpeter and his aerial sound may have belonged momentarily to the street audience, but Ben Charles thought he may like to stake his claim on both. Was it too early? Too presumptuous? Early, yes, but hardly presumptuous, he decided. After all, Baby Back had already ridden roughshod over his wife, taken possession of two poems, and been incited to vengeful jealousy over a prostitute. Baby Back was the one who had staked a claim. Ben was only responding in kind.

The improv session ended with backslapping and handshakes among the musicians and frenzy from the crowd. Ben and Baby Back walked away, heading south. It started raining in sprinkles.

"When did you know?" Ben asked. "That you were . . ."

He couldn't say the word. Partly because he didn't *have* a word for it. He didn't want to keep calling it *this thing,* and there was something unsavory about *sodomite*.

"Young," Baby Back said. "You?"

"Fourteen years old exactly."

"What, it suddenly hit you the day you turned fourteen?"

"Yeah, actually."

They kept walking and talking, their shoulders brushing against each other with frequency, the first time unintentionally when Ben swerved out of someone's way. After that, the brushing became part game, part affection.

"You been in love?" Baby Back asked.

"Yes. I was fourteen."

"That magic age again. What was his name?"

"Willful."

"What kind of name is that?"

Ben sighed. "That, Mr. Baby Back Johnston, is a long story."

"We all got one of those, don't we?"

Baby Back put an arm around Ben, only for a moment, but it was enough to quench Ben's need to be touched by this man whom his heart was growing big over.

"What do we call ourselves?" he asked. "*Pansies? Fairies?*" He cringed. "*Sodomites?* Ain't there a nicer word?"

"*Queer.*"

Ben thought about this. "Well. Beats *sodomite.*"

They walked a little more and then Baby Back said, "I want to take you someplace. Come on."

He led Ben to a place in Jungle Alley. The lighted sign out front read THE CLAM HOUSE.

"You're taking me to a seafood joint?" Ben said. "I ain't complaining or nothing."

It was a club, not a restaurant, with the requisite amounts of reefer, cigarette smoke, and low light. A long bar ran along one side, tables lined the wall on the other. A slim aisle slinked between them. The tables seated two each and were loaded with men. A piano rose above the chatter. Heavy. Moody. The sound distant, like an echo. And above that, a growling horn (a trombone?), its timbre husky as it moaned out blues. Ben couldn't see the piano or the trombonist.

A hostess stood behind a podium in a green velvet evening gown, arm-length white gloves, and a necklace of diamonds and emeralds.

She looked like a colored version of a moving picture actress with her exuberantly coifed, near-blond hair. She took occasional puffs from a cigarette in a silver holder, nonchalantly blowing out smoke like she was just too damn beautiful. She screamed and threw her arms around Baby Back.

"Baby Back Johnston! How you doin', doll?"

"Good to see you, May. How's my girl?"

Ben was immobile. May, all makeup and glamorous getup, possessed the bellowing voice of a man.

"This is Ben," Baby Back said. "Ben, meet May Hem."

May extended a gloved hand, gripped Ben's like a boxer. "Lovely to meet you. Follow me."

She walked ahead of them. Her gown, low-cut in back, unmasked a network of toned muscle on a body well over six feet tall. She moved with the grace of a bear as she led them up the slim aisle. The moan of the trombone increased, dipping into low notes and then wailing high, the piano loping underneath. Ben still couldn't see the musicians.

The long, slim aisle led to a larger room. An assorted crowd—coloreds and whites, men and women, queers and non-queers—partied at a flock of tables. The dance floor was mostly colored on colored with one or two mixed couples and even a pair of white guys waltzing.

The low lighting softened and blurred the place around the edges. And that moaning trombone bedeviled Ben, a sound that might insinuate its way into his dreams. He followed the direction of the music and found a stage in back. At the piano sat a three-hundred-pound man dressed in a white tux and white top hat, his fingers romping across the keyboard, providing backup to the trombone's yowling. But Ben still didn't see the trombonist. Then, watching the pianist, seeing his mouth open and close in exact time with the wailing horn, Ben realized that it wasn't a trombone he'd been hearing. A voice, words, became clear.

> *"The man's a good cook,*
> *Gals like him a lot,*
> *'Specially with his big piece of beef in their pot.*

He stirs it up good,
They know he's the boss,
'Specially when he pours in his salty good sauce."

The pianist's voice was as fat as he was, and growly and warbly. A voice like a muted horn.

May brought Ben and Baby Back to a table and then departed with bulky steps in her high-heeled shoes.

"We need some drinks," Baby Back said. "Hey! Anna!"

A waitress squealed and pranced over as quickly as size eleven feet in three-inch heels would allow. "Ooh, Baby Back! Where you been, child? Ain't seen you in the longest. Thought you finally went to Paris or maybe some lucky guy snatched up your big, sweet ass!"

The words bounded out in a brawny baritone. Every waitress in The Clam House was too tall, had legs much too muscular, or a back way too broad.

"Ben, meet Anna Mossity."

"Hi, Anna. Nice to meet you."

"You too, child." Then to Baby Back: "He's cute. Go on with your copasetic self!"

The pianist's singing distracted Ben. The man looked foolish—all that flab in a white tux and top hat—but his fingers somersaulted across the keys and his voice nailed every note.

"My man won't use my front door.
Thinks too many been through there before.
The entrance don't nobody use
Be the one he always choose.
That's how I got me these backdoor blues."

"She's something, right?" Baby Back said.

"She?"

"That's Gladys."

"Is she a real 'she'?"

Anna Mossity brought their drinks and Ben swirled in the whirlwind of Baby Back and dancing and men and Gladys's dirty, lively blues. The edges of things, blurry before, now melted and overlapped into one another, distorting boundaries.

They left The Clam House. Five minutes later a hard rain soaked them, but Ben cared only about Baby Back and about the light wind twirling inside him. He laughed out loud. *This thing,* after years of battle, was now a light wind. Baby Back must have taken his laugh as a signal because he plucked him off the sidewalk and into an alley, placed him against a wall, and planted his tongue in his mouth.

"Come on," Baby Back said. "Let's go home."

Home was a boardinghouse on 131st, not far from the corner where the impromptu musicians gathered.

A quilt lay on the bed. It looked like somebody's grandma had infused it with all her skill and all her soul. It was square after square of every conceivable pattern and fabric—plaid, stripes, gingham, polka dots, tartan—all sewn into a creative whole. A writing desk against one wall was stacked with a phonograph and a mess of records. A hat rack hosted a slew of rakish hats. An assortment of books lived on the nightstand—all volumes of poetry by Negro writers. Ben couldn't hold back a smile, but when Baby Back touched the small of his back his body locked up. Nervousness choked him. He was relieved when something across the room caught his attention.

"What are these?" he asked, fleeing to the bureau. On top stood three photographs in simple wood frames. Their sepia coloring burnished them with a dreamy quality. The middle picture was a full-body portrait of a colored man in a suit, spats, and gloves. A three-cornered handkerchief peaked out of the front pocket of his suit jacket. He looked off to the side, his expression composed of a mild smile, a look of tranquil confidence. His snazzy suit put him on par with any gentleman guest at The Pavilion. And he was extraordinarily handsome.

The photograph to the left showed the same man engaged in some kind of stage skit. Dressed in a tux with tails, he carried a trumpet and was flanked by a half dozen chorines in broad-brimmed hats and floor-length gowns. They carried voluminous feather fans and they ogled the man adoringly. His mouth was opened wide as if the picture had been snapped in the midst of a ringing high note.

The third photograph was probably the same man, again performing, this time wearing a top hat and an outrageous checkered suit. He was made up in blackface. The overtly dark makeup contrasted with the whites of his eyes. The lips were painted on in that exaggerated minstrel fashion. He held a watermelon that he seemed to be sneaking off with.

"Who's this?" Ben asked.

"Roland."

"He's . . . beautiful."

"I know," Baby Back said.

"He's an actor, huh?"

"He was. He's dead."

Baby Back stood in front of the photos, head bowed as if paying his respects at a shrine.

"Was he someone you loved?" Ben said.

"I don't talk about him."

Baby Back fell silent, but his hand found the small of Ben's back again. It rested there a moment before rotating Ben around to face him.

"Well," Baby Back said.

"Well."

Nervousness paralyzed Ben. Their tryst in the alley had vitalized him. But here in this comfy little room, there was no adventure, only intimacy.

"You all right?" Baby Back said.

"Yeah. Yes. No. I don't know."

"This ain't your first time, is it?"

"My first time in a long time," Ben said.

"Willful? Tell me about him."

*If you tell me about Roland.* "Later."

Baby Back began to undress, taking his time shedding each article of clothing. He made a production of it, a burlesque almost. Ben became more and more aroused with each disappearing garment. And he didn't just discard his clothes into a pile on the floor—he hung them in the closet and folded them methodically into the bureau, lengthening the burlesque, maddening and exciting Ben, the trumpeter's impish smile evidence that he loved it.

With all the layers stripped away, he was all sumptuous dark skin and muscle. Powered by this and by the still-fresh sensation of their frolic in the alley, Ben shed his own layers. Baby Back smoothed the back of his hand on Ben's face, his neck. Glazed his finger along his collarbone and the vague outline of his pectorals. Ben fought the urge to compare his slight body to Baby Back's muscular physique, and chose instead to embrace this moment the way Baby Back was now embracing him.

Once in bed, once he saw how hungry Baby Back was, the nervousness returned.

"Wait. I don't want . . ."

"Don't want what?"

"It might hurt . . . *back there*. I'm scared."

Baby Back cooed in his ear. "Don't you worry. We'll keep everything aboveground tonight."

Water avalanched out of the black sky. A monsoon. The room was black except for momentary slashes of lightning, silent except for the thunder.

"Where you from in Georgia?" Baby Back said.

"Town called Dogwood."

"Been back since you came here?"

"Nothing and no one to go back to," Ben said.

"Friends? Family?"

"They don't want me."

Baby Back held him closer.

The wind snarled. November wind. The kind that chills you from the outside in, makes you grateful to be with a good man under a grandma-made quilt.

"What you gonna do about Mrs. Charles?"

"I can't think about it right now. Can we just have tonight to ourselves?"

Baby Back kissed Ben's temple. "I don't want just tonight."

Outside this room was rain and cold and uncertainty and Angeline. Inside, an oasis. Ben never wanted to leave this room.

It rained all night and most of the next day. They spent all of it in bed. The rain didn't diminish to a drizzle until after eight o'clock at night. With the end of the storm and the impending arrival of Monday, their time in The Oasis ended.

"I gotta go home," Ben said, "but I don't want to. Baby Back, I don't want to go."

He was like an animal that's been delighting in the safeguard of hibernation and must now reenter the world. They dressed together, purposely slow, treasuring each remaining moment. Ben walked around the room, taking everything in, trying to preserve it all in his memory so he could replicate it at will on those lonely nights he wasn't with Baby Back.

"You're acting like you ain't never coming back here again," Baby Back said. "You'll be back. Better be."

The big trumpeter didn't want him to go, and that made the going easier.

They left the boardinghouse together, Baby Back with his trumpet because he had Teddy's that night. He walked Ben most of the way home.

"Come to the club Tuesday night," Baby Back said.

"You gonna play something special? Just for me?"

"Yeah. And you bring me a new poem. No cheating."

They wanted to hug, to kiss. But they made do with a very long handshake.

Ben continued on home. He took his time. Hands in his pockets. A smirk on his face. Effortless confidence in the slow stride of this victory lap. Images of the buffet flat, Baby Back's arms, and the blurry-edged Clam House bombarded him, tenderly. New friends accompanying him as he cruised like an explorer onto the coast of a brand-new world. But was this world really new? You learned in school that Columbus discovered America, but that was a lie. How can you discover a place that's already inhabited? This world may have been new to Ben, but others already lived here. Maybe secretly, or quietly, perhaps dangerously, but they were here. Now Ben was, too. Like any new resident, he had to find his way around, get directions, get lost, get familiar, learn the rules and the shortcuts and the protocols. And then would he be happy? He didn't know, was convinced happiness was more aspiration than destination, but was also convinced that the sublime turmoil of everything he was feeling at this moment was, perhaps, as close as he would ever get to achieving happiness, so he reveled in it, rolled it around in his mouth and ground it up like candy.

Night had fallen. Sunday was winding down. The merriment of Friday and Saturday had run its course as Harlem and the rest of New York girded themselves for Monday. No flotillas of taxis zooming from downtown. No reefer smell whirling in the air. Passersby looked tired and grim whereas on Friday and Saturday they would have glowed.

He was almost home. He had to fight to keep the newfound confidence in his stride, the victory in his lap. He didn't know what he would say to Angeline. Or what she would say to him.

He commanded the image of himself in Baby Back's arms, wrapped it around himself like a protective layer of skin as he turned onto his street, then climbed the stairs to his building.

He stepped into the apartment, cautiously, as if stealing uninvited into a stranger's home. The only light in the house came from a lamp in the bedroom. Angeline sat on the bed, her back to him. Ben approached, but stayed just shy of the Neutral Territory.

"So now you're staying out all night and all day," Angeline said. "No regard for me? Like I don't matter? I was worried."

He hadn't meant to worry her. He hadn't meant to hurt her. She didn't deserve it. He had fought *this thing*. Spat in its face. Run from it. But now, electrified by his night with Baby Back, he no longer wanted to run. He didn't despise *this thing* anymore. *This thing* was *him*.

The light wind twirling inside him last night was a hurricane now. It stormed through him, razing his old perceptions even as its rains bathed and fertilized him. Before last night he'd been drought-stricken. Now he was verdant. The rains soaked him through, weighing him down with peace. And peace mobilized him against his wife's hurt. Didn't make him impervious to it, but it desensitized him so that his own grand luck would not be tainted by her misfortune.

It *was* misfortune. God was cruel and untrustworthy. Ben knew that, had always known that. Angeline knew it, too. It was as victims of godly cruelty that they had initially found each other, loved each other, saved each other. Ben loved Angeline, yes, with every ounce of blood shooting through every vein in him. Just not in the way that she loved him. And that was something she'd always known, too. From their very beginning.

Before age fifteen, Ben had never ridden a train and never traveled more than twenty miles from Dogwood. When he arrived at the train station after leaving the Zachary plantation, he bought his ticket then walked out to the platform. He wasn't sure what to do or where to board, so when he saw folks—white folks—entering the huge, iron machine, he followed them. As he climbed the steps, the white uniformed man standing in the doorway pushed him to the ground.

"Go to the nigger car," he said, as offhandedly as he had pushed.

Ben dusted himself off and started toward the back of the train.

"Not that way," the uniformed man said. "The nigger car is at the front, right behind the locomotive."

Dust hung in the air inside the "nigger car," accompanied by an odor like burning trash. It grated his eyes, dried his throat. The car's seats were decayed with age. He took a seat by a window and waited for the journey to begin. Folks boarded. Folks poor like himself, but carrying themselves with dignity. They wore their best clothes—jackets and bowties for the men, Sunday hats for the women—as if headed someplace special. Excitement shimmered through the car. It made the dusty air quiver.

A man his pa's age sat next to him. No bowtie, and threads frayed from the seams of his old jacket, but it was buttoned up and his white shirt had been pressed.

"Hello, young man," he said.

"Good day to you, sir."

"Where you headed?"

"North."

The man chuckled. "We's all headed north. Where you hopin' to end up?"

"New York City. You?"

"Washington. Got family there."

Ben nodded, then looked out the window.

"Well," the man said. "Good luck to you, son."

The train pulled out of the station and away from everything Ben had ever known.

The train's motion twisted up his stomach. Steam and cinders from the locomotive whooshed into the car and accumulated. It was smoke, not dust, that clung to the air. The passengers coughed and wiped their irritated eyes, but none complained.

"Yes, sir, it's a smoker," his seatmate said. "Us coloreds have it all to ourselves. Been ridin' 'em all my life. What you gone do? Demand to sit in a white car? Ha!"

Hours passed. Georgia sped past Ben's window as the train plummeted into the night. People gave up coughing for sleep as a crescent moon lit their way north. Ben awoke in the middle of the night. His seatmate's snoring and the chug of the engine stopped him from returning to sleep.

And there was another noise.

A child was crying. He heard its whimper and quick intakes of breath as it sobbed. The volume of the crying came in waves, getting loud, and then subsiding, only to get loud again. A few passengers shushed, but the crying persisted. Annoyed, Ben sat up and scanned the car to locate the source.

He found it. But it wasn't a child. Sitting by a window on the opposite side of the car was a girl—a young woman—alone, her face in her hands, her body shaking as she wept. She seemed his age.

He walked over. "Hey. Hey." She didn't reply. He crouched next to her. "Why you cryin'?"

She removed her face from her hands, revealing large eyes milky-red from the tears.

"What is it?" Ben asked, keeping his voice low. "You all right?"

"No."

Her felt hat sat lopsided on her head and her wrinkled dress looked as if she'd pulled it from a crumpled pile. A small carpetbag hid under her seat.

"Anything I can do?" Ben asked.

"Ain't nothin' nobody can do."

She seemed so lost, so helpless. An unprotected thing. Impulsively, Ben sat next to her. "I'm Ben. What's your name?"

"Angeline."

"Where you from?"

"Spurgeon County."

"Good to know you, Angeline."

Her crying lessened as he talked. He admitted he had run away from home, told her about Dogwood and the Zachary plantation.

"But why you runnin' away?" she asked. "Your folks beat you?"

"No."

"Gotta be runnin' away for *some* reason. I'll tell you why *I'm* runnin' and you do the same. All right?"

Ben was wary. Confession posed risks. But before he could answer, she inhaled deeply, as if steeling herself.

"I'm . . ." She placed a hand on her stomach, firmly. She looked at him, then tumbled into his arms. "I *had* to run. I ain't never been so ashamed in my life."

Her tears came again. A fed-up passenger shouted, "Shut up that damn cryin'! Don't you know folks is tryin' to sleep?"

Angeline stood up, hands on her hips, and screamed, "Why don't you come over here and make me!"

The fed-up passenger didn't.

She returned to her seat and to his arms. "Please don't hold my . . . situation . . . against me."

"You made a mistake. A bad one. I did, too."

"What'd you do?"

*I can trust you. You're as alone as I am.* "Come here. Sit up. I need to look you in the eye."

He confessed. The afternoons in the dogwood groves. The night at the house with the red door.

"Why'd you do it?" she asked, without judgment.

"I thought I loved him."

"You must've been mighty lonely. If you'd had someone to talk to and be with, you wouldn't have done those things. If you'd had brothers and sisters . . . or a pretty girl . . . you wouldn't have needed him."

She placed her head against his shoulder, yawned, and went to sleep.

The train raced northward. Moonlight and starlight stole into the car, combining with the smoke to make a silvery vapor. While Angeline slept, Ben stayed awake, calculating:

Both were outcasts.

Both had something to be ashamed of.

Both were young and all alone and headed to a strange place that may or may not be a promised land.

But Angeline hadn't said where she was going. She had hopped on the train with no plan. She hadn't said what she would do about her *situation*. Ben prayed she wouldn't follow Trina Ledger's path. *No. I won't let that happen.*

He had just met her but, as she snoozed on his shoulder, he decided to do what Trina's fiancé would have done had he been given the opportunity: take responsibility for Angeline and her child, if she would let him, if she would have him. And right then, right there, on that Jim Crow train car with its smoke and cinders and poor colored folks on a northern pilgrimage in search of milk and honey, he resolved to bury his unnatural feelings. He would bury this . . . *thing*. He and Angeline had both sinned. But they could redeem each other.

The next day, he asked her to marry him.

"You ain't gone be doin' nothin' with no more boys, is you?" she asked.

"No. Never again."

"Promise."

He looked in her eyes. He didn't flinch. "I promise you. I promise myself."

They agreed to marry once they reached New York. They were both fifteen years old and had known each other for one day.

Attachment grew quickly. Ben, attentive and protective, ensured Angeline always ate even if he sometimes went without due to the dwindling stash of money. And Angeline proudly introduced herself to the passengers as *Mrs. Benjamin Charles,* even though they were only engaged.

Ben was happy. Willful began to disappear. *This thing* began to disappear. Angeline had freed him. He wanted to give her some proof of his gratitude, so he opened his satchel and produced the only valuable thing he owned.

"Here," he said as he placed Willful's locket around her neck. "For you."

"Oh, Benny. I ain't never owned nothin' this pretty. I'll wear it every day."

They needed to get to Washington, DC, and switch to the Pennsylvania Railroad line to complete the journey. For many passengers, the train ride was monotonous. But for Mr. Benjamin Charles and the soon-to-be Mrs. Charles, the ride was their time to plan their life.

"First thing we gotta do is get a place to stay," Angeline said. "A roomin' house or somethin'. Then we gotta get jobs."

"*I* gotta get a job. I don't want you workin'."

"Benny, we ain't got no choice. I'll work as long as I can before the baby comes."

He gave in on that point. He gave in on *a lot* of points. The future Mrs. Charles had definite ideas about how things needed to be done.

"After we on our feet, we'll move out the roomin' house and get a bigger place, but not real big. We won't need nothin' too big till the baby's older. Then we both might have to get two jobs so we can afford it. And I'm good with hair, so I can do that on the side and bring in extra money."

All Ben could say was, "Yes, Angel."

One day as the train steamed through North Carolina he asked, "What we namin' the baby?"

She considered. "Benny. We gone name him Benny."

"But what if it's a girl?"

She took his hand, inserted her fingers between his so they meshed perfectly. "It'll still be Benny."

In that moment he fell in love with her. The next moment her eyes closed so tightly, the lids wrinkled up with the strain. One hand flew to her stomach, the other clawed Ben's thigh as she clamped her knees shut and gnashed her teeth. A thin line of blood trickled down her leg.

"Help!" Ben shouted. "We need help over here! Please!"

Passengers gathered around them. Some of the women tended to Angeline. The conductor was summoned. He took one look and said, "Nothin' I can do."

"You can't stop the train?" Ben asked.

"What good would that do, boy? We're in the middle of nowhere. There's a nigger doctor in Fauset, the next town, couple hundred miles up."

They rushed to the doctor as soon as the train arrived. He confirmed what they already knew.

They stayed in Fauset while she recovered. The doctor and his wife, seeing the young couple had no means, sheltered them.

"I guess you's headin' on to New York," Angeline said.

"*We's* headin' to New York. Nothin's changed."

"But I didn't think you'd still—"

"Nothin's changed."

Ben was devastated. The child, his means of redemption, was gone. But there was still Angeline.

They married in Fauset. Instead of a ring, Ben placed Willful's locket around her neck. Their wedding night was Ben's first time with a woman. It was different and it wasn't easy. He was nervous. But Angeline taught him.

They stayed in Fauset, both working odd jobs and living with the kindly doctor in a spare room, paying a few cents each week for rent. It took four months for them to earn enough to continue north. In New York, things worked out almost to the letter the way Angeline had scripted them. They found space in a tenement slum in the Bowery that they shared with three other families. They worked multiple jobs and saved every cent. They moved to a better place. They worked hard. They loved each other.

Six years later, it had come to this: Ben just outside their bedroom, Angeline's back toward him, her perfect, oiled marcel waves glimmering in the small light of the nightstand lamp. How long had she been sitting on this bed that, for him, had more often been a scene of terror than of rapture? He thought of Baby Back's grandma-quilted bed and the twirling-light-wind-hurricane stormed again.

"I'm so sorry I've hurt you, Angeline. But this won't be the last time I stay out like this."

"Did he play his trumpet for you? Or maybe you gave him another one of my poems. Must have been doing *something* all night and all day besides . . ."

She didn't finish it, but she had affirmed it out loud nonetheless. *Is that progress?* Ben thought, and then he closed the bedroom door. Closed it softly. So softly, he didn't hear it click.

# come with me

## 1926

# 15

January. The opening stanza in an abundant new poem. An obedient virgin Ben could have his way with. The chance to write his life and bend it to his desire.

And his desire was Baby Back. He wanted him. Wanted every bit and bite of him. Every jazz phrase of him. Every year. Every memory. Every kiss. Every moist pearl from him. Every urge of him. Every sunny, dark, bitter, and sweet mood in him. Every shade of black, brown, and beige on him.

They couldn't be together on New Year's Eve. Each had to serve and entertain drunk carousers, Baby Back at Teddy's, Ben at The Pavilion. Neither left work till six in the morning. Ben arrived at The Oasis first and poured two glasses of the bootleg champagne Mr. Kittredge and David-Nicholas had given him as a New Year's gift. As he waited for Baby Back, he examined the photographs of the mysterious Roland for the hundredth time. Who was this man? Had he been a friend? Lover? Baby Back refused to talk about him, leaving Ben to hypothesize, fantasize, invent.

Baby Back arrived, exhausted from his marathon sets, steaming with the gamy odor of sweat.

"Well," Ben said.

"Well."

Too tired for sex, or even to undress, they clambered fully clothed underneath the grandma quilt, latched their arms around each other, and slept.

With opposite work schedules most of each week, their overlap of mutually free time often amounted to only a few hours—sometimes less. Dear time that had to be used productively. Through experimentation as deft as it was plentiful, they learned the most concise, efficient ways to pleasure each other. These moments were too rushed and not romantic, but the frenetic urgency brought them to a blood-stirring sweat every bit as rewarding.

Bodily recreation didn't consume all of their time. They passed many hours lolling on the floor of The Oasis—sometimes clothed, most times not—taking turns playing their favorite music for each other. Baby Back loved Louis Armstrong: the piercing sound, his lovely shaded nuances. Ben played song after song by Alberta Hunter, marveling at her mix of cosmopolitan finesse and low-down grit.

Or, in a mood for poetry, they attended readings at the Harlem Library. Impassioned discussion always followed.

"That poem about Africa," Baby Back said once as they departed a reading, trampling through snow left over from a mid-January blizzard. "It didn't move me. Unoriginal."

"You're wrong. He used some of the most beautiful language I've ever heard."

"Please. When are Negroes gonna stop talking about Africa like it's just a big ol' jungle?"

Baby Back always got the last word and it was usually, as now, "*You* could've written that poem better."

Since Baby Back had liberated him, he wrote more than ever.

> *The river brought me home.*
> *It put the moon in my mouth,*
> *Sugar and spice in my blood.*
> *It seared light into a dark place,*
> *Made castles of what was once a slave ship.*
> *The middle passage on the vast, unfeeling ocean has ended*
> *And I have slipped*
> *Onto the vein of this river.*

*A medley—jazz-bright and friendly—*
*Rides shotgun on the current*
*As the river bleeds its wet brown body over me,*
*Under me, on top of me.*
*As it leads me to its mouth*
*And releases me.*

Baby Back sometimes critiqued his poetry, but mostly just loved it. "You know, it's killer hearing you recite your poems, but when am I gonna *see* them? In print?"

"I'd have to send them out and hope someone likes them enough to publish them."

"Well, then."

So Ben restarted the barren work of sending his poems to any publication that would consider a Negro writer, and a few that he knew wouldn't.

January made Ben powerful. He looked into its face and reveled in its eyes fine-tuned to the future. But January is a two-headed god. It looks forward, but is incapable of closing its other set of eyes on the past.

"What you gonna do about Mrs. Charles?"

Baby Back asked this frequently. He wanted Ben to move in with him. But Angeline held fast to their in-name-only marriage. He had approached her about a divorce a few months earlier. She refused, fiercely, as if he'd asked her to go to hell.

"This marriage is a sham. Always has been," he'd argued. "Now that everything's out in the open, it's time to set us both free."

"Easy for you to say. You got someone. You got *him*. If you leave, I ain't got nobody."

"You're young. Beautiful. You'll find someone."

"I told you before: Nobody wants another man's used goods."

He could have filed for divorce anyway. Or moved out at the very least. But he couldn't bear to hurt her any more than he already was. So he was biding his time, waiting for the opportunity to win his freedom. But he wouldn't wait forever. Because Baby Back wouldn't.

"Mr. Poet, I asked you a question," the trumpeter said. "What you gonna do about your wife?"

An edge of impatience that Ben had to tread delicately.

He hugged Baby Back, nuzzled his head on the big man's shoulder. "Don't know yet. But I promise I will soon."

If not listening to records in private or poetry in public, they took long walks. The early-February air bit them as they walked along the Harlem River one evening. Baby Back was talking about Paris again with starry-eyed fondness, even though he'd never been there.

"They got beautiful parks that are really just big gardens. And the city's old. Ancient. Lot older than New York. A river flows right through Paris. The Seine. Cuts it in half. Left Bank and Right Bank."

"The East River cuts New York in half. Manhattan on one side, Brooklyn and Queens on the other," Ben said, anxious to equalize the two cities and keep Baby Back on the ground with him.

Baby Back stopped. He looked north across the river, into the Bronx. He shook his head. "Ain't the same."

Passing reefer between them in The Oasis later, he said, for the millionth time, "They love Negroes in Paris." He inhaled too hard and coughed, but didn't lose his train of thought. "Not like here with these fuckin' crackers up in your face. Every time I get a letter from down home, they tell me about another colored boy who got lynched because he was 'uppity' or he looked at some white bitch the wrong damn way."

He passed the reefer to Ben, who was careful to inhale conservatively. "But President Coolidge wants to pass a law against lynching. And anyway, things ain't as bad up here, in the north."

"It ain't that much better either. Don't be stupid."

He took the reefer back, relit it, hauled a huge drag.

Reefer blunted physical sensations, but not hurt feelings. If anything, it augmented the hurt, gave it legs so that, no matter what Baby Back said after, all Ben heard was *don't be stupid*.

# 16

Saturday morning and Ben awoke with a rampage inside his head, the product of too much reefer and bootleg the previous night. Anna Mossity had kept their teacups full all night. The Clam House was their late-Friday-night routine now. Anna always waited on them unless otherwise indisposed, in which case Ella Vader, Della Kit, or Testa Monial did the honors. And there was always Gladys's horn of a voice as it sobbed out songs:

> *"My little hole of a home one night caught on fire.*
> *Believe me, dear friends, my desperation was dire.*
> *Then who came to save me, do you suppose?*
> *A fireman, luggin' a big, long hose.*
>
> *He swung that big hose all over the place.*
> *That man even put it right up in my face.*
> *He shook that big hose in my hole of a home.*
> *That hose seemed to move with a mind of its own.*
>
> *Then he sprayed out his water and put out my fire.*
> *By the time he was done, we was both wet and tired.*
> *If your home catches fire, child, you can be sure*
> *That a fireman's hose is your ready-set cure.*

*Where my fireman went, I ain't got no clues.*
*And that's why I'm singin' these fireman blues."*

Baby Back wouldn't let Ben out of his arms. "Stay here. You don't work today."

"I need to put in an appearance at home."

The arms tightened. "Do that later."

"I have to write."

"You can write *here*."

"My typewriter's *there*."

"Write longhand."

"Baby, I need to go."

"You need to bring that goddamn typewriter over *here*."

He hated leaving, but looked forward to writing time alone in the apartment. Angeline would be at work. He heard a scratch of a voice behind him as he was about to let himself in.

"Only one reason a married man stays out all night."

Ben didn't bother turning around. "What reason is that, Mrs. Harrisburg?"

She came up beside him and then steadied herself with her ubiquitous walking stick. "Men. All alike. Even my dear late husband. Couldn't keep it in his pants for anything."

He stepped back, surprised by her indelicate language and the tears drenching her cheeks, and then astounded when she leveled her walking stick at him.

"Don't you know how to treat a woman?" she asked. "Don't you know when you run around, you make her feel bad about herself?"

The screech in her voice must have surprised even her because she collected herself, smoothed her hair down, adjusted her shawl, which had slipped askew. Then she deliberately turned her nose up at him. A gesture so formal, so invested with contempt, it almost hurt his feelings. Evelyn Harrisburg hobbled into her apartment and shut the door. Not with a *slam,* but an aloof *click,* as if Ben rated no better effort.

He entered his apartment, so ruffled by the episode that he couldn't immediately comprehend the scene that fanned out in front of him. The table had been set with Angeline's best linen and the good china they'd saved over a year to purchase. Smells of bacon, smoked ham, eggs, and coffee assailed him. Angeline stood beside the table, a frilly apron over her dress, her marcel wave done up fresh. The locket shone against her chest.

He had never seen her this beautiful. It was as if time had shifted and in that tiny drop of space, Willful, *this thing,* and Baby Back were all reduced to footnotes in the book of his life with Angeline.

"Join me for breakfast?" she said.

"Yes. Yes, I will."

They didn't know what to say or how to act with each other. It used to come so naturally. It used to be so lovely. Now they bumbled through conversation about their jobs and the weather. But pieces of the old friendship returned.

"Remember when we first moved up here?" Angeline held back a giggle. "And we felt the subway underneath us?"

"We thought it was an earthquake!"

"We ran for cover."

"Everyone thought we was crazy!"

"Couple of hicks from down South."

They laughed out loud, recalling their first frightened, naïve days in the big city.

Angeline brought him another slice of toast and buttered it the way he liked it. He knew she had sacrificed to prepare this banquet: Saturday was her most lucrative day at the beauty shop. *This breakfast ain't worth the rent,* Ben thought, and then felt bad.

"How's your poetry?" she asked. Her eyes drooped to her lap. "I miss it."

A picture assembled in his mind: he and Baby Back, nude on the floor of The Oasis, Ben reading his poems out loud as some pretty tune played on the phonograph.

"I just got published," he said. "Two poems in *Opportunity.* And I'm reading at the Harlem Library on Thursday."

"You got published? Benny, that's wonderful!"

She swooped onto his lap and laced her arms around him. She pressed her forehead against his neck. He smelled her perfume—

vanilla with a dash of rose. Too sweet-smelling and she wore too much. She began to feel heavy on his lap and he didn't know where to put his hands.

"We need to celebrate," she said. "Exactly what we need to do."

He heard the charge, the longing in her voice, and knew he was in trouble.

"Why don't I clear the table and then we'll go to the bedroom? Or I can leave the table till later. What do you say, Benny? Benny-boy?"

She lifted her head from his neck and put her tongue in his ear. He drew away from her. "Don't. You know I can't."

She swooped off his lap with the same velocity with which she had swooped on. "You mean *won't*."

He went to the door.

"No, please don't leave yet," Angeline said. "Not without some more clothes and books. You've taken half your things to *his* house already. Might as well take the other half. You only use this place for storage these days. Like I'm in the fucking storage business."

The landslide of tears made her sputter the words when she meant to shoot them. She held herself tall and valiant, but was really an abandoned little girl. Ben felt sorry for her, yet here it was: the opportunity he'd been sitting in wait for. He snatched it.

"Then I should move out. Don't want to impose on you."

He remained calm, held himself as tall and valiant as she, looked directly into her eyes, wouldn't allow himself to look away. He held his breath. His heart beat savagely. They stared each other down with molten-hot glares that melted what was left of the marriage. Angeline blinked first.

"Get out, Ben. Get on out of here."

She began to clear the table, her movements slow, blasé, as if none of this had ever mattered.

"All right," Ben said, and breathed, and let his valiant height slip a little.

# 17

"And we'll need to get you new suits," Mr. Kittredge said.

David-Nicholas kept his head bowed. "It's not necessary."

"Nonsense. We can't send you off on a business trip without new suits. Can we, Benjamin?"

"Sure can't. Gotta have new suits." He placed food in front of each man—grapefruit for Mr. Kittredge; bacon, eggs, and toast for David-Nicholas. "You're going away, Mr. David?" He couldn't help smiling, tried to hide it.

"He certainly is," Kittredge said. "To attend to some of his family's business interests. We're going to Wanamaker's after lunch. I'm going to outfit him with a stunning wardrobe. All those magnates and company chiefs will know exactly who they're dealing with when they see you in your handsome clothes!" He trailed his finger along David-Nicholas's arm, stopping just before he reached the young man's hand. "You'll cut quite a figure. But you don't need new suits for that."

Ben returned later to find Mr. Kittredge still ablaze about David-Nicholas's wardrobe. The young man listened, eyes downcast. He hadn't touched his breakfast.

"Geoffrey, I wish you wouldn't bother about the suits," he said.

"Don't be absurd. It is imperative that you make a good impression." Kittredge softened. "I'm so proud of you, Nicky."

David-Nicholas grasped one of the older man's hands with both of his. The public display unnerved Ben. More so when David-Nicholas said, "Ben, you'll look after Geoffrey when I'm gone, won't you?"

The pianist was the only musician onstage when Ben arrived at Teddy's. He cut loose on a variation of a Scott Joplin rag, improvising embellishments, hands zigzagging over the keys as his body listed to the syncopated beat.

"Hey, swinger!"

"How you doing, Fanny? Where's Baby?"

She pointed. Baby Back sat in a corner of the quarter-full bar with a man in a suave double-breasted suit. A velvet hat lay in front of him on the table. His gold-tipped walking stick leaned against the table as he and Baby Back engaged in what looked like serious talk. Ben tensed as he observed the youngish man's lustrous brown skin with its reddish tint, his hair—partly straight, partly kinky—brushed back in crinkly waves.

Fanny slapped his arm. "It's nothing. You know Baby Back: always schmoozing."

"This is Mr. Leroy Jasper," Baby Back said when Ben walked over. "He owns a jazz club. In Paris."

Baby Back lounged back in his chair, hands up and behind his head, poised, cocksure. As if the man had offered him a gig and the ink on the contract had already dried.

"I must correct you. It's Le*Roi,*" Mr. Jasper said. "Accent on the *second* syllable. And my club is called Chez LeRoi. Appropriate, no? It's the hottest club in Paris, if I do say so myself. And I do."

LeRoi Jasper's speech bloomed with eloquent vowels and curt consonants. His dialect was a hybrid between Negro musicality and the formality of upper-class white speech. Ben thought if he listened with his eyes closed, he'd be unable to discern this man's race with certainty.

"Let's have drinks," Jasper said. Without breaking eye contact with them, he lifted a smooth, diamond-ringed hand and snapped his fingers. "Waitress," he said, without raising his volume.

LeRoi Jasper was genial and he demonstrated admirable patience with Baby Back's endless inquiries about Paris. His laughter, though low and conservative, trickled easily, and he was generous in offering them cigars and more drinks. But snobbishness offset his hospitality. He spoke *at* Fanny instead of *to* her. When Baby Back sought assurance that Negroes could make it in Paris, Jasper replied, "Yes. Provided they're not lazy." And when Ben wondered if he'd seen Josephine Baker's show, Jasper looked at him like a child asking a silly question, then answered, "I don't go for that kind of thing."

Baby Back sighed. "Paris. God almighty. I've wanted to go there since my uncle Roland told me about it when I was a kid."

Ben was startled. *Uncle* Roland?

Baby Back elbowed him. "I'm trying to convince Mr. Jasper to hire me for his club."

LeRoi Jasper sipped his drink like a bourgeois gentleman. "You're a talented musician, Mr. Johnston. I'll keep you in mind."

In bed that night, Ben tried to temper Baby Back's hopes from speeding too high too soon.

"He said he'd *keep you in mind*. Don't sound like no firm offer to me."

"Just gotta work on him."

A minute of quiet.

"Hey, Baby Back? You're taking me with you, right? If you go to Paris?"

Baby Back got on top of him. "*When* I go. And hell yeah you're coming with me." He kissed his cheeks, his neck, began working his way down.

Ben was determined to ask the critical question before they became lost in intimacy where important matters had a tendency to die.

"Baby? Why didn't you tell me Roland was your uncle?"

Baby Back stopped kissing him. "You know I don't talk about him."

"But I've told you everything. About Angeline, Willful."

"That was your choice. I choose not to talk about Roland."

Baby Back flipped off of Ben. He lay on his side, facing the opposite direction.

Ben sat up. "You told a stranger you met tonight that Roland was family. But you wouldn't tell *me?*"

\* \* \*

> *"Open the door to the motherland.*
> *See her.*
> *Peel away the exotic jungle.*
> *Peek behind the curtain of drumbeats.*
> *See the milk streaming from her rock."*

The basement reading room at the Harlem Library was at capacity. Ben had begun his first poem shyly but then found his momentum with his second.

> *"Touched with earth-toned hands.*
> *Gazed upon with eyes the color of Egypt."*

He was having fun by the time he started his final piece. Baby Back sat in the front row, cheering him on with a big, proud smile.

> *"The Blues seduced me*
> *With a whisper.*
>
> *Lured me, vamp-style,*
> *With glinting smile, mahogany hips.*
>
> *It waltzed me to the cliff's tempting edge,*
> *And then, with a shimmer*
> *And a sashay,*
> *Caressed me into jumping."*

He stopped mid verse when Angeline walked in.

The audience mumbled its concern at the poet-gone-mute while Baby Back's disbelieving eyes pursued Angeline as she took a seat at the back. Ben concluded the piece and sat beside the podium with the other writers. The last poet read what seemed like a dozen pieces while Baby Back looked behind at Angeline, as if itching to confront her. While the poet droned, Ben schemed: As soon as the reading ended, he would hustle his lover out of there and handle his wife later.

He hadn't counted on a meet-and-greet.

The audience converged on the writers, blocking him from Baby Back. But the attention outdid his worries: To his surprise, Mr. Benjamin Marcus Charles was the hit of the evening. The audience fawned on him, sidelining the other poets. After several minutes of compliments and handshaking, Angeline emerged out of the morass. She attached herself to him and kissed him full on the mouth. A kiss so ardent, it dispersed the crowd.

Baby Back appeared.

"Mrs. Charles. Been a while. What you doing here?"

"Supporting my husband."

"*I'm* here. You can go."

"You'd like that, wouldn't you?"

"Yes. I would."

"Stop it," Ben said. "We're in public."

Angeline cozied up to him, took her time straightening the knot in his tie. "Benny, let's go home. We need to talk."

Baby Back cringed. Ben said nothing.

"Benny," Angeline said. "Don't you think I still deserve a little something?"

Evelyn Harrisburg was camped on the stoop when they arrived.

"Well, well," she said. "Look who's here. Together. Must be a full moon out tonight."

She sat bent over at the waist. The walking stick shook in one hand; in the other she held a silver picture frame with a photograph of a couple on their wedding day. It looked fifty years old. Mrs. Harrisburg coughed. The sound was liquidy like phlegm.

Once in the apartment, Ben stepped no farther than the doorway.

"Can I fix you something?" Angeline asked. "I got oxtails. And there's greens. And rice."

He shook his head *no*.

She took his hand and pulled him. He thought she was convey-ing him to the bedroom and dragged his feet, but she led him to the sofa instead.

"I really did come tonight to support you," she said. "I wasn't trying to cause no trouble."

But she had done just that. Right now, Baby Back was some-where seething.

"Benny, I've been thinking about that train ride north. That smoky Jim Crow car. Remember?"

He did, of course, but was reluctant to feed this bit of nostalgia.

"You came out of nowhere. One minute I was pregnant and disgraced, the next I had you. I couldn't believe my luck. You had no obligation at all. You could have done whatever you wanted. I thought: This is a good man; a man I can always depend on."

Was she compiling this list of his former virtues to compare and contrast them against his transgressions? He wanted to hide.

"I know I ain't the man you married no more," he said.

"I thought if I was a good wife—"

"You *are* a good wife."

"—then you wouldn't have those desires. If I was a good wife, you wouldn't choose to be that way. But I failed. I ain't a good enough wife or a good enough woman and I can't have children, so you've chosen to . . ." Tears spurted down her cheeks. "Benny, I want a divorce."

Ben couldn't explain why he craved a man's kiss, a man's bed in-stead of hers. So he said nothing. He was sorry for her, yes, and guilty, too, because the happiness of gaining his freedom prevailed over anything he felt for her.

She removed the locket from her neck, placed it in his hand. In-stinctively, he wiped her tears and hugged her. Then he kissed her cheek, keeping his lips there a long time. *One last kiss.* Angeline veered her lips onto his, lips both foreign and familiar.

The kiss was lasting longer than it should. Her smell was subtle, lacy. Different from Baby Back's musky smell of sweat and muscle, which he preferred. But that preference didn't stop him from de-lighting in his wife's scent one last time.

"This won't change nothing," he whispered.

"I know."

Ben rubbed his face against hers. Its smoothness struck him. He had become accustomed to Baby Back's stubbly skin. Skin that bruised you if you weren't careful. Skin that bit.

Having nothing to lose liberates. Gives you the bluster to do what you need to; puts an added swing in your thrust. Ben left knowing that he had finally and really satisfied her. A perverse pride heartened him as he walked to Baby Back's. He had bathed before leaving, telling Angeline that his nervousness during the reading had caused him to sweat a lot. But the truth was that he couldn't return to Baby Back awash in her scent.

He readied himself for an ugly reception, rehearsed his arguments in his head as he walked up the stairs to The Oasis. The door swung open just as he arrived on the landing.

"Start packing!" Baby Back said.

"Come again?"

A smile stretched across Baby Back's face till there was almost no face left. "I heard from LeRoi Jasper. We're going to Paris. And we ain't coming back no time soon."

# 18

Mr. Kittredge held up a sealed envelope like a trophy as Ben poured his Earl Grey tea. "A letter from David-Nicholas. Just delivered."

"Wonderful. When will he be back?"

Kittredge tore at the envelope. "Hopefully this will shed some light on that very subject, my dear Benjamin. Grapefruit, please. Make it a double."

Ben returned to find Mr. Kittredge staring at the empty seat that David-Nicholas would have occupied. His knuckles sharpened as he strangled the letter in his hand.

"Mr. Kittredge? Sir, what's wrong?"

Kittredge winced as if in pain. His Adam's apple tottered up and down like he was choking. Ben was about to run for the hotel physician when Kittredge stammered through pale lips that trembled.

"His family wants him away from me. He won't be back."

"Where is he?"

"Los Angeles. He's married."

Mr. Kittredge tilted back his head, opened his throat, and released a fearless, smoldering wail. Tears splurged. He went prostrate on the table, face sunk in his outstretched arms while the gentlemen and ladies in The Pavilion's dining hall tried their sophisticated best to suppress their horror, their interest. The letter lay on the table. Ben spied a passage: *Geoffrey, please know how very much I love you.*

Ben thought a moment, then sat in David-Nicholas's empty chair. He touched the back of Mr. Kittredge's neck, let his hand lilt there. Smooth skin, just the littlest bit flinty, its warmth good against his hand. He had never touched Mr. Kittredge before. Not even a handshake. As the Englishman cried and cried, Ben's hand slid down his warm white neck until it rested on the small of his back.

He hadn't cared if the ladies and gentlemen or his boss objected: He had only three more weeks in New York.

"Mr. Jasper sent two tickets for the boat," Baby had said. "First class. One for me, one for my *girlfriend.*"

"What's he gonna say when you show up with *me?*"

"Nothing. I'll tell him I broke up with the girlfriend and brought my *cousin* along."

"Baby, we're jumping across the ocean to a country full of nothing but white people."

"I keep telling you: They *love* Negroes over there. You'll see. Trust me."

Baby Back. His lover. His muse. Admirer. Critic. His antagonist. His protector. Defender. His savior.

His.

He *did* trust him. Loved him, too. He often recalled their first night together, the fresh and bouncing seed that was planted as Baby Back sent jazz rocketing on the 131st Street corner. The seed had erupted into a fully grown tree, mostly flowery and fragrant, but just as often top-heavy and unwieldy. This was a love that Ben would not, could not live without, even with its juggernaut of complexity. He would go anywhere with Baby Back. Scared as he was, he couldn't imagine not. And he *was* scared. Because even after several years in New York, he still occasionally looked in the mirror or caught an inadvertent glance of himself in a shop window and saw the same dumb hick who'd migrated from the backward back-woods of Georgia. How would Paris—the cosmopolitan capital of the world—receive him? How would *he* receive Paris?

Preemptive action was best, so he went to the 135th Street Li-brary and staggered back loaded down with every book he could find on Paris and France and French history. But his fright notched up at the thought of language. When he and Angeline first came to New York, other Negroes savaged them for their countrified Eng-lish. Now he would have to start over with a new language. He bought a French/English dictionary, a book on French grammar, and began teaching himself the basics. *Un, deux, trois, quatre, cinq.*

Baby Back balked when Ben entreated him to learn as well.

"I speak the language of jazz," he said as he adjusted his tie in the mirror, readying himself for Teddy's.

"That's killer. Till you gotta ask for directions."

Baby Back admired himself in the mirror. "Hey. You tell Ange-line we're leaving?"

"Yeah."

"And?"

"She wished me luck. Fixed me a last dinner of pork chops, greens, and black-eyed peas. Then we took a walk to Striver's Row. We used to do that when we first came up here. Go to Striver's Row and look at the fancy houses; dream of living there one day."

"Mmm-hmm."

Baby Back thumbed through some sheet music. He didn't ap-preciate Ben's excursions down the highway of Angeline memories.

He had informed Mr. Kittredge, too. The past few days, his fa-vorite guest had been despondent. Face unshaved. Clothes wrin-kled. His pristinely sculpted hair in disarray. Instead of dry toast or grapefruit, he now gorged himself on multiple helpings of eggs and bacon. When Ben gave him the news, Mr. Kittredge looked him up and down, slow-like.

"It seems both of my lovely young men are deserting me."

The band at Teddy's took a break between sets, but the banjo player remained onstage, playing and singing a down-home coun-try blues.

*"My wife, she done left me,*
*I don't know where she done gone.*
*My wife, she done left me,*
*I don't know where she done gone.*

*But my girlfriend still loves me—*
*She'll be movin' in 'fore dawn.*

Ben and Baby Back talked and laughed and drank. Fanny, with hardly any customers, stood by, joining them in their fun.

"He's been learning French," Baby Back said. "He'll be my interpreter, 'cause I ain't gonna bother."

"How do you say 'I want another whiskey'?" Fanny asked.

"Um . . . *Je voudrais* . . . another whiskey . . . *s'il vous plaît.* That last part means *please.*"

They smoked reefer and listened to the banjo player.

*"I love me some women,*
*Send me three or six or nine.*
*I love me some women,*
*Send me three or six or nine.*

*If you can't send a woman,*
*A sissy-man will do me fine."*

Baby Back touched Ben's arm, nodded toward the entrance. Angeline. She hurried over, looking scared.

"What you need, Mrs. Charles?" Baby Back said. "Oh, wait. You ain't Mrs. Charles no more. Least not for much longer."

Angeline banged her fists on the table. The impact upset Baby Back's teacup and sent it careening into his lap as she screamed, "Fuck you!"

The banjo player stopped singing. The few people in Teddy's looked over. Fanny slinked away. Baby Back stood, his pants and jacket stained with whiskey. He moved toward Angeline, but Ben inserted himself between them.

"Go outside," he said to her. "I'll be out in a minute."

When she was gone he rounded on Baby Back. "Don't you ever talk to her like that. Don't you ever disrespect her." He barged out.

He took her in his arms right away, a vestige of their happily married days, their I'll-always-protect-you days.

"Mrs. Harrisburg died," she said. "Thought you'd want to know. The landlord came over yesterday because she hadn't paid the rent. Knocked on her door. No answer, so he let himself in—you know how he is. And he found her. Looks like she died in her sleep."

"Can't honestly say I'm sad to see her go."

He was unsure of the appropriateness of his comment until Angeline said, "Yeah. I hated that bitch."

They laughed. But tears filled her eyes, tears that couldn't possibly be for Evelyn Harrisburg.

"Angeline. What is it?"

She closed her eyes. Tears stole from beneath the lids. "Benny . . . I'm pregnant."

# 19

"How could you?"

They sat side by side on the grandma-quilted bed. Ben was rigid—back straight, both feet flat on the floor, hands on his thighs, eyes staring ahead like an Egyptian statue. But Baby Back contorted himself toward him, his entire posture imploring him.

*"It can't be true."*
*"My cycle was late. I went to the doctor. I'm as surprised*
*as you are."*
*"But you can't conceive."*
*She threw up her hands. "A miracle?"*
*"Liar!"*
*"Have I ever lied to you?"*

Over the next hours Baby Back screamed at him for his infidelity, denounced Angeline for her gall in getting pregnant, and raged at the mutilation of their Paris plans. Ben didn't defend himself. He couldn't. Nothing he could say could justify his actions. And he found the sole means of reversing the result unthinkable. Baby Back suggested it, then quickly backed off when confronted with Ben's ferocious refusal.

The screaming ended. A beastly quiet settled on The Oasis. They went to bed, but didn't sleep much. The odd absence of street noise intensified the quiet between them. Both lay awake. Ben feared his lover, so much that he kept his breathing shallow in an attempt to hide. It surprised him when Baby Back spoke.

"You didn't need her."

Ben took a chance, reached over, touched him. "Forgive me?" A request so trite, he regretted opening his mouth.

Baby Back didn't withdraw, didn't reciprocate either. "Even if I can, even if I do: What then?"

He went to Angeline's. On the way in, he saw the nameplate on Mrs. Harrisburg's door had been changed to *Jackman*. The landlord had rented out the place already.

"I didn't do this on purpose," Angeline said.

"I didn't either."

He'd been trying to rationalize a reason for why, how. The only answer was that God was farther away than anyone realized and the prayers they'd screamed as Angeline miscarried years ago were only now being heard.

"You tell *him?*" she asked.

"Yes."

"And you're here for one last good-bye before you ship off?"

"I ain't going. I'm staying. And I'm moving back in."

They negotiated an agreement: They would not divorce; they would raise their child together. But they would not share a bed. And he forbade her to ever ask about his life outside the apartment.

He slogged up Seventh Avenue. Forty-eight hours since The Revelation. They were scheduled to leave for France in four days. He heard the street musicians jamming as he approached the 131st Street corner. It sounded richer, though, than the usual amateur fare. A trumpet discharged a spectacular barrage of notes that skidded into the night. This cat couldn't be any street corner amateur. Ben pushed to the front of the crowd. The virtuoso was none other than Baby Back Johnston, soon-to-be star of the Paris jazz scene.

He was in performance mode: eyes closed, knees bent, hands cradling his horn. His eyes opened and landed on Ben standing right at the front, then closed again like a slow-descending curtain.

The improv session ended. Baby Back approached him. "Let's walk."

They headed north on Seventh. The pleasant June night forged a happy medium between May's spring coolness and the pulverizing heat that July would soon bring. They zigzagged around a group of hopscotching girls, passed a homeless husband and wife begging from a line of people at a food cart stationed at the curb. Ben wanted to give them some coins, but Baby Back moved quickly, with intent. Ben didn't want to get left behind.

"Here's what we're gonna do," Baby Back said. "We'll go to Paris like we planned. I'll be working. You'll get a job. We'll send money to Angeline every month to take care of the kid for as long as we have to. Problem solved."

Ben supposed it was easy to strategize other people's lives if the result didn't disrupt your own. "Problem solved, huh? And you still get to go to Paris."

"*We* get to go to Paris."

Ben explained his arrangement with Angeline and offered a compromise. "Go to Paris without me, do the gig, and then come home. We'll pick up where we left off."

"No. I'm going forward. Without you if I have to."

Ben stopped in front of a brownstone with a stoop-full of people, all fanning themselves vigorously, although it wasn't anywhere near warm enough for that. "You would do that? Go away and stay away and leave me here?"

"*I* wasn't unfaithful. *I* didn't fuck that woman. *I* didn't get her pregnant. *I* didn't get us into this mess!"

His volume reared so high, the people on the stoop stopped fanning and tuned in. Though awful to admit, Baby Back's solution would be easiest: Go to Paris as planned and let Angeline and his child exist as an amount to be accommodated in his budget each month.

"You're right," Ben said. "I fucked up. But I ain't leaving Angeline to bear this on her own. I will be a father to my child. I want to be a lover to you, too. Go to Paris. Do the gig. Hell, keep going back. Make it a regular thing. But make this the home you come back to when you're done."

Tears spilled down each of the trumpeter's cheeks. "A home without you in it. That ain't no home."

They went back and forth and around in circles, forcing their arguments, each campaigning to convince the other of his own superior reasoning. The poet and the trumpeter employed a creative arsenal of tactics: pressure, guilt, cajoling, hysteria, threats, sympathy, apology, insults, flattery. Sensing failure, they modified their words, refined their phrasing, finessed their inflections. But the essence of what each argued remained constant.

Neither could convince the other.

Ben decided to move back to Angeline's right away, that night. He packed his things as Baby Back beseeched him to reconsider.

"You're the one who won't budge," Ben said. "Paris is more important to you than I am."

"I *have* to go!"

Ben had been stuffing a book in a satchel, but now slung it against the wall, so hard it dented the plaster. "Why the hell is Paris so goddamn important? Why are you obsessed with it?"

Baby Back looked across the room at the photographs of his uncle. Tears launched out of his eyes. He felt his way to the bed like a blind man.

# 20

"Baby Back. Baby. Please talk to me. Please tell me about him."

Baby Back was fifteen when his pa's younger brother returned to Locke's Creek, South Carolina, after a sixteen-year absence. Uncle Roland had clowned on vaudeville stages, been a song-and-dance man in ritzy music halls and nightspots in Chicago, New York City, and even abroad. He had left Locke's Creek in overalls and returned in a tailored suit and spatted shoes—all the worse for wear after weeks of travel, first on a transatlantic ocean liner and then in sweltering Jim Crow railroad cars. He claimed he came back to be with his family, but Baby Back's pa sneered at Roland and his fashionable, crumpled clothes.

"What happened? You outta money? Ain't got no place else to go?"

"How about a welcome-home hug?" Roland said.

Baby Back's pa puffed on his pipe. "How 'bout you earn your keep? If you gone live here, you gone have to get your pretty hands pretty dirty."

Next morning Uncle Roland went out to the fields with the rest of them. Baby Back, big for his age, gave him a shirt and pants, but didn't have a spare pair of shoes. Roland had to wear his own—a pair of wingtips, the most casual shoes he owned. The men laughed.

"Hey, Roland. That how they plow fields in New York?"

"Hell, this a farm, not no fancy party."

Roland ignored them. Baby Back admired that he went out to the fields on his own terms. His uncle had class even while sweating in shabby clothes. His bearing distinguished him from everyone Baby Back knew.

Lunchtime the first day. Everyone ate outside, sitting or squatting in the fields. Roland secluded himself from the others. Sweat and dirt had already wrecked the wingtips. Baby Back joined him. Roland didn't acknowledge him, didn't speak. After five minutes, Baby Back said, "Tell me 'bout the places you been."

A full minute passed without any response. Baby Back almost gave up and moved away. Then Roland said, "Chicago's cold. The wind slices you to ribbons. But it's a fun town. New York City is wild. They travel on trains underground. But, Baby, you haven't lived till you've seen Paris."

"Where's that?" Baby Back asked, embarrassed that his knowledge of the world extended no farther than the next county.

"Across the ocean, in a country called France."

"That where you was living? Before you came home?"

"Yes."

"What you like about it?"

"The Champs Élysées. The music halls. The brasseries after hours. Baguettes in the morning. The Seine. Everything."

Baby Back understood none of it. But he was hooked. "Tell me more."

They became constant companions, working in the fields side by side and always together at lunch, although Roland didn't always speak.

Baby Back's bedroom—a tight space serving the dual purpose of sleeping quarters and storage room—was a tiny shed behind the family's shack. A second sleeping pallet was crammed in and Baby Back and his uncle became roommates. They slept each night with their backs to each other, Baby Back's spine taut with the effort of not touching his uncle—nearly impossible in that cooped-up space. At first they went to sleep right away, but before long Baby Back begged for stories about Paris and Roland obliged with tales that ran all night. When more at ease, Baby Back relaxed his back, allowed it to touch Roland's, lightly at first, but soon, without thinking, without realizing, without worrying about it, their backs cuddled densely against one another as they lay in that makeshift bedroom each night. Uncle Roland's back was strong, comfortable, comforting.

Baby Back was curious about his uncle. Roland talked about the shows he'd performed in, the places he'd been, but said nothing about *who* he'd been with. All the men Baby Back knew bragged about the women they'd had or aspired to have. He winced each time he was asked which girl he thought the prettiest, what he would do with her, to her, if given the chance. Dodging the questions would be suspect, so he told lies pumped high with creativity and armed with bravado. He didn't dare tell the truth: that he wanted nothing to do with girls; that the prettiest girl had nothing on a nice-looking boy; that he had messed with boys a few times and loved it.

His uncle never talked about women, but women in Locke's Creek tittered about the handsome Roland.

"He the marrying-est man in these here parts. Wish he'd marry *me*."

"Good-looking man like that: You know he'd make some beautiful children."

"He's so handsome, don't matter that he don't never say nothin'."

They threw themselves at him endlessly. He didn't return their flirtations or care. Long before his return, Baby Back had heard the gossip that his uncle was *funny;* that Roland, too, had messed with boys when he was Baby Back's age; that sixteen years ago he up and joined a minstrel show that toured through Locke's Creek because there were men in the troupe who liked to lie with men.

One night, Baby Back's gnawing curiosity prompted him to ask, "Uncle Roland? You ever been in love?"

Roland said nothing for the longest. Baby Back thought he'd

fallen asleep or into one of his quiet spells. Then, at last, "Yes, Baby. I've been in love. I'm still in love."

"Somebody in Paris?"

"Yes. Loving. Tender. Beautiful. Young. Maybe too young. For *me*, at least. Loved me. Touched my body and it opened right up." Another quiet spell then, "Dead. My love . . . Dead."

"That why you left Paris?"

The only answer was the heaving of his uncle's back against his as Roland wept.

Uncle and nephew. Inseparable. Baby Back was the only person Roland talked to. Baby Back became protective of him. When folks pestered him about his quietness, Baby Back fended them off. If someone teased him about his wingtips or his washed-up career, Baby Back interceded. Anyone making a sly crack about men in minstrel shows risked a bashing from Baby Back.

Folks watched the pair's closeness and whispered.

One day Roland opened his trunk, removed two items, and gave both to his nephew. A book entitled *The World's Best Negro Poetry*: "Negroes need poems more than anyone else in this world. Never forget that, Baby." And a trumpet from his vaudeville days: "Your ticket out. Learn to play this and you may get to Paris one day. Or at least away from *here*."

"I can't play no trumpet, Uncle Roland. I ain't got no music in me."

But he wrapped his hands around the polished brass, kissed his lips into the mouthpiece, pushed down on the valves, and fell irretrievably in love. Baby Back played the trumpet and felt his knees sink. Baby Back played the trumpet and never wanted to come up for air.

They did their lessons at night, though dizzy with exhaustion after a long day toiling in the sun. Roland taught with urgency, pushed him as if time was running out. Baby Back didn't understand, but he didn't mind. He loved having his uncle all to himself.

That monopoly ended the day they went to town for supplies.

The crackers liked their niggers humble, so they kept their heads down as they walked through Locke's Creek, Roland limping along in his butchered wingtips. They Uncle-Tommed as required and bought what they needed. On the return trip home, they ran into Edwin Gracely, son of the richest family in town.

Edwin Gracely was *funny*. The rumors were prolific. Locke's Creek fumed in a perpetual state of scandal.

"You know he goes to New Orleans, with that French Quarter and all that nigger voodoo."

"He buys men in the Quarter."

"And right here at home, too. Naomi Eldridge—down at the hotel—she swears it. Says he brings 'em in from outta town. Rents a room for a night or a weekend. Checks in in broad daylight. Checks out the same way. That's nerve."

"That's *money*. The Gracelys is too goddamn powerful. Can't touch 'em."

Gracely leaned against the rail of a short bridge that led across a shallow creek. His shirt was unbuttoned halfway down his chest, exposing a downy meadow of hair on his slim body.

"You the nigger used to sing and dance in Paris?" he said.

"Yessuh," Roland said. He and Baby Back kept going, heads bowed.

"Stop walkin'. A white man's talkin' to you."

They did. Baby Back prayed this would end quickly; that Edwin Gracely would hurry up and humiliate them, have his fun, and let them get on home. But when he spoke again, Baby Back was shocked to hear not taunts, but tenderness, and something that sounded like pleading.

"My ol' man sent me to Paris one summer," Gracely said, eyes set on Roland. "I had a good time. I wasn't lonely there. You know what I'm talkin' about. Don't you?"

Roland unbowed his head, looked Edwin Gracely square in the eye. He started walking, Baby Back at his side. When they reached the other side of the creek, Roland stopped, looked back.

Next day, Baby Back and Roland looked up from their work. Edwin Gracely stood on the crest of a small hill, watching.

Later, Roland bathed. It wasn't his usual night. He dusted his wingtips. He limped up the road.

\*   \*   \*

Over the next weeks, the mood on the farm and in town darkened. Folks didn't whisper or tease anymore. They shot Roland and Baby Back hateful looks. Baby Back sensed something terrible was about to happen, was already happening.

One night after Roland bathed and left, Baby Back overheard his folks.

"The crackers ain't gone stand for it," his pa said. " 'Specially now that Mr. Edwin doin' that depraved shit with a nigger."

"We don't know what that man doin' or who he doin' it with," Ma said. "Could all be lies. And I ain't never believed them rumors 'bout your brother."

"You mean you don't want to."

"Tell me you believe that about Roland. Tell me you believe that about your son."

Ma fought, but Pa made the final decision, as was his duty and his right.

"Roland gotta go," he said.

"You gone kick your own brother out?"

"Woman, we ain't got no damn choice."

Baby Back waited up for Roland.

"They gone send you away," Baby Back said. "I don't want you to go. Least not without me."

"You can't go with me."

"Why? I'm doin' good with the trumpet. We could go to Paris. Work in the music halls."

"Getting to Paris—getting anywhere—is impossible. We have no money."

Uncle and nephew perspired in the muggy shed. Baby Back took charge. He had to. Enemies were closing in and Roland was too tired and too weak to fight them. But Baby Back was tough. He was resilient. So he switched places with Roland, became the adult, and schemed their way to a solution.

"Mr. Edwin. Get the money from him," he commanded. "Go to him tomorrow."

Roland was unfazed by the switch. He welcomed it. Uncle obeyed nephew. "I will. I don't need to go back to Paris. But I need to get you out of here. This is no place for a boy like you. For people like us."

They didn't have a chance to execute their plan.

Next morning a lynch mob ambushed the shack. They pulled Roland from the house and dragged him to a field. Baby Back and his parents followed, screaming, crying, begging. A horde of whites in Sunday finery had gathered. Women in flowery bonnets. Men in starched shirts. Children in knickers and pinafores and carrying dolls. The horde laughed and cheered like revelers at a carnival. Only the souvenir booth was missing.

"Friends and neighbors, this nigger's a degenerate and he's 'bout to learn what good Christian white folks do to degenerate niggers," the head cracker proclaimed, performing for his audience. An ebullient master of ceremonies. "This here Roland Johnston's been corruptin' young men all over town."

His ma tried to stop him, but Baby Back marched right up to the man.

"Liar! Mr. Edwin the one been doing the corruptin'. If you gone kill my uncle, kill him, too."

The day was all cloudless sky and August sun, but Baby Back saw nothing but black when the cracker flattened him with a single punch.

His pa crouched next to him and hissed, "Shut your goddamn mouth, boy. They'll kill you, too."

The mob piled on Roland. He collapsed in on himself on the ground, tried to shelter his face and eyes. They hauled him to his feet, confined his arms behind his back, buffeted him with fists. He retaliated with kicks and spit and curses and they hammered him to the ground again and clubbed him, each assailant wielding his favorite weapon. Bat. Brick. Chain. Knife. Foot. Every weapon turned slick with blood. They battered his head with rifle butts. Baby Back heard the crunch of skull with each blow. They hacked his chest with boards spiked with protruding nails, slashed his face, his genitals. They beat him to something less than a pulp, something less than human while men held guns on the family and forced them to watch.

"Don't turn away," a gunman said, smiling, jubilant. "Open them eyes!" He cocked his rifle. "Now, goddamn it!"

Beating complete, they dragged him to a patch of sycamores and stripped him to the waist. What used to be Roland was now a wreckage. He was barely conscious as they tied his hands behind his back. He couldn't hold his head up, so they kindly did it for him as they fitted his neck with a hemp rope. They mounted him on a chair that Baby Back recognized as one from the shack. Someone kicked the chair. Roland's eyes bulged to life as he danced in the air. Seconds later, his body swung limp and lazy in the dank air.

But the mob wasn't done.

They sawed through the rope with a knife. Roland crashed to the ground. They slopped him with gasoline, lit a match. He gusted into flame in an instant.

The crackers congratulated each other—backslaps, handshakes—and dispersed, leaving behind a crackling mound of roasting human flesh. The seamy smoke slithered up to the sky. Vultures picked up the scent, began circling overhead.

Ben was usually the one who got held, but this time a trembling Baby Back sought shelter.

"What happened to Gracely?" Ben asked.

"His pa sent him away. Nobody ever saw him again. I gotta get to Paris, Ben."

"Then go. I want you to. But come back."

"And have to share you with that woman and her kid? Hell no."

So Ben finished packing. More like stuffing everything into his suitcases as quickly as he could. The trunks they had bought for Paris remained in the middle of the room, a reminder of what might have been. It took three trips to get everything into the taxi. Baby Back didn't help. Ben didn't expect him to.

"Good-bye," he said, typewriter in hand, about to begin his final trip down the stairs and out of Baby Back's life. "I'm sorry. I love you."

Baby Back pressed something into Ben's free hand. A ticket for the boat to Paris. He put his lips hard against Ben's ear and whispered, "I love you, too. So come with me. This is our chance to be together in a place that wants us."

Ben's desire to go with Baby Back was so severe, he had to shake himself. "What about Angeline?"

"What about *me?*"

A perfectly selfish, perfectly valid question.

"The boat leaves Sunday at three o'clock," Baby Back said, his mouth still against Ben's ear. "Change your mind. It ain't too late."

# 21

Friday evening, two days before Baby Back would sail. Ben sat on the stoop in Mrs. Harrisburg's wicker chair. He couldn't bring himself to go inside. The night had cooled. A trace of humidity remained. It was late, but children played on the sidewalks or out in the street, compelling automobiles to caution their way forward. Some parents shouted at their kids to be careful while others, too busy with their conversations or not present at all, did nothing.

In a few years, Ben's son or daughter would play ball or hop-scotch or jump rope and he would be the parent watching astutely. The world was full of good parents and not-good parents. He would be one of the good ones. He would nurture and dote. He would be grateful for his child, grateful even for the careless error that had brought it to existence. But not now. Not yet. Right now he wanted to flounder in the mud of self-pity. He wished he could be as selfish as Baby Back and leave the kid and Angeline in the lurch. But it wasn't in him.

But then, yes, it *was*. Hadn't he abandoned his ma and pa, forcing them to guess his fate? Before that, he had cut Willful out of his life.

It was darker now. All of the young kids had gone in. Only the older ones remained and they sat on their building's steps, trying to act grown—smoking, sneaking kisses with boyfriends or girlfriends. Ben's child would do that, too. He would have to chaperone his daughter and repel the boys with wandering hands; keep his son away from kids who offered him liquor or worse.

Ben rose from the wicker chair feeling as old and stiff as Mrs. Harrisburg. He went inside. The table was set with steaming platters of food.

"I fixed dinner," Angeline said.

"I see that. I ate already."

Her face withered. "All right."

She ate alone, then seemed ready to talk or spend time together.

"I'm whipped," Ben said. "I need sleep."

"Sure." He could barely hear her.

She retired to the bedroom and he to the sofa—a bitter fall from the spacious, grandma-quilted bed. And he had only his own arms to bundle around him.

*I love you, too. So come with me. This is our chance to be together in a place that wants us.*

Suddenly he was so very lonely and he tightened his arms around himself. He would have to be his own lover now. He had begun the drift into sleep when a brutal vision intruded: Baby Back with another man sealed against his chest; his Baby loving someone else underneath that grandma quilt. Ben turned onto his stomach, stuffed his face against the sofa cushion to muffle his sobs. Angeline heard them anyway.

"Benny?"

A moment later she had crossed the boundary of the Neutral Territory and her hands were on his back. Lightly. Comfortingly. But he didn't want her comfort. He turned over and slapped her hands away.

"Go away. Go back in the bedroom," he said, making no effort to hide the cold threat in his voice. "Don't come out here again."

Mr. Kittredge didn't show for breakfast, lunch, or dinner. It occurred to Ben that he had checked out, but he refused to believe he'd leave without a good-bye. He sought out Reggie the bellhop who knew all the gossip and comings and goings at The Pavilion.

"He cut out, jack. This morning. Early. Hired a car to go to Penn Station. I'm telling you, my back ain't never ached so much. I had to bring down trunk after trunk after trunk from that suite. Why white people gotta have so much stuff?"

Ben upbraided himself for thinking a white man found him worthy enough to say good-bye to. But when his shift ended, his boss handed him a sealed package. Inside he found a small leather-bound book. The title *Les Poèmes d'Amour de Pierre de Ronsard* was printed in gold lettering on the black cover. The pages were thin, almost translucent, edged in gilt. Ben flipped through it. Each poem was in French with an English translation beside it. The package also contained an envelope. Inside that, a handwritten note.

> *Dear Benjamin,*
> *Please forgive my abrupt departure. I do not know when I shall return. Frankly, I do not know that I want to.*
> *I was distressed when you told me that you will not be going to Paris. I hope that this is a decision you are comfortable with and that you do eventually visit that wonderful city.*
> *Thank you, dear boy, for everything. I do consider you my friend.*
> *Yours,*
> *Geoffrey Wells Kittredge*

Enclosed with the note was a card with a London address and five crisp ten-dollar bills.

\* \* \*

> *What about me?*
> *You have whispered*
> *Misty blessings in my ear,*
> *Given me possession of*
> *Your triumphant verses,*

*Allowed me deep into the*
*Most vulnerable parts of you.*
*Don't I, therefore, deserve your heart?*

*Come with me.*
*Come with me, sweet.*

He had composed the lines in his head the night before as he lay on the sofa in the dark, and now committed them to type. It was exactly noon. Baby Back's departure day. Ben was alert to each minute, each second that skulked by. The boat ticket lay on the desk, next to the typewriter. He hadn't been able to throw it away.

After work the previous night, he had defaulted to his old walking routine and found memories everywhere. He ended up under the streetlamp across from Teddy's. It wasn't the same, even from outside. Music filtered out from the speakeasy, but it didn't swing without Baby Back. It had been too early for a big crowd. Ben had pictured Fanny and the other waitresses roaming the place, bored. The hostess would be saving her saltiest jokes for later.

Baby Back would be home, preparing for his big day. Ben had considered going to see him, but what was the point? He had come home instead and lay on the sofa and composed his poem, mouthing the words as he chose them.

*Come with me.*
*Come with me, sweet.*

Angeline set a cup of coffee on the desk. He couldn't comprehend why she insisted on doing these wifely things.

"Can I read it?" she asked.

"No."

"Oh, come on, Benny. I know it's good."

She stood over him and began reading. He tore the paper out of the typewriter.

"I said no!"

She backed away, seated herself at the dining room table. "Is this the way it's gonna be? For the rest of our lives?" The question seemed directed at herself rather than him. "I thought the baby would make things different."

His instinct was to go to her, beg forgiveness. But he stayed put. "It's gonna take a little time for me to get used to this."

"How could I be so stupid?"

"Angeline, please—"

"I ain't pregnant."

Years later, whenever Ben recalled this moment, he would try to isolate the feelings that assailed him. Then, taking his analysis further, he would try to determine, exactly, the very first thing that upended him in that suspended half second after Angeline's declaration. It took years of musing to pinpoint that one overriding feeling.

Hope.

"What?" he said, low, menacing. "What the hell did you say?"

"I. Ain't. Pregnant." Her voice was as low and as menacing as his. And she dared look straight at him. "I said I was so you'd stay. But you don't want to be here. And that ain't about to change."

He wanted to hit her. His hands shook with the desire and he crushed them into fists and locked them behind his back to calm them. She had destroyed his life. It was too late to be with Baby Back. He looked at his watch. 1:17.

No, it wasn't too late. The boat didn't leave until three o'clock.

He flew up from the desk so fast, the chair fell over and hit the floor with a *boom*. He got a suitcase, dumped clothes in, then sprinted all over the house, collecting books, papers, toiletries, more clothes. He could barely close the thing with everything wadded up and crammed in and his hands shaking. He put his typewriter in its case and set it next to the luggage and then stripped out of his clothes and jumped into a traveling suit and he didn't button the shirt all the way and didn't tie the tie and he plunked his hat on his head and he knew he looked like hell and he didn't care because the only thing that mattered was getting to that pier by three o'clock.

He swiped up the boat ticket from the desk, stuffed it in his jacket's inside pocket. Angeline hadn't moved. They looked at each other now. She was crying.

"Good-bye, Benny. You don't want to hear this. But I love you."

No, he didn't want to hear that. Because he didn't want to soften toward her.

"Take care of yourself," she said. "Please. Good luck."

She was sobbing the first time he ever saw her and she was sobbing the last time he'd see her. He said nothing as he opened the door and took up the heavy luggage and left, not bothering to close the door behind him.

# ambition
## 1926

## 22

He couldn't believe it. He tapped his foot, impatient, and checked his watch. 2:20. Forty minutes until the ship sailed and he'd been stalled in a subway train somewhere beneath Seventh Avenue for the last twenty. Stalled and perspiring, although he didn't know if the sweat came from the heat or his anxiety. He was the only one fanning himself. The only one tapping his foot in manic, percussive rhythm. Two white women sat across from him. One read *Show Boat,* the other knitted. Each paused her activity, watched his foot, and frowned. He stopped tapping.

Without that distraction, Angeline's revelation barged to the front of his thoughts. He hated her. But he suspended his hatred, momentarily, to savor the knowledge that he was so worthwhile that she had lied to keep him; that *two* people loved him and had fought for the right to have him. But that gust of self-worth dithered in the face of his current dilemma. He checked his watch again: just thirty-five minutes till that boat carried Baby Back across the Atlantic and out of his life.

A train conductor strode through the car, very official in his spotless uniform, shoulders thrown back, chin elevated, as if he worked for the military instead of Interborough Rapid Transit.

"Excuse me? Sir?" Ben said. "Can you tell me why the delay?"

"Something's going on at Fourteenth Street. Where are you headed?"

"Fourteenth Street."

"Twenty-third's next," the conductor said. "If this train ever gets moving again, that is. You should get off there." He looked at Ben's luggage. "Especially if you're in a hurry. We might stall again before we make it to Fourteenth."

And the boat might leave before they moved again at all.

Ben tapped his foot again and didn't stop when the reader and the knitter frowned their objections. He thought about what he would do if he missed the boat. Go back to Angeline's and get the rest of his things. Rent a room somewhere, maybe Baby Back's old room. Keep working at The Pavilion. Get a side job. Save until he had enough for a ticket to Paris. Pray Baby Back didn't meet another man in the meantime.

That last thought made him wince just as the train rumbled back to life and bolted forward. It rolled into the Twenty-third Street station at two thirty. Ben had to decide quick: take his chances and stay on this train until Fourteenth, or get off now.

Passengers exited. The doors were about to close. The knitter's hands had gotten tangled in yarn and she hurried to gather her handbag and knitting paraphernalia. She ran off the train just as the doors were about to close. In a moment of decision that felt dangerously like a whim, Ben followed.

He got up to the street and froze. *What now?*

The boat sailed in less than half an hour. He'd never make it on foot, even if he ran, so when he spotted a cab idling at a light, he sprinted toward it, opened the rear door, shoved his stuff inside, and got in, all in what felt like one swift, elongated move.

"Pier Fifty-seven," he told the driver. "It's at—"

"I know where it's at," the driver said, sounding mildly offended, as if Ben had tried to teach the teacher. "What time's your boat leave?"

"Three o'clock."

The driver looked at his watch. "You didn't give yourself much time, did you?"

"Just get me there, OK?"

"Hey, pal, I'm a driver, not a magician."

"Then drive!"

The light changed. They turned from Twenty-third Street onto Seventh Avenue and headed south in the direction of Greenwich Village. Traffic was sparse and moved quickly, but time ticked by. To ease his panic, Ben kept his eyes off his watch and on his surroundings. This part of Seventh Avenue was all cheap hotels and luncheonettes and apartments. Advertising thrived on billboards and signs.

HOTEL ROOMS: $1.00 AND UP.

ALBERT HIRST SELLS FORD CARS, B'WAY AND 68TH STREET.

EGYPTIAN PRETTIEST CIGARETTES: PACKAGE OF 20 FOR 25 CENTS.

"Hey, pal," the driver said. "What happens if you miss your boat? Will you get fired? Or they'll just put you on another one?"

"Fired? What?"

"You work on the boat, right? In the kitchen or cleaning rooms or something?"

He wore a newsboy cap on his bald head. A network of grooves lined the back of his neck. He spoke with the accent and working-class gruffness of someone from the Bronx or Jersey.

They were passing Twentieth Street. Ben peeked at his watch: 2:37.

"I'm going to France as a *passenger*," he said.

"I didn't know darkies did that."

"*Negroes* do. Guess you ain't kept up with current events."

"Guess not."

Nineteenth Street.

Eighteenth Street.

At Seventeenth they stopped at a red light. It took so long to change, Ben feared it was broken. They hit another red light at Sixteenth and when it turned green, they remained stuck because an old man hadn't made it across the street in time. Ben tried to resist his watch, but couldn't: two forty-five.

The old man crossed and the taxi drove on. They turned west onto Fifteenth. By the time they got to Fifteenth and Ninth Avenue, they had landed in the Meatpacking District. The pier wasn't much farther. But at Tenth Avenue, they hit a tantrum of traffic. Cars and trucks and pedestrians and horse-drawn wagons swarmed the avenue, kicking up a flurry of dust. Gasoline fumes, horse manure, and the stink from the slaughterhouses soured the air.

"Hey, pal," the driver said. "Looks like you're one *Negro* who ain't going to France this time around."

Ten minutes till three.

In yet another second split-second decision, Ben grabbed his wallet, threw money into the front seat, gathered his stuff, hopped out of the taxi, and plunged into the traffic, spiraling his way around the maelstrom of barely advancing vehicles. He crossed Tenth Avenue, made it to Eleventh, and raced toward the pier. He considered ditching his suitcase to boost his speed.

It was really a series of piers, each serving a different cruise line. Ben ran until he saw the terminal building at Pier 57 that housed the French Line. A sea of cars packed the area in front. He ran inside.

"The boat to Paris—please tell me it ain't left!"

Customs officers stood nearby. One approached. "Not yet. But you're cutting it awfully close. Ticket and passport, please."

Ben produced both.

The officer confirmed he was on the passenger list. Another inspected his luggage. His ticket was verified, his passport stamped. The first officer told him he'd escort him to the ship.

"Ain't necessary," Ben said. "Just tell me where it is."

"Trust me, son: You'll never get through the crowd by yourself."

He was right. With the officer in front shouting, "Make way! One more passenger! Make way!" Ben muscled through the morass of well-wishers, all shouting and waving up to their loved ones who waved back and blew kisses from the deck of the ship. The rabble hemmed him in on all sides as a blizzard of streamers and confetti swirled in the air.

"Make way! Make way, please! One last passenger!"

They bullied their way through the crowd and approached the ship, a gargantuan thing floating on the water, light and carefree as a leaf. The hull was solid black. BONAPARTE was etched onto the hull in white letters that slanted to the right. Three red and black funnels rose up from the ship's top, gushing steam.

They got to the ship just as the gangplank was lifting up and away from the dock. The officer blew a whistle and waved his arms.

"Lower the plank! One more passenger!"

It lowered.

Ben started up the gangplank, giddy, spent, woozy, galvanized. The confetti and the streamers continued swirling. The crowd below shouted joyfully, as if they were the ones embarking on this trip.

Someone was in the entryway at the top of the gangplank. Just standing there, as if waiting. A man. Ben got closer, saw the man was colored. And tall. And broad-shouldered.

Ben reached the top.

"Well," Baby Back said.

"Well."

They looked at each other as if neither believed the other stood before him. Ben could barely see the tears in Baby Back's eyes because of the tears gathering in his own.

They attacked each other before the door to their cabin was even shut good and fell into a ferocious round of fucking. Ben tasted a glimmer of blood on his lip where Baby Back got carried away. As the *Bonaparte* sailed out of New York Harbor, Ben couldn't tell if the topsy-turvy motion was the seesawing of the waves or the in-and-out, rolling-and-rocking of him and Baby Back as they tumbled and flopped over each other with the clumsy poise of playful kittens.

He couldn't believe his luck. The turmoil of the last weeks was like a chronic pain that had suddenly vanished. A miracle? It didn't matter. He had been a dying man who found out he was going to live; a pauper who now possessed gold. It was as if he had tricked the clock, sneaked a few weeks back in time to that happy period before their lives were upended by a lie. They were back to the way they should be, as if they had never been uprooted.

The kittens bit and growled and scratched. Insatiable. Better than it had ever been. Was that possible? To pick up where they left off and be better than before? Baby Back had waited for him. He had left Harlem without him, yes, but then parked himself at the top of that gangplank, praying for an off chance to pan out. The sight of him had made Ben think the notion of their separation was just that: a notion, and nothing more, case closed.

The kittens growled their last, then fell against each other, beat. Baby Back was the first to speak.

> *"I got love runnin' through me,*
> *Like a river,*
> *Like wine,*
> *Like sweet jazz in an uptown dive.*
> *Runs through me, and through me, and through me.*
>
> *May I kiss your pretty cheek?*
> *May I kiss your pretty lips?*
> *Your pretty hips?*
> *Be my beauty,*
> *'Cause I got love runnin' through me."*

"I didn't know you memorized it," Ben said.

"I didn't either. It suddenly came back to me. Like you did. And it's gonna stay with me. Like you are."

So it *was* possible to pick up where they left off, reverse time and circumstances, redeemed, stronger, the slate licked clean and glistening like honey. Ben felt invincible, his life with Baby Back assured. Only one bit of unfinished business: forgiveness. A formality, but necessary.

*Mr. Poet, please, please forgive me.*

Forgiveness was like charity: You could dispense it, or not. And, as with charity, the one dispensing held the power. Ben wallowed in Baby Back's arms and in the power he wielded over the big, handsome trumpet player who so often took the lead, took control, made Ben subservient. Ben's power to forgive (or not) was an equalizer: It raised him to Baby Back's level.

*Mr. Poet, please forgive me.*

The request was imminent. Ben would grant it. But he'd make

Baby Back suffer first. Just a little. Payback for his offensive rejection of compromise; for gambling on an off chance at the top of a gangplank when they should have ascended it, side by side. When Baby Back begged his forgiveness, Ben would climb onto a high horse and gently educate his stubborn lover on the merits of compromise and selflessness; use his status as charitable forgiver as a mechanism to change the man.

But that could wait. Exhausted Ben began descending into well-deserved sleep.

"Mr. Poet, I want you to know something: I forgive you."

The descent halted. "Come again?"

"Everything's all right now, Ben. I forgive you."

He sounded like a king granting an imperial pardon. Ben wormed his way out from under him.

"You forgive me? *You* forgive *me*? It should be the other way around."

"The other way around? You got Angeline pregnant—"

"But she ain't really pregnant," Ben said.

"The point is you were unfaithful. For that, I forgive you. Why the hell you think that *you* should be the one forgiving *me*?"

"Because you were gonna leave me. You *did* leave me. You wouldn't compromise. Baby Back, when you love someone, you compromise."

"When you love someone, you don't fuck somebody else."

They swatted accusations back and forth.

"You didn't think about nothing but yourself. You didn't think about *us*."

"Well, you didn't *think*."

And they defended themselves.

"I came up with a solution I thought would work for both of us."

"I was trying to make the best of a fucked-up situation."

They stopped. Stumped, they said nothing. They couldn't, wouldn't look at each other. Ben had thought the slate had been licked clean. Now he just felt licked.

Minutes passed. The interlude allowed him to get his first good look at the cabin. LeRoi Jasper had arranged their accommodations in first class; said if Negroes were coming to Paris on his dime, they were traveling in style even if it cost a fortune. This room certainly did. Chest of drawers and desk made of rosewood. Damask on the walls. Silk linens on the bed. A private bath with a marble floor and sink, and a tub of lustrous porcelain supported by four silver claw feet.

Ben knelt on the Persian rug, rested his head in his lover's lap. He could smell his sex as he kissed the inside of his thigh.

Baby Back rose. "I gotta get dressed."

"Oh. Why?"

"Rehearsal. There's a bunch of musicians on board. Europeans is crazy about jazz, so we're performing in the evenings. Extra money. Ain't saying no to that."

Ben remained on the floor. Back in The Oasis, he had often watched the production that was Baby Back's grooming: starched shirt always buttoned from the bottom up; shoes ushered onto his feet with a shoehorn to preserve the shape; jacket slipped on, buttoned up, smoothed down; hat placed at a jaunty angle. But there was none of that self-indulgence now. He simply got dressed and walked out, leaving Ben on the Persian rug, still naked from their lovemaking.

# 23

A palatial, carpeted staircase with mahogany railings provided entrance to the first-class dining hall. The hall soared three decks high. As spacious as it was elegant, all its furnishings and décor—tables, chairs, chandeliers, artwork, even the pattern on the carpet—boasted that Art Deco style so in vogue these days. A string quartet played on a small stage. Every table was full. Older, conservative gentlemen and ladies in full formal attire—tuxes, spats, full-length gowns, tiaras—looked askance at younger men and women in white dinner jackets and sparkly, sleeveless dresses with necklines that dipped rebelliously low.

The string quartet's stately melodies did not suit the room's festive pulse or the mood of travelers with nothing on their hands but time and champagne. The brash younger set, with their modern clothes and lawless good looks, laughed and drank and bounced in their seats. Even the stodgy older set seemed to sway.

Maybe ten Negroes—mostly musicians—sailed aboard the *Bonaparte,* and all were invited to dine at the captain's table that first evening. They stood out because of their color, their status as the captain's guests, and their clothing. None owned a tux or dinner jacket, but each wore his very best suit spruced up with a flower on the lapel. Except for Baby Back and Ben, their quarters were in tourist class. Captain Olivier held court, sparkling on and on about his treks through Harlem's clubs while on shore leave. But his dinner companions sat silent, hands imprisoned in their laps, on guard against this foreign white man who had thwarted the natural order of things by inviting them to break bread.

"We have *le jazz-hot* in France, too," Captain Olivier said, "but I wanted pure Negro jazz. Harlem did not disappoint!" He leaned forward, professorial, hands folded on the table, his distinguished, mid-fortysomething face aglow. "You see, musicians of *my* race study and practice and learn music theory and such. But a Negro musician's gift is primal and instinctive. Music comes from deep within you. *Mon dieu.* You have been gifted with a native abandon that moves listeners and makes them dance. Having musicians on board who can perform such miracles is an honor. We are honored to take you to our France." He lifted a glass of champagne. "To *le jazz-hot!*"

"Told you they love us over there," Baby Back said, his first words to Ben since the fight.

An opening. Ben raced through it. "Sorry about earlier," he whispered.

"Yeah, I know that."

Captain Olivier's welcome helped his guests breathe. Hands left laps. Bodies loosened. Elbows sidled onto the table top. The table began bubbling with conversation and Baby Back put himself in the center of it, discarding Ben on the outskirts. The captain played host like a virtuoso, but Ben's attentions shifted around the hall. Two tables in the immediate vicinity fascinated him, one filled with French speakers, the other with Americans. Members of the French party smiled and nodded if Ben caught their attention, but the Americans' eyes shot ice at their ship's captain sitting so amiably with a table full of Negroes.

A Negro couple approached the captain's table.

"I'm Clifford Treadwell. My wife, Millicent."

Olivier stood. "*Bienvenu, Monsieur et Madame Treadwell. Enchanté.* Sit down, *s'il vous plaît.*"

Millicent Treadwell wore a heavily brocaded, long-sleeve brown gown and a cameo brooch. Her ensemble made her the most matronly looking young female in the room. But her husband snazzed it up in a white dinner jacket and full-cut pleated slacks. The Tread-wells were very light-complexioned—not light enough to *pass,* but close. Both had *good* hair—not a kink in sight.

Mrs. Treadwell regarded the table's guests with skeptical eyes, then chose the seat beside the captain. The musicians elbowed each other.

"She don't want nothin' to do with us dark-skinned niggers," one mumbled.

"Something tells me those two ain't stayin' in no tourist class," another said.

Waiters commenced serving. The Treadwells behaved as if being served by whites was nothing extraordinary, but Ben and the musicians tittered at the role reversal.

"Can't wait to write the folks back home and tell 'em about this."

"Shoot. This is too damn good to be true."

"I feel like I done died and gone to heaven."

"Hey, y'all, watch this." To a passing waiter: "Oh, excuse me, *garçon!*"

Champagne flowed ceaselessly. The musicians, so bashful be-fore, now bantered with the captain with the cozy irreverence of cohorts. Coziness was contagious in the rest of the dining hall, too. Old coots mixed it up with the younger set; flappers taught ma-trons how to smoke cigarettes; a feisty gentleman teamed up with a hot-blooded young man at the lip of the stage to bawl out the string quartet for remaining behind the times with its waltzy minuets.

For Ben the lilting-on-air strings were a change from hard-driving jazz and blues. He didn't mind the minuets. He did mind that Baby Back wasn't paying attention to him. He craved the surreptitious public affection they had perfected back home: holding hands and rubbing knees under a table; whispering naughty bits in each other's ears under the outward guise of discussing serious business. But Baby Back immersed himself in the table's conversations. It felt like a slight. When a waiter brought a tray loaded with champagne glasses, Ben took two.

"As soon as you arrive in Paris," Captain Olivier said, "you must go see Josephine Baker at the Folies Bergère. Magnificent.

She bends and undulates her body and crosses her eyes like you have never seen. She performs a jungle dance dressed only in a belt of bananas. Very sensual. Absolutely authentic. Ironically, rediscovering the primitive is the key to advancing the modern. Avant-garde thinkers and artists agree on this." He folded his hands on the table again. "And I tell you, *mes amis,* the European must embrace the primitive sensuality that comes naturally to the African. That is essential to reinvigorating a white race that is becoming, quite frankly, boring. Mademoiselle Baker is doing Europe a great service."

The musicians' reactions ranged from befuddlement to annoyance. The Treadwells, neutral, sipped their champagne. Ben opened his mouth to question the captain, but Baby Back kicked him under the table.

"I just want to ask him what he means by *primitive,*" Ben whispered.

"Keep your mouth shut. Don't make no trouble for me. You've made enough."

The waiter came with another tray of champagne. Ben took two more.

Somebody mentioned a section of Paris called *Montmartre.*

"That's where a lot of the jazz clubs are," Clifford Treadwell said.

"Montmartre is not a respectable neighborhood," Millicent Treadwell said. Her pretty, light, young voice was a profound contrast to her matronly garb. "That's why the jazz clubs are there, naturally."

Elbows bounded around the table again like a circle of falling dominoes.

Millicent appealed her case to the captain. "My husband and I prefer the classics."

"My wife doesn't speak for both of us," Clifford said. "I love me some down-home jazz!"

"Clifford, you needn't contradict me in front of people."

"And you needn't speak on my behalf about my musical preferences."

The corners of Millicent's mouth ticked up in an attempt at a smile. She picked at her crème brûlée.

"Madame Treadwell," Olivier said, "I appreciate your love of the classics, but I am tired of this violin music." He engaged the musicians. "*Mes amis,* you will be so kind as to entertain us."

Strings were out. Jazz was in. At last, the music from the stage jibed with the mood in the room, so much that the maître d' intervened when some of the younger set kicked up the Charleston, threatening to transform the first-class dining room into a dance hall. Millicent conversed with the captain, at ease for the first time. But engrossed in *le jazz-hot,* he didn't pay her much mind.

First time Ben had seen Baby Back perform in weeks, though the multiple double doses of champagne blurred his vision. He was anxious for later tonight. They had to talk. He might have to junk the idea of the trumpeter begging forgiveness. Might have to be subservient again. Maybe that didn't matter. Maybe being in Baby Back's center and not on his outskirts was all that mattered.

"Your friend," Clifford Treadwell said.

He startled Ben. "You talking to me?"

"Obviously." But his attention was locked on the band. "Your friend—Baby Back?"

"My *cousin.*"

Clifford's gray eyes shifted to Ben. The man inhabited a nebulous realm of in-betweens: He was neither attractive, nor unattractive; not tall, but not short; he wasn't fat, nor was he particularly trim; not acceptably white, yet not verifiably Negro. What was it like, Ben wondered, to live that way, never solidly one thing or the other?

"I see," Clifford said. "What's your *cousin's* real name?"

"Well . . . everyone always calls him Baby Back."

The gray eyes shifted back to the band. Clifford smiled. "Killer. So will I."

The party roared on the Atlantic. The band pumped out jazz. Jazz got the passengers dancing. Dancing got them thirsty. Thirst compelled them to drink preposterous amounts of champagne. Preposterous amounts of champagne made them as buoyant as the

*Bonaparte* itself. Baby Back and the band picked up on the buoyancy, fed off it, which got them jamming harder, which got the people dancing more deliriously till pellets of sweat shimmied off their
bodies and they were forced to replenish the errant moisture with
more champagne, which ratcheted up the buoyancy, which fired
up the band which escalated the dancing which exacerbated the
thirst which made them guzzle more champagne and the cycle repeated and repeated and repeated all night long and Ben got snagged
in the cycle like getting snagged in a powerful whirlpool and he
danced and drank and he drank and danced (right alongside *white
people!*) until he extracted himself from the whirlpool by flat-out
force of will and called it quits at two a.m.

He dragged himself back to the cabin. Whipped, out of breath,
and dementedly, joyously drunk. When he closed his eyes he spun
out of his body and up to the sky and looked down on a fortress of
bright light floating, elegantly, on the undulating water.

He wanted to sleep, but needed to wait up for Baby Back.

What a night. What a *day*.

The night may have beaten down his body, but it was the day
with its drama and counter-drama, its checks and checkmates, that
kindled his emotions. They were all over the place; he needed a
map to chart them. If they were colors, they'd run the gamut: bonfire-
bright, moonlight-cool, every shade in between.

What about Baby Back, his map, his spectrum? Where in the
overlap with Ben's did the lines intersect, the colors still mix har-
moniously? All Ben was sure of was that they loved each other, and
that love had stationed Baby Back like a sentinel at the top of the
gangplank, but hadn't been sufficient to mitigate the forgiveness
wars.

Ben sighed. "Yes, indeed. What a day."

He plummeted onto the bed, fought to stay awake by stringing
together a new poem in his head.

> *I am a barge floating toward a city of light,*
> *I carry the pulse of Africa,*
> *Reinvented on the avenues*
> *Of New Orleans and Harlem.*

He was too soaked with champagne to stay awake. He undressed and went to sleep, then awoke later (an hour? two?) to the scent of the ocean breezing in through the open window.

Then the sea scent filled out and darkened into the earthy, muscular funk of a man.

Through the window, Ben saw the moon. Its light dallied into the cabin and onto Baby Back, sitting on the bed's edge.

"A second chance," Baby Back said, low, mournful. "Who gets that? I thought I could forget about everything. I thought, *If I can just be with my Ben, everything'll be all right.* But I can't forget that you rejected me. For that woman."

Ben broke out in a rash of cold sweat. At last he recognized how blind he'd been. With the blindness lifted, he could see—clearly see—for the first time and all at once—just how brutally his betrayal had cut Baby Back, exactly how deep the blade had gouged. He felt guilty. And his guilt embarrassed him. And his embarrassment made the apology that Baby Back was so valiantly entitled to rot in his throat like a thing dead.

Ben reached for him.

"Don't," Baby Back said.

He walked away, only to the window, but it seemed a thousand miles.

# 24

They slept and woke on separate sides of the bed. Ben wondered if that was the new way of things as he watched Baby Back commence his grooming routine—a listless exercise without a speck of the swaggering, Harlem hepcat. Ben cowered on the silk sheets, afraid of being repelled again. He lowered his head each time Baby Back turned in his direction.

Baby Back finished dressing. He checked himself in the mirror, then let out a heavy sigh. He walked over to the bed, looked down at his lover. Ben tried to read him, but his face was neutral. Baby Back tickled Ben's head.

"Mr. Poet," he said, "come on. Let's see what these French folks can do with breakfast."

Clifford Treadwell waved them over as soon as they entered the dining hall. Millicent glowed with an ember of hostility, then quickly cooled. They ordered big bowls of hot chocolate, a pitcher of grapefruit juice, and tartines, which they spread with jam.

"I guess you folks been to Europe before?" Baby Back said.

"Why, yes, of course," Millicent said in her light, pretty voice. "Our honeymoon was Paris. We've been back a number of times, as well as other European cities, naturally. This trip is an anniversary gift from Clifford's parents. They insisted we go, wouldn't take no for an answer." She took her husband's hand, eyed him sweetly. "This is a second honeymoon, isn't it, dear?"

"Indeed," Clifford said, extracting his hand. He addressed Baby Back. "Your first time to Paris, I take it?"

"Yeah. Wanted to go all my life."

Clifford laughed. "What? All sixteen years?"

"Thanks for the compliment," Baby Back said.

"I'm just telling you the truth, Mr. Johnston."

Baby Back relaxed back like he was in an easy chair. "I like your truth. And it's Baby Back."

Clifford relaxed back, too. "I'm here to please."

Baby Back's mouth spread into a grin, wide and sly and bordering on lewd. "Might have to take you up on that."

"Do."

Millicent's ember returned. It burnished her light skin a humid red.

"Gotta love this!" Baby Back said, lounging in his deck chair, arms up and behind his head like he'd hit the high life. "If the folks in Locke's Creek could see me now." He closed his eyes. He wore a big, toothy grin.

The first-class deck was lounge, game room, and playground all at once. Passengers in fur-trimmed coats relaxed in deck chairs, legs covered with blankets, while stewards served tea. A round of shuffleboard was in progress on one section of the deck while on the other children engaged in three-legged races and tug-of-war. Ben and Baby Back were the only coloreds, but Ben barely noticed. The novelty of congregating with whites was already thinning. Besides, he was too furious.

"Did you enjoy flirting with him?" Ben said.

Baby Back remained with his eyes closed, arms up and above his head. "You sound like a guilty man, Mr. Poet. A man who knows he did wrong and tries to take the heat off himself."

Ben concentrated on the *plink* of the shuffleboard pucks as he contemplated what to say. "He's one of us, you know."

"Treadwell? Hell, I knew that as soon as I saw him last night. All it took was one look. Like when I met *you*. But I ain't hardly interested in that half-white man."

"You acted like you were," Ben said.

Baby Back sat up. "Uh-oh. I do declare that Mr. Ben Charles is colored, and that color is green." He tickled Ben's side, his neck, his ear, and made him giggle. "Mr. Jealous. Afraid of that light-skinned nothing with the uppity wife." He affected a half-falsetto, faux-aristocratic voice: "*And of course we've been to Europe thousands of times and Clifford's parents sent us on this trip because they think it'll make him want me. But all Clifford wants is a juicy dick up his butt. Oh, so sorry. Didn't mean to curse. I meant* penis. *He wants a juicy* penis *up his butt.*"

They disintegrated into a reckless bout of giggling. It took flight in the deck's open air. They clapped hands over their mouths to stifle it, but each time they looked at each other they disintegrated again. Before long everyone on deck was looking at the two gleeful colored men. Ben turned inadvertently to the couple next to them. They began laughing, too. And then the people next to *them* started. And the people next to *them.* Within moments half the deck was in mirthful uproar.

Perhaps the mirth prevented Ben and Baby Back from noticing the white American couple nearby. Maybe laughter drowned out the American woman when, in a flowery and affronted Southern drawl, she said to her husband, "Dear sweet Jesus. Samuel, there's *niggers* sittin' right there." And Baby Back's antics must have distracted Ben so that he only vaguely noticed when the American man stood and said, "What the hell you boys think you're doin'?" But the mirth and the antics could not block out the man when he roared, "Get out of here, you dumb-fuck niggers!"

His outburst cut the air like a shotgun. The deck went silent.

"Your darky asses shouldn't even be on this ship."

He had fat cheeks, a graying mustache, trench-like lines on his face. Not a tall man, but his straight back and sturdy weight planted soundly in his feet gave the illusion of height.

Baby Back rose.

"Baby, no!" Ben said, leaping up.

But Baby Back approached the man. "Sit your fat ass down and leave us be. Fuckin' white cracker."

An awful smile dirtied the Southern man's face. "Where I come from, I would kill you for that. Hunt you down like a deer, string you up from a sycamore, and savor every goddamn minute." He stepped closer. "Filthy nigger."

Baby Back turned as if to walk away, then pivoted back and swung his fist. The man intercepted the punch and struck one of his own deep in Baby Back's gut. He began thrashing with unrelenting speed as Baby Back struggled to protect his eyes and face. Ben tried to run to him, but a group of women circled him, holding him from jumping into the fray while a quartet of male passengers subdued the assailant.

"Get off me!" the Southern man yelled, squirming in their grasp.

Ben freed himself from the women and went to Baby Back. Captain Olivier, accompanied by a troop of first officers, strode onto the scene, demanding to know why hell was raging on his ship. Bedlam ensued as witnesses asserted their explanations—the Europeans in languages Ben didn't understand, the assailant and his wife in Southern accents he understood too well. He didn't detect any other American accents, but saw groups of whites, observing from a distance.

"Niggers sit with whites, but *I* get assaulted for doing something about it?" the Southern man said.

"*Monsieur,*" Olivier said, "this is a French vessel and in France, we treat *everyone* with respect. Now, kindly cooperate while my officers escort you from the deck."

Assailant and wife were led away amid protests from both.

"I will send the ship's physician to administer to you," Captain Olivier said to Baby Back.

"No, I'm fine." He held out his hand. The captain grasped it. "Thank you. Thank you very, very much."

As soon as the captain left the deck the Europeans surrounded Ben and Baby Back. The men gripped Baby Back's shoulders, slapped his back. The women took Ben's hands in theirs. They guided the two colored men to the deck chairs, sat them down, babied them, fawned over them, took care of them.

# 25

For the first time, *ever,* Ben was on vacation. He had either worked or looked for work almost every day of his life. Having nothing to do but eat, sleep, and lounge felt unnatural. There had to be a catch.

"Ain't no catch," Baby Back said. "And it ain't gonna last forever. Best enjoy it."

While Baby Back rehearsed, Ben toured the ship.

The *Bonaparte* was a self-contained dream civilization coasting on the Atlantic. Ben discovered a beauty parlor; a library with everything from Chaucer to Gertrude Stein; a full-size, working carousel for the junior passengers; a restaurant that was a fully functioning replica of a Parisian outdoor café complete with a sidewalk and potted trees. Smoking rooms. A music room where passengers listened to ship-to-ship broadcasts of phonograph records. A radio room for sending and receiving telegrams. Even an airplane that brought and delivered mail when the ship was in range of the shore and a swimming pool that Ben didn't dive in, though he longed to. The Europeans wouldn't mind, but he could imagine how white Americans would react to a Negro swimming in the same water as they. Anyway, he hadn't brought a bathing suit.

Baby Back joined him when he wasn't rehearsing. They lunched at the sidewalk café; smoked cigars in the smoking room though they would have preferred reefer; rode the carousel, to the amusement of the adults and the kids.

Everything was good again.

They had returned to their cabin following the Southern man's assault. Baby Back sat on the bed. Ben knelt in front of him to apply iodine to his wounds.

"Baby, I'm so proud of you. The way you stood up to him."

"Wasn't exactly *standing*. He thrashed me pretty good."

"Don't matter. You didn't back down. You was brave. I couldn't have done it. I'm so proud to be with a man who's brave and strong. What happened on that deck makes me see how lucky I am. Makes me see how wrong I was to put you through that mess with Angeline. Strong man like you deserves better. I ain't have no business expecting you to compromise. And I was wrong to think you should apologize. Baby Back, please forgive me."

Baby Back smiled down at Ben like a father so proud his son has, at last, become respectful enough, man enough, to own up to his sins. Ben's humble admission of wrong made things right. Baby Back lavished him with forgiveness, summoned him back from the outskirts.

They strolled the promenade one afternoon along with folks who walked as leisurely as they would the Fifth Avenue Easter Parade. Women in fur stoles and cloche hats over bobbed curls. Men so sporty in single-breasted button-down jackets, plus-fours, and argyle socks. The string quartet played, its stately tunes much more appropriate to the austerity of the promenade than for evenings in the first-class dining hall.

They left the promenade to stand near the prow and watch the water as the ship carved through the Atlantic, as the distance between them and America expanded. Could distance be reversed? Ben sensed that, even if they returned to America, the distance between them and their homeland would remain. Because on the *Bonaparte* they had nibbled on a morsel of freedom. If that morsel represented what they'd find in Paris, then the distance from America would seep into their blood. It would change them. They could never go back.

Baby Back stared across the water, rapt, as if he could already see the French shore. Impatience gripped him. He grasped the railing like he would strangle it. Ben knew what he was thinking.

"He'd be proud of you," Ben said. "He *is* proud of you."

"Sometimes I still see him hanging from that tree. Sometimes I dream about him and when I wake up I can smell him burning. That smell got in my nose that day and I swear to God it ain't never came out. The least I can do is to get over there and play my music and be a success. Then I'll *know* he's proud. And I ain't stopping at LeRoi Jasper's club. Hell, no." He looked at Ben. When he spoke again, it was chilly, low, explicit. "You listen to me, Ben Charles, and you listen damn good: This gig at Chez LeRoi—it's only the beginning. I'm gonna play every big spot in Paris. Every big spot in Europe. Make records. Tour the world." He was nose-to-nose with Ben now. "You think I can't? Think I won't? Watch me."

Ben had never seen him exhibit such ambition. There was something shrewd about it. Something careful and cunning and glossed with ruthlessness. Ben wondered where all this ambition left *him*.

"Let me tell you something: Anybody—and I mean *anybody*—who's in my way," Baby Back said, "had better get the fuck *out* of my way. 'Cause ain't nothing gonna stop me."

"*Comment allez-vous? . . .* How are you? *. . . Je suis de l' États-Unis . . .* I am from the United States. . . . *Quelle heure est-il? . . .* What time is it? *. . . J'ai vingt-deux ans . . .* I am twenty-two years old."

He had to distract himself, so he sequestered himself in the cabin and plunged into French. What a strange language. Adjectives followed the nouns they described instead of the other way around. You could address someone in either a formal or familiar way depending on their age or class. Every single noun was either masculine or feminine and you had to memorize which was which. But French was beautiful, too. He recalled the French guests he had served at The Pavilion, their nasal tones, the melodiousness of their speech.

"*Excusez-moi, mademoiselle. Comment arrive-je à la gare? . . .*

Excuse me, miss? How do I get to the train station? . . . *Pouvez-vous me dire combien cela coûte?* . . . Can you tell me how much this costs?"

Were colored people supposed to talk this way? In Dogwood, any colored person speaking French would be derided as some kind of strange creature. Human, surely, colored, yes, but only on the outside. Colored Dogwood wouldn't approve. Neither would the whites. An uppity French-talking nigger would qualify as an impeccable candidate for lynching. Both coloreds and whites would perceive it as trying to fly higher than you had the right to. A bird flouting the boundary of the sky in a profane attempt to reach the moon.

That's what Baby Back wanted. To crack the sky, reach the moon, then reach higher, fly farther. *How far?* The question bedeviled Ben. Baby Back's ambition bedeviled him. Not the ambition itself, but its magnitude, its greedy and still-evolving shape buttressed by his discipline, his talent, his majestic confidence. Baby Back would be a star. It wasn't in him not to be.

Ben admired him. He envied him. He feared himself unworthy, that he may not be the lover Baby Back needed. Deserved. He couldn't match the trumpeter's ambition. He wasn't confident or big and broad-shouldered. He lacked the moxie to electrify a room. He was talented, but his talent was a quiet one, an intimate gift that might make people cry (if he was lucky), but never dance.

Ben would never be a Baby Back Johnston.

Until now, he hadn't known how much he wanted to be. What would become of him when Baby Back outdistanced the moon?

The question tormented him as they lay in bed later after making love. Though early morning, outside remained the color of night. Baby Back had entertained passengers jolly, drunk, and ravenous for jazz until the wee hours, then sought Ben. He had been gentler than usual, though no less zealous, his blood still rumbling from the performing high, the audience high, from having roused the very essence of his artistry that simultaneously invigorated and exhausted him; that shot him up and burned him down.

"Why do you love me?" Ben asked. He hadn't planned to. It popped into his head and out his lips before he could think.

"Your quiet soul. Your poetry," Baby Back said. "I love how you give in to me. I love your body: It's nice and slim and smooth and pretty and muscled."

"I ain't got muscles."

"You got more than you think. You got a lot more of everything than you think."

A beautiful thing to say. And reliably true since Baby Back always told it straight. It heartened Ben. With heart came the courage to ask the un-askable.

"What *don't* you love about me?"

He had imagined an uncomfortable silence, maybe a full minute or two, while Baby Back wrangled with what to say and how to say it. But with no hesitation—not a sliver—he said, "Weakness."

Ben had asked for it; had voluntarily rambled across a floor he knew could be riddled with trapdoors. Baby Back now released a barrage.

"You already had everything: a good man who loves the hell out of you; a chance to start over in a place that wants us. And you risked it all. 'Cause you were weak. Even if that bitch had really been pregnant, you didn't have to stay. You gotta be cold—gotta be *able* to be cold—to get what you want. You can't be weak. Even asking why I love you—that's weak, Ben. Shows you ain't sure of yourself."

The barrage stung. It triggered Ben's defenses. "Then why the hell are you with me? Why the hell are you with someone so damn weak and so damn unsure of himself?"

The hesitation and uncomfortable silence that would have been appropriate earlier now settled in. Ben waited, weighed down by his own hypocrisy: He couldn't disagree with what Baby Back had said, but he hated him for saying it.

"Well?" Ben said.

"I already told you."

"Oh, because you like my poems and I got so much muscle."

"Ben. I love you. We're on our way to Paris. This is our chance to be together—"

"—in a place that wants us. I know."

Silence again. Not uncomfortable or appropriate. Just plain quiet. Ben was on the floor, knees up, his head resting against them. He wasn't sure when he'd gotten off the bed, moved away from Baby Back. He was lying next to him one minute. The next minute, he wasn't.

# 26

Baby Back and the band spent the next day performing in private lounges for the *Bonaparte*'s wealthiest passengers. A treat for the elite. Ben stayed in the cabin, practicing French. Verb conjugation. He'd mastered present tense and now toiled on past, struggling not to confuse the two. His brain, a well-guarded fortress of English, wasn't letting French in without a fight. So much to remember, so much to keep straight. He'd listened in on a few French conversations on the *Bonaparte,* trying to pick out words or strings of phrases, and had gotten horribly discouraged. For Ben, learning French was like seeing with new eyes that displayed the world in colors he wasn't used to.

Ben looked up the French word for "weakness." *La faiblesse.* The noun was feminine. The adjective form was *faible.*

"*Je suis faible:* I am weak. If I want to use the noun: *J'ai la faiblesse.* I have weakness. Or if I want to use the plural form of the noun: *J'ai des faiblesses.* I have weaknesses." He remembered he was supposed to be studying past tense. " 'I *was* weak' would be *J'etais faible.* But it ain't past. I *am* weak. The almighty Baby Back Johnston said so."

He couldn't concentrate. He left the cabin, roamed the ship, ended up on deck. He found the string quartet, now permanently banished from the dining hall by Captain Olivier, had forsaken minuets for "Dinah." The musicians smiled along with the lilting tune, backs swaying. A half-moon had plunked itself in the constellation-laden sky. The moon wasn't pretty tonight. It was gray and standoffish, half in shadow as if hiding. A shiftless, untrustworthy moon.

*La faiblesse.*

What Baby Back said hurt. The way he said it hurt worse. Like *weakness* had been squirming on his tongue, chomping at the bit for release. No hesitation. Ben detested his candor and his drilling down on the accusations with such exactitude; was insulted by the moralizing and condescending tone, as if he was lecturing some naïve child. Being told what he didn't want to hear was one thing. Being told with relish was another.

Even if it was the truth.

What was "truth" in French? *La vérité.* Baby Back could have withheld *la vérité,* but he needed to keep himself strong and Ben weak.

That wasn't true. Baby Back told the truth because he needed a lover who could support, who could withstand, the coming onslaught of his ambition. *He told the truth to put me on notice, to build me up.* And in building Ben up, the trumpeter implicitly helped *himself.*

The quartet had segued from the lilting "Dinah" to the mushy "I'm Coming, Virginia." Why were these French classical musicians infatuated with sentimental songs about Dixie?

He checked his watch. Dinnertime. He went to the dining hall. Baby Back was onstage with the band. Captain Olivier was at his table, hand drumming the tabletop, head bobbing in rhythm with the band's beat. Ben saw Clifford Treadwell waving him over.

He took a seat. "Where's Millicent?"

"Lying down, having one of her headaches." Clifford spread foie gras on a thin piece of toast and popped it in his mouth. His attention went to the stage. "How did you and Baby Back meet?"

"In childhood. We're cousins, remember?"

Clifford laughed. "*Cousins*. I adore code."

They ordered dinner. Clifford gave compressed biographies of himself and Millicent.

They came from prominent old colored families in Washington, DC, an exclusive world of Negro gentry where light-complexioned skin was akin to grace.

"Africa? Please. My family doesn't want to know the place exists. They think people *your* complexion are beneath them. They'd be appalled that you're eating with me instead of standing by with a tray."

Still a bachelor at twenty-seven, his family pressured him to marry.

"Let's just say I had gotten into some compromising situations that could have jeopardized my family's social standing. And Millicent's family's fortune had dwindled. Bad investments or bad . . . something. I don't know. The solution was obvious. She needed to shore up her family's bank accounts and I needed—"

"—a cover."

Clifford stopped in the middle of prying open a clam. "Such a tasteless way of putting it, however accurate." He smirked like a rascal. "I'm a tad darker than she is. Married five years and she's still not happy about that."

The smirk flattened. Clifford looked adrift, as if he'd woken up in some desolate place, positively stumped about how he'd gotten there. "It's tough. Living a life that's not you. You wouldn't understand. You have Baby Back."

Ben took a pass on the raw plea for empathy. "Got kids?"

"That's what this second honeymoon business is supposed to be about."

Ben lifted his champagne in a toast. "Have fun."

Clifford scowled at him, then snapped open the clam with such force, pieces of shell went flying.

They ate in silence as Baby Back and company played "I'm Just Wild About Harry." As Ben watched Clifford watching Baby Back.

Did the trumpeter find Clifford weak? Would he tell him so? Would he hesitate?

"I can help him," Clifford said, eyes feeding on the trumpeter. "I have connections in Paris. Agents, promoters, record people. You tell him I can help him."

Suspicion caught Ben's tongue. He distrusted this man. His extravagant audacity in not even attempting to conceal his attraction to Baby Back. The rudeness with which he—somewhat understandably—treated his wife. Something else, too: Ben had never met a rich, powerful colored person. He knew they existed but, till now, had never seen one up close.

"That's generous," he said, at last.

Clifford took a final sip of champagne, dabbed his mouth with his napkin. "Yes. It is."

He left. A moment later, Baby Back dove into the chair Clifford had vacated.

"Hey, good-lookin'. What did Treadwell have to say?"

Ben didn't hesitate. "Nothing. Small talk."

# 27

"Shit! I can't wait to see Chez LeRoi," Baby Back said. "Big club. Big stage. Dozens of tables. All those spiffy, high-class folks there to hear me play. God*damn!* Mr. Jasper said it was the hottest club in Paris."

"What the hell's he supposed to say? That he owns the *worst* club in Paris?"

"Why you trying to bring me down, Ben? Please don't do that."

A genial request infused with a dose of menace.

A waiter came by with Ben's bourbon—his third.

"Hey. Take it easy. OK?" Baby Back said.

"No. *You* got high. *I'm* gonna get high."

A musician gave Baby Back some reefer he'd smuggled aboard. He had indulged, but saved none for Ben.

They relaxed on a leather couch in the first-class smoking room—a room Ben had expected to be an all-male domain. But cigarette-smoking young women on one side of the large, Art Deco room counterbalanced the cigar-wielding old fogies on the other. Ben and Baby Back sat in between.

"Sorry I didn't save no reefer for you," Baby Back said. "Guess I got carried away."

His eyes were red. He smiled stupidly.

Ben downed a big slug of bourbon. It scorched his throat so bad, he thought it might leave a scar. "You gotta think about yourself, right? Gotta take care of *you*. I mean, all that ambition—it ain't gonna get you nowhere, ain't gonna make you no star, if you're busy taking care of anybody else. And wouldn't that be a damn shame?"

Ben recognized he'd poked a nerve because Baby Back went mute. The stupid smile shriveled. His reefer-red eyes minimized to the size of dots and then fastened on some vague spot in front of him as he popped his knuckles one by one.

"I take care of the people I love. You're here, ain't you? Instead of back in Harlem with that lying bitch."

"Don't you call her that again. I ain't having that."

Ben could see Baby Back was ready to shoot back, that he stifled the urge.

"Ohhhh," Baby Back said, as if suddenly enlightened. "This is about that conversation the other night. Yeah. You been acting strange ever since."

Ben knocked back more bourbon. "*Notre conversation de ce que je suis si faible.*"

"Come again?"

"That was French for *our conversation about me being so weak*. You might know that if you bothered to learn French. Don't make no sense to me how you can go live in another country and not even bother to learn the damn language. But Baby Back Johnston does whatever the fuck Baby Back Johnston wants to do!"

He had raised his glass and shouted. The young women and the old fogies looked at them. Baby Back scooted closer and took the bourbon from Ben so fast, some spilled in their laps.

"What's wrong with you?" Baby Back said, with rage, with fear, with disappointment.

The disappointment struck Ben the most. There was pleading in it, and sorrow. As if Baby Back mourned something lost.

"We'll be in Paris day after tomorrow," he said. "We're about to have the time of our lives. Don't you fuck it up. Don't you dare."

The pleading again. The menace. His face was in Ben's. Ben was scared of him. He wanted to move away. He couldn't. He was sub-servient, defenseless, *faible*. But he managed to say, "You mean you're about to have the time of *your* life, don't you?"

"No! No! This is *our* chance to be together. . . . Finish it. FIN-ISH IT!"

Everyone in the smoking room watched them. The waiter hur-ried over.

"Go away!" Baby Back yelled. When the waiter stayed put, Baby Back stomped toward him. "I said go!" The waiter took off. Baby Back pulled Ben up by the arms. "Come on."

He marched him toward the exit like a truant child. The three bourbons had started to take effect. He had drunk too much, too fast. The scar in his throat itched. They were almost to the door when Clifford Treadwell walked in.

"Strangers. Haven't seen you gentlemen in a couple of days." He scrutinized them. "You guys OK?"

"Yeah. Sure," Baby Back said. "How you doing, Clifford? Say, where's Millicent?"

Clifford laughed. "She wouldn't be caught dead in a smoking room. Too unladylike, she says. Hey, Mr. Jazz Man, I can't believe you've been so elusive. What, you don't want to meet important people who'll help your career?"

"I'm sorry? Come again?"

Clifford looked from Baby Back to the nauseous Ben. "Looks like someone neglected to tell you about a certain conversation. Allow me to fill in the blanks."

"Start explaining."

Ben sat on the bed. Baby Back stood over him, arms crossed.

"I don't trust him," Ben said.

"You don't trust him? *You don't trust him?* Hell, I don't even *like* him. But if he knows people who can make me a star, I don't give a damn."

Maybe it was the bourbon or the nausea or the raw memory of Clifford Treadwell's triumphant face in that smoking room, but the ease with which Ben spoke his next words surprised him. "I wanted to hurt you."

He kept his eyes in his lap. He didn't have to look at Baby Back to know the rage, fear, and disappointment of earlier now siphoned down to simply rage.

Baby Back grabbed up his trumpet case, so fast it seemed to fly into his hands. He was almost out the door, but he came back, knelt down, got nose-to-nose and eye-to-eye with Ben.

"Don't you ever, and I mean *ever,* do nothing like this to me again."

# 28

<u>Sand</u>

By Benjamin Marcus Charles

Shatter the hourglass.
The sand tumbles out,
The grains minute, sharp-edged,
As many-pointed as a snowflake.

What now?

Sweep up the sand?
Try, but some will remain,
Elusive and uncatchable.
Glue the shards of glass,
But they will cut you.

Fairy tales lie:
Magic words cannot undo destruction.
Regret is no elixir.

Because the truth,
That two-faced witch,

Enlightens and provokes,
Incites even as she purports to
    civilize.
Fall under the wrong spell
And invite catastrophe.

What now?

War comes as naturally as the seasons
    now,
It rides the air, deftly, like an
    infection.
It permeates.
Reason stumbles.
Pleading fails.
Prayers rise, then fall, then evaporate
    like dew.

What is left?
The remnants of love in a field of
    broken glass,
A heap of parched sand,
The scraps of a dream.

# 29

"Millicent. Hello. May I join you?"

Her lips twitched in and out of a nervous smile. "My husband isn't here. He'll be arriving shortly."

"Well, is it all right if I join you?" Ben asked.

Her attitude was a definitive *no,* but she said, "Why, certainly."

He asked if she was enjoying the voyage; which ship's activities she had participated in; if she and Clifford had friends in Paris and would they be visiting them; living in Washington, DC, must be really nice, right? She shunned his small talk by snapping short answers and not once lifting her nose from her dinner menu. Millicent made clear that first night at Captain Olivier's table that she was complexion-conscious. *She don't want nothin' to do with us dark-skinned niggers,* Ben recalled one of the musicians saying. He lamented that her husband didn't share that view.

A waiter appeared. Millicent shooed him away, avowing that she would not order until Clifford arrived.

Ben detested the Treadwells. Their snobbery, their machinations. Their presumption of entitlement based solely on their wealth and their "superior" skin color. How were they any different from whites? He wanted to excuse himself, go back to the cabin to practice his

French, but extending friendship to the Treadwells could be his bridge back to Baby Back.

Since Millicent refused to be engaged, Ben concentrated on the band. Something was amiss. The music meandered without a coherent through line. It sat weighted on the air. Ben scanned the stage. Baby Back wasn't there, and without his beacon of a horn to guide them, the musicians drifted lost.

Ben tried again with Millicent. "Clifford made Baby Back a very generous offer. Both of us appreciate what he's gonna do for him."

She lowered her menu. A ripple of nastiness wrinkled across her face. She looked him flat in the eye. "Of course you do. Naturally. Although I doubt there's anything *natural* about this."

Ben was so relieved he almost laughed in her face. He no longer had to feel guilty for hating the Treadwells. Millicent had just proven his hatred justified. She had lowered her menu and also her mask, exposing the private Millicent, the *real* Millicent, who normally stayed hidden and discreet but had flared up unexpectedly. She was ominous and unsightly. He couldn't look at her.

He shifted his attention back to the stage. Baby Back was still absent, the band all but useless without him.

Clifford arrived. Millicent recomposed herself into the meek guise of her public self. "I can only imagine what kept you, dear," she said. She smiled. Affection toppled off of her bride-sweet mouth. It was clear then: She loved Clifford. It was the one sincere thing in her. The travesty of it caused Ben to detest her slightly less.

"Thanks for keeping Millicent company," Clifford said. "She's been positively starved for good conversation this whole trip. I'm sure you filled that void."

"I'm sure I tried."

And then he saw it: the purplish bruise at Clifford's neckline, peeking out just above the collar of his starched, white shirt. A love bite. Recently administered. It scorched his light skin. Ben studied his menu but his eyes kept shuffling back to Clifford's neck and Millicent's now-public face. Both alarmed him. He focused on the band for distraction and finally heard cohesion because Baby Back had taken to the stage. He was in performance mode—eyes shut, knees bent—as passengers clapped and snapped.

Ben regarded the Treadwells again. His eyes alighted on Clifford's neck once more as Baby Back purred on his horn and the *Bonaparte* sailed toward Paris through the jazz-slicked night.

# distance & color
## ═1926═

# 30

The open-air taxi curled through the narrow, hilly streets of the Montmartre section of Paris, weaving around unexpected corners and through alleyways, as if maneuvering the corridors of a labyrinth. The brick streets made the ride bumpy. The place seemed deserted. A sleepy village. Only a few people out and about. A mother with two children in tow, a large basket hanging from her arm. A young man carrying a long loaf of bread that rested against his shoulder like a fishing pole. He whistled as he jaunted along.

They drove on. The sights of Montmartre blurred by. Houses with paint flaking off soiled stone walls. Front stoops strewn with liquor bottles and drunk, sprawled-out figures. A young woman with plump breasts and plumper hips on the stoop of one house, hair loose and falling about her, legs spread farther apart than a young lady's ought to be. The buxom woman took long drags off a cigarette. As the taxi neared her, she spread her legs wider, then blew a long seam of smoke at them as they passed her.

They told the driver they needed inexpensive accommodations and he dropped them at a three-story boardinghouse in rue Constance run by a woman somewhere between middle and old age. Madame Gautier wore painted-on eyebrows and too much rouge, her dark hair constrained into a tight, unyielding bun. She escorted them to a small room on the second floor. A washstand, wardrobe, bureau, a deep window seat. One double bed.

"We'll take it," Baby Back said.

Madame Gautier raised one painted-on eyebrow. "Are *messieurs* sure they would not prefer *two* rooms?"

Ben noted the heavy French accent, the way the "r" rasped in the back of her throat.

"*Merci, madame,*" Ben said. "but we can only afford one. We'll manage fine here."

The other eyebrow arched as she inspected them. "*Oui,* I am sure you will."

Wordlessly they unpacked. Wordlessly they crisscrossed the little room, delivering items from their trunks to the wardrobe and bureau, ambling out of each other's way to avoid collision, to stave off contact. Ben retrieved the grandma quilt and tucked it onto the bed. He had thought The Oasis would receive a seamless transplant to Paris but, more and more, it seemed to have been tossed overboard during the passage to France.

*Did you fuck Clifford Treadwell?*

The need to know brutalized him. He closed his eyes and gripped the bed to steady himself. But behind his closed eyes, he conjured the sick image of Baby Back and Clifford carousing with each other. "No," he whispered, clasping the headboard as he wrestled suspicions built on evidence that was circumstantial at best: two men's brief absence, a directionless band, a love bite. "No," he said again with a finality designed to will the suspicions away.

"You say something?" Baby Back asked.

Ben regrouped, walked over to his lover, opened his arms, and waited.

"Yes?" Baby Back said, terse and irritated.

Ben had wanted a hug, a kiss, sex. Anything. Something. But now he dropped his arms as Baby Back glowered at him.

"We're here," Ben said. "This is our chance to be together. . . ."

He wanted him to finish it, but Baby Back gave him a soulless smile and walked back to the trunks. He lifted out the three framed photographs of Uncle Roland, balancing them like fragile porcelain figures, and placed them on top of the bureau. He preened them into the exact formation they had occupied in his Harlem room, then stepped back and acknowledged them as if paying homage to a saint.

"I'm here, Uncle Roland. I made it."

Roland's phantom crowded out of the picture frames and into the room, squeezing Ben out.

"This is it? No way this is it."

Baby Back paced the room, hurling disgusted looks everywhere. "There must be some mistake. This *can't* be the club."

LeRoi Jasper tapped his walking stick on the parquet floor as Baby Back scowled around the room. "Mr. Johnston, there is no mistake. This *is* Chez LeRoi."

In his velvet hat and flashy double-breasted suit with broad lapels, Mr. Jasper was as dapper now as the night they met him in Harlem, but his elegance hardly prevented Baby Back from whirling on him.

"There's only twelve tables in the whole damn club! This place would fit in my room back in Harlem."

Ben looked around. The place *was* small. Bar on the right, kitchen on the left, and a cramped space with twelve tables in between. At the rear, a spiral staircase cascaded straight to the floor of a tiny stage.

"There's no shortage of musicians in Paris," LeRoi Jasper said, "so if the size of this club is a problem for you, you are more than welcome to go back to the States."

"The size of the club *is* a problem for me, so maybe I will board the next ship back."

"Mr. Jasper, excuse us a minute," Ben interjected. He gripped Baby Back's arm and pulled him aside bodily. "Calm down. This place may be small, but it's nice. Hell, it's *real* nice."

He didn't lie. The bar was mahogany. White linen dressed each table. Crystal and shining china topped them off. Every now and then two colored kitchen helpers appeared, performing odd jobs beneath chandeliers made of prismatic sparks of glass.

But the gorgeousness of the little club didn't move Baby Back. He kept on scowling like a sulky child offended at not receiving the exact gift he wanted.

LeRoi Jasper tapped his walking stick as Ben and Baby Back conferred.

"You want to blow this?" Ben said. "Your big chance?"

"Real big. Twelve tables."

"Stop it! Stop being stupid. Giving up this gig would be the worst mistake of your fucking life."

His forcefulness caught Baby Back's attention. He seemed flummoxed that his normally subservient lover had confronted him. He didn't say a word. Ben used his speechlessness as an opening to press him.

"You been driving me crazy talking about Paris ever since the night we first met. And now that you're here, you're gonna throw it all away? After all the hard work. Everything you've been through. Come on, Baby. Remember what you said on the ship: Chez LeRoi is just the beginning; ain't nothing gonna stop you. And now you're gonna stop *yourself?*"

Baby Back slumped, fidgeted with his cuffs.

Ben took a risk, dove in for the kill. "What would your uncle say if you gave up?"

It worked.

Baby Back's chest lifted. He reappraised Chez LeRoi, and then, as if it was his own idea, said, "You know what? I'd be crazy to pass up this chance. This place will do. For now."

Triumph. Ben still had clout. Relief flew him upward on new wings. Until Baby Back said, "Clifford's connections will get me into bigger clubs," and clipped his wings midflight.

"All right, Mr. Jasper," Baby Back said. "You got yourself a trumpet player." He strolled the club once more, this time like he owned it. "Guess there's worse things I could do than headline my own club show in Paris. I'd like to see the marquee: My name's on it, right?"

LeRoi Jasper's mouth opened, then shut, then opened again and hung there. "Mr. Johnston, I believe there's been yet another misunderstanding. You're *not* headlining. I never ever said a thing about you headlining. However, you *will* be leading the house band."

Ben put a hand out to restrain him, but Baby Back slapped it away.

"You're telling me I came all the way here just to be a member of a band?"

"I hired you—*brought you here*—to be part of—*to lead*—the band backing my star attraction."

"And who the hell is your star attraction? Who was I *brought here* to back up?"

Before Jasper could answer, a voice chimed out from above them.

"*Me*. You was brought here to back *me* up, sugar."

All eyes catapulted to the top of the spiral staircase. A pair of pink high heels containing two brown feet materialized on the top step. Someone began a slow descent, clicking down the steps, regal-like. *Click. Click. Click.* A full-figured colored woman rounded the curves of the staircase and swerved into view wearing a sleeveless pink dress and pink cloche hat pulled down to her eyebrows. *Click. Click. Click.* She reached the stage and took in the three men with a colossal smile.

"Which one of you fools thought you was headlining?" She looked first at Baby Back, then Ben.

Neither answered.

"Has colored people back home gone deaf and dumb? Or is y'all just tired from the trip? You fools just got off the boat, I can see that."

Her Southern, down-home accent evoked cotton fields and sugar cane and collard greens; banjos and spirituals and stifling nights on the front porch praying for a hint of breeze.

She laughed. "Y'all still ain't answered me. Which one of y'all thought you was headlining? Mr. Jasper, can *you* answer since these fools done got laryngitis?"

"I don't appreciate being called no fool," Baby Back said. " 'Specially by someone ain't even introduced herself yet."

"Gloria Ida-Mae Eloise Henrietta Littleton Fairchild. Call me

Glo. I sing. Now, *fool,* is you the one thought you was headlining? If so, you was sadly mistaken. Chez LeRoi's *my* place." LeRoi Jasper cleared his throat. "Well," Glo said, "it's Mr. Jasper's, but I'm the star of this show." She stepped off the stage, advanced on Baby Back, got within a foot of him. "Hope you ain't got a problem with that."

Baby Back advanced, closing the gap to six inches. "Actually, I got a big problem with that. See, I didn't cross a damn ocean to play backup."

Glo narrowed the gap to three inches. Her colossal smile glittered. "Then take your nappy ass back across the damn ocean."

"Take yours. Or is it too wide to fit on the damn ocean liner?"

"Son of a bitch! I'ma beat you to within a inch of your sorry-ass life!"

She meant it. She scratched and swiped and clawed at Baby Back, who scratched and swiped and clawed right back, with Ben trying to drag him away and LeRoi Jasper planting himself in the middle of the fray.

"Stop it! Right now or I'll fire you both," he said. "Glo, I'll get that redheaded woman from the Grand Duc club in here to replace you in a heartbeat."

Her fist stopped mid-swipe. Ben swiveled Baby Back into a chair while the kitchen helpers poked their heads out from the kitchen and giggled.

"That's better," Jasper said. "There's no need to be uncivilized. This isn't some juke joint. Mr. Johnston, you go on tonight. The rest of the band will be here shortly for rehearsal. Gentlemen. Glo."

He swept out of the club. Through the big front window, Ben saw him climb into a glossy-black two-seat convertible roadster with white-rimmed tires and gold spokes radiating out from the hubcaps. A woman sat in the passenger seat. A woman impeccably dressed, beautiful, and white. Ben froze. LeRoi Jasper kissed her full on the mouth, then he gunned the engine and careened down the street.

Ben remained at the window, paralyzed and gawking.

"All right, Peeping Tom," Glo said. "You gonna get struck blind, you keep eyeballing them like that. I didn't catch your name, sugar."

"Ben. Nice to meet you, ma'am."

"*Ma'am?* Child, you better call me Glo or we gonna be fighting. I'm already fighting with that one." She tossed her head at Baby Back, now inspecting the stage.

"Sure don't want that," Ben said. "Good to know you, Glo."

She stepped back, sized him up. One eyebrow soared, just like Madame Gautier's. "So. What *is* y'all? Friends? Roommates?"

Ben swallowed. "Cousins."

"Mmm-hmm. Must be *kissing* cousins."

# 31

*I'm a long way from Dogwood.*

With Baby Back working, Ben was on his own. He left Chez LeRoi, spied a street sign that said RUE FONTAINE. *Rue. That means street. Remember that.* He started north. Nervous. Scared. Head bowed a little. He wished he and Baby Back could explore their new world together. *New world. New home. I live in Paris. In a section called Montmartre. Montmartre is on the right bank of Paris. La rive droit means right bank. And rue means street.*

Eleven a.m. and the sleepy village was waking up. No hordes scampering about like in Harlem at this time of day. But a housewife talked quietly with a man in a white apron in the doorway of a shop. The sign said POISSONERIE and the odor of fish frothed out from inside. *Poissonerie. Fish store? Yes. Poissonerie means fish store.* A bicyclist whooshed by. *Bicycle. La bicyclette.* A basket filled with those long loaves of French bread hung on the bike's handlebars. *Baguettes. We had them on the ship.* A man set up tables and chairs outside a café, each table adorned with a small vase containing a single flower. *Flower. La fleur?* He took his French-English dictionary from his pocket to confirm. *Oui. La fleur.*

He kept north and landed on the Place Pigalle, a public square couched at the foot of a big hill. Street vendors hawked their wares.

At outdoor cafés patrons sat in chairs that faced straight out toward the street rather than each other. Busy shopkeepers darted in and out of their stores as they set up their displays. An idle shopkeeper lazed outside a door with a sign that said TABAC, smoking a cigar while automobiles rattled by and buses rattled by and trucks with lumber rattled by and bicycle carts filled with flowers or food rattled by and people rattled by clothed in drab garments. Most buildings were rundown with crumbling pillars and plaster shedding off their exteriors. Above, women hung laundry on balcony railings or on lines strung from one balcony to the one across the way. The windows of many buildings were clotted with grime as thick as dough. Ben passed one window where it was so thick, someone had sketched a naughty picture of a nude woman with mammoth breasts and mischief in her dusty eyes. In the distance, smoke from factories blemished the sky with veils of soot. And the cars and the buses belched smoke from their tailpipes and the people walking up and down the brick streets smoked cigarettes and the kitchens of the cafés spouted out smoke and the bicycles whizzing by churned up dust and Ben wondered, *This is Paris? This rundown, ramshackle, grimy place?* Where was the glamorous, romantic city he'd read about? The Paris of the Uncle Roland fantasies and Baby Back's assurances?

*Will we—will I—be happy here?*

He was hungry, but nervous about entering a café. He'd been treated with supreme courtesy aboard the *Bonaparte,* but what if that had been a floating fantasy different from the reality on land? He walked into a café that faced the Place Pigalle. It was empty except for two old ladies sipping coffee inside and a trio of men at a table outside. A waiter in a white shirt, black pants, and black bowtie approached him.

"*Bonjour, monsieur,*" the waiter said. He was young. A smile chirped on his face.

"*Bonjour,*" Ben said. "*Je voudrais* . . . eat . . . um . . . *si'l vous plaît* . . . *dejeuner* . . . please?" His tongue trampled all over itself, producing gibberish.

The waiter's chirping smile opened out into a laugh as he took

Ben by the arm and led him to a table outdoors. "Welcome to Paris. This is your first time in France, I see."

English. A relief.

A menu appeared followed by a glass of champagne that he hadn't even requested.

So. This was a Paris café. A *real* one. In the midst of dust and traffic and street noise, unlike the apparently idealized version on the *Bonaparte*. Ben worried that other aspects of Legendary Paris may also be idealized, romanticized, untrue. He sipped champagne, scanned the Place Pigalle. His eyes fell on the building with the red windmill on its roof. He'd seen it earlier. It was called Moulin Rouge. A theater or nightclub of some kind. Placards out front advertised risqué extravaganzas featuring a superabundance of sparsely clad women. Ben fantasized that Moulin Rouge produced similar fare with sparsely clad *men*.

"*Monsieur,*" the waiter said. "Those gentlemen ask that you join them." He pointed to the trio of men. They were smiling and waving him over. The waiter transferred Ben's champagne to the trio's table before he could protest.

"*Bonjour,*" he said as he joined them. "*Moi, c'est* Ben."

They besieged him with French, unaware at first that he spoke none. He couldn't keep up. It was as if his hours of practice, the interminable lists of vocabulary words, his drilling of verb tenses, meant nothing. But, as the men spoke, tiny epiphanies glinted as Ben recognized a word here, caught a phrase there.

"*Êtes-vous un Américain ou un Africain?*" they said, then repeated it five times and slowed it down considerably before he understood.

"The United States," he said. "*Je suis de l'États-Unis.*"

"*Ah! Un Américain!*"

He had made himself understood. A small, priceless victory.

The next hour was spent with the trio feeding Ben fragments of French and all four smoking cigarettes and laughing and guzzling tankards of beer. They were manual laborers as evidenced by the ruddy sunburn overlaying their tawny skins, their giant hands with lines on the palms etched as deeply as trails. Their rolled-up shirtsleeves revealed muscular forearms. The hair there grew dense and thick.

"Ben, *êtes-vous marié?*"

Ben looked it up in his dictionary. *Are you married?*

The most stolidly built of the trio had asked. The top buttons of his shirt were undone, spears of hair piercing out. His mustache was a line of fur spanning his upper lip and then snaking slightly down either side of his mouth.

"*Oui,*" Ben said. "*Non. Oui.* Well . . ."

Ben had never kissed a man with a mustache. Just for fun, he mused how the fur would feel as it scraped his lips and tongue.

Montmartre north of the Place Pigalle was hilly. The streets inclined and declined so steeply, that when Ben reached the top of a hill and looked down, he thought he'd get vertigo. Shabby homes, storefronts, boardinghouses, and cheap hotels nuzzled close together along the narrow streets. People went about their day, toting groceries, pushing wheelbarrows, sweeping the sidewalks in front of homes. Many smiled and said *bonjour* as Ben passed. Twice he saw Negro men, at a distance. Each time, the men waved and Ben waved back and it seemed the men might approach. But Ben would bow his head and swing onto another street. Most of the Negroes in Paris were musicians. He was embarrassed to admit he was merely the "cousin" of one.

He climbed a hill, turned onto rue Constance, and returned to the boardinghouse. He found Baby Back in bed. Nude, on his back, one arm behind his head. A sheet covered him from the waist down, a half-inch patch of pubic hair just visible, his dark skin in luminous opposition to the dove-white sheets. His eyes were closed, but Ben didn't know if he slept. He removed his shoes quietly, then his jacket and tie, and prepared to glide into the bed.

"Undress before you get in," Baby Back said without opening his eyes.

Ben obeyed and then fastened himself to him.

"Well," Baby Back said.

"Well."

"Paris."

"Paris."

At only four words and six syllables, it was among their few conversations in days. Ben now moved to parlay those syllables into a lessening of the distance between them. A distance that sometimes flooded them all at once, other times trickled in like an insidious leak until they found themselves floundering in a foot of standing water.

"We've been mean to each other, Baby Back."

"I know."

The water receded a little. Ben pressed on.

"I ain't asking you for no apology. But I've given you mine. Over and over. I can keep saying I'm sorry, and I can keep meaning it, but if you ain't gonna forgive me . . ."

Baby Back rolled on top of him, smoothly, as if executing a willowy dance move. His dick unfurled against him. A dollop of moisture splashed onto Ben's stomach before bleeding down his side.

"Mr. Poet, you've fucked up a lot. But I really love you and I do forgive you."

Now Ben really resented this thing called *distance*. Because closing it required giving in, conceding to the arrogance of the stronger lover. The stronger lover never conceded. That was the obligation of the weaker, the one desperate and scrambling like a goose to rebuild the ravaged nest.

Baby Back began grinding on him. A slow friction. "We're in Paris. This is our chance to be together. . . ."

"In a place that wants us."

Baby Back's mouth found Ben's neck, first teasing it with his tongue, then taking a fold of skin in his teeth and discharging a sustained bite. A delicious pain, but it made Ben think of Clifford Treadwell.

# 32

He took extra time to dress, imitating Baby Back's self-indulgent routine. Suave styling of the hat. Buffing the cuff links. Fastidious knotting of the tie. He felt entitled to a little self-indulgence.

He stepped out of the boardinghouse, took in the night, the three-quarter moon trifling above, and headed to Chez LeRoi. Eleven p.m. Montmartre was awake. The streets and cafés and storefronts were beset with people. Rowdy shouts and laughter raged out of a brasserie where men downed tankards of ale. Someone somewhere played a record of a woman wailing in nasally French as a jazz orchestra backed her.

Ben walked down rue Constance where street vendors straddled the curb, haggling to sell their cheap trinkets, then descended into the madness that was the Place Pigalle. He joined the masses of people swarming the square. The madness engulfed him. Slovenly prostitutes locked illicit eyes with any man or woman who looked in their vicinity. One eyed Ben and scratched her privates. He giggled to himself and kept going and nearly ran into an elderly accordion player hobbling about, seeking tips. Ben dropped one centime in his tin cup.

Over here an artist exhibiting work, some of his canvasses on easels, some on the ground propped upright by bricks. And over there another, striding the square, carrying a canvas in paint-smeared hands as he leapt in front of potential buyers to display his masterpiece.

To Ben's right, a group of flappers—young girls brandishing bare arms and bare curvy legs and hoards of fringe lopping off their scant dresses. To his left, a mime with a face painted chalk-white and stained with black teardrops. He performed a skit—something tragic that ended with the poor soul prostrate on the dusty ground. People clapped and the mime sprung up from his deathbed and stepped daintily among the crowd with a black bowler hat, begging for coins. Ben drew another centime from his pocket and threw it in the hat.

On the west end, expensive goods and drugs were peddled out in the open by slick men in slick suits, a moody aura of danger ghosting them like a dark halo. On the east end, young men slouched against streetlamps, cigarettes hanging limply from their slack mouths, hands fingering their sloping hips as middle-aged and old men in-spected them. Rich slummers and tourists—out of place in their top hats and tails—pointed and gaped, wide-eyed and happily scandal-ized.

Ben looked in the doorways of some of the shoddy bars lining the Place Pigalle. Seamy places clogged with workmen, sleeves hiked up, shirtfronts open, their sweaty odors steaming out into the square.

So much here, such an over-exorbitance of color and sound and smell, that the brain had to parse everything into component parts and then reconstitute them into some kind of seeable whole. Ben's attention was pulled and jerked and pushed and contorted in mul-tiple directions all at once by this circus of sensations. He was afraid to look at any one thing too long for fear he'd miss out on something else.

Chez LeRoi was packed. Twelve tables, five times the people. They laughed and bragged and sucked down oysters and cham-pagne while waiters paraded from the bar to the tables with bottle after bottle after bottle of it. And the people kept coming. Limou-sines deposited patrons dressed in tuxes and satins and diamonds.

They crammed in where they could: at the bar, in corners, or on other people's laps.

LeRoi Jasper cruised through the club, chitting and chatting with patrons, feeling up women, and directing waiters. Otherwise, he spent time at his own private table with a slim white woman—different from the one earlier—with dark hair styled in a sleek bob cut. Jasper nosed in close. They kissed with the sweet restraint of people who know that discipline exerted now will earn them a more ravenous night later.

The band cranked. Baby Back went at his trumpet, leading the band like it was the *last* jam session. A woman in flapper regalia hauled herself onto a table, threw back a glass of champagne in almost one gulp, then let fly a spirited Charleston. Finished and sweating, she imperiously held out her glass to a passing waiter to be refilled.

Ben had arrived late. There was no place to sit and he chastised himself for his tardiness. He found a foot of unoccupied space near the bar and just stood in it until LeRoi Jasper bumped into him.

"Don't look so serious," Jasper said. "You're in the hottest club in Paris. Come over here. I'll introduce you to some people. They'll love you." He lowered his voice, accomplice-like. "You know the French adore us coloreds, right?"

He escorted Ben to a group headed by the tabletop Charleston woman.

"LeRoi, come here," she said and kissed him on one cheek and then the other in quick succession. As earlier, Ben gaped at them, certain he'd never adjust to seeing such intimacy between a colored man and a white woman.

"Ah, Baroness Deneuve," Jasper said. "Lovely to see you. Although I'm quite upset with you. You have not been here in some weeks and I suspect you've been patronizing Chez Florence instead. I feel positively neglected."

"*Mon cher,* you know I always find my way back." She batted green eyes fringed with a quantity of eyelashes. She looked forty.

Jasper laughed. "*Je vous présente* Ben Charles, the new bandleader's cousin. They arrived from the States this morning."

Baroness Deneuve's group cried, "*Bienvenu!*" as she guided Ben into a chair.

"This morning? You must be exhausted. You *must* have some champagne." She seized a glass from the tray of a passing waiter and shoved it into his hands.

"*Merci, mademoiselle,*" he said.

"*Mademoiselle?*" A seizure of laughter. Her entourage followed suit. "*Mon cher,* I am *la Baronesse Juliette Deneuve.*" She tapped Ben's chin with her finger. "But you had better call me Denny." She retrieved her own champagne and toasted. "To Ben and *le jazz-hot.*"

Her friends raised their glasses and cheered as if Ben was a soldier returning from the front.

"Are you from Harlem?" someone asked.

"Yes."

Curiosity sizzled as chairs scooted closer and cigarettes were removed from mouths mid-puff.

"Josephine Baker is from Harlem. Do you know her?"

"Afraid not," Ben said.

"I hear there are parties in Harlem every night."

"And waiters who dance the Charleston as they bring the food."

"And everyone sings the blues."

Ben laughed. "Well, that last one might be true."

Denny sat with legs crossed, one arm on the back of her chair. A lovely man was next to her. He looked twenty. When Denny placed a cigarette between her lips, he lit it automatically, as if by reflex.

"As you all know," Denny said, "I've been to Harlem. I went to a divine spot called the Cotton Club. All of the entertainers are Negroes and they are *wild*. The music is jungle-like. Authentically African. The sets have a jungle motif and the chorus girls are dressed like natives. I think LeRoi should do something like that here. What do you think, Ben?"

"Can't say. Ain't never been to the Cotton Club. They don't allow Negroes."

"*C'est ridicule.* All of the musicians and dancers were Negroes."

"They're allowed on the stage, but not in the audience. They don't let Negroes in."

His revelation sobered the tipsy group. At first dumb with disbelief, the people offered Ben their pity, their outrage, which made him feel ecstatic but guilty, too, for ruining the party.

Denny perked up. "Do not worry about it, *mon cher*. You are in Paris now! *Garçon! Encore du champagne!*"

He had started his fourth glass when the lights dimmed and LeRoi Jasper took to the stage.

"*Messieurs dames, bienvenus à Chez LeRoi!* Thank you so much for coming to the hottest club in Paris. We have the best of everything. The best champagne, the best food, and—needless to say— the best-dressed, best-looking people! *C'est vrai,* this crowd tonight may be the most beautiful Chez LeRoi has seen in recent memory. But with beauty comes danger. You stunningly lovely ladies had better beware because I see a number of wolfishly handsome gentlemen whom I suspect are on the prowl! It's never a good night to go home alone, is it, *mes beaux messieurs?* Forgive my irreverence, *s'il vous plaît.* I am only trying to loosen you up—as if drinking up every last drop of my champagne isn't accomplishing that already! I swear, *mes amis,* I stock and restock enough of the stuff each week to intoxicate a small country. Well, just as important as having beautiful people and an ocean of champagne is providing the finest jazz in Paris—which we do each and every night. *Alors,* with that in mind, Chez LeRoi presents to you *l'oiseau chanteur de Paris*—the songbird of Paris—Mademoiselle Gloria Fairchild!!"

The crowd thundered. The lights darkened. The band swelled to a frantic tempo. Glo shimmied down the spiral staircase to the stage. What a sight in her sleeveless gown of golden, flashing, clinging material. The low-cut bodice hugged her breasts. Her snug skirt amplified the slope of her round hips as it draped to the ground. A short train trailed in back. Her hair was fashioned into a simple, graceful bun.

Glo *glowed*.

She and the band discharged a snappy number:

> "*Nights are for lovin', so be sure to treat me right,*
> *Touch me sweet and tender and I won't put up no fight,*
> *Come on, baby, squeeze me till the early morning light,*
> *Papa, if you're satisfied, come back tomorrow night!*"

Glo's voice was robust, with low and middle notes that bellowed or growled and high notes that rang. The big smile on her face opened up her voice, added some light. And she enchanted the audience by singing to specific people in the crowd and winking or flirting.

> *"They say rainbows come from heaven,*
> *But I don't believe that's true,*
> *I believe that rainbows happen*
> *When I think of lovely you.*
>
> *My misty heart beats like a drum,*
> *My blood warms up like fire,*
> *Papa, come on, love me quick,*
> *And quench my soul's desire."*

Then the band took over, igniting a wildfire. From the pounding of the piano keys to the bludgeoning of the drums to the thundering brass to the thrumming banjo. The heart of the wildfire: Baby Back. He was the match that lit the flame, the gasoline that maddened it, the wind that fanned it. His trumpet stormed above the band, cutting a musical path right through Chez LeRoi. It was his big night and he worked it: eyes closed, knees caving to the floor because he couldn't control the music roaring through him.

That first number put the crowd on its feet. They just about mobbed the stage after the second. But the third blasted Chez LeRoi off the map. It opened like a dirge. A low-down, slowed-down blues.

> *"My man treats me evil, I won't even tell you no lie,*
> *My man treats me evil, I won't even tell you no lie,*
> *But if he ever leaves me, I'll lay my body down and die."*

Glo sang like she was already dead inside. Her plaintive tone made you want to belt the guy who broke her heart.

*"Steals all my money, gambles every dime away,*
*Steals all my money, gambles every dime away,*
*But when he comes home broke, I give him more anyway."*

Glo's vocal was the main attraction, the band a partner that affirmed her lament. But out of that affirmation, Baby Back's trumpet dawned. She would feed him a phrase and he would take it, embellish it, feed it back. If Glo contributed the main theme in this blues concerto, then Baby Back applied the variation as they, phrase by phrase, seduced the audience down the primrose path to the blues. The song was part gritty gospel-shout from the back alley bars of New Orleans, part sophisticated ballad from the chi-chi nightspots of Manhattan. Part earth, part air. All blues.

*"Goes out with other women, leaves me by myself alone,*
*Goes out with other women, leaves me by myself alone,*
*I just pray when morning comes, he'll bring his loving*
   *self back home.*

*"My friends tell me 'leave him,' 'cause he only makes me*
   *blue,*
*My friends tell me 'leave him,' 'cause he only makes me*
   *blue,*
*They don't understand it—that man's the best that I*
   *can do."*

When it ended, the audience brawled into cheers. Glo and Baby Back descended from the stage and into a lovefest. They greeted the crowd—separately—shaking hands, giving and receiving kisses.

Denny took to the tabletop again while her entourage gushed.

*"C'est fantastique!"*

*"Mon dieu.* You can tell they are from Harlem, *n'est pas?"*

*"C'est vrai.* I am so glad they have come to Paris!"

Baby Back's Paris debut. A smash. Ben cheered and whistled and screamed and stomped and clapped along with everyone else. He couldn't stop. Nobody could. He was fat with pride, lost in it.

He wanted to never find his way out. Wanted to remain in these woods, directionless. North, south, east, and west useless. He didn't need the North Star. Incandescent Baby Back was his North Star.

More champagne. More inquiries about Harlem. More French words to store away. More food and laughter and cigarettes and celebration and crazy Denny clowning up the Charleston on the tabletop as Ben downed the last drop from his umpteenth glass of champagne, raised his hand to signal a waiter for more, and saw him: Clifford Treadwell. Near the entrance. He spotted Ben, nodded aloofly, and kept looking around until Baby Back marched up to him, hugged him like a buddy, and shepherded him over to LeRoi Jasper.

Ben had already drunk a bucket of champagne, but now he needed a real drink, not this fizzy stuff. He excused himself and went to the bar. He downed bourbon while watching the three confer like confidantes. They formed a triangle: Mr. Jasper at the apex, Baby Back and Clifford side by side, shoulders almost-touching, Clifford's eyes lodged on Ben's lover.

He knocked back a second bourbon. It slow-burned down his throat. He waited for Baby Back to wave him over and recruit him into the business being conducted. Clifford's shoulder still almost-touched Baby Back's. His eyes seemed addicted to him.

*Did you fuck Clifford Treadwell?*

He was about to crash their triangle when someone next to him said, "Shit. You must really hate one them guys, sugar."

Glo.

"Let me see if I can guess which one. Hmm. Can't be Mr. Jasper—you ain't known him long enough to hate him. Obviously ain't that fool Baby Back. And I don't care if he *did* bring this house down in that first set. He still a fool. And on top of that, he big-headed, arrogant, and too damn big for his britches. But where was I? Oh, yeah. That leaves that high-yellow gent standing next to him. Now, Benjy, tell Glo why you hate that poor little high-yellow man so much that you're throwing back straight bourbon like it's water even though I know you already been drinking champagne all night."

He didn't know which was more shocking: that she was all up in his business after knowing him a day, or that she had called him *Benjy*. He stared at her, inarticulate, as she grinned that giant smile of hers. Close up, she was a little blinding in her gold getup.

"Never mind," she said. "I *know* why you hate him. Mmm-hmm. See how he standing right next to Baby Back? Shoulder right up on him? Can't take his eyes off him? That's why you hate him. You think he after your man."

She seemed content with her assessment, but Ben heard alarms go off.

"No, you got it all wrong, Glo. The high-yellow...uh...Clifford, that's our friend. We met him on the ship on the way over. Me and my cousin did, that is."

"Lord have mercy. Benjy, if you and me gonna be friends, you gotta stop with this *cousin* shit."

"We're gonna be friends?"

"We sure is. Starting tomorrow when you come to my house for coffee and tell Glo *all* about this high-yellow Clifford who you think wants to steal your boyfriend."

# 33

The pastry was of deep-fried dough and jammed with a fruit filling. A "beignet," the waiter had called it. *Another word to remember. Beignet.* It was probably delicious, but Ben couldn't be certain. Alcohol had soaked the taste out of his taste buds. Odors fumed from his mouth, a grotesque mix of champagne and bourbon.

"How's the head?" Baby Back asked, sipping coffee as they lounged at an outdoor café on the Place Pigalle. He sat back with his legs crossed at the ankles, grinning big as a floodlight, eyes sweeping from one end of the square to the other as if he had conquered Paris and now surveyed his new kingdom.

"*My* head just hurts," Ben said. "Yours looks a little oversized."

"Damn right. I tore up that club last night. Tore it *up!*"

"You and Glo."

Baby Back groaned. "She did all right. For a girl singer."

Ben bit into his beignet. Fruit filling oozed out. Baby Back, without so much as tilting his head away from the square, and with the floodlight still shining, said, "Saw you talking to her. Careful. Might not be a good idea. You know, consorting with the enemy."

Ben returned fire. "I was surprised to see Clifford last night. Guess you two got pretty close on that ship. Ain't right, leaving me out when you was talking to him and Mr. Jasper."

Baby Back's floodlight diminished like a scene from a movie: It faded rapidly, smoothly, to black. "I didn't want no mess. I may have fucked you yesterday, Mr. Poet, but that don't mean I trust you again."

He had fired back with the cutthroat precision of a marksman. Ben took another bite of the beignet. The attack had jarred the sensation of taste back into his tongue and he discovered the filling was way too sweet. He sipped his coffee, cold now, through trembling lips.

A monumental building hunkered on the crest of a hill immediately north of the Place Pigalle. Three domes sat atop it like crowns— one giant dome in the center, two smaller ones on either side that seemed to play attendant to the dominant one. The building was white and looming as an iceberg. It looked like a palace or a mausoleum or a fortress. He'd never seen anything so large. It sat on that hill like it ruled it; as if it had been there always and had condescended to let Montmartre spring up around it. Ben stared up at it, stupefied, while Baby Back shifted his weight from one leg to the other and continually checked his watch. Two sets of stairs crawled up either side of the grassy hill to the palace-mausoleum-fortress. The climb looked daunting.

"Let's go up," Ben said.

"I ain't climbing all the way up there. Gotta save my breath for my horn. You go on."

"I want us to do this together."

"I want to rehearse."

As Ben climbed, bells rang out, reverberating in a majestic clang. Others climbed the steps as well. Some were well-dressed tourists who had underestimated the stamina required for this quaint adventure; others drably clothed Montmartre residents who had long ago learned to pace themselves for the trek. The bells continued to clang.

"*Excusez-moi, monsieur,*" Ben asked a fellow climber. "*Qu'est-ce que c'est?*"

"*La Basilique du Sacré-Cœur.*"

It took several patient repetitions on the man's part and a mad flipping of pages through Ben's dictionary to determine that the edifice was The Basilica of the Sacred Heart. A church.

"*La Basilique du Sacré-Cœur. La Basilique du Sacré-Cœur.*" Ben repeated it until he could reproduce it with only a fraction of stuttering.

"*Mon ami,*" the man said, "we call it *Sacré-Cœur* for short."

It turned out to be the highest point in Paris.

Ben reached the summit, then proceeded up to the basilica's portico. From behind the heavy wood doors came the surge of an organ and an exhilaration of voices in song. Ben looked out beyond the crest of the hill. The rest of Paris lapped below like an electric tapestry, sewn with a surfeit of colors and textures, some creamy, some jagged; all distant and shadowy, yet touchable. The city rippled out, far, vast, grazing the world's corners.

The apartment was in rue Blanche, not far from Chez LeRoi. The girliest thing he'd ever seen. A tyranny of lace. And ruffles. And pink. *Everything* was pink—the drapes, the tablecloths, the wallpaper, and beyond.

"What you think of the place?" Glo asked. She set two pink mugs on the coffee table, filled them with coffee from a pink urn, and spiked them with gin.

"You have . . . you possess . . . a certain . . . flair," Ben said.

What she possessed was a skyscraping self-regard. Pictures of her inundated the smallish apartment: a gigantic portrait in a gilded frame above the sofa, several smaller photos parked on accent tables and shelves, a showstopper of a painting in the entryway. Smaller than the monster above the sofa, it illustrated Glo in the midst of a dance step with bold hues that vaulted across the canvas. The artist had ditched realism—Glo was just some drawn lines and flourishes of color—and instead endeavored to capture her sass.

"I know that painting is as irresistible as I am," she said, "but I want to talk. Sit down, drink your coffee, and tell Glo why you think this Clifford's trying to steal Baby Back from you."

Ben laughed, confounded and weirdly charmed by this woman's

presumption. "How about this: You tell me a little something about *you* first."

She sighed. "All right, Benjy, if that's the way you want to do this. Lord, Lord. Where to start? Well . . ."

She was born in Cleo, Mississippi. At sixteen, she married a banjo player.

"Floyd Fairchild. The homeliest man you *ever* did see. Plain as a mule and about as smart. But a kind man. A good man. I loved him. And he had a way with his . . . instrument." She winked.

The couple moved to New Orleans when they heard its music scene paid. With his banjo-playing and her voice, they worked right away—in dive bars and brothels in downtown Storyville.

"Joints so low-down, you had to dig your way in with a shovel. Whores and thieves and killers. And then the rough folks showed up."

After New Orleans they toured the colored vaudeville circuit. Tent shows in the summer. Tiny, rickety theaters in the winter months. Riding Jim Crow smokers and bunking at colored-run boardinghouses.

"We did all right. Made a name for ourselves. Cut a few records. Made a little money."

Then Floyd enlisted and came to France to fight in the Great War.

"Got his brains blowed out. Ha. Never had much anyway. They buried him here. I came over to lay flowers on his grave, pay my respects."

And she stayed.

"Sugar, this town went jazz-crazy after the war. I had it made. I ain't never once thought about going back to the States. Never once." She refilled their coffee and added another generous draught of gin to both cups. "That's my life story, Benjy. Your turn."

Was it the high from the gin, or was she growing on him? Ben took a gulp of coffee and gave her the rundown. Dogwood. Angeline. Harlem. *This thing*. Baby Back. Even Willful, tactfully skirting the more raw details.

"*This thing?* That what you called it?" Glo said. "Sugar, you should have been in New Orleans. There was sissy-men running around all over the damn place. Nobody cared. Least not in Storyville or the Quarter. Now tell Glo all about this Clifford!" She was almost salivating.

"Why you so anxious to get up in my business?" Ben asked.

She batted her eyes like a coquette. "Because that's what friends do, Benjy."

Yes, she was growing on him. He had said her decorating had flair. That seemed true of her, as well. Lighthearted devilment tiptoed behind the sass. Irreverence was her calling card. She was presumptuous and nosy, and even that charmed him. He had known lots of nosy women, but had never found one endearing. Perhaps Glo could chaperone him through this strange world he'd sailed into or counsel him across the capricious terrain of this new distance with Baby Back. Hadn't she bested the trumpeter, even as she clicked down those spiral stairs? Called out his inflating ego and won?

Ben drank some more gin-laden coffee and told his new friend all about Clifford. All about the distance.

"You ain't got a thing to worry about," Glo declared, a judge who had heard the evidence and now presented her ruling. "Baby Back done come all the way to Paris with *you,* right? Distance, hell. He ain't gonna toss you aside that easy. But I don't know what you see in him. He arrogant as all shit."

A woman with a home chock-full of pictures of herself complaining of someone else's arrogance? It made Ben snicker.

> *Shake your bluesy thing.*
> *Lover of life.*
> *A new light in my life?*
> *An ebony star shooting across the Paris skyline.*
> *Glow, Glo.*

# 34

*The moon rides on the arc of night.*
*In this city of light, shadows kiss.*
*Jazz slinks up and down the city's veins*
*And Charlestons through cobblestone arteries.*
*Brown skin shines,*
*A grateful bird set free.*

Ben sat on the steps of Sacré-Cœur, writing. He looked up from his tablet and out over the panoramic view, in love with it. The August air was summery, but a bit cool, the sky clear except for the factory haze. Buildings clustered together along the streets that threaded the city. The Eiffel Tower ascended above all, puncturing the sky like a needle. Two months in Paris and this spot on the steps of this church surpassed all others. It was his favorite.

He checked the time. He had a few hours before he had to be at work. Work: as in waiting tables—at Chez LeRoi. It happened because of Clifford Treadwell.

Since his arrival, Ben had spent his days exploring Paris and his nights wading through the tumult of the Place Pigalle to get to

Chez LeRoi where he hobnobbed with Denny's set. When that crowd was absent, LeRoi Jasper trotted him over to other groups to exhibit him like a prize horse.

"*Mes amis, je vous présente* Ben Charles," he'd crow. "He's from HARLEM!"

Chairs would scuffle against the parquet floor as the people scooted aside, frantic to make space for an authentic Harlemite.

"You've all heard of wild, jungle nights in Harlem, yes?" Jasper would say. "Well, this young man was downright *savage!*"

Champagne would be ordered and the now-familiar questioning would ensue:

"Do you know Josephine Baker?"

"Did she always dance in a belt of bananas?"

"*Le jazz-hot* was born in Harlem, *n'est pas?*"

"Why are Negroes more sensual than Europeans?"

"Do you dream of Africa?"

This querying about Harlem in particular and Negro life in general made Ben think he'd been appointed the official representative of both.

Clifford came to Chez LeRoi frequently, usually with his oft-mentioned connections. Between sets, Clifford and Baby Back and the connections would huddle like conspirators. They never included Ben. If Clifford came alone, he assessed the scene from the doorway before deigning to make his entrance. Whether commandeering a table or parked at the bar, he always kept in his sights that big, bad wolf of a trumpeter spewing jazz dynamite from the stage.

"I gotta be there every damn night," Ben told Glo one day. "Because *he's* there every damn night. I gotta keep an eye on him."

She poured him coffee from the pink urn. "Sugar, just work there. It kills two birds with one stone: You can keep an eye on Cliffy and get paid for it, too. And Melvin just quit, so this is your lucky day."

Baroness Deneuve—Denny—once his patroness, became his customer. It didn't take long to get the gossip from his new coworkers.

"Baroness" may have been her title, but controversy percolated over its validity. In what had become a catty guessing game in the *haute* parlors of the rich Parisian set, some debated whether she had inherited the title from family or acquired it by marriage. Others sniped that she had invented it: a ruse for accelerating up the ladder of Paris society. But with her chauffeur-driven, snakeskin-upholstered Renault town car and couture from Jeanne Lanvin and Coco Chanel, faux title or not, no one could deny that Denny possessed egregious wealth. She was in her mid forties; her male escorts (she cavorted with a different one almost every night) were half that and always the most stellar men in the room.

And Ben got the low-down on LeRoi Jasper from Norman, the bartender, when they passed a cigarette back and forth before work one evening.

"I knew him when he was *Leroy* Jasper. We was in the 369th Infantry Regiment during the Great War. All through training, Leroy was timid and quiet. Awful nervous, too. Whenever somebody made fun of him or played a joke on him—which was all the time—I swear he'd look like he was 'bout to break down crying. I felt bad for him. I thought, *Might as well send the telegram notifying his next of kin 'cause ain't no way this boy's gonna make it through no war.* When we got over here, a French soldier told him *Leroy* was a corruption of *le roi,* which is French for *the king.* It went to his head and stayed there. He made everybody call him *LeRoi.* And no more Mr. Scaredy Cat. No, sir. He turned out to be the most vicious fighter out of all of us. Them krauts ain't stand a chance against him. When the war ended, he scraped the money together and opened this place."

Baby Back was displeased at not being consulted about Ben's hiring.

"Just keep a low profile when Clifford comes in with people, hear me? Clifford says his contacts might not, you know, understand about you and me."

"Baby, you're the one that's been keeping a low profile."

They worked in the same place, lived in the same room, but rarely saw each other on account of Baby Back's constant meetings with record people or impresarios or club owners or Ben didn't know who. Or he spent his days at the club obsessively practicing his trumpet and rehearsing the musicians, driving them—and himself—like a plantation overseer.

"Clifford says I gotta be ready. Never know when one of his contacts might make an offer."

It was afternoon. They were in their room in the boardinghouse in rue Constance.

"Here we go again," Ben said. "*Clifford says. Clifford says.* If Clifford said you should jump in the Seine, would you?"

"If it would help my career: hell yeah."

He sat on the bed, buffing his horn with a soft cloth. Ben took the horn, laid it aside, sat on Baby Back's lap, and kissed him.

Ben became aroused. Baby Back didn't.

"Get up," he said, patting Ben's thigh, then nudging him away. "I gotta go practice."

Ben watched him retrieve the shining horn and place it in its case. It occurred to him that Baby Back spent more time with his trumpet than he did with him. Was more intimate with it, too. For exactly one split second, Ben hated that trumpet.

"Hey. Would you jump in the Seine to help *us?*"

Baby Back opened his mouth, but didn't answer. A minute later he was out the door.

Paris. Full. Filling. Rational. Daft. It could be conservative as a mortician's suit and then you'd round a corner and it was a brazen flapper. It could be itinerant or intransigent; tamely feral or wildly civilized. Paris was vast, eternal, but also small and annoyingly provincial. It soared multifaceted and diverse and eclectic, and it was homogenous as hell. Ben discovered all of this once he broke out of the fishbowl of Montmartre and dove into the rest of the city—a painter's palette streaked with colors: brilliant, moody, audacious, tantalizing, inviting, alienating. Reds and blacks and pinks and that milky gray that belonged both to the cloudy Paris sky and the pearls entwining a rich socialite's neck.

But he felt rather than saw its colors.

He felt pastels—peach, pink, diaphanous yellows—when he traipsed up the Champs Élysées with its fashionable shops full of wealthy customers radiating easy grandeur. Something light and airy hummed about the Champs Élysées, dancing up and down the street and in and out of every expensively appointed shop window.

Older conservative women climbed out of limousines in long skirts whose hems skimmed the pavement. Young women stormed the boulevard in boxy hats and dresses that stopped just above their knees. But it was the men at whom Ben marveled. Slim young men, slicked hair glistening and distinctly parted, wearing the new jazz suits—pants hemmed high and cuffed at the ankle, jacket waists pinched tight to flaunt their slender contours. Ben refrained from staring until he didn't.

Then there was the black of Notre Dame. Its gothic weight oppressed and fascinated him as he perused altars and artwork handcrafted with such intimate specificity that even the details had details. The cathedral was somber. Its dim light spoke elusiveness and distance. You had to strive toward the light, aspire to it. He sat in a pew, decimated by the dark beauty, and thought of the distance with Baby Back. It was a tunnel, the poet at one end, the trumpeter at the other, and in between lay an unnavigable expanse of dense black. They couldn't see through it to get back to each other. They didn't talk anymore. They didn't fuck anymore. The only time Baby Back seemed alive was when he was performing or scheming to advance his career. Or when Clifford Treadwell came around.

One evening, Ben complained to Glo. He was lolling on the chaise longue in her dressing room while she made up her face and took swigs of gin from a silver flask. She stopped in the middle of applying rouge.

"Benjy. Oh, sugar." She said the three words like she pitied him. "That bigheaded fool gonna keep on hurting you. He ain't no good for you. And be honest with yourself: *You* ain't no good for *him*. Baby Back Johnston needs somebody as ambitious and bloodthirsty as he is. I know that ain't what you want to hear, but Glo gotta call it like she sees it."

"I love him."

She shook her head like he was the most tragic thing she'd ever seen. "I know. Poor child. All the worse for you."

Ben rose. "You have a good night."

He walked out and down the spiral staircase as she called after him.

"Yeah, that's right. Just walk on out when you don't like what ol' Glo has to say! Mmm-hmm. Even when you know she's right!

Just walk your little skinny ass on out, like that's gonna change anything!"

Pastels again when he discovered Le Jardin des Tuilleries. People
strolled the garden's grounds amid sculptures and fountains, or busied
themselves with the food and entertainments: puppet shows, acro-
bats, lemonade stalls. Ben walked to the edge of the garden, looked
west, and saw the Champs Élysées clogged with automobiles stream-
ing toward the Arc de Triomphe. The bottom of the Eiffel Tower
was visible, but a light-blue mist obscured its top.

It started raining. He sought shelter in an orchard of trees. The
leafy boughs shielded him. A few feet away, a man also sought pro-
tection under a tree. He extended one hand against the trunk, the
other on the half-moon of his hip, which jutted out as if waiting for
someone to claim it. His body was slim and lithe and pliable, his
hair a light brown. He was close enough that Ben could stare into
his light green eyes. Close enough for the man to return the favor
with a gaze, steely and carnal, as rain began to invade the sanctity
of the protective trees.

Ben thought how easy it would be to do something with and to
this man. Nobody had to know. Baby Back didn't want him these
days, hadn't touched him in weeks.

And Ben craved to be touched.

He broke the impasse, offered the man a nod. The man puck-
ered his pink lips, smooched a kiss, then walked off into the rain.
He turned and teased Ben a look, then continued on until he was
swallowed by distance and the pallid white wall of rain.

Everything in the Latin Quarter shone gold. The fiery haggling
in the marketplace and the exchange of coins, one tawny hand to
another; the gilded intellects of artists and students and aesthetes
blazing glitter against the backdrop of the dark, twisting, medieval
streets. Ben ate in the Latin Quarter's literary cafés to eavesdrop on
the intellectuals, though he cared nothing about their philosophies,
their theories, their socialistic complaining.

He listened in order to master French.

Not the spiritlessness of tourist French, nor the workaday French gleaned from grammar books. Ben aspired to its tricky nuances, its artful cadences, so he could one day skate the slopes of its slippery idiosyncrasies. He listened and uncovered new words and imitated the accent and practiced the inflections until he sensed new muscle forming on his soft palette and at the back of his throat. He wanted to flex the part of his brain that stored English and make room for French. He'd know that he'd mastered it when he could skate the slopes in his head, when he dreamed in it.

And if he dreamed in it, couldn't he write poetry in it, too? Recently, he'd been startled to find he couldn't even write in his own language. Long accustomed to poems sailing off his fingertips and onto the page, lately he'd sit at his typewriter or with his notepad, waiting for a wind to charm his sails. Sometimes it came as a languid breeze, sometimes not at all, leaving his paper either flecked with listless verses or blank. He wasn't sure which was worse, or what to do. Baby Back never suffered any loss of artistry. Why had *he?*

He went to a café in the Latin Quarter one afternoon, a cramped room with rough wood floors and the odor of coffee in every corner. He chose a table near the entrance. In the middle of the dining area were tables with benches on either side like picnic tables. One hosted a group of male students from the Sorbonne. Clean-cut boys with clear white skin and rosy, dimpled cheeks. Clichés, but lovely nonetheless.

A literary debate ensnared the table: one side advocated romanticism, the other defended modernism.

"Chateaubriand, Hugo, and Dumas, *père. They* are the masters, *mes amis.*"

"The *old* masters. Their words, their styles are gray-haired and decrepit! Give me Breton and Cocteau. Give me Apollinaire. Hell, give me Fitzgerald."

"Fitzgerald? Bah! Ninety years from now, no one will remember him or care. American writers: bah!"

The students smiled through their entire argument, then closed their topic with a chummy clinking of coffee cups. The Fitzgerald-endorsing student stood out. His tie askew. Longish hair falling in front of his eyes. A dash of scruff on his ruddy face.

Something in Ben's pants smiled.

He went downstairs to use the lavatory, the basement dark and medieval-dungeon cool. The Fitzgerald boy was at the sink when Ben came out of the stall. They studied each other through the mirror's reflection.

"*Bonjour,*" Fitzgerald said.

"*Bonjour.*"

Silence. Studying.

"I need to wash my hands," Ben said.

"What were you doing in that stall to make them dirty?"

He stepped aside. Ben moved to the sink. As water poured over his hands, he felt a nice slap on his backside. Sharp and quick, the sound like a whip. Ben looked in the mirror, saw Fitzgerald at the stall cocking his head in its direction, renegade hair flailing. He went in, left the door ajar.

Ben finished at the sink and moved to exit. He looked back at the stall, felt the smile in his pants again. He hesitated, then hesitated some more, then walked toward the stall with purpose, then reversed course and left.

Montmartre was brown. And beige. And tan. And bronze. The majority of Negroes living in the city called the jazz-drenched province in northern Paris home. Mostly musicians or show people, but former soldiers, writers, painters, and sculptors, too. Ben ran into many Negroes during his explorations and, regardless of their height, they all walked tall, carrying themselves with the poise of those who are welcome. If he saw someone at a distance, he didn't go out of his way to introduce himself. But at close proximity, he had no choice. It was *de rigueur.*

"What instrument you play?" was often the first question asked of him.

"I ain't a musician," Ben would say, then quickly add, "But I'm here with my cousin; he's a trumpeter. Baby Back Johnston? He's playing at Chez LeRoi over in rue Fontaine?"

"Oh, yeah! I been hearing all about that cat. I'm piano man over at Zelli's, myself. Come over and catch the show some night. Tell 'em you're a friend of Lawrence. By the way, what do *you* do?"

"I write."

"Songs?"

"No. Poetry."

"Killer. Working on something now?"

"No."

The brown, beige, tan, and bronze exploded in the black night in rue Fontaine, rue Blanche, rue de Clichy, rue de la Trinité, rue Pigalle, and rue des Martyrs. The Jungle Alley of Paris. Jazz clubs ruled those streets. Drunk partiers would tumble into a club with their own booze glass in hand, listen and dance for a spell, then tumble back out and into another club to do the same thing all over again, all night. Some clubs drew top-drawer patrons in dinner jackets and ermine; others were holes-in-the-wall where hand-me-downs and yesteryear's fashions reigned. Both attracted the set that prowled their way to Montmartre to slum and gawk and then, the next week, host a *fête* at their Neuilly estate where they would shake their heads and tell their buttoned-up friends, "*Oui,* Montmartre. *Très décadent.* I have seen it firsthand."

But whatever the patrons' incomes or intentions, the Negro musicians jammed with a freedom Ben didn't hear back home. A devilish finesse in the pianists' riffs, a little extra jive from the brass, a saltier bump from the singers' hips. Even that genius Baby Back seemed to jam harder in Montmartre.

"*Bonjour, mademoiselle,*" Ben said. "*Nous voudrions deux billets, s'il vous plaît.*"

The ticket seller produced the requested tickets, then appraised Ben and Baby Back. "*Êtes-vous de l'Afrique ou de l'Amérique?*"

"*D'Amérique.* New York," Ben said.

"Harlem?"

"*Oui.*"

"*Des musiciens de jazz?*" she asked.

He patted Baby Back's arm. "*Il est un musicien. Et il joue le jazz le plus sublime dans le monde!*"

"*C'est magnifique. Bienvenus à la Louvre et à Paris.*"

"*Merci, mademoiselle.*"

Ben assumed the Louvre would feel like a many-colored tantrum. But it was sinless-virgin white. The museum itself was a blank world, a stark white canvas on which empires of color had been grafted. The walls writhed with paintings, hung one above another above another, from floor to ceiling and from end to end. The eye didn't know where to start, what to latch on to. A chaos of art. *How do I absorb all this?* How does one distinguish between a piece that's very good and one that's superlative?

*Which of my poems is superlative? Or very good. Or just good. Any of them? How can I tell? How could these artists tell? Baby Back, he can always tell when his music's superlative. He always knows. Baby Back Johnston. He's always superlative.*

They were touring the Italian Renaissance wing. Curious Ben surrendered to the reverie that was the Louvre, but Baby Back made a theatrical production of his boredom. He shoved his hands deep in his pockets and scuffled his feet abrasively against the floor; pointedly checked his watch; yawned so melodramatically that eyes at the gallery's far end temporarily abandoned the Da Vincis and Bellinis and shifted toward him.

Thirty minutes into the visit, while Ben inspected a dark male beauty peering out of a Caravaggio painting, Baby Back said, "You and that ticket girl was having quite the conversation. It all had to be in French, huh? When you speak French and all I can do is stand there, I feel like a fool."

"You *chose* not to learn it."

"I'm sick of looking at this white-folks' art, so now I'm choosing to get the hell out of here."

They fought all the way back to Montmartre.

"You love making a fool of me, don't you?" Baby Back said.

"You make a fool of *yourself.*"

"Why'd you drag me to that stupid museum? So you could act like you're better than me? So you could act white?"

"I dragged you there so we could spend time together," Ben said. "Won't make that mistake again. Trust me."

"Yeah. Trust *you.*"

The battle escalated by the time they reached the boardinghouse. They cut each other off mid-sentence, shouted over one another, launched bullets of sarcasm that exploded like shrapnel.

Tenants in the next room beat their complaints on the wall, and the landlady, Madame Gautier, appeared at their door threatening eviction.

"You don't give a shit about the language. You don't give a shit about the culture. So why come to Paris?" Ben said. "Why are you here?"

"To be a star. My uncle Roland wanted me to come."

"Your fucking uncle is dead."

Ben's senses suddenly swam loose in his skull. He perceived only blurs and smudges. A cloudy, muted gauze. The spot where his head pressed the floor (or was it the other way around?) throbbed. He felt himself being hefted off the floor and seated on the bed; he sensed more than heard Baby Back's voice—*Oh God. Oh God, Ben. I can't believe I . . . Oh God, I didn't mean to*—and then Baby Back stumping around the room, ransacking drawers. Sound and vision began to sharpen. A prick of liquid stung his forehead, then his bloating lip. He licked it and tasted the metallic fusion of iodine and blood.

# 35

Over the next weeks Baby Back reverted, in part, to the doting lover Ben had originally gone crazy for. They rediscovered intimacy, waking each morning and gravitating to each other, without thinking, without opening their eyes, without effort or creativity. Like a puzzle they had memorized, they knew where all the pieces fit and eased them into place automatically. But Baby Back's niceness was medicine that relieved the symptoms and left the disease untouched. On the steps of Sacré-Cœur, as he tried to coax a poem out of hiding, Ben pondered whether it was possible to sustain love in the throes of change.

"Why do things have to change? Why did Baby Back have to change?"

Perhaps it wasn't that people changed, but that they revealed themselves; that fertile ambitions bloomed and clamored to be harvested. Maybe this dark side of Baby Back had existed all along and Ben had been too naïve, too much in love, to see it.

He gave up coaxing the poem. It didn't want to come. He glowered at the blank page as if it had wronged him.

He missed Harlem and the haven of The Oasis. He wished they'd never come to Paris. Then he looked out over that panoramic view from the portico of that church on the crest of that hill. And Harlem vanished. It just went away. Like a whisper in a dark church, or a light, pastel rain sprinkling down on an orchard of trees. It was gone. There was only Paris.

Clifford didn't come to Chez LeRoi during the weeks of Baby Back's niceness, giving Ben space to breathe.

"You want to know what I think, Benjy?" Glo asked. He opened his mouth to answer, but she kept talking. "He ain't been here in two weeks, so that means him and his wife done took their high-yellow asses back to the States."

He tested her theory.

"Haven't seen Cliffy in a while," he baited Baby Back one morning.

"Left Paris. Him and Millicent."

"What about his contacts?"

"They're *my* contacts now. I don't need him."

Baby Back gloated, but Ben sensed he was relieved as well. As if Clifford was a hurdle he was glad to have cleared, glad to have gotten clear of. He became more immersed in himself. Instead of leading the band, he acted as though he owned it. He reduced the musicians' parts to give himself more solo time; substituted his own arrangements for songs the band had been playing long before he arrived. The club's staff withstood his screaming orders and watched, speechless, when he castigated the young technician for not keeping the spotlight on him enough. And he and Glo waged repeated skirmishes about material and tempos and musical styling.

The staff grumbled to LeRoi Jasper, but there was nothing he was willing to do. Glo may have been the official star, but it was Baby Back who now packed the place. Audiences talked or drank through Glo's vocals, but came alive for Baby Back's solos.

"Is this the club with the big Negro trumpeter?" arriving customers asked, or "This is the Baby Back Show, *n'est pas?*"

The uninterrupted flood of talent-scouting show business people proved he'd been right: He didn't need Clifford. And when he hooked an agent and then a contract with a small record company, his ego rioted. He demanded recognition as Chez LeRoi's official star or he'd jump to another club. After suffering through negotiations with Baby Back and weathering Glo's threats to quit, LeRoi Jasper invented a solution: He put Baby Back's name on the marquee after Glo's. But Baby Back's name was slightly bigger.

Glo complained at Ben as she ranted around her apartment and boozed from her silver flask. "I been singing for Mr. Jasper for years and he does this to me?" She stamped and stomped, but beneath the thin skin of her anger lurked fear. "And why? Just 'cause Baby Back got hisself a contract with some two-bit record company?"

"That *is* a selling point. *Chez LeRoi is proud to present recording artist Baby Back Johnston.*"

"Yeah, Benjy. That's right," Glo said, her speech slurred. She took another swig of gin. "Defend a man who beats you."

But Baby Back never hit him again. Instead, their life devolved to cycles of war followed by silence. Ben continually picked fights about his refusal to learn French. Baby Back pointed to Ben's camaraderie with Glo as evidence of disloyalty, which prompted Ben to rail about the trumpeter isolating him in regard to his career.

"You signed with that record company without even telling me," Ben said. "How could you leave me out of a decision like that?"

"I ain't gotta consult you. This is *my* career."

"And this is *our life*. What you do affects *me*."

"You fucked Angeline after you and me had already got together. Remember that? Huh? Then you kept Clifford's offer to yourself. So why should I give a shit what you think?"

Then days of silence.

Mornings they would wake, decline to say a word to each other, then dress and go their own ways. Nights they lay in the same bed, but locked in separate realms. Unless Baby Back needed release. Then he would climb onto Ben, satisfy himself, then climb back into his own realm. He didn't let on but, secretly, Ben craved those times, prayed for them. Because he didn't trust himself not to succumb to the orchard men in Le Jardin de Tuilleries or the men in jazz suits on the Champs Élysées or the men at Chez LeRoi who, after he took their orders for champagne and oysters, might surreptitiously slip a card with a name and phone number into his pocket, or leave it on the table in addition to—or in lieu of—his tip. Often, they were members of Denny's set.

"Ben, *mon cher,*" she said one evening. "I do not believe you have met Édouard."

Of course he hadn't met Édouard. He was her latest toy and she played with a different one almost every night. This one was as young as the rest with a head of brunette curls.

"Édouard, Ben is from *Harlem.*"

He guessed the next question before it was uttered.

"*Connaissez-vous Josephine Baker?*" Édouard asked.

"*Non, monsieur,*" Ben said. "*Malheureusement, je n'ai pas cet honneur.*"

"Not only that," Denny said, "but Ben is a very bad Negro. He has not seen La Baker's show. Bad Negro. Bad, bad, bad."

Édouard and the rest of the entourage shook their heads at the shame of it. Denny sat forward. "But listen to this." She paused, let the suspense hover, and then dropped the bomb. "Ben loves the Louvre. *The Louvre! Real* Negroes do not love the Louvre. *Real* Negroes play jazz and dance and act wild. The Louvre is not wild."

She laughed. Her entourage did, too. Laughed at the Negro from Harlem who didn't know how to act like one.

Denny held a cigarette to her lips. Édouard lit it instantly. Then winked at Ben.

He went to the Folies Bergère to see about tickets, to shut Denny up. Two big posters for the production hung outside the theater. The first depicted Baker dancing. Her skirt of bananas flared yellow against her brown skin. A crescent of light dappled her short, black hair. The artist had rendered her from behind, but mildly in profile, so you saw her bare back and a hint of her uncovered breasts. Baker's body was silky, sexy, fluid. She bled sensuality.

"She is amazing. *Incroyable.* Have you seen the show?"

A man in a snappy three-buttoned, double-breasted overcoat stood close by.

"*Non, monsieur,*" Ben said. "*Pas encore.*"

"See it before you die. *La Baker est une force de nature.*"

Ben viewed the second poster. In this one, Baker's face was visible, her mouth a boastful red, her figure clothed in a skimpy white dress hitched a mile up her thighs. The poster depicted two men alongside her, each with dark black skin and fat, monstrous lips the same scarlet as Baker's. One's mouth was spread open in a clownish grin, exhibiting an animal-like abundance of oversize teeth colored a searing white. His white hat tipped forward in jocular fashion. Ben's eyes kept returning to the lips.

He told Baby Back about that poster. "The way the men was painted, they looked like monkeys. Is that what they think of us?"

"Who cares? They pay us. We're in *their* country—like you keep reminding me—so we give them what they want. Everybody wins. Don't be an uppity nigger."

"Don't call me that!"

"Uppity nigger. Uppity niggerrrrrrr. What you gonna do? Huh? What you gonna do about it?" Baby Back towered over him, leaned down, and stuck his face right in Ben's. "Uppity, French-talking nigger."

Ben wanted to hit him, but Baby Back would pulverize him. He tried to think of something witty to cut him down. He couldn't. All he could do was say, "Fuck you," as tears fell.

Baby Back left. Ben sat at his typewriter, tried to convert his pain to poetry. He couldn't.

# 36

On Sacré-Cœur's hilltop, Ben watched the sun set in an immolation of orange and scarlet. The sky tempered into calm blues and violets, then darkened to an endless depth of black, clearing out room for the moon. A current pulsed through him. It made him edgy. Restlessness bloated up. He couldn't control it. He ached for release. Ben looked down at the city. Lights blinked against the skyline. Corners and grooves brooded with shadows. He was off from the club tonight and glad. He was sick of Chez LeRoi. Sick of jazz and champagne and being asked about Harlem and treated like an enlightened savage. He was sick of not being able to write.

He had to get out of Montmartre tonight.

Le Jardin des Tuilleries was quiet, but not empty. Couples promenaded. Elderly folks assembled on some benches, their conversations dotted by tinkles of laughter. A full-bodied moon loitered in the sky, shining like a freshly minted coin.

Men pervaded the orchard, each one standing by a tree as if it was an island he'd claimed. There were delegates from every class of Parisian society: rich men in Oxford suits; middle-class men in everyday office suits; workmen in heavy, soiled boots. Mostly young men, but a few who were older or old. Ben's dark skin rendered him almost invisible under the thick tent of branches, but he received many winks and loose nods and many loose, knowing smiles as he roved the orchard's gallery of men.

"*Venez-vous ici, mon Africain,*" one said as Ben passed.

He rambled deeper into the orchard. The men grew sparser, but two to an island instead of one. He smelled reefer, sniffed around to detect the source. Someone reached out, pulled him onto an island, and inserted a mouth onto his in a swelling kiss. Ben squirmed and resisted, and then didn't. The man's mustache scraped his upper lip. Ben was about to be subsumed when he felt his pants being undone, a hand slithering in. The shock woke him. He backed away.

"*Pourquoi vous vous arrêtez?*" the man said.

"*Je m'excuse. Je dois aller,*" Ben said, and fled the orchard.

He needed release. The urgency propelled him toward the boardinghouse, but he had to press through the anarchy of the Place Pigalle. He wound around prostitutes who mixed with the urchins and the criminals and the bourgeois tourists who came to Montmartre to ogle. He passed a brasserie where a brawl had enticed an audience who watched from outside through the picture window, commenting and cheering and taking bets on the outcome.

A man on the corner near the boardinghouse sold cocaine and reefer. Madame Gautier was forever shooing him away, but his product was popular and he feared the loss of his livelihood more than he did a sniping old woman. Ben wanted reefer, but that would delay getting back to the room, a delay that posed the hazard of him descending into madness right there on the street.

His hand shook as he inserted the key. He opened the room door. Baby Back and Clifford Treadwell sat on the bed, glasses in their hands, a bottle of cognac tottering between them on the grandma quilt. Both were fully clothed, although Baby Back's shoes were off.

"Look, Baby Back," Clifford said. "Your cousin's here!"

The two laughed. It was indiscreet, pitched high enough to shatter glass. Ben idled in the doorway. He couldn't talk. He couldn't take his eyes off Clifford. The door remained open.

"Uh-oh," Clifford said to Baby Back, "looks like your cousin's gone dumb. He's lost the use of his mouth."

"Believe me," Baby Back said, "he *knows* how to use that mouth!"

They laughed again, the obscene laughter of drunkards. Except they weren't drunk. The cognac bottle was almost full.

Ben closed the door. "Thought you left Paris."

"I did. Millicent and I went to Marseille. And then I left her there. I think *high and dry* is how we say it back home. And now I'm here again. With you two cousins."

Ben hadn't entered any farther into the room. What he'd walked in on infuriated him. Its tacit intimacy infuriated him. Clifford's smugness and Baby Back's shoeless feet and the cognac spilling on the precious grandma quilt infuriated him. Not a raucous fury. Rather, it collected in a tight whorl as quiet as a hum.

"Have a drink," Clifford said. He looked around. "Is there another glass?"

"No!" Baby Back shouted.

They laughed that intemperate laugh again. It compelled Ben toward the bed. When he got close, he saw Clifford's feet were shoeless as well.

"Get out," he said, his volume low, a whisper, deadly. "Get the fuck out."

The cohorts' laughter ceased. Baby Back sipped his drink. Clifford rose, located his shoes, put them on, and then exited sans a good-bye.

Neither Ben nor Baby Back moved.

"Did you fuck him?" Ben said.

Baby Back's head swiveled toward him, his face a dagger. "You got eyes, Ben."

"I ain't talking about now. Did you fuck him when we was on the ship?"

At last. The question—the accusation—was out in the world after incubating for months.

Baby Back finished off his cognac, shrugged. "Yeah. I did. You fucked Angeline. I fucked Clifford. So we're Even Stephen. How do you say that in your high-and-mighty French?"

He poured more cognac, raised it in a toast.

Ben walked out.

The dealer was still on the corner and now he *did* buy reefer, went to the Place Pigalle, and smoked it openly. No one gave a damn. Good reefer. Did its job quickly, sharpened his senses and numbed him at the same time. A crowd snaked through the Place Pigalle. Ben allowed it to carry him along. The reefer made people and things and sounds seem like impressions. His mouth and throat dried up. Everything in him felt dry. He smoked more to prevent diminishment of his high. He scorned ebb, desired only flow. The fresh injection of reefer waded through his body and found his dick. He was of a mind to return to Le Jardin des Tuilleries. But something caught his eye. Some*one*.

A young colored man swished through the crowd. He wore white pants, white shoes, and white jacket with blue vertical stripes. His backside swung like a pendulum. He moved with purpose, head high, nose needling the air as he headed east of the Place Pigalle, toward the Boulevard de Clichy. Ben wasn't attracted, but he was fascinated. He followed the pendulum hips up the Boulevard de Clichy and then down a short brick side street lined with rundown houses. Young men milled about on the steps of some. Hawks on the lookout, primed to catch prey. They noticed the two colored men instantly.

"*Regardez-vous! Des nègres!*"

"Come, *mon cher.* Come to my room and show me *une nuit sauvage!*"

"*Non!* Come to *my* room. Let me see if it is true what they say about you."

"Come to *my* room. I have jungle records from America. And I will not charge you. At least not much!"

Pendulum Hips made a spectacle of his voyage down the street. He played to the audience, lagged his walk, swerved his hips harder. But as he flaunted himself at the French boys, Ben realized it was *he* receiving the attention. They looked directly at Ben as they tossed their propositions. Pendulum Hips was merely the sideshow but didn't know it. He stopped performing when he reached the dead end of the street. He entered a building and vanished.

Ben followed.

The handwritten paper sign glued to the wall next to the stair-case read MON CLUB. An arrow pointed down. As Ben traveled down the ramshackle steps, piano licks wandered up. He reached the bottom step and found himself in a basement lit with harsh, dim bulbs. A long wood board supported by cinderblocks stood at one end, stocked so heavy with booze it bowed in the middle. A piano player and a girl singer occupied the other end. She wore a leopard-print caftan with a matching turban and she sang a torchy song in raspy French. Florid makeup highlighted an angular jaw and a pronounced Adam's apple.

Two dozen men clothed in the hand-me-down suits of clerks and office workers occupied Mon Club. Some talked and laughed in groups. A few couples stood apart, groping, kissing. Two men in a corner snorted cocaine from a small metal tray they held between them. Wallflowers, drinks and cigarettes in hand, evaluated the action and strategized their opportunity to hop in.

Ben watched the show from his roost on the bottom step. He spotted Pendulum Hips with two men. They were nudging in close, grating against him, while he closed his eyes and submitted.

Ben headed to the bar. While en route almost every face scrutinized him. The guys playing with Pendulum Hips did, too. Ben received a few tart spanks on his backside and at least one pinch.

"*Un Africain.*"

"*Très exotique.*"

"*Très sensuel.*"

The bartender cast a lewd smile and waived payment for the drink. Ben faced Pendulum Hips's admirers, lifted his glass in a toast. They promptly deserted their plaything, who opened his eyes, perplexed to find them gone.

"*Moi, je m'appelle François,*" the one on Ben's left said. He couldn't have been over thirty, but his hair was completely silver. "*Et vous?*"

"*Moi, c'est* Ben."

The one on his right—a very tall, robustly built blond—grunted something in a guttural tongue.

"His name is Dietrich," François said. "From Berlin. He speaks only German."

Dietrich inspected Ben's backside, then stepped right up in front of him, grazed his cheek with his fingernail, the graze long and ungentle. A smile, not unlike the bartender's, prowled on his lips as he looked down at Ben from his substantial height. He grunted again.

"He says you need another drink," François interpreted. "He will buy it for you."

Dietrich left them.

The silence between François and Ben might have been awkward if not for the reefer stirring through him. It walled off his bashfulness, even in the face of François's dogged stare and curl of lips that he moistened every few moments with a decadent gloss of his tongue.

"Dietrich's visiting from Berlin?" Ben asked. "You guys are friends?"

"He is my lover. He lives here, but he refuses to learn French."

"Sounds familiar."

Something was happening. Mon Club's shadows purred. Men were leaving the lighted areas in twos and disappearing into the dark, then reemerging, sometimes with their partner, most times alone, sometimes with a different partner than the one with whom they'd disappeared. The disappearance screamed urgency, heated impatience, but the reemergence dawdled with the lazy indifference of a yawn.

Dietrich rejoined them with Ben's drink. He downed it. Cheap, drab champagne without the crackle of the stuff LeRoi Jasper served. Dietrich bought him another. And then another. And another. They dallied on the outskirts of the basement's overspilling shadows.

Ben lifted reefer from his pocket, lit it, shared it with his new gentleman friends. Reefer made them playful. Lips and cheeks brushed, hands wound their way to private places. A coy rendition of the heaven taking place in the shadows.

Dietrich grunted.

"He says he wants to go to Harlem, in America," François said. "He wonders if you have been there."

"No. *Jamais,*" Ben said. "But I've always wanted to. I hear they have parties every night and everyone sings the blues."

More champagne. More translation to and from German. More couples purring in the shadows accompanied by the chanteuse's French rendition of "I Wonder Where My Baby Is Tonight." Ben perspired, rubbed his cold champagne glass across his forehead to cool off. He smoked more reefer.

"You two were talking to that other Negro," he said. "Well, not *talking* exactly. *Alors,* what happened?"

François slipped an arm around his waist. His thumb skidded airily up and down Ben's side. "We like African *men,* not girls. He would have sufficed, but since *you* are here . . ."

As if Negroes were interchangeable. What was the word for *interchangeable* in French? He didn't know. What he *did* know was that this room—these men, this Frenchman, this German, that leering bartender, these shadows—inflamed him. Ignited the craving in him. In this room craving didn't frustrate because the means of fulfillment was available, his for the taking. All he had to do was be here, be present, want it, allow it. It excited him. The danger. The escapade of instant intimacy. But something else, too. In a few moments he would step into the shadows where this Frenchman and this German would have their greedy way with him. And he would let them. Not simply for the sake of release; not just because he was lonely or because the loss of Baby Back's touch had left him bereft.

He would step into the shadows because he was curious.

Mon Club overflowed. A continuous cavalcade of men tramped down the basement stairs. The temperature warmed, making the air closer, mustier. A collective odor of bodies swamped the room. Not only couples in the shadows now, but threesomes and quartets. More champagne. More groans as chests quivered out of shirts and trousers puddled at men's feet. François still held Ben about the waist as the groaning in the shadows intensified, as the temperature rose tenfold.

"*Mon beau Africain,*" François whispered, "do not think. Allow."

Dietrich's teeth and prickly tongue bombarded Ben's neck. François dug his tongue into his mouth. Ben cloaked his arms around him and reciprocated.

Then the Frenchman and the German escorted him into the shadows.

# 37

He paid no attention to the boys on the steps on his return trip up the street. He tried to inhale the night air, but the smells of Mon Club sealed up his nostrils. He rejoined the crazed crowd on the Place Pigalle and drifted back to the boardinghouse. Ben clumped up the stairs and opened his door. There sat Baby Back, a glass in hand, the cognac bottle before him, looking as if he hadn't moved at all since earlier, except his shirt was off.

Ben's sudden appearance seemed to startle him. He inspected the poet, head to foot. "Where were you?"

Ben caught a glimpse of himself in the mirror above the wash-basin. Doused in sweat. Shirt untucked and unbuttoned down to his navel. Tie hanging about his neck like loose string. Pants fly un-done. He started to button it, then didn't. Was it the Frenchman who undid his pants? Or the German? He didn't know. Once they had him in the shadows, once they'd gone to work on him, it hadn't mattered.

"I said, where were you?" Baby Back's eyes settled on the un-buttoned fly. He approached, took a big whiff, and Ben knew the stinky musk of those two men covered him. The way their hands had. Their mouths, their bodies. Funny. He couldn't remember their names. This was the first time he'd been intimate with anybody and then couldn't remember a name. He was shocked at his lack of shame. But the shock couldn't compete with the pleasure—gluttonous and fever-bright—that he'd devoured in those shadows. He should have felt dirty. Instead, he was delighted.

"Where were you?" Baby Back asked for the third time, louder, moving closer, using his height and his bigness to intimidate an answer from his silent, wayward lover.

"*Even Stephen*. That's where I was."

Baby Back grabbed the lapels of his jacket and tugged him in close. Their foreheads and noses touched.

"Pack your things," he said. "Get out. I don't want you back."

"I used to sing at Mon Club, sugar."

Glo held the gin bottle, Ben the reefer cigarette. They exchanged substances in one dexterous move. Except for the streetlamp light straining through the windows, the apartment was dark. Glo sat in her pink easy chair. Ben sprawled on the pink sofa—his new home.

"*You* sang in that dump?" He upended the bottle. Gin rinsed down his throat. The reefer inoculated him against the burn.

"Sure did," Glo said. "When I first came here."

"I hope you dressed better than that thing they had singing."

"Probably didn't. Glo hadn't become the maven of fashion that she is now." She coughed as she sucked in a lungful of reefer.

Ben emptied the gin. "We need that other bottle. I'll make myself at home and get it."

"I remember one night," Glo said. "I was in the middle of a song. None of them sissies was paying attention. They was too busy checking each other out and doing their business in them shadows. All of a sudden this man comes tearing down the stairs. Everyone thought it was a raid. Them sissies buttoned their pants up right quick. The man screams, '*Aidez-moi! Aidez-moi!*' and goes running into the shadows. Not a minute later, two more guys in suits come running in—gangsters—looking for the first guy. They knew exactly where they'd landed soon as they got down the stairs. Everybody was scared. Whole place got quiet. The gangsters started walking around, checking it out. Then they went to the bar and ordered drinks and mixed with the sissies, talking to people like they was just two guys out on the town."

"Were they queer?"

"No, sugar. They was thirsty. The owner told me to keep singing, so I did 'Tain't Nobody's Business If I Do.' Them gangsters was drinking and laughing and having themselves a good ol' time. Before they left, they told the owner they was shaking the place down for a five-percent cut per week."

"What happened to the guy they was chasing?" Ben asked.

"Good-looking guy, hiding in the shadows of a sissy bar. What you think happened?"

Without a word they switched substances again in a seamless exchange. Ben relit the reefer and dragged hard until he floated in near oblivion. He couldn't move, couldn't think. He could feel, but only the periphery of things.

"What you gonna do without that big-headed trumpet player?" Glo asked.

He sucked and sucked and sucked on the reefer. Smoked it down to an ash that singed his fingers. "I ain't doing shit tonight. Tomorrow I'll probably cry."

And so he did. Woke up late with a demonic hangover, went up to Sacré-Cœur, and hemorrhaged tears.

*I've lost my Baby. All that color's gone.*

Before Paris, it was Baby Back who supplied color to Ben's world. Baby Back was saturated with color. It was the trumpet glowing gold and boiling red-hot and cooling down with blues. It was the blue in his blues. It was the savage, blinding, starlit orange of his jazz genius. It was the cold wrought-iron black of his bad moods, his ambition, his selfishness, his cruelty. It was so many rainbows. It was the rainbow pastiche of the grandma quilt. It was the rainbow delight of loving him. It was the rainbow bruise of loving him.

*How will I ever replenish the color? How will I ever recolor my world?*

After the hemorrhage, he looked up at the sky. At that late hour of morning he could still see the moon. A light imprint. Ben wondered about the other side of the moon. He could only speculate. Or fantasize. But he was certain it wasn't uniform, perhaps not even predictable, in its terrain, its textures. Perhaps something (new colors?) on that other side, that far side, both complemented and contradicted what he saw from his perch on earth.

He felt like the moon: a stray and lonely body.

His gaze slid down to the Paris skyline.

Paris. Bright miracle. But behind every bright thing creeps its shadows. The moon had its shadows and Paris hers. They lurked in her back streets and back alleys, in parks and in basements. The shadows attracted Ben like a snake cajoled from a basket by the arousing notes of a flute. He had his shadow side. Just like Paris. Just like that pesky, double-sided moon.

# shadows
## 1926–1927

# 38

Harlem had truly, finally come to Chez LeRoi. *Chocolate Jubilee of 1926,* an all-colored musical revue from New York, had sailed into Paris and anchored at the Music-hall des Champs Élysées. The cast and crew christened Chez LeRoi their official after-performance watering hole. Denny and her set adopted them, then proceeded to suffocate them with champagne and attention. The troupe was bewildered by the welcome, their instant celebrity. Ben envied them. He recalled that he had been the celebrity just six months ago. With an entire passel of Harlem Negroes to pet, he was now relegated to mere servant. "Ben!" Denny would snap. "Bring more champagne! Right now! We have *real* Negroes in the house!" On these occasions, the impulse to discharge a crisp reply would set Ben's lips tingling, until he remembered that Denny was Chez LeRoi's most important customer and his biggest tipper.

The cast of *Chocolate Jubilee* displayed a bewitching parade of attitudes and temperaments, moods and natures.

The women:

There were girls—late teens, early twenties—whose first show this was. Ben could tell by their fresh, pretty, unblemished faces; by their pertness and laughter that tinkled like the *ping* of a crystal goblet. They were still too naïve to grasp that their fresh, pretty faces might harbor the formula for fulfilling their ambitions.

The foils to these fresh buds were women a little older and miles wiser. Pretty, too, but they had partied too much, worried too much, loved harder than they should have. It weighed on their careworn faces, in the silk-fine creases prickling under their eyes like unruly lines on a map. They once nurtured ambitions, but learned that ambitions beget consequences. Survivors, these tough-skinned women slung mean words at anyone foolish enough to mess with them and spoke their minds as if firing a weapon, as when Denny asked the *de rigueur* question of whether they knew Josephine Baker.

"I know that heifer," one of them blasted, primed to unleash a massacre. "Worked with her on the road back in '21 or '22 in *Shuffle Along*. Bitch thought she was better than everybody else. She fucked anybody—male, female—as long as it had something between its legs and a wallet full of cash or a way to get some. Hope she chokes on that banana skirt."

Ben expected mortification from Denny's set at the butchering of the Queen of Harlem, but they poured more champagne for the butcher, drew their chairs closer, and licked their lips over the delectable gossip.

Then came the saucy colored girls. Neither as naïve as the buds nor as hardened as the survivors, they wisecracked and chicken-necked and their laughter clattered off the walls in reaction to their own salty jokes. They smiled a lot, drank plenty, thrusted themselves into life, and held back nothing. It made them lovable, seemingly invincible, and vulnerable.

The men:

The guys of *Chocolate Jubilee of 1926* were men in the basest sense: fluid in desire, ever-wavering in commitment. They were mysteries, yet transparent and easily deciphered. One of middling height, handsome as a king and quiet as a kitten, kept an arm around a certain saucy girl and his eyes on a particularly ripe bud. Then there was the male couple, sometimes affectionate and inseparable, other times snuggling up to the men of Denny's set. Denny's men would amble outside with one or the other of these guys for some fresh Paris air, then return with their hair mussed, their white dinner jackets rumpled. Rumors spread that the male couple could be had—one, the other, or both together—for a price.

These *Chocolate Jubilee* men were stage people: transient and itinerant by nature. They didn't know what would become of them three, five, six months from now, so they lived and ate and loved while they could, as much as they could. Ben watched the couple's suavely lean dancers' bodies and cheered them on.

He understood them.

Since the split with Baby Back, Ben had sunk himself in Paris's shadows. Daily. Nightly. Loving while he could, as much as he could. Not *loving,* really. More like feeding. Being fed. Being fed on. The shadows welcomed him, offering delights and guiltless pleasure. Even in daylight the shadows hummed, like the afternoon in the Montparnasse train station restroom. Men entered and set about their business like automatons, looking into no one's eyes, saying nothing except, perhaps, *excusez-moi* if they stumbled into someone's way. And even this was said quickly, with their eyes on their shoes and a sharp pivot left or right to get out of the way. A man he'd been casing held his gaze steady like a rope to reel him in. Ben halfheartedly washed his hands in the sink. A mirror hung above it. They looked at each other in the reflection. The man walked to a urinal and paused, put a finger to his temple, scratched deliberately, then proceeded inside, leaving the door ajar. Ben dried his hands, walked into the urinal. It was over quickly. It usually was. And, as always, in that transitory moment right after, Ben asked himself if it was worth it. *Why am I doing this? To forget Baby Back? Maybe just to forget.*

The moment over, Ben smoothed down the sleeves of his jacket, adjusted his tie, cocked his hat, and exited the urinal.

Chez LeRoi could have been renamed Chez Baby Back. His hit records had cemented a loyal following and secured him occasional gigs in some larger venues. Glo received less stage time as the show—formerly *her* dominion—became Baby Back's.

"What the fuck am *I* there for?" Glo screamed, waking Ben, as she thundered around the apartment one morning in her housecoat and slippers, flask in hand. "That big-headed fool done took over!"

She screamed and pleaded as if he could reverse time, transform things to the way they were before Baby Back barnstormed Chez LeRoi. He squashed the pink pillow onto his head and tried to go back to sleep.

"You're ignoring me?" Glo said. "Excuse you. You're living in *my* house and sleeping on *my* couch and your little, skinny, poetry-writing ass is ignoring me? Fuck that. You can find somewhere else to live."

That afternoon, he did.

A boardinghouse in rue Condorcet, way south of the Place Pigalle, almost on the outskirts of Montmartre. The room occupied the rear corner of the first floor where sunlight waged a losing battle. The lone window looked out onto an alley fortressed by a stone wall. Shadows bathed the room. But it had warmth. It was clean. The hardwood floors had been kept up. The cherrywood desk, chair, wardrobe, and headboard were worn with age and use, but still lovely.

Ben unpacked his things, stood back to admire his new home. He smiled until he saw the double bed. A bed with no grandma quilt. He missed it. He missed Baby Back.

They hadn't spoken. If they happened upon each other at Chez LeRoi or out and about in Montmartre, they kept walking. No greeting. No sidelong look. He stayed at the club because he wanted to be near Glo. And he refused to back down from Baby Back yet again.

"Looks like he done moved out that boardinghouse y'all was living in," Norman the bartender had said. "Making so much money from them records, he rented a fancy place in rue des Abbesses."

What Norman omitted, but Ben had heard through gossip, was that Clifford spent a lot of time in Baby Back's new, fancy place.

He thought of their breakup as The Demise: capital *T,* capital *D*—investing it with all the weight it deserved. One more notch in the increasingly vivid history of one Ben Charles, the current phase being solitude in a warm room flush with shadows in a city with its share of them. A miracle city where Negro skin could illuminate the shadows like a torch, attract white moths to the flame. In those moments Negro Ben was strong, handsome, worthy.

* * *

A blizzard had deposited a cargo of snow on Montmartre. More was falling. Ben trudged across the tightly packed snow on the Place Pigalle. It crunched as he walked. He looked up at Sacré-Cœur, its white façade nearly invisible against the falling blur. He wondered how Paris's snow-filled ruts and grooves looked from that hill. He wanted to go up there, but didn't.

Christmas was coming. It was December, but the thought of Christmas hadn't occurred to him until last night. He had spent last Christmas with Baby Back in Harlem, but this year the trumpeter would be with Clifford. Ben had been trying to write—a tepid poem with no marrow in its bones, the only sort he seemed capable of lately—when he realized it. The thought had tormented him away from his typewriter, through the snowstorm, and into Claire de Lune, known for its large contingent of sailors and the old crone who acted variously as advice-giver and raconteur. He smoked reefer, snorted cocaine, and awoke that morning in a bed, some-where, with three muscular sailors. He wondered if he'd ever see them again, and if he'd recognize them if he did. Wasn't one mus-cular sailor just like any other? In the end, only one thing mattered: that fleeting, cardinal moment of release.

He looked up at Sacré-Cœur again, then walked to work. Nor-man was behind the bar, polishing champagne glasses.

"Hey, Norm. How you doing?"

Norman put a glass down as Ben went to the spiral stairs. "Ben. I gotta tell you something."

"Tell me in a minute. I want to say hi to Glo. Don't get to see her as much since she kicked me out."

"She ain't up there."

Ben continued up the stairs. "Sure she is. She's singing tonight."

"Damn it, I'm telling you, she ain't up there!"

He had been taking the steps two at a time, but now made a cau-tious descent. "What happened, Norm? Why ain't she up there?"

"LeRoi fired her. Just happened a half hour ago. When he told her, she cussed him out, threw shit at him. Screamed something about how Baby Back took over and how unfair it was." Norman chuckled. "Told LeRoi he could go to hell and then fuck himself when he got there. Looks like that dressing room gonna be Baby Back's now."

Ben visualized him strutting down the spiral stairs and onto the stage to mad applause. The royal *entrée* of Chez LeRoi's undisputed king.

"I sure is gonna miss Glo," Norman said. "I hope she lands on her feet. Jobs is scarce. Even for talented colored folks."

Ben sat on the bottom step. Norman shook his head and went back to polishing glasses, as if he had played his part in the drama and could be of no further use.

# 39

Chez LeRoi was wild that night. Virus-wild. The band rampaged like it was on the warpath, slinging out songs with a velocity and volume that felt like the club would blow up. Everybody—patrons, waiters, Norman—*everybody*—was drinking or drunk or high or striving to be. Snooty patrons, normally quick to censure poor etiquette in others, ate steaks with their fingers and wiped them on tablecloths. Neckties loosened. Men exiled dinner jackets to the backs of chairs. Women kicked off high heels and tossed them into a pile near the bar. A woman over here sat with her legs loosed wide apart, torso tilted forward as she smoked a cigar, while one over there placed a hand on one hip as she gobbled champagne right from the bottle.

The *Chocolate Jubilee* troupe was there. A young bud took to the stage to teach a rich gentleman the Charleston, although he persisted in appropriating her waist as if a lesson in close waltzing better suited him. One half of the male couple slipped outside with a man in Denny's set while Denny herself luxuriated in the lap of the actor whose arm normally lived around the saucy girl. Said saucy girl was triangulated in a corner between Madeline and Charlotte—two stalwart members of Denny's set. The threesome snorted cocaine from a sterling-silver cigarette case. Madeline obsessed over the girl's soft brown arms while Charlotte probed her breasts.

Ben, drunk as everybody else, tripped and dropped a tray of langoustine, spilling them on the floor. He delivered them anyway to a table of *Chocolate Jubilee* women—some of the hardened survivors who observed the mischief in Chez LeRoi with much shaking of heads and clucking of tongues as they smoked cigarettes and tossed back double shots of bourbon.

"Here you go, ladies," Ben said, placing the langoustine on the table. He noticed a minute speck of dirt on one of them. "Let me know what else I can get y'all."

They ignored him, like uppity house niggers turning up their noses at a field slave. In the States he was their equal; here he was the help. His presence gifted them with the coveted opportunity to pretend they were white. Ben smiled, thinking they ought to thank him. If Glo had been there, they would have laughed about it.

En route to the kitchen, he saw Baby Back sitting at the bar, Clifford Treadwell all but in his lap. Baby Back touched Clifford's face with a languid air, fingered his knee without heat, without heart. His hands, always greedy on Ben, acted stingy on his new lover. But Clifford acted like a man in love. His touch was possessive. He stood in the gap between Baby Back's outspread knees and massaged the trumpeter's neck, kneading it with strokes that were firm, slow, significant. Clifford Treadwell had staked his claim and now buttressed it with menacing looks that he hurled around the room like bolts, taunting anyone to challenge him. A bolt struck Ben. The two contemplated each other, two adversaries who had warred over a prize, one now the victor. Baby Back stared emptily. A heartless hand fingered Clifford's waist.

He was no longer Ben's. The confirmation sent him fleeing into the kitchen.

"This pain ain't never going away, is it?" he said aloud.

The chef looked at him like he was crazy, then returned to seasoning a pot of bouillabaisse.

Later, the band swung notes into the crowd, then segued into a marchlike beat, as if a king was about to enter. Because a king was.

A spotlight hit the top of the spiral staircase, lingered there, empty, and then Baby Back stepped into it. Chez LeRoi erupted as he tramped and vamped his way down. When he reached the stage, it erupted again as he moved into position. He turned his back to the crowd and wiggled his big backside in a bump-and-grind. Ben half expected him to strip. And then rapture exploded out of his horn as he slugged out one number after another. The crowd consumed them—*him*—like addicts. Ben watched, addicted like everyone else. His star of a former lover had never radiated more powerfully. His light eclipsed everything.

"Ben!" Denny shouted. "My glass is empty. I cannot continue to exist without more champagne."

Ben fetched more.

"*Monsieur,* more champagne?" Ben asked her escort du jour.

This escort was an oddity. He hadn't rushed to light her cigarettes, laughed at her jokes, or paid transfixed attention to her. All night he had stared around the club, a cigarette between his fingers.

"*Monsieur?*" Ben said again. "*Encore du champagne?*"

The man returned to earth, searched for the person who had dragged him to attention, and found Ben. His gaze started at Ben's face, plummeted to his feet, and moseyed its way up to his face again.

"*Oui, s'il vous plaît,*" the escort said.

Ben poured.

"I am Sebastien. *Et vous?*"

"*Moi, c'est Ben.*"

Denny cleared her throat, inserted a cigarette between her lips, and waited.

"*Vous êtes de l'Amérique?*" Sebastien said.

"*Oui, monsieur,*" Ben said. "And, yes, I lived in Harlem."

"Then Harlem was extremely lucky."

Ben knew better than to feel flattered. He was aware that Sebastien had barely looked at Denny all evening, directing his attention instead to the *Chocolate Jubilee* men. His eyes had been stuck to them. Sebastien's flirtation made Ben feel second best. He was insulted. But it didn't matter: He had no desire to play with Denny's toys.

She cleared her throat again, still waiting for a light.

Sebastien touched Ben's arm. "It was very nice meeting you. *Excusez-moi, s'il vous plaît.* I have neglected Baroness Deneuve."

He smiled at Ben. He struck a match.

Ben went to the bar to collect champagne for some *Chocolate Jubilee* people—a clutch of fresh buds whom he had watched grow up. He'd eavesdropped as their voices became progressively raspier and grown alarmed (though by no means surprised) at the cheerful venom that sparked off their now quicker-witted tongues.

"Hey, Norm. Bottle of champagne when you get a chance."

Norman, in the midst of mixing a drink, nodded.

"I bet a certain girl singer's sitting home right now, sopping up champagne. To ease the pain. Or gin, more likely."

Clifford. He sat with hands folded on the bar like a schoolboy, a snifter of brandy in front of him. Ben had been too preoccupied to notice him.

"Norman!" Clifford said.

The bartender placed Ben's champagne on the bar. "Yes, Mr. Treadwell?"

The staff was now required to address Baby Back and Clifford as *Mr. Johnston* and *Mr. Treadwell.*

"I think the show's really good tonight," Clifford said. "With Glo gone, there's a lot less trash on our stage. You agree, don't you, Norman?"

Norman looked from Clifford to Ben.

"Norman," Clifford said, "I asked you a question. Don't you agree that, without Glo, there's a lot less trash on our stage?"

Sweat pimpled the bartender's forehead. "Yes, Mr. Treadwell. I agree."

Caught between his job and Ben, he chose the job. Ben couldn't blame him. What he *could* do was take that champagne to the fresh buds. But he stayed put. His hatred tacked his feet to the spot. He viewed Clifford in profile, taking in the treasured light skin; the gray eyes; the nose, smaller, pudgier, much less elegant than he'd noticed before. But it was the grin—mean and self-satisfied—that turned his stomach. This was indeed Baby Back's new lover. The king's consort who had engineered his ascent and now powered his reign. The force that Ben never came close to being.

"I'm glad I got her fired," Clifford said.

"*You* got her fired?" Ben said.

"Norman. Refill." Clifford didn't speak again until the bartender refilled his snifter. Ben waited. "I went to LeRoi, told him, 'Fire Glo or Baby Back quits.'" He looked at Ben dead-on. "No one's going to miss her. No one's going to miss that fat, black drunk."

He reached for his snifter, but Ben was quicker. He grabbed it and sloshed the brandy in Clifford's face, then yanked him off his stool by the lapels of his jacket. The shock paralyzed Clifford's legs and they caved under him as Ben wrenched him away from the bar.

"Ben! Ben! No!" Norman shouted as he hurried from behind the bar, but in loud, crazy Chez LeRoi, the fight blended in with the rest of the hijinks and no one else noticed.

He held Clifford by the throat with one hand, squeezing tight as his enemy tried to dislodge his grip. Ben pulled back his free arm, knuckled his fist, took a moment to look Clifford in the eyes, and then socked him a grand punch that leveled him. But Clifford picked himself up and charged at his opponent with a wildness that Ben hadn't thought him capable of.

And now the denizens of Chez LeRoi *did* notice as the two battled. Norman tried to pry them apart, but Clifford shoved him hard and he crashed headfirst into a table, then lay unmoving. Everyone else stayed on the sidelines, some shouting at them to stop, others egging them on, no one intervening. A few climbed onto tables for a better view as Clifford grabbed Ben by the throat with both hands and began to strangle him. At last, someone intervened. Baby Back flung Clifford to the floor, seized the wheezing, coughing Ben in his arms, and held him. He caressed his neck and back. He wouldn't let go.

"What the hell's going on here?"

LeRoi Jasper stood at the entrance in a black wool coat with a fur-lined collar, a white woman wearing chinchilla at his side. Ben pulled away from Baby Back and surveyed the havoc. Norman was sitting up with a bloody gash on the side of his head, the contents of the table he had crashed into scattered about the floor.

"Vance! Get Norman in the office," Mr. Jasper said. "Kyle, you cover the bar. Baby Back, Clifford, Ben—into the kitchen." He flicked on his charm and addressed his customers. "*Mes chers amis,* I apologize for what has happened here this evening. Please forgive us. You know at Chez LeRoi we care only for your entertainment and your comfort. Two bottles of champagne for each table—on the house!" To the band: "You guys onstage, play something. Anything. Now!"

Once in the kitchen, Clifford wasted no time. "He attacked me. Get rid of him. Now, LeRoi."

"Ben, is that true?"

Panic froze in Ben's chest. But when he looked at Clifford— face bleeding, lower lip swelling, and yet holding himself with the imperious air of the privileged—it thawed. "Hell yeah. I attacked the bastard. And I'd do it again."

"You're fired."

He should have expected it, but it blindsided him. He couldn't let it happen. Far more significant than the loss of a good job, being fired meant that Clifford Treadwell had won.

"Baby Back," Ben said, "you can stop this. You're the only one who can."

From the dining room came the band's rendition of an up-tempo number. In the quiet kitchen, Clifford seemed to dare Baby Back to defy him, Mr. Jasper looked nervous, and Ben maintained a stern eye on his former lover. All three awaited the trumpeter's decision.

"Good luck, Ben," Baby Back said.

As he left the kitchen, he did something Ben had never ever seen him do—he hung his head like a man with no confidence. A moment later, his horn slowed, slowed, slowed that up-tempo tune down to something like a funeral dirge.

# 40

He dreamed of arms. Arms confident and possessing, encircling him in a defensive grip, draped around him with snug familiarity, as if part of his own body, as if they knew him.

He began to wake and fought it. He wanted to stay in those arms. As he ascended out of sleep and into the morning, the maelstrom of last night played in his head. He gloated over the triumph of Baby Back tossing Clifford to the floor. It made him smile. He felt so good. And then, eyes still shut, he yawned and stretched. The yawn triggered pain in his throat and jaw. The stretch made his abdomen hurt.

Then he remembered.

He sat up, shaken by his new circumstances: unemployed in a city with its share of unemployed people. Parisians loved Negroes, but job-hunting Negroes held an advantage only if they could sing or dance or play an instrument. But he didn't have to panic yet: He had hoarded his generous tips from Chez LeRoi's wealthy patrons and still had most of the money Mr. Kittredge gave him. The exchange rate favored those blessed with American money: A single dollar netted nearly fifty francs.

He wanted to write. He closed his eyes, tried to will a poem into existence. When that didn't work, he looked at his typewriter as if a muse would spring from the keys. None did. So he grabbed a bottle of whiskey and some reefer. Sedated, the dream of arms reclaimed him.

He should have known Glo's Christmas tree decorations would be pink. Pink bulbs. Pink ribbons. Pink electric lights. Ben and Glo attached the ornaments with the enthusiasm of mourners.

"Ain't we a sight?" Glo said. "We got about as much Christmas spirit as we got jobs."

"You know, I was thinking."

"Uh-oh."

"Maybe you could go back to singing at Mon Club."

"Fuck you, Benjy." She poured them coffee, spiked it with gin. "Yeah, that's what I need: to see you shaking your thing in them shadows."

They placed the last ornament, then stepped back to review their work. It was a parody of Christmas with its overload of cheap pink baubles. They lit some reefer. Snow fell outside, making the gray day grayer.

"You going to Mon Club tonight?" Glo asked.

"Girl, I ain't got no job, remember? I can't be spending money at Mon Club."

"But the urinals is free, ain't they? Mmm-hmm."

She got him. Got him so bad, he didn't attempt a response.

He was inhaling a helping of reefer when she blurted out, "Hey, Benjy. Why? Why the urinals and Mon Club and all that? I mean, do whatever the fuck you want, sugar—Glo ain't judging. But wouldn't you rather be in love?"

Glo's cute curiosity allowed him to forgive her intrusiveness. He reclined on the sofa, head lounging against the pink cushions. He dragged on the reefer, then looked out the window and watched the snow as it evolved from flurries into something that might accumulate.

Love.

You could have love, or you could have pleasure, and rarely did the two commingle. Love was difficult. Pleasure was not. And Ben's pursuits in the shadows had unloosed a coldhearted desire for it. Pleasure had to be mined where it was found. It couldn't be bypassed. You had to pursue it, take it, relish it, bite hard on each morsel and glean every sliver of paradise. Pleasure was instant, achievable. And when you had your fill or you got bored or it wasn't fun anymore, you could just walk away. In that way, it was a lot like love.

He used to retreat to his writing to find pleasure. But as he sought refuge more and more in the shadows, his poetry receded. The more he went to the urinals, the less he seemed able to write. Or was it that the less he was able to write, the more time he spent in the urinals? All he knew was that the loss of his poetry was like a precious child gone missing.

"Benjy? You ain't answered me."

"Sure, I'd rather be in love. But the urinals is closer. And free."

Weeks later, he had inquired at every club, restaurant, and shop, and exhausted every job prospect in Montmartre. Then he checked around the Louvre and along the Champs Élysées; crossed the Seine and searched in Montparnasse, St. Germaine, and the dimly lit cafés of the Latin Quarter. Nothing. It depressed him. On his way home from his inquiries one day, the depression converted to anger and the anger escalated into something that needed venting. He sat at his typewriter as soon as he arrived in his room in rue Condorcet.

Good words, the right words, wouldn't come. Shapes of poems formed in his head, and then cheated him. A mound of crumpled paper accumulated on the floor.

"Damn it. Damn it. Damn it. Damn it!"

He tore the latest attempt from the typewriter, looked at the sorry excuse for a poem, and then kicked the chair so hard it thudded to the floor. He picked an empty whiskey bottle out of the trash and smashed it against the door. He had lifted up the typewriter to hurl it against the wall when someone banged on the door.

"Ben? What's going on in there? Ben! Open up! Open this goddamn door!"

The voice was resonant, concerned, familiar. Baby Back's. Ben tiptoed over the broken glass and opened the door. The trumpeter stood on the other side, big and handsome and looking younger, as if living his dream agreed with him.

He pushed past Ben, almost got snagged on the broken glass.

"What the hell? You by yourself? I thought you was getting beat up. I was ready to bust somebody's head in."

Ben buried himself in Baby Back's arms before he could stop himself. He inhaled his scent, as familiar as his own. Then he remembered that Baby Back belonged to Clifford and he broke away.

"You're in here breaking shit, throwing heaps of paper on the floor," Baby Back said. "And unemployed to boot." He winked. "You sure is lost without me, ain't you?"

That devilish smile. That evil, gleeful wit. Ben felt their pull. He almost retraced his steps back to his former lover's arms.

"What you doing here?" he asked. "How'd you know where I lived?"

"When you're Baby Back Johnston, it ain't hard getting information." He winked again. "When you're Baby Back Johnston, it ain't hard getting whatever you want."

That plush baritone. That seductive arrogance.

"Maybe I should try that sometime," Ben said. "Being Baby Back Johnston."

"You should." He looked around the room. "You wouldn't be living in this dump."

Ben ditched himself on the bed and laughed. Baby Back laughed and ditched himself there, too. He wore a fantastic suit and a pair of two-toned wingtips—dark black and shameless red. Ben lay back on the bed, both feet on the floor. Baby Back did, too, but was careful not to wrinkle his suit.

"I may not have a place to live at all—dump or otherwise— since your Cliffy got me fired and I can't find no job."

Baby Back sat up quick. "Don't do that. Don't try that shit. You know you hit him first."

Ben fretted that he'd leave, but he lay back down.

Quiet.

"You ever think we'd be in bed together again?" Baby Back said.

"You call this *in bed?* We got all our clothes on and our feet on the floor."

Baby Back removed his shoes and jacket, then laid down fully. Ben did the same. They lay side by side, facing up, not touching.

"The job hunt ain't going so good, huh?" Baby Back said.

"Should've kept your fist to yourself."

Ben's turn to sit up quick. "Is that why you're here? To rub it in?"

"You used to like it when I rubbed it in."

*That devilish smile. That evil, gleeful wit.*

Ben lay back down. "Does Cliffy know you're here? Why *are* you here?"

He closed his eyes. Something tickled his foot.

"I'm sorry I didn't stop LeRoi from firing you," Baby Back said.

Ben wanted to climb up to Sacré-Cœur and shout *Hallelujah!* The first time Mr. Baby Back Johnston had *ever* apologized to him, and with humility at that. Then he recalled Baby Back's conniving, and everything he did to Glo, and the humility seemed a sham. He wanted to be in bed with the man he first met in Harlem. Then he remembered that he was.

"But the big reason I'm here . . ." Baby Back said.

"Finally."

Baby Back kicked him. "I know a guy owns a jazz club. Needs a waiter. Job's yours if you want it."

"I definitely want it. Thank you."

"Café Valentin on rue Frochot. You start tomorrow. Ask for Monsieur Rameau."

"*Rue* Frochot? *Monsieur* Rameau? Baby Back, you spoke French! I guess I *was* a good influence on you."

Baby Back yawned. "You sure as hell was. Is. Mr. Charles. Mr. Poet."

The room was quiet until the big man began to snore. Ben let the sound lull him. He didn't know he was smiling as his eyelids drifted down, down, down, down.

When he woke up, Baby Back was gone.

# 41

Café Valentin was off the Place Pigalle on a murky side street trolled by cocaine peddlers and prostitutes. It was a hole-in-the-wall, a little larger than Chez LeRoi, and as dog-eared as its surroundings, but its wood floors and walls of peeling plaster gave it a bohemian class.

Baby Back told Ben he'd be the new waiter, but neglected to mention that he would be the *only* waiter. He also left out that Ben would be the bartender. And the kitchen boy. And the cashier. The cooking and the entertainment would be the only areas not under his charge. He panicked when the proprietor informed him of this legion of responsibilities.

"Do not worry, Monsieur Charles," Monsieur Rameau said. "You will find Café Valentin far less taxing than that man's—please forgive me—*LeRoi Jasper's*—establishment."

Ben repressed a snicker and wondered what unpleasant history existed between the two entrepreneurs.

Monsieur Rameau's shiny black hair was forged into place with oil, then divided down the middle by a part so severe it looked as if it had been carved into his scalp. He had massive black clumps of wool for eyebrows, a matching mustache, and a monocle on his right eye.

"I am not here much. It will be up to you to open and close and order supplies. You will work six days and be off one. On that day, another waiter will run the club. *Vous avez des questions? Bon. Vous commencerez ce soir.*"

The place was even darker than Mon Club. Shadows outfoxed light. Ben needn't have worried about the quadruple threat of waiting tables, tending bar, cashiering, and playing kitchen boy. While steady, Café Valentin lacked the craziness of Chez LeRoi. The Baroness Deneuves of Paris didn't congregate there. Neither did entertainers, tourists, or slummers.

Café Valentin's clientele was comprised of people of the night.

Prostitutes wandered in alone, then wandered back out with a gentleman in tow. On Ben's inaugural evening, a man in an expensive suit slinked in, met minutes later by another. They leaned in close, spoke in low notes. There was an exchange of items, but in the somber light, Ben couldn't make them out. Later, a stylish young woman came, soon joined by a stately and commanding man in his fifties who looked accustomed to getting his way. They ate dinner, then left together. But the man paused in the doorway and looked up and down the street before exiting.

At the back of the room, a quartet of musicians jazzed it soft and easy. No star soloists. No vocalist. Just a steady repertoire of low-key tunes that suited the temperament of Ben's new workplace. The musicians wore hats with the brims pulled down so low, Ben perceived only shadows where he assumed faces lived.

At two a.m., just a few customers huddled about. Business was so dead, Ben sat on a stool behind the bar with a cigarette in one hand, a snifter of brandy in the other. He took a puff, then a swig, a puff, then a swig, as the band teased out jazz.

He was bored. But it was a clean boredom. Uncluttered and white with quiet. Paris was rarely quiet. The same was true of Harlem, and Dogwood, too, really. It wasn't often he found a virgin space to nest in, free of noise and floating on a lake of peace. Peace. An elusive and fragile thing to claim. If you wished to hold it long, you had to hold it carefully, and who in this world was capable of that? So he let this ephemeral slip of peace rest in his palm like a baby bird. Soon it would open its wings, take to the air, be gone, gone, gone. It would return, eventually, and in the interim he would seek its substitute in the shadows. It wouldn't be the same, but a poor substitute trumped none. Temporary intimacy topped nights alone beset by the affliction of failed love and unborn poems that mocked.

Another puff, another swig.

The bird had flown. Peace hightailed it. Its absence instantly embittered him. With peace gone he was left with plain old boredom, and not the clean kind. But the itchy, restless kind that begged to be filled.

A customer entered and sat at the bar. The brim of his straw boater obscured his face. He kept his head down. Ben swallowed the last of his brandy and greeted him. He didn't bother to hide the snifter.

"*Bon soir, monsieur. Qu'est-ce que vous voudriez boire?*"

"I will have whatever *you* are drinking," the man said.

Ben poured him a brandy.

"*Merci.* Harlem was, indeed, extremely lucky to have you, Monsieur Ben. And now Paris is, as well."

He removed his hat, lifted his head.

"I'll be damned," Ben said. "Denny's escort. The one who wouldn't pay attention to her."

"Norman said that I would find you here."

"Find? That means you were looking."

"Indeed."

Ben refilled his own brandy. The band ebbed into winding-down mode. Not *le jazz-hot,* but cooling-down, cooling-off music. Music of the night. A prostitute sat at the bar's far end. She smoked a cigarette as she eyed the two men.

"Why were you looking?" Ben asked.

"I wanted to talk to you about Harlem. It fascinates me."

"You and everyone else. Sometimes I think if one more person asks me about Harlem or if I know Josephine Baker—which I don't—I'll shoot them."

Sebastien recoiled. "You sound resentful."

"A little. There's more to being Negro than Harlem and Josephine Baker." Then, mostly to himself, "More than jazz and nightclubs, too."

Ben stubbed out his cigarette, retrieved another. Sebastien lit it for him.

"Denny had to move heaven and earth to get you to light hers. I must be special."

They appraised each other by the dim electric light and the full moon sidling in through the window. Sebastien was about Ben's age. A dab of ruddiness tinged each cheek. His dark, slicked-back hair curled slightly. His high forehead held eyebrows set low over his eyes. A prominent *V* in the center of his upper lip dramatized his mouth. The folds of his chin tried to gather into a cleft, but didn't quite. His neck, slender and long, was mounted to a pair of narrow shoulders that sat atop a lean torso.

"Are you going to tell me how you ended up with Denny?" Ben asked. "Or just sit there looking at me?"

"How do you Americans say? I can walk and chew gum at the same time."

Ben topped off their brandies. "You like Americans?"

"*Oui.*"

"Especially the colored ones."

"Does that make me awful?" Sebastien said.

"It makes you a French cliché." He took a fat drag off his cigarette. He saw from Sebastien's downcast eyes, the flood of ruddiness to his cheeks, that he had hurt him. "I shouldn't have said that. Forgive me?" He extended his hand, expecting a handshake. But Sebastien leaned in and kissed it. The prostitute at the end of the bar smiled.

"I am a painter," Sebastien said. "I had a showing of my work at a very small gallery in Montparnasse. On opening night, only two people attended. They liked my work—or so they said—and told me they had a rich friend who would love my paintings and could possibly serve as my patroness and would I like to meet her. *Oui, certainement,* I said."

"Then you found out what you had to do in exchange for her patronage."

"*Oui.*"

"And you did it anyway."

Sebastien took a long drag off his cig. "My rent was late. No one wants to be homeless. But I will not see her again. I cannot bear to."

Ben opened a new bottle of brandy, took a swig, passed it to Sebastien. He swigged, passed it back. Low, dark notes trickled off the piano, italicized by the murmur of the brass and the banjo's steadying strum.

"Where do you live?" Ben asked.

"Montmartre. A boardinghouse in rue la Bruyère."

"I thought all the artists moved to Montparnasse." Ben took another, deeper swig.

"Careful," Sebastien said. "You are working."

Ben gestured at the mostly empty club. "You call this work? You should see what I had to do when I waited tables in New York. Or Chez LeRoi, for that matter."

"You lost that job. After that fight with that horrible man."

"I forgot you were there that night. You should have come to my rescue."

"Someone beat me to it. It seemed the fight was caused by... what do you Americans call it? A love triangle."

Ben laughed out loud. The prostitute leaned toward them, as if she wanted in on the joke. The brandy caught up with Ben. He closed his eyes, feeling woozy. Something touched his cheek, something light and warm. He opened his eyes. Sebastien was caressing his cheek, his touch just firm enough, just tender enough. Ben closed his eyes again and let him. Sebastien's fingers feathered random loops up, down, and across his neck and throat, pressed his temples, cradled his cheek. Before he could help himself, Ben turned his face into the cup of that hand and kissed it. Sebastien's finger meandered to his mouth, then took one full minute to travel the length of his bottom lip. Ben got dizzy, started to swoon, opened his eyes to steady himself. The prostitute placed some coins on the bar and left, nodding her approval.

Sebastien looked around. Café Valentin was empty. "It is just us and this band." He leaned in toward Ben, close, as if he would kiss him. "Tell me, what do you do? Besides wait on tables?"

He had dropped into a whisper so patently suggestive that Ben wasn't sure which to address—the question or the innuendo.

"What do you mean? What do you really want to know?"

"I want to know who you are."

He still felt the impression of Sebastien's feather touch. He lifted the brandy to his mouth, but thought better of it. "I'm a writer. I write poems. Or try to."

"That is very close to what I do. I paint with a brush and colors. You paint with words."

"Strange," Ben said. "You were escorting Denny and now you're here with me, in this hole-in-the-wall, talking about poems and painting. I've seen her with many, many other handsome young men. *Elle a une collection*."

"Ahh. You find me handsome."

Ben was caught.

"I find you handsome, also," Sebastien said.

"Handsome? Not wild or exotic? Not sensual? Or primitive?"

Sebastien eyed him, perplexed. "*Non*. Bitter perhaps. Angry. Hurting, I suspect. But no less handsome."

The band played something airy and quiet. It floated through the walls of Café Valentin like breath. The tune was lean and spare, like carefully selected words in a poem or thoughtful strokes on a canvas.

# 42

The room was tiny. Paintings everywhere. Hanging on the crude, plaster walls. Perched on easels. Stacked upright on the floor, one after another like dominoes. Some completed, others sketched in chalk outline, waiting to be filled in with color. A washbasin rested on a stand in one corner. Nearby a freight of books weighed down a chest of drawers. More books in orderly loads on the floor. In the middle of the floor was a rug, faded and unraveling at the edges and splotched with spilled paint, but thick and warm and soft. The floor underneath was rough wood. By the room's lone window sat a small table with pens and paper and more books. It seated two.

The window gave a perfect view of the moon, but it was the art that held Ben's attention. He took his time examining each brushstroke, each dab of color, as if by studying the art, he could learn Sebastien.

His style married the grace of the Impressionists with the jagged electricity of the Cubists, the result the mixed-blood offspring of the Old Masters and the new modernism. There were landscapes whose breadth and detail dazzled; portraits whose subjects seemed live flesh and bone on the canvas. In one series of paintings, the Eiffel Tower held court above the Paris skyline while another presented patrons—sometimes refined, sometimes ornery—drinking it up in cafés.

And there were nudes, so many, divided into two camps. The first consisted of slender-waisted young men—some white, some Negro—with smooth, flat chests and skin that glowed in a bath of sunlight or moonlight. The boys frolicked on boats and in verdant forests or lounged on rocks or beaches, sometimes solo but more often in pairs and groups. The settings were idyllic, pastoral; the subjects idealized and rosy.

The other camp was all ruddy-skinned youths with dark curls and sex in their eyes, partnered with sailors or workmen in seedy rooms, a nearby bed always prominently featured. The sailors had big backs and hair on their barrel chests and in the pits of their arms. Often a sailor sat or stood while a youth knelt before him. Ben could almost smell the grimy rooms, the sailors' sweat. In both camps of nudes, the men's privates were teasingly, frustratingly ob-scured. A leg placed just so, a piece of furniture that happened to be waist-high.

Overwhelmed by the amount of art in the small room, Ben asked, "Do you paint every day?"

"Most every day, yes."

And now Ben felt envious and unworthy because of his own gift held hostage. His hardheaded child who refused to come when called. He began to cry. Sebastien had been shadowing him as he perused the paintings. But now, from behind, Ben felt hands on his back, a kiss on the back of his neck.

"Why are you crying, *mon chaton?*" Sebastien said.

"I love your work. I love that you *can* work. It's been months since I've been able to write. It's terrible. I miss it."

Another kiss.

"I'm afraid that I've lost it. That it'll never come back."

Sebastien wrapped his arms around him. "It will come back. I promise."

The reassurance felt good, the pressed warmth of it, even as he doubted it.

The room was quiet, except for the bustling Montmartre street life intruding from outside. A string of jazz notes from a nearby club flounced into the room.

"How do you know?" Ben said. "You don't know me."

"Come here."

He took Ben's hand and led him to the table by the window, sat him down, positioned a piece of paper and a pen in front of him, then sat in the chair opposite. "Let art inspire art." He smiled, patient, waiting.

The expectation spooked Ben. "I can't. Not like this. I—"

He turned away and Sebastien's paintings flew into his sights. Even in the darkening room, the colors shone. Wild colors: blood-red, wine-red, rust.

He picked up the pen. His fingers trembled with desire. Then, almost on their own, they began to scratch out words. He allowed the momentum to cruise through his fingers and the words surrendered themselves into verses.

> *Eclipse my shadows*
> *With your poignant day,*
> *With points of flame that dance on the peaks of candles.*
> *Light my way.*
> *Blind me.*

A poem! Rough, yes, and lopsided, but a poem still. Momentum stung his blood. He kept scratching out words, afraid finicky momentum would betray him if he stopped. He wouldn't let the pen leave the paper. He wrote and wrote and wrote. And Sebastien smiled, and waited.

# art
## 1927

# 43

Café Valentin's singer-less band gave Ben an idea.

During his fourth week of work, he wrote to Monsieur Rameau. He expressed gratitude at being hired for such a good position, humility at being entrusted with so much responsibility, and assurance that he loved the job. He drenched the band with praise for its understated power, its nuanced styling, which, Ben gushed, was steeped in the very fiber of the blues. But he wondered if a *singer* might add a bit of spice. He begged Monsieur Rameau's forgiveness for his presumption before requesting permission to hire a vocalist, asserting that that would distinguish the club from venues—like, say, Chez LeRoi—that did not feature one.

Rameau replied. He affirmed his satisfaction with Ben's work (the criteria being that Ben was sending him the receipts on time and the police had not raided or shut the place down) and granted permission to proceed with hiring a vocalist.

By week's end, Glo had begun her newest gig.

The band, initially perturbed by what it considered unnecessary musical intrusion, was soon won over—first by Glo's irreverent tongue and then by her talent. Word spread that a sassy, jazz-and-blues-singing colored woman had set fire to a shady hole-in-the-wall that served inexpensive drinks—and where one could, just as cheaply, purchase one's dessert of choice: crème brûlée, cocaine, reefer, or prostitutes. The nightly receipts at Monsieur Rameau's little club soared. An across-the-board win: Glo revived her career; Ben got to see her every night; Monsieur Rameau took more francs to the bank.

Just as the musically refurbished Café Valentin drew a new clientele, Ben drew Sebastien. Encouraged by the reception of his feather touch, he visited the club nearly every night. He'd loiter in the doorway, nervous and fidgety, until he spotted Ben waiting on a table or chatting up a customer. Then he'd glide to the bar and seat himself with the cheeky, upright pride of a man who's found exactly what he's looking for.

During the club's waning hours, as Glo and the moody band slow-jammed, Ben and Sebastien talked and smoked and took liberties with Monsieur Rameau's liquor. They got to know each other in those slow hours before closing, with after-midnight music drawling and only a few customers whispering in lightless corners. They talked art and music and poetry; discussed Paris, dreams, goals, hopes. But it was their hurts, their hardships, that connected them.

"I rarely had a conversation with my parents," Ben said one evening. "My father hardly spoke. My mother shouted orders at me, like I worked for her. But sometimes I forget it wasn't always like that."

He told Sebastien that he remembered a time—before the deaths of their offspring—when his folks were good to him. He had loved his ma's voice, its cushiony softness even when she laughed, which was often because his pa was a cutup, always ready with a joke or a story that was as funny as it was dumb. His folks had worked so hard the sweat stains on their clothes were permanently soaked onto the fabric. But they had been content with their lot. Or had accepted it, at least.

"Then their children started dying."

Pa's jokes stopped. Ma's mellow voice hardened like a stick that she leveled, daily, hourly, at her lone surviving son (because *he* was the lone survivor, instead of some other, more favorite child?).

"And when I needed them most they couldn't summon up love,

even then. All they could do was be ashamed. They sent me to that plantation because they were ashamed."

Sebastien didn't speak. He didn't take Ben's hand or rub his cheek or say, *It's all right. I understand.* Instead, he nodded. And that solemn nod bore an empathy too mighty to live in words or touch. The nod slumped. He hung his head. His lips creased into a smile laced with both sneering and sadness.

"My family was—*is*—renowned and extremely rich," Sebastien said. "So rich, they own estates all over Europe. So powerful, they insert themselves into politics with ease."

The family's fortune, he confided, was built first on slaving, then the modern slavery of colonialism and, finally, shipping.

"All I wanted to do was paint. But I was required to go into the family business."

His father sent him on an extended business trip to Abidjan in Côte d'Ivoire—Ivory Coast—the hub of the company's West African operation, to learn everything in preparation for one day running the business. He was attended to by a Monsieur de Lonval.

"De Lonval's role was both teacher and chaperone. He ran my family's operation in Ivory Coast. He saw to my every need and he despised me. He was very ambitious and he saw himself—not me—running the company one day. And now he was being ordered to train his competition."

Sebastien lived in Monsieur de Loval's house and was with him every day.

"I came to despise him as much as he despised me. I hated the work. My father forbade me to take my paints to Ivory Coast. He instructed de Lonval to make sure I did not paint and he demanded a report each week on my doings. I did not paint for six months. My father might as well have cut off my hands. At night I dreamed I was painting."

But he found solace.

"Akossi. A servant in de Lonval's house. Nimble of body, keen of mind. Young and beautiful and strong. Obviously no one could know about us. When Monsieur de Lonval or the other servants were present, Akossi and I were all business: master and black servant."

Akossi lived in the servants' quarters—a hut—behind de Lonval's house. At night, he sneaked into Sebastien's room.

"He could never spend the night. The possibility of getting caught was too great. That was our saddest regret: that we could never spend an entire night with each other."

But one night, they accidentally fell asleep in each other's arms. The next morning, de Lonval caught them.

"I was sent home *immédiatement*. De Lonval played the righteous, disgusted Christian, but I knew he was rejoicing because now I was out of his way. I do not know what became of Akossi."

His parents disowned him the moment he returned to France.

"I was allowed to take nothing with me. Can you imagine? Someone born rich and privileged, who has never been without means, having to fend for himself?"

He quickly learned what a young, attractive man could do to survive. And with whom. And how much to charge.

"Obviously I preferred men. But if I had to do it with women, so what? Bread costs the same regardless, *n'est pas?*"

So. They were both alone. Both orphans of a sort. Instead of an empathetic nod, Ben refilled their brandy snifters, lifted his in a toast and said, "Here's to loneliness. I didn't know it was color-blind until now."

Ben studied Sebastien's paintings. Every line and every texture, every acute and nuanced shade, while Sebastien pored over each verse in the poems Ben brought him. One day Ben examined a painting of a colored boy on a rocky stretch of beach. The boy's back was to the viewer as he stared out at the ocean, nude, lazing on a rock as the sun scattered a shower of rays that created both pools of light and shadows on his lissome body.

"I could write a poem based on this painting," Ben said.

"And I could paint a picture based upon this poem."

Three weeks later, Sebastien had a substantial sketch of a scene of two men slow-dancing, the shorter man's head against the chest of the taller, a pianist and sax player losing themselves in their serenade, the waltzing men—one was white, the other colored—finding themselves. And Ben presented his poem.

*Rough winds chafe*
*Your bronze skin.*
*You stare out at the sea,*
*A rock for a throne,*
*Exposed, forbidden,*
*As clouds skim the muted line of the horizon*
*And the tide rushes forward, seeking you.*

He knew Sebastien loved him. Or was falling in love with him. Or would. All Ben had to do was let him. While a romantic may have embraced the expedience, he distrusted such effortlessness. It was too easy. He had parachuted into every relationship he'd had, without looking, without seeing, without bothering to. Like shooting yourself from a cannon without considering what thorns you might land in. He distrusted love; its sugar promises; the way it commenced with a swelter, but then dissipated, far too quickly, to a lukewarm muddle.

So, for a while, he split his time between Sebastien and the instant intimacies in the shadows. Kiss Sebastien in the morning; fuck a sailor at night. Breakfast with Sebastien; tryst with a gentleman behind a statue in Parc Monceau at lunchtime. He didn't know if Sebastien knew. The shadows were his insurance against betrayal, against Sebastien's arms closing. The arms of the shadows, the arms *in* the shadows, never would.

But things began to change.

After Glo came aboard and made Café Valentin hop, the slow times grew few, replaced with hours that kept Ben crisscrossing the club, running from table to table and from the dining room to the kitchen to the bar and back again. During those hours, Sebastien sat at the bar or occupied a table in a corner, always keeping Ben in his sights even as he ran loops around the club. When he worked behind the bar, he felt Sebastien's eyes on him. Returning to the main room after an errand to the kitchen or the cellar, Sebastien's rigid shoulders relaxed, as if Ben's absence had been turmoil, his return a blessing.

One busy evening, Sebastien occupied himself by sketching at a corner table. At two a.m., Ben looked up to find him gone. He went to clear the table and found a rendering of himself. Sebastien had captured Ben in one of those harried moments when he rushed about fulfilling ten tasks at once. The penciled lines—some light and wispy, others durable as carving—streaked and shimmered on the paper. The effect endowed Ben with an authority, a worth, he wasn't sure he deserved. A worth he never felt from even the most inviting arms in the shadows.

—

# 44

Everything was as it should be at Café Valentin. The house was packed. Glo and company jammed a blues about tortuous, unrequited love.

> "Love treats me bad, and it ain't hardly fair.
> Love treats me bad, and it ain't hardly fair.
> But I won't live without love.
> Baby, that's more than I can bear.
>
> Come back, lover, I'll treat you like a king.
> Come back, lover, I'll treat you like a king.
> I promise I'll give up these blues,
> Find me a happy song to sing."

Ben went to the cellar for champagne and supplies. On his way back up, he heard the trombone firing out notes. But the sound was too piercing, not the muffled bleat of a trombone. He listened hard.

It was a trumpet firing out notes like shooting stars.

Ben rushed up the stairs. When he saw Baby Back onstage in his iconic performance mode—eyes shut, knees sinking—he hoped it was a mirage. Baby Back played with a beastliness that Ben had never heard from him. It enslaved the audience. Mesmerized eyes stuck to the trumpeter who filled the stage like it had been built for him.

Glo wasn't in sight. Ben snapped out of his trance and went to her "dressing room," a former storage closet haphazardly converted to accommodate Café Valentin's new singer.

"Glo?"

"I ain't coming out till that big-headed fool gets the fuck off my stage!"

He did two more numbers, kept the musicians on their toes with his twisting and turning of rhythm, the liberties he took with melody. Baby Back led, they followed. When he was done, the band paid him homage like new disciples. He shook hands and signed autographs as the audience hollered for more.

"What'd you think?" He plopped himself on a barstool.

"I think it takes a hell of a lot of nerve to waltz in here and take over," Ben said.

"Ain't my fault. I came in, folks recognized me—you know, from my picture on all those posters and record covers—and insisted I play. When fans insist..." He threw his hands up in faux innocence. "Gimme a drink. Brandy. And not no cheap shit either, Ben Charles. I got a image to keep up."

The man's egomaniacal charm still moved him. He fetched the drink.

"So. You're with a white guy now," Baby Back said.

"How'd you know?"

"When you're Baby Back Johnston, you know everything."

"I keep forgetting that. Yeah. He's white. You don't approve?"

"Frankly, no."

"*You're* with a white guy," Ben said.

"*Half*-white."

"Yeah. In the States, he'd only *half* ride them Jim Crow smokers. He'd *half* sit in the balcony at a Broadway play. He'd only get *half* lynched."

Baby Back's eyes fixed onto Ben's. The shade of Uncle Roland's mutilated body hovered between them.

"I shouldn't have said that," Ben said.

The trumpeter waved it off, sipped his brandy.

He looked good. Another fantastic suit. Diamond-studded cuff links. Rakish hat. The women didn't bother hiding their attraction. A few male customers wrestled their glances away from him, but their rogue eyes kept crawling back.

Baby Back downed some brandy, then hung his head. When he looked up, tears wet his face. "Got a letter today. My mama died. She got sick. Then sicker. They couldn't do nothing for her."

He laid his head on the bar and cried. The men sneaking looks and the women whose eyes had been plastered to him quickly looked away. Ben touched the big man's head, fought his instinct to climb over the bar and take him in his arms.

"I'm so damn sorry," Ben said. "But I know she didn't want for nothing in her last days."

Baby Back whisked the three-cornered silk handkerchief from his front suit pocket, wiped his face, and slung back a jolt of brandy. "You got that right. I did every thing I could for my folks since I made it big. New house. Money. Would've sent a doctor all the way from Paris to South Carolina if I'd known in time. Hey? Ben? You ever write your folks?"

"No."

"No? Not since you left Dogwood?"

"Excuse me. Gotta work my tables."

When he returned, the trumpeter was getting ready to depart.

"Thank you, Mr. Poet."

He headed for the door. Ben wanted to stop him, or at least delay his going. Wanted to have him for the tiniest moment longer.

"Baby Back. Why me? Why didn't you go to Clifford?"

Baby Back's lips parted. He seemed confused. His mouth hung open a while before he said, "That never even crossed my mind."

# 45

Ben was at Café Valentin by nine each evening to prepare for opening at ten. He worked until three a.m., with Sebastien joining him in the last hours, eating soup and drinking or sketching, the up-and-down, right-left sweeps of his pencil almost in rhythm with the band's after-midnight music. By four a.m., they'd leave together and go to Ben's room in rue Condorcet to play and then sleep and then play again until ten. From there they'd head to the Place Pigalle for a light breakfast—coffee, bread. Light because Sebastien had no money. Painting was his life, but not a reliable living. Rent and bills—many overdue—devoured whatever was generated from the occasional sale of his work. He worked odd jobs now and then, but was loath to take time away from his painting. He remained dreadfully, joyfully poor, but also proud, so though Ben could afford to provide a substantial meal for them both, Sebastien declined.

"You won't let me buy you a good breakfast," Ben said, "but you don't complain when I give you Monsieur Rameau's soup and liquor for free."

"That is different. That is, how do you Americans say? A fringe benefit." Proudly: "I am the lover of the man who runs the establishment. I am entitled to eat and drink for free."

They were in the middle of the Place Pigalle and surrounded by people, but Sebastien placed his hands on the soft skin of Ben's neck. His hands traveled up to Ben's cheeks, then descended to his shoulders before sliding down to his arms and squeezing.

They would arrive at Sebastien's room by noon for painting and writing. They thrived in that creative refuge, in their ambitious, disciplined work. Ben produced poems that he rejoiced over as he would over a lost child, thought dead, who had miraculously returned home.

> *My river was dammed.*
> *Some criminal god deterred my waters.*
> *My intrepid torrent got siphoned down to a sprinkle.*

But it was back, resurrected by his own will and the need to compensate for the time lost, the energy wasted, the poems still not yet conceived, because of his addiction to the shadows. Spurred also by a competitiveness that drove him to keep up with Sebastien's constant output.

This was different. Sebastien was different. Willful and Baby Back had enthralled Ben with their self-consumed swagger; demanded his subservience and gotten it. But Sebastien didn't swagger. He wasn't aggressive or confident. Melancholy roved beneath his surface. It was there when he smiled or laughed or kissed Ben or painted. Physically he was different, too, from Ben's previous lovers, his body's loveliness owing more to a svelte shapeliness than to the heady musculature of a Willful, the imposing size of a Baby Back. And so, during intimacy, they were equal. Neither dominated the other. Intimacy was a partnership.

"How is that, *mon chaton?* Is that all right? Are you all right?" Sebastien might ask as they loved.

"Yes. I'm all right." Tears would bubble up because Sebastien had the sensitivity to ask. The sensitivity sang and the lyrics said, *You're falling in love.*

*Lord. That phrase. Je déteste ça,* he thought.

*Falling in love.* As if love was some awful pit and the inevitable direction was down. Why not rise in love instead of fall? And even

that was inaccurate because love didn't do either. It unfolded, like
a story. It had plotlines and plot points and points of view; was pop-
ulated with supporting roles like Glo and colorful auxiliary characters like Café Valentin's patrons and band. Their story unfolded
with drama, like the night they argued at the club in front of everyone. Sebastien had charged Ben with flirting with a handsome male
customer, a charge Ben had at first laughed off before being lured
into the fight.

"I am neither stupid, nor naïve," Sebastien said. "You know
that *les tapettes* find you charming and attractive and you use that."

"Oh, I use my masculine wiles?"

"If you want to call it that. Or perhaps your exotic wiles or jungle wiles would be *appropié.*"

"Let's add *primitive* while we're at it," Ben said.

By now, the normally liquid voice of each man had hardened,
stopping everything in Café Valentin. The patrons and Glo and the
band became engulfed in their fight as if it was a stage play.

"Fine," Sebastien said. "Primitive. *D'accord.* It suits you."

He walked out. Glo and company resumed their set, but everyone in the place was so stunned, the only song they could do was
the saddest one in their repertory.

> *"Please, lover, don't forsake me,*
> *Or I don't know what I'm gone do.*
> *Please, lover, don't forsake me,*
> *Or I don't know what I'm gone do.*
> *Lord, have mercy on his soul*
> *For what this man done put me through."*

Ben went home at evening's end, numb, horrified. *Primitive.* He
cursed himself for believing Sebastien incapable of such an insult.
Sebastien didn't join him that night in the room in rue Condorcet,
but crept in the next morning, pale and hungry and perspiring,
looking so abject that Ben immediately opened up his arms and
his bed.

"I am . . . I am so sorry. For what I said." He clung to Ben as his
shards of tears fell onto Ben's chest. "Can you forgive? Forget?"

He ran his fingers through Sebastien's hair. "I can forgive."

The moisture accumulated on Ben's chest, some running down the sides of his body, but most of it pooling like a stagnant pond. It occurred to him that Sebastien wore the same clothes as the night before.

"Have you been home? Where did you spend the night?"

But Sebastien had cried himself to sleep.

Their unfolding story had its joyous episodes. They scaled the hill to Sacré-Cœur, the first time Ben had taken anyone there. But before he could show Sebastien that beloved cityscape, the painter threw open the giant doors of the church, cloaked an arm around him, walked him inside and, for the first time, Ben stood on the *inside* of La Basilique du Sacré-Cœur. He had never considered going in, maybe because he'd been raised Baptist and thought he would somehow be barred from entering. He knew nothing of Catholicism, except that Catholics worshipped saints and the Virgin Mary and went straight to hell if they ate anything other than fish on Fridays.

The rows of pews extended up the nave for what seemed like miles. The altar was enthroned on a large dais. High above it rose a fresco of a white-robed Jesus surrounded by kneeling supplicants, a gold heart aglow in the center of his chest. He seemed to levitate. People were arriving for weekday morning mass. Mostly old women carrying heirloom rosaries, a few young women with small children. Many kneeled in the pews, eyes closed, pious lips mouthing prayers.

"I used to go to church," Sebastien said. "When I was young."

Ben laughed. "You're still young."

"*Et tu? Tu allais à l'église?*"

"In Dogwood, with my parents. When I used to believe."

"You no longer do?" Sebastien seemed startled.

Ben gazed at the high-flying Jesus and recalled walking to church with his folks and his sister before she died. Pa wisecracking. Ma smiling and shaking her head. Emma Jane and Ben giggling. But after Emma Jane passed, he and his folks walked to church in silence.

"I no longer believe that it matters," he said, gazing at Jesus.

Sebastien took in the grandiosity of the church as if in awe. Ben played along while thinking, *Notre Dame's better.* But Notre Dame didn't sit on a hill at the highest point in Paris. He extracted Sebastien from his reverie and led him outside. They looked out over the panorama as sunlight darted among the crags and edges and grooves of the city, creating shadows that courted Ben with promises of pleasure; pleasure that, unlike love, did not cost and would not take on a life of its own.

He didn't answer the shadows. Answering would be majestic. But it was too easy.

With his poetry he shunned the easy words and phrases that just anybody could embed in a stanza. He took his time to shape each verse so that it shone, so that he could say, *I did this. I made this. I'm proud of this. I love this.*

# 46

June brought summer, if you could call it that, summer in Paris being nothing more than a warmer, slightly drier, version of spring. Not like New York and Dogwood where summers seethed. Along with warmth, June delivered news. One afternoon on the Place Pigalle, Ben ran into Norman, Chez LeRoi's bartender, only too happy to gossip about Ben's former lover: Baby Back's record sales had spiked in France, England, and Italy. The voluptuous influx of money bankrolled ridiculously expensive suits and a brand-new Packard automobile paid for in cash.

"Each record he sells feeds his bank account *and* his ego," Norman said. "That thing's a goddamn monster. Gets bigger and hungrier with each swallow." And Baby Back lorded it over Chez LeRoi like a despot. "He's made enemies of everyone—from the musicians to the chef to the kitchen boys."

Soon, word of a rift between Baby Back and Clifford Treadwell swarmed the Montmartre jazz scene. The story was that they had argued on the street. Passersby, arms loaded with baguettes or fish wrapped in paper and tied with string, stopped and witnessed the colored man with shoulders as broad as the sidewalk high-stepping it as Clifford slunk to his knees, blithering like a discarded infant.

June was also the month when Ben and Sebastien rejoiced because the drought officially ended: Ben received notification from the *Deux Amours Review,* a journal publishing work by expatriate Americans in France, that two of his poems had been accepted for publication. That night, in celebration, Glo and the band played two entire sets comprised of Ben's favorite tunes and he and Sebastien helped themselves to more than their usual portion of Monsieur Rameau's liquor.

"I am so, so proud of you," Sebastien said later. They were in the room in rue Condorcet, getting ready to play. *"Félicitations, mon chaton."*

His pride, Ben knew, was in part because Sebastien could claim some of the credit for his success, success that served as proof that their creative partnership worked.

In mid-July, another journal accepted his work. Notification coincided with *La Fête Nationale*—Bastille Day. To salute his adopted country's freedom and his most recent success, Ben and Sebastien joined hordes of celebrants along the Champs Élysées. They watched the military parade from the Arc de Triomphe to the Place de la Concorde as the crowd waved an infinite fluster of French flags on both sides of the boulevard and someone held up a banner inscribed with the French national motto: *Liberté, Égalité, Fraternité.*

Afterward, they went to a café. Sebastien allowed Ben to treat him. They sat outdoors and ate ham omelets and salad while a waiter stood nearby, greeting passersby. *"Bonjour, monsieur. Bonjour, madame,"* he intoned, his voice fraught with boredom and more nasal than the typical Frenchman. *"Bonjour, mademoiselle. Bonjour, les enfants. Bonjour, tout le monde."*

"You have attended your first *Fête Nationale,*" Sebastien said. They clinked their champagne glasses together. "You are a Frenchman now."

"And proud to be."

"I wonder what they would think about that in Dogwood. I wonder what your parents would think."

Ben shrugged.

"I'm sure they would be proud of your literary success," Sebastien said, "if they knew."

*Perhaps they will soon,* Ben thought.

The death of Baby Back's ma had prompted an ache for his own folks. It aggravated a longing that gnawed. Over the years he'd convinced himself he didn't want, need, or love them; that the surplus of hurtful times invalidated the good ones. Then why the longing? It was rather like *this thing* once upon a time: too massive, too prominent a part of himself to ignore or contain. It had to get out. And, like *this thing,* the more he ignored it, the more it would gnaw until it hollowed him out.

So he had paused his hurt and written to his parents.

The words had stuttered from his pen. Fragments, incoherent on their own, strung themselves to one another and expanded into a letter. *Been so long... Shouldn't have hurt you.... Shouldn't have left like that.... Forgive me?... Can you?...I...I love you.*

He had mailed it, weeks ago, but not heard back. He hadn't told Sebastien for fear of jinxing the outcome. And what if regaining his ma and pa piqued Sebastien's loneliness for his own parents? What if he became jealous? They already competed for Glo's mothering attentions. They fought about it once. During coffee at Glo's one afternoon, Sebastien had monopolized her with stories and advice-seeking and narration of his own history. By the time they left, Ben had barely talked with her.

"She's *my* friend," he said, on their way back to Sebastien's. Ben set the pace, walking at a clip and a little ahead.

"It is stupid to be jealous," Sebastien said.

"I don't mind sharing, but—"

"—you would like me to take a smaller share? As if she is a thing to be divided?"

Ben stopped walking. Sebastien didn't.

"She's the closest thing I have to a mother!" Ben shouted at the painter's back, pleading, ridiculous, mad at himself for his ridiculousness.

"Same for me!" Sebastien shouted back.

The *bonjour* waiter resumed his weary greetings. "*Bonjour, madame. Bonjour, jolie fille. Bonjour, tout le monde.*"

"I should not talk about our parents so much," Sebastien said.

"I suppose I do because I miss mine. Imperfect and impossible and cruel as they were—*are*—there is still no substitute."

A month after *La Fête Nationale,* Ben learned from Norman that Baby Back quit Chez LeRoi to star at a larger, swankier club in rue de la Gaîté in Montparnasse.

And that Clifford Treadwell had moved out of Baby Back's house.

"From what I heard, it wasn't voluntary," Norman said. "Ain't nobody sure where he went. Is he still in Paris? Did he leave France? Go back to his wife in the States? Nobody knows." Norman smiled, villainous, victorious. "And let me tell you something else: Don't nobody give a shit."

Ben smiled, too: his nemesis defeated. But he also pitied Clifford Treadwell because he knew what it was to love and to lose Baby Back Johnston.

"I wonder why it is," Sebastien said when Ben told him, "that you take such interest in what happens with your *former* lover."

Ben said nothing, locking out, momentarily, Sebastien's jealousy of Baby Back—a cover for the more insidious jealousy that had folded itself into their unfolding story: A third batch of Ben's poems had been accepted by another journal at the end of July, a fourth in September for an anthology, but Sebastien hadn't sold a single painting.

"You should try to sell your work to the tourists and slummers on the Place Pigalle," Ben said. "Or set up shop on a street corner."

Sebastien cringed at the suggestion as a quiet torch of the former rich, spoiled scion still blazed. But he took Ben's advice. The results were minimal. Mornings he left with loads of canvasses under his arms and evenings he returned with the same ones. Depression staked its claim on him. He was grumpy and silent or he vented his frustrations on Ben. He would stay away from Café Valentin and then appear in Ben's room the following day, pale and weak and looking dazed and strangely tranquil. More than once, Ben detected a sweet aroma trailing him. He wanted to follow that trail and see to what—or whom—it led.

"You do not know," Sebastien said, "how humiliating it is to place your life's work on the sidewalk and watch as people pass by as if they are walking by trash. Or they stop and look and give you a courteous smile and then keep going. I do not want their courtesy. I would rather they spat in my face."

He gave up the street corner sales, took odd jobs, lived off Ben, and grimaced each time Ben paid for a meal. Ben felt bad, but was more jubilant about his own success than sorry about Sebastien's rut.

His poetry was back. He was whole again. His poetry was a star out in space that he had worshipped, prayed to. As with ships' navigators of old, its place in the sky was a marker of where he was, where he was going, how long and far he had traveled. For a while the marker had disappeared, snuffed out by God.

> *Who turned out the light?*
> *Whose malice spun me into*
> *This boundless gorge of black?*
>
> *I used to frolic with the spheres.*
> *I rested my head on the breast of the moon.*
> *Light was sugar.*
>
> *This darkness cuts.*
> *It blinds.*
> *It empties and does not replenish.*
>
> *Who turned out the light?*
> *Why are my eyes no longer sweet?*

He never wanted that starlessness again. So Sebastien terrified him. His erstwhile pride in Ben's accomplishments had reshaped into an ax. Ben thought about ending it. *But he set me on the starlit path home. And I . . . I love him.*

He did not want to crush their unfolding story. But he hoped he was not in love with love. That was like wanting to read, but only good news. Love could fill, but not make whole; it could cushion loneliness, not cure it. What it did was broaden your circumference of concern beyond yourself to encompass another person. Even if—when—that person caused you grief.

He so often felt as though he hailed from a different species, not quite human. He'd always been different, had never fit. Negroes looked at him askance, questioning his credentials as a Negro man. Whites did, too. For both groups, he wasn't Negro *enough*. They didn't know what to make of him, what category in which to box him. And queer to boot! Benjamin Marcus Charles was something that shouldn't exist but had slipped through the mesh of the evolutionary net. As such, he was a natural and perpetual outsider. It was in the very cells that composed him.

And then came Sebastien, another exile. They were of different races; one had been rich, the other poor; one was French, the other American (if Negroes counted as Americans), but they were of the same outsider species. Their circumference of concern naturally encompassed each other.

They inspired each other. Ben scoffed at the cliché: *love as inspiration; love inspires.* It sounded like a passage from a Romantic play from the last century. But wasn't inspiration an ingredient of love? Perhaps itself a form of love? If you embarked on the fool's errand of defining love, wouldn't inspiration be one of the roots? Without Sebastien, without Sebastien's art, Ben would still be blundering in the wasteland, starless, guideless.

In November, just as winter settled in, Norman gave Ben the latest news: Chez LeRoi was dying.

"We ain't had a packed house since Baby Back quit."

LeRoi Jasper's patrons had deserted him. Denny and her menagerie of escorts and hangers-on were gone. The tourists and rich slummers sought other venues. *Chocolate Jubilee of 1926* had long since moved on to Brussels, London, and Berlin as *Chocolate Jubilee of 1927,* although a few cast members—inspired by Baby Back's stardom—stayed behind to try their luck in Paris. Most nights the joint LeRoi Jasper had anointed the hottest in Paris sat empty, the music from its stage reverberating in the hollow shell of the club.

"And the few folks who do come," Norman said, "think they gonna hear Baby Back. When they find out he ain't there no more, they turn right around and walk out."

\* \* \*

Ben sat up in bed. The room was chilly even with the radiator hissing steam heat. Another night had passed without Sebastien. It had become a ritual: the painter staying away all night and then straggling over Ben's threshold the next morning, a snippet of some sweet aroma (whose?) straggling with him.

He hadn't sold a single painting or attracted the interest of any gallery. His melancholy now dwarfed his ability to paint. He would sit at his easel, waiting for a stab of creativity with which to slay his canvas. It rarely came. Ben understood that. Resented it, too: He was supposed to inspire Sebastien and took it personally when he didn't, couldn't.

But this morning, he just wanted Sebastien to come back.

"One-thousand-one. One-thousand-two." He counted to calm himself, hoping Sebastien would come.

At *one-thousand-twelve,* he did.

"Where were you?" Ben asked as he held him, sniffing covertly for a trace of that sweet scent. There it was, nearly camouflaged by Sebastien's strong body odor, but there nonetheless. Too sweet for a man's scent, but not a woman's either.

"Do not worry, *mon chaton.*"

"Why won't you tell me? Were you with friends? Family?"

"Family," Sebastien said. He polished the sour-candy word in his mouth. "You know I was not with family."

Ben awaited an explanation, received none, counted *one-thousand-one, one-thousand-two* in his head. He wished he hadn't mentioned Sebastien's family. It roiled memories of his own; of how his ma and pa had retreated into themselves, retreated from him, until they were changed, distanced, gone, shells. The worst memory was his own helplessness as he witnessed each retreating step.

He shook himself. "Sebastien. I want to tell you a story from when I was with my wife."

"Angeline. You never talk about her." His voice was muffled, his face pressed close against Ben's chest. His whole body was pressed close, as if he'd given up control and let all of his weight mass onto Ben's.

"I sent some poems," Ben said, "to a literary journal. They were rejected. I wanted to give up. And Angeline"—he couldn't help laughing—"she wasn't putting up with it. She told me, 'Shut up with that nonsense. Work harder. Try again. And again. And again.'"

"Did you try again and again and again?"

"I sure did. It paid off, too. Just like it will for you. But you have to try." He began to cry. He tried to stop, but couldn't. "Sebastien, you have to try. Or else."

The painter lifted his head from Ben's chest. His body was stiff with alarm. "Or else what, *mon chaton?*"

The room was no longer chilly. It was too warm now. They both perspired. Ben's sweat slid down his face along with his tears. He wondered if Sebastien could distinguish one from the other. The tears flowed, the sweat flowed, and now mucus ran out of his nose, as well. He didn't wipe any of it. He wanted it all to flow, until he was drained, limp, a mess.

"Or else what, *mon chaton?*" Sebastien repeated, almost a challenge.

Ben rose to it. "Or else it's over." Carefully: "Here's what I want you to do."

He told Sebastien to try again on the Place Pigalle.

"But it is winter," Sebastien said. "It will be awful to be outside all day."

Ben was sympathetic, but didn't budge.

# 47

Ben peered in the window of a top-drawer gallery, the type where sought-after artists of the moment showcased their work. Mostly modern and abstract art, swollen with color and segmented by stark, discordant lines. One painting of two disembodied heads reminded him of African masks: the long, exaggerated oval faces; the stylized eyes and mouths projecting lethal serenity; the sense that a god breathed behind the mask, a god that might watch over you protectively or smite you dead.

A couple exited the gallery, both clad in full-length fur coats, the swelter of wealth smoldering about them. A uniformed chauffeur stood at attention, holding open the door of a shining black Delage limousine. The husband assisted his wife as she stepped onto the running board and into the car, then followed her in. As they drove away, Ben wondered what it would take for Sebastien to get his work into a gallery like this, into the homes of people like those.

He was on Boulevard Haussmann, in the chic world of Paris's 9th arrondissement, not too far south of Montmartre, yet many incomes away. Montmartre was fish stores and brothels and jazz clubs; callous-handed workmen hauling coal and housewives quibbling with shopkeepers over the price of bread. But lavish window displays of jewelry and couture animated the expensive shops on Boulevard Haussmann while ritzy gentlemen and ladies eased through the posh department stores that dominated the boulevard like stone monoliths.

Ben walked farther down Boulevard Haussmann, then turned onto rue Scribe. Across from the Paris Opera was the behemoth structure housing the American Express office where visiting Americans exchanged dollars for francs and expatriates gathered to read newspapers from the States, cash checks, send and collect mail.

Expatriate. Is that what he was? Didn't one first have to be a patriot before he qualified to put the *ex* in front of it? Could a colored American even be a patriot? Ben wasn't sure. He chuckled at his conundrum as the colored doorman ushered him inside.

He joined the queue of people lined up at the waist-high counter. Clerks sat behind it, separated from the customers by a metal grille. The building was austere, all stone and marble and rounded arched doorways. A quartet of white American tourists—two couples—had just changed money. One of the women noticed Ben. She nudged her husband who looked over. So did the other couple. The men wore business suits; the women furs and feathered hats, their curled hair poofy in back. They seemed taken aback at the sight of Ben: *Coloreds in Paris?* They stared and whispered, not sure how to process this anomaly. Ben smiled big and nodded.

"*Bonjour, messieurs dames,*" he said. "*Bienvenue à Paris. J'espère que vous aurez un temps merveilleux.*"

The quartet's faces froze, mouths open, in horror or simply shock, Ben couldn't tell. Then they giggled like children amused by the sophisticated antics of a pet, and left.

"I want to see if I have mail, please," Ben said when he reached the counter. "Ben Charles. Or Benjamin Marcus Charles."

The clerk went away to check, then returned moments later and handed Ben the thing he'd been waiting for: a letter from Dogwood.

In the months he'd waited for his folks' reply, he'd tried and failed to restrain himself from fantasizing. Spectacular, idiotic fantasies. Him and Ma and Pa and Sebastien and Glo living together, as a family, in Paris. Buying Café Valentin and running it together. Ma directing the kitchen, Pa and Sebastien taking charge of the dining room, Glo singing, and Ben the impresario tasked with cultivating Café Valentin as Paris's premier jazz enterprise. Or he and Sebastien moving to Dogwood to help his folks run the farm. They'd add a room onto the house for them. Pa would strategize the construction. He was good with building, a master at the intricacies of planning and measuring and cutting. Ma would assist with furnishings and decor. Sebastien could paint the groves of dogwood trees and Sugarfish Pond where Ben once swam. He'd like that. He'd think the rural landscape beautiful.

Whether in Paris or Dogwood, Ma and Pa would accept Sebastien. Of course they'd raise silent eyebrows when witnessing the two men retire to their bedroom and then saunter out next morning with lucent faces. The painter's whiteness would certainly trouble them at first. But joy at the return of their sole surviving child would trump everything. Judgments, disapproval, and shame would be shunned. Ma and Pa would let it be and get on with the business of contentment.

None of that would or could happen. He knew that. He wasn't stupid, just a dreamer realigning the borders of what was possible.

But the dreams had to stop, now, for always.

Ben sat on his bed in the room in rue Condorcet and reread the letter.

> *Dear Ben.*
> *I'se so sorry to tell you dat your ma and pa done passt on. Ben Sr. took sick in '22 and died later on dat year. Maggie wuz misable. She wouldn't take care a herself. She passt de nex year. Dey always misst you. Nevah knowd wut happend to you. Dat made em so sad. But by God's glory dey is now at peace.*
> *Truly,*
> *Missus Paula Sue Thurman*

\*   \*   \*

*Loss.*
*Island of loss.*
*Wandering the shore.*
*A nomad.*
*Connective tissue severed.*
*Ties untied.*
*The frayed, brittle strings disintegrate to powder,*
*Fly away on the island wind,*
*Blown out to sea.*

*You killed them.*
*You killed them.*

*grief kills . . . murder . . . murderer . . . fugitive, give*
*yourself up . . . patricide . . . matricide . . . you cared*
*only for your own selfish side . . . left them spinning in*
*the deathtrap of unknowing . . . not-knowing . . .*
*aching for a taste of you . . . self-consumed warlock*
*of words . . . you sent none to the grieving . . . you*
*have spent years luring words . . . like a predator . . .*
*trapping them . . . fondling them like clay . . . but*
*you could not spare even one for the grieving . . . even*
*one would have . . . might have . . . could have . . .*
*saved them . . . you should have . . . could have . . .*
*saved them*

*Can forgiveness reach down from the sky?*
*Will the lofty moon relay your love?*
*Or block it?*

"Ben. Ben. *Mon chaton.* You were having a nightmare. Come here. I will hold you."

"I don't deserve it."

"Ben, please let me—"

"My pa died first. I'm sure my ma held him. But when she died, did anyone hold *her*? I hope somebody was with her. Anybody. It's better to die with your worst enemy in the room than to die all alone, right? *Right?*"

"I do not know. I—"

"Pa was gone. All her children were dead. Almost all. At least she knew where the other kids were. She could put flowers on their graves, she could say, *Emma Jane Charles: That girl is buried right here. I know where that child is.* Not knowing where your child is . . . that must be the most awful thing in the world. Sebastien?"

"Yes?"

"Do your parents know where you are?"

"No. Nor do they care."

"Mine did. Mine cared. Oh. Dear God. Dear, dear God . . . They cared. And I didn't know. How could I not know?"

"You can only know you are cared about if you are told and shown. Your parents did neither."

"That wasn't their fault. Everything they went through. Losing all those children. Of course they couldn't give me the love I needed. Love-wise, they were bankrupt. That I *did* know. Yet I still . . ."

"Ben. I would very much like to hold you. Will you let me? Please?"

"Two of the children died during childbirth. Another one died when he was a few months old. My folks named him Jeremiah. We called him Li'l Jerry. Then Emma Jane died a year after that. So much death. I'll never forget the looks on my folks' faces at Li'l Jerry's and Emma Jane's funerals. Nothing. There was nothing on their faces. No life. No light. Like it'd been shut off, leaving two blanks where my ma and pa had been. I'd never seen anything like that before. Or since. Faces writhing with nothing."

"Ben—"

"So I should have been more understanding when they closed themselves off. But *I* was still here. *I* still needed them to love me. And I was mad when they couldn't, at least not in the selfish way I wanted."

"It was hardly selfish for you to want love."

"Don't tell me what it was! I know what it was! Just like I know what it was that made me hop on that train that took me north: It was revenge. I was getting back at them. I would imagine how their faces might shift a little—their nothing faces—when they realized I wasn't coming back, and satisfaction rose up in me, warmed me. I was hurting my own folks and I loved it! That's the most selfish thing I've ever heard of."

"You must forgive yourself."

"Stop telling me that. You don't know what this is like. You could go see your parents tomorrow if you wanted to."

"Ben. *Mon chaton*. It is true that my parents are a car ride away. But, believe me, they are as dead to me as your parents are to you. Perhaps much more so. You and I are both grieving."

"Don't compare your grief to mine."

"My intention is only to help. Perhaps I can best do that by leaving you by yourself. I will go home to my room now. I will see you tomorrow? I love you."

"Good night, Sebastien."

# 48

"I just heard."

"How? Let me guess: When you're Baby Back Johnston, you hear everything, right?"

Baby Back came in. Ben closed the door. Baby Back hugged him from behind before he could turn around. It was nice being held by a big, strong man. But he belonged with Sebastien. He wanted Baby Back to let go, and he wanted to stay in that backward embrace. He thought of Sebastien freezing for his art on the Place Pigalle. Staying in Baby Back's arms any longer might lead to something he'd have to feel guilty about.

He already had enough guilt.

He stepped out of his former lover's embrace and sat on the bed. Baby Back removed his shoes and his coat—a full-length, dark brown raccoon fur—and joined him.

"When did it happen?" Baby Back said.

"Years ago. While I was living it up in Harlem, they was already gone."

"Ben, you wasn't *living it up*. You was working your fucking ass off."

He placed a big, heavy hand on Ben's thigh. Ben liked its weight, its presence on his body.

"I should've sent word to them."

"Yeah. You should've," Baby Back said. "But that don't mean it's your fault they're gone."

Merciless honesty after days of Sebastien's babying. A relief. He was grateful for it and for the heavy hand and for the big shoulder his head now rested against.

"When your ma died," Ben said, "you came to me, not Clifford. Sebastien keeps trying to comfort me and I shut him out. Why is it that you and me can comfort each other, but we shut out the men we supposedly love?"

Baby Back lay back on the bed, pulled Ben to his chest. "Because we come from the same place. Been through the same shit. Clifford and Sebastien, they don't know nothing about what we been through."

Snuggling against this chest he knew so well—it was wrong, but betrayal was never so good, so warm. Innocent betrayal. It would go no further than this. They would not kiss. They would not undress. They would not fuck. They would not be tempted to. They would be content with this. Two former lovers—a small flower of whose love bloomed still and would always—dawdling in each other's warmth this final time, purged of regret, burning with forgiveness, and grateful to and for each other.

"I'm leaving on tour," Baby Back said. "Southern France first—you know, Marseilles, Nice. Then Italy. Then swing back through France and hop over to Germany and England."

Nothing had changed. Baby Back was supposed to be soothing Ben's grief but, as usual, it became about himself. Ben couldn't be mad. He recalled that day on the *Bonaparte,* when Baby Back had first laid bare his herculean ambitions. It had frightened him. Not because the trumpeter wasn't capable of fulfilling them, but because he was. *Yeah, not a damn thing has changed,* Ben thought. *And I guess that's OK.*

"You got everything you wanted," he said. "Roland's proud of you. I'm proud of you." He yawned. "I'm so tired."

"Grief wears you out. When my ma died, I spent most of the day, every day, sleeping. Clifford didn't like that."

"Cliffy's gone? Back to the States?"

"He's gone. All I care about. Go to sleep."

Ben was almost there when Baby Back said, "Remember the first poem you gave me?"

"You *took* it from me, if I remember right."

"Only took what you couldn't wait to give."

"I remember it. Do you?" Ben said.

> *"I got love runnin' through me,*
> *Like a river,*
> *Like wine,*
> *Like sweet jazz in an uptown dive.*
> *Runs through me, and through me, and through me.*
>
> *May I kiss your pretty cheek?*
> *May I kiss your pretty lips?*
> *Your pretty hips?*
> *Be my beauty,*
> *'Cause I got love runnin' through me."*

"Can't believe you remember it," Ben said.

"Go to sleep. Mr. Poet."

"Ben. You're in trouble. Wake up. Come on. Mr. Poet. We got company."

Ben's eyes snapped open. Sebastien was at the foot of the bed. A mess of snow covered his coat and hat. He had tracked it into the room and it melted in puddles on the floor. He said nothing as he watched Ben lie carelessly in Baby Back's arms.

"Guess it's time for me to go," Baby Back said.

The trumpeter nudged the painter out of the way as he collected his shoes and his fur coat. "Excuse me, Sebastien. I got that right, didn't I? It's Sebastien, right? I still ain't no good with these French names." He went to the mirror above the washbasin, took his time fine-tuning his tie. "Hell, I ain't no good with French, period. Ain't that right, Mr. Charles? You should've seen some of the fights we had about that, Sebastien. You'd best be careful with this one. Don't mess with him, and don't be fooled neither. For a poet, he got a mean right hook. Punched me out once. Sure did. And all I was doing was enjoying the Louvre." He looked over at Ben and winked, then smoothed down the sleeves of his fur. "Yes, sir. Mr. Charles here is a handful. Hey, Sebastien, my hat's behind you, on the desk. Hand it to me, please. Uh, Sebastien? Hello? All right. I'll get it myself." He groomed his hat into the perfect, jaunty posture, then turned to leave. "Ben, see you when I get back from my tour. Sebastien." He slapped him on the arm, pointed at Ben, and spoke in low, foreboding notes. "You take care of him, you hear me?"

And he was gone. And the room felt a thousand times smaller.

Neither Sebastien nor Ben moved. Ben couldn't look at him.

"Nothing happened," he said.

"Meaning you did not have sex with him."

"Yes. Exactly," Ben said, relieved, excited that Sebastien understood. "He heard about my parents. He was being nice. We weren't intimate."

"There are other ways of being intimate besides sex."

"He was comforting me."

"I see. I see. You would not allow *me* to comfort you, but you accepted comfort from your *former* lover. Your former lover who mistreated you. Betrayed you. Yes. It makes sense, *mon chaton,* that you would accept consolation from him."

Ben's eyes closed of their own accord. His head shook itself in disbelief. He'd done it again: become so consumed by his own needs, burrowed so deep inside his own cozy hell, that he willfully disconnected from someone he loved and caused hurt. Angeline. Baby Back. His folks. Now Sebastien. A consistent and unbroken track record.

Sebastien turned his back on him. Only now did Ben see the canvasses that he had brought into the room. He must have left the Place Pigalle early when it began to snow.

The painter picked up his canvasses. Ben almost slipped on the puddles as he scrambled to insert his body between Sebastien and the door. He tried to think of something to say, any reasonable thing at all, but the only thing he could think of was as cliché as it was desperate.

"Don't go. Don't leave me alone."

He knew Sebastien's reply, knew it before the painter uttered a sound. Knew it practically word for word, as if he'd magically gained the ability to read minds.

"You do not have to be alone, *mon chaton*. Perhaps you can accompany Baby Back on his tour."

# 49

Sebastien didn't come to Café Valentin that night. He didn't join Ben in the room in rue Condorcet later, nor did he straggle in the next morning. When Ben didn't see him at the Place Pigalle, he went to his boardinghouse, hoping he was painting, but prepared to find him pouting. He wasn't there.

Ben sat on the floor, surrounded by paintings, and waited.

He studied the paintings, analyzing each stroke, following every line's curve. Where shadows fell, he searched for the opposing light. The urge to critique sneaked up on him. He began finding flaws in the perspective; shadows and highlights that couldn't logically exist where they'd been placed. Some pieces screamed for more color. Others had been oversaturated. A few would have benefited from a simpler touch, and in a handful Sebastien had needlessly held back. Ben pondered how to present his critiques; how to be honest, yet constructive.

One thing he could be honest about: Baby Back. His former lover was like wildfire: The light and the heat tantalize, but stray too close and face obliteration. Ben didn't love him. He loved Sebastien. He'd make him believe it; tell him he'd been undone by jealousy of a man who was a vestige from Ben's past and press his case until Sebastien was convinced.

Hours passed. Dusk came. Then evening. Then night.

They didn't bring Sebastien with them.

"Fine," Ben said. "I'll see him at the club tonight."

He rehearsed a scolding speech. "Don't ever stay away like that again, you hear me?" he'd say. "People who love each other can't just run away when they get mad." The part about *people who love each other* would be a good touch. Then he'd fetch Sebastien some soup and his favorite wine and close the argument with "Nothing's going on between me and Baby Back. I love *you*."

He practiced it in his head, mouthed it to himself all night while he worked until he knew which words to punch, which to tap, which to massage. He perfected it, but never had a chance to perform it: Sebastien didn't show.

He amended the speech for the morning, but Sebastien didn't come.

Ben dressed and ran to his usual area on the Place Pigalle. He didn't find him. He went to his boardinghouse, inspected the room for evidence of Sebastien's presence since yesterday. Nothing. Back at the Place Pigalle, he made the rounds, inquiring if anyone had seen him. No one had. He went back to the boardinghouse, knocked on neighbors' doors. No one knew anything. He returned to the Place Pigalle and then to his own boardinghouse just in case and then searched at Sacré-Cœur.

That night at Café Valentin, his hands shook so bad, he could barely write down customers' orders. *One-thousand-one, one thousand-two,* he thought as he fought to calm himself. He held his breath each time the door opened.

He went to the *Préfecture de police* on day three of Sebastien's absence.

"*Ces artistes,*" the officer said. He shook his head in sympathy. "You will probably find him passed out in a bar or a brothel, *mon ami*. Come back in a few days if you do not find him."

Ben did search the bars and every café and back alley in Montmartre. He searched around Chez LeRoi, the Louvre, Montparnasse, Île de la Cité. He returned to Sacré-Cœur, tried to pray to the gold-hearted Jesus, then went home and pounced on his typewriter.

*I have tried to be*
*As soft as feathers*
*To cushion you from the rocks howling inside you.*
*You have no idea how beautiful you are.*
*You paint pictures*
*With a brush tipped with rubies.*
*Your mouth on mine is a diamond.*
*And still you flee from me.*
*One-thousand-one.*
*One-thousand-two.*
*I lose my breath.*
*I search for you.*

\* \* \*

The house was in Neuilly, a suburb seven kilometers west of the center of Paris. It was mausoleum-like, more monstrosity than home with its rows of gravely symmetrical windows set in three stories of sterile beige brick. Balconies hugged both ends of the edifice. An enormous, overly ornate clock stared out from the center of the roof like an ugly face. Sebastien had said his parents were blasphemously wealthy, but that didn't prepare Ben. Gratuitous wealth remained an abstract concept for him even as he'd witnessed its trappings at The Pavilion and Chez LeRoi. This was the first time he had seen such wealth in solid form, close-up. It intimidated him.

He approached the tall front double doors—heavy wood, framed by a marble column on either side—and rang the doorbell, the chime as extravagant as a symphony. A butler appeared, a stooped-over old man, his age somewhere north of seventy. His mustache and surprisingly full head of hair were completely white.

"*Bonjour,* young man."

Kind eyes. Kind smile.

"*Bonjour, monsieur,*" Ben said. "*Je m'appelle* Ben Charles."

"What can I do you for you, Monsieur Ben Charles?"

An expansive marble-floored entryway fanned out behind the butler. Paintings that looked as old as the Renaissance hung on its walls.

"May I please speak to Monsieur and Madame Crespin?" Ben said. He took a breath. "About their son. Sebastien."

The butler's smile waned. "What about him?"

"I'd prefer to talk to *them*."

The butler looked down at his feet and said, "*Attendez-vous ici, s'il vous plaît.*"

He closed the door, then returned several minutes later and led Ben around the side of the house to a patio in back.

"*Monsieur et Madame vous parleront ici,*" the butler said.

"*Merci.*"

The old man turned to leave, then stopped and pulled up his stooped back. He gripped Ben's arm with surprising strength.

"Monsieur Sebastien . . . is he all right?"

"I don't know."

The butler's hand fell. He resumed his stoop and walked away.

It began to snow. Ben shivered and waited. Several minutes passed before a man and woman appeared through a set of glass double doors. The man wore a black suit, the woman a gray dress. They were older than Ben had imagined and both tall, their statures as stiff and straight as the old butler's was bent. They held themselves so royally, Ben wondered if he should kneel. Despite the cold, they didn't shiver.

"*Monsieur et Madame Crespin?*" Ben said. No answer as they evaluated him with prim, expressionless faces. "*Je m'appelle* Ben Charles."

He stepped forward, his hat in one hand, the other outstretched. Monsieur and Madame stepped back.

"We know your name," Monsieur Crespin said. "Erneste told us. What do you want?"

"I'm here about Sebastien. I—"

"He told us that as well," Monsieur Crespin said.

"Answer my husband's question," Madame said. "What is it you want?"

Ben recognized their rudeness for what it actually was. The couple's words and tone, the malice with which they eyed him, the way they kept their physical distance—he had lived this in the States. Seeing it now was like resuming relations with a treacherous old acquaintance. After all, he hadn't been invited inside the house to meet with the Crespins, but outside, in back.

"Sebastien has been missing for days. I don't know where he is. I wonder if you've heard from him."

He'd never heard his own voice sound so meek. His stomach felt sick. Snow fell harder. Even in his heavy coat he trembled with cold, while the Crespins, who wore no coats, were as still and rigid as the house behind them. Ben made himself look them in their eyes.

"I'm aware that . . . that you haven't been close in a very long time."

"That is a private matter," Monsieur Crespin said.

"And no business of yours," his wife added.

Their voices were controlled and stinging. They stood in close proximity to each other, in total solidarity. Two Crespins operating as one unit. How many other enemies had they faced off against this way? How many had they vanquished?

*One-thousand-one. One-thousand-two.*

"It's not my intention to intrude," Ben said. "But he's been gone for days. I thought, just maybe . . ."

"That he would be *here?*" Madame Crespin said, and the control slipped a little as her volume tacked higher, accompanied by a contemptuous grin.

"If you know our son," Monsieur Crespin said, "and you know our history, why, like an imbecile, would you think he would be here?"

"Because, *mon cher,* he *is* an imbecile," Madame said.

Now they *both* grinned. An insect had flown voluntarily into their web. It was time to feast.

"*Monsieur et Madame,*" Ben countered, "in spite of everything, Sebastien loves you and misses you greatly. That's why I thought he might have come here."

Madame Crespin stepped forward. "What is the nature of your relationship with our son?"

She snarled the words. They were husky and guttural. Capsized by her brusque inquiry, Ben averted his eyes, ashamed.

She walked back to her husband. "*J'avais raison!* He has become . . . intimate . . . with yet another black degenerate."

"*Oui,*" Monsieur Crespin said, lightly, sighing. "Sebastien does seem drawn to these aborigines."

The couple lifted their haughty noses at the same time, as if they'd planned it. The snow was really falling now. Ben's dark coat was alive with white. Annoyed, the Crespins brushed it off their own clothes like some bothersome pest, but didn't seem to feel the cold. He hated these people. He didn't comprehend why Sebastien missed them so. Monsieur and Madame Crespin were monsters.

"Get off our property," Monsieur Crespin said.

"And if you do find Sebastien," his wife said, "tell him to go to hell."

He was shaking when he returned to Montmartre. He needed a drink. Or reefer. Or both. But then, maybe not. Drink and reefer would medicate him and possibly shave down the rough edge of his hatred, and he didn't ever want to hate those people any less than he did right now.

He considered going back to the police or checking the Place Pigalle again, but then headed to Sebastien's boardinghouse. *Maybe? Just maybe?* Snow still fell, the sky smoky with it. It had accelerated since he left Neuilly. He was a couple of blocks from Sebastien's place when he saw a hill of rubbish on the sidewalk in front of the building, lit with reds, yellows, greens, oranges. A tempest of color. Someone was dumping loads of bright clothes. Two someones, men, making repeated trips from the building to the pile and back. Something was odd. The men strained as they heaved the clothes, and each item banged onto the pile like wood hitting wood.

Ben was half a block away when he realized it wasn't clothes. It was Sebastien's paintings.

"*Arretez!*" he screamed. "Stop! These don't belong to you!"

"Who the hell are you?" It was the older man, in his fifties with a stevedore's muscle and a fat man's gut, coatless, his shirtsleeves rolled up to the elbow. He wore suspenders.

"I'm a friend of the man whose paintings you're trashing," Ben said. "Who the hell are *you?*"

"His former landlord."

"Former?"

"The vagrant has not paid rent in two months."

Snow accumulated on the mass of paintings. When it melted and the water soaked into the canvas, would the paint run? Fade?

"I'll pay it for him," Ben said. "How much?"

"*Trop tard,*" the landlord said. "A new tenant moved in this morning."

Pleading: "I'll give you what he owes plus another two months."

A delaying tactic. At the moment Ben's pockets contained not much more than lint.

The men threw the last of the paintings on the pile, then lit cigarettes as they walked away.

Ben collected as many as he could, shoved them under his arms, took them home, ran back for more. But the pile was gone, the spot where it had been now blank and rapidly filling with snow. A truck sped up the street, the paintings loaded onto it like garbage.

# 50

Ben, alone in his room. Evening. Sebastien's rescued canvasses sat in a corner on the floor. All but one: an unfinished, nude portrait of Ben. He held it lightly, but with the gravity with which one holds an infant. Sebastien had replicated the exact hue of his skin, the distinct pink of his lips, his long limbs. He captured the subtle but distinct ridge of muscle curving around the pectorals; the svelte midsection with only a morsel of flab; shoulders broader than Ben had realized; his winsome, arresting, handsome face. At first he dismissed the painting as idealization. Then he accepted—with a depth of satisfaction that felt like an epiphany—that this was no idealized rendering. It was the truth. He had never thought himself beautiful. Sebastien's portrait changed his mind.

More than the beauty, Sebastien had captured the complexity of his subject. Ben looked into the pensive face of his portrait self and recognized the intelligence, the curiosity, the hunger, the restlessness. The multiple layers enriched the portrait with the kind of brio that is possible only when an artist loves his subject.

But Ben was tired of love's vexations and illogic. There was love in this painting. The colors had been mixed lovingly. Love breathed on every brushstroke. And none of it mattered. The love was here; where was the lover?

\* \* \*

Café Valentin was winding down. Down so low that an audacious dealer inventoried his remaining merchandise right there at a table in the shadows. Down so far that Glo and company had begun their last set, letting loose a love-blues, consummate in its yearning, appalling, pitiful, mesmerizing in the yearner's shameless blaze of anguish.

> *"Please, lover, don't forsake me,*
> *Or I don't know what I'm gone do.*
> *Please, lover, don't forsake me,*
> *Or I don't know what I'm gone do.*
> *Lord have mercy on his soul*
> *For what this man done put me through.*
>
> *If his sweet self don't come back,*
> *Put a gun right to my head.*
> *If his sweet self don't come back,*
> *Put a gun right to my head.*
> *If he still don't come on home,*
> *Pull the trigger, shoot this poor gal dead."*

Ben smoked in the open doorway. The cold air sobered him from the day's calamities. He wished it would snow again, an incorrigible blizzard that would bury everything. Euphoric destruction. End of the world. A sneaky twist on the traditional apocalypse narrative: the world destructing in a furor of snow, not fire. Ben leaned against the doorjamb, took a puff on his cig, then submitted to a fantasy of where he'd like to be the day the world ended.

A sidewalk café. Coffee. Beignets. A favorite book of poems, the pages edged in gilt. A serenading band. Wistful jazz. Happy jazz. Glo. Gin. A poem dancing off the nib of his pen. The sun and moon holding hands in the sky. A tickle of champagne. A stroke of reefer.

And Sebastien.

Sebastien.

*One-thousand-one, one thou—*

Something down the street caught his attention: a man, walking briskly, if a little unsteadily. A familiar something—long neck, narrow set of shoulders, lean torso—caused Ben to first remove his cigarette from his lips, then discard it altogether.

"Sebastien?" he shouted. "Sebastien!"

Sebastien stopped, looked around him, confused. He spotted Ben and ran, dodging down the street and over the snow while Ben raced to keep up.

"Sebastien, come back!"

Sebastien took an unexpected left and vanished. Ben took the same left and found himself in an alley lit by a few lanterns. The smell of trash almost made him vomit. A herd of rats dined on the remains of a dog. Shoddy, threadbare laundry hung on clotheslines strung across the alley. Sebastien swooped through a door. Ben ran to catch up and almost slipped in a puddle of foul, unidentifiable liquid. Huffing and puffing, he reached the door and was stopped by a thick-set Chinaman.

"Ten francs," the Chinaman said.

"I need to talk to someone. He just came in here."

"Still ten francs."

Ben didn't have enough cash with him. "I need to talk to my friend! *C'est urgent!*"

"Ten francs. Pay or go." The Chinaman opened up his coat. The glow from a lantern reflected off the metal of a lean, sleek, exquisite gun.

"A Chinaman? A back alley?" Glo said. "That was a opium den."

"Down the street. He's been down the street the whole goddamn time."

"We don't know that, Benjy. But we *do* know Sebastien got hisself a bad habit. I ain't no praying woman, but I'll pray for Sebastien. And you should, too."

The next day he walked right up to the Chinaman and held out a ten-franc note.

The door closed as soon as he stepped through it. A bolt locked into place on the other side. A flimsy candle mounted to the wall provided the only light. He waited for his eyes to adjust, then took the staircase down. He descended, cautiously, the wood creaking with each step. A large room opened up when he reached the bottom, better lit, but still dark. A sweet, pungent odor struck him. The basement was saturated with it.

The grimy concrete floor was littered with dozens of pallets that were nothing but piles of putrid sheets. People lay or sat on the pallets while holding the stem of an arm-length pipe to their mouths. A Chinese woman in traditional garments carried trays loaded with pipes, scissors, bowls, and decanters filled with a green liquid.

Ben scanned the room. He didn't see Sebastien.

"This way."

A Chinaman stood in front of him. Ben hesitated.

"This way," the Chinaman said, impatient, and directed him to a pallet.

He took a seat on the wad of rancid sheets. People around him lay on their backs, eyes closed. The man to his right moaned and groaned; in pain or reverie, who knew? The woman on his left giggled and conversed with herself. The Chinese woman came to Ben. She handed him a pipe and an oil lamp to light it. As soon as she left him, Ben set off in search of Sebastien.

Every person down here simmered in a delirium. Some mumbled and gesticulated. Others lay corpse-like. A man lay on his side, unconscious, as vomit poured from his mouth. A large rat skittered about, scavenging among dazed smokers while an attendant shooed it away with a stick. The sweet stench of opium weighed close and heavy. The darkness was a black quilt pricked here and there by the glow of the oil lamps.

He kept searching for Sebastien and found him.

He lay on his back, seemingly at peace. Like a dead man. He moved suddenly, an odd, jerky movement. He twitched again, but remained unconscious. Perspiration swam off him. The twitching evolved to violent convulsions—hands and arms and knees flailing. Ben crouched next to him and tried to restrain him.

"Help!" Ben shouted. "Help! This man needs help!"

The female attendant and the guard came running.

"Get a doctor!" Ben said. He felt Sebastien's face. It was cold.

Neither the attendant nor the guard moved.

"Did you hear me? He needs a doctor! Hurry! Why are you standing there?"

"I will bring water," the attendant said.

"He needs more than water, you stupid bitch!"

Ben took charge. He slapped Sebastien's face. He slapped him again. And again. Harder and harder until his face turned crimson.

The convulsions slowed. His eyes half opened. Ben lugged him to his feet, then propped him up by draping him around his shoulders. But Sebastien couldn't move his legs. The convulsions started again. Ben lowered him to the ground, placed his hands under his armpits, and dragged him. He weaved around the pallets to the stairs, then pulled Sebastien up, step by step. He reached the top, out of breath, his lower back and legs on fire. The door was locked from the outside. He banged on it, he kicked it. It didn't open, so he battered it with his whole body.

"Let us out! Open this fucking door!"

The door opened so fast, Ben fell onto the ground outside. The Chinaman stood there with the gun aimed at his head.

"Please. I just want to get him out of here," Ben said.

"Go!"

He dragged Sebastien through the alley, fearful the rats might latch on and tag along for the ride. Just before he reached the street, Ben lugged him to his feet again and propped him up.

"Taxi! Taxi!"

The taxi stopped.

"You have to help me get him in the car," Ben said.

The driver was a very dark-skinned colored man. He examined the pair. "What the hell is wrong with him?" An African accent.

"Too much champagne." Ben laughed, attempted to sound jovial. "You know how it is."

"Too much champagne makes you pass out. It does not make you twitch like that."

The driver faced forward, placed his hands on the steering wheel in preparation to leave.

"Please!" Ben shouted. "Just help me get him to my house. It's not far. I'll pay you double."

The driver's skeptical eyes took their time sliding from Sebastien to Ben, then back to the twitching Sebastien where they lingered. Ben's arms and neck and shoulders ached from propping him up. His lungs began to sting from holding his breath, awaiting the driver's verdict.

"You will pay me triple," the driver said. "Get in."

# 51

The doctor produced a needle and a vial of clear fluid. "Morphine." He injected Sebastien, whose agitation immediately ceased. "You will be attending him?"

"Yes."

"You will have to inject him several times before the withdrawal is over. I will show you how."

The doctor gave him more needles and a few vials of morphine. "Be extremely careful with the dosage. Administer less and less each day. Morphine soothes the withdrawal pain, but if you give him too much he will become addicted to that, too. And that would be far worse than opium addiction, I promise you."

Ben paid him for his service and his silence. The vigil began.

Hours later, Ben's hand trembled as he filled the hypodermic needle. He tapped a vein in Sebastien's arm, then pierced the needle into his clammy flesh. The reaction was almost instantaneous—Sebastien's convulsions calmed and he drifted into sleep.

A few hours of calm, then Sebastien awoke and vomited. The cramps in his gut curled him into a tight ball. Pain wracked him. He howled and vomited some more. Ben injected him with morphine, cleaned up the vomit. He filled the washbasin with cold water. He undressed Sebastien and saw that he'd defecated. He was emaciated. Already slender, Sebastien had lost so much weight, his ribcage almost tore through his skin.

Ben sent a message to Glo. She came over with soup she'd made. "Something he can keep down," she said.

The cramps returned as soon as Sebastien woke again. He curled up so tight, Ben and Glo had to pry him loose from himself. It went on all night. Waking and injecting. Waking and injecting. By morning, they had cleaned up vomit and defecation twice, attempted to feed him to no avail, and covered him with every blanket they could find to warm his shivering.

That night, Ben sent word to Café Valentin that he wouldn't be in.

By the next day, Sebastien was conscious most of the time, which made his withdrawal more agonizing because he was fully awake through it. The cramps and the sweats and the shivers left him begging for morphine.

"Please," he said as the cramps sliced his insides. "Another injection."

Ben, torn between easing the torment and heeding the doctor's warning, said, "Not yet. A little later."

"Hold me."

Ben climbed into the sweat-sodden bed and rocked him. Sebastien needed reassuring, too. He didn't think he'd get better; the pain would never end; he regretted everything; he thought he'd die; might as well die; wanted to die; was terrified of dying. Ben rushed to cool Sebastien's rising panic. Rushed to cool his own.

"I'll tell you a story. Listen to *me,* not to the pain. *D'accord?*"

"*D'accord.*"

"The first time I heard jazz, I had just moved to New York. One day I was wandering around Manhattan, looking for work, and there were these two guys on a corner. One played the banjo; the other was on the clarinet, improvising. There was a hat for people to drop coins in, but I was the only one paying them any attention. Even though I didn't know a thing about jazz I could tell they were amateurs. But there was something about the music. It was sweet. And spicy. Kind of complicated. A little low-down. And intricate.

And a little naughty. I threw a penny in the hat, which I had no business doing because me and Angeline were broke. She would have killed me. After that I started hearing about jazz clubs. There sure as hell wasn't money for that, but I went to a club one night and stood outside and listened. It was a lot better than the street corner cats. I was hooked. When Angeline and me started doing better, we went to clubs all the time. Almost lived in them. Ha. Now I work in them."

A surge of cramps hit Sebastien. He shut his eyes and grinded his teeth as he growled in pain. His body tightened so violently, it seemed his bones might snap. The stink of fresh defecation filled the room. Ben kept rocking him. At last, the surge subsided. When Sebastien spoke again, his voice was ragged and aged.

"Tell me about Angeline."

*Angeline. Beautiful. Bawdy. A whiff of vanilla with a dash of rose.*

"She was my best friend. She saved me. At least for a while. She enabled me to hide. And that's what I needed at the time." He shook off the bout of nostalgia. "I told you how she tricked me, almost prevented me from—"

"—coming to Paris. With Baby Back."

The first mention of Baby Back since Sebastien's return.

"Thank God her trick did not work. We would not have met," he said.

Ben steeled himself. "Sebastien. I'm so sorry. What you walked in on—it shouldn't have happened. I hurt you terribly. But you shouldn't have left."

Wind howled. The radiator hissed.

"I wanted to punish you," Sebastien said. "I wanted you to feel as abandoned as I did. I stayed away because I found peace. Yes, in that opium den, in that wretched place, I found peace. Some measure of it anyway."

"You wanted peace more than you wanted me."

Sebastien's tears came in spasms that rivaled the cramps. "*Oui.*"

Damning disbelief shook Ben first. Then outrage, quiet and quick-boiling. But hurt outdid them both and coaxed him to retaliate.

"I went to your parents." He let it dangle, like a Christmas ornament.

Sebastien hefted himself out of Ben's lap, his eyes alarmed and red. Dark blotches swelled beneath them. He reeked of shit and salty, dirty sweat. "How did they treat you?"

Ben's eyes cut into Sebastien's. "How do you think?"

"Oh God. If I had known you would go to them . . ." He shriveled into Ben's lap again and cried.

The room was too warm. It stank. Ben wanted to open the window, let in the fresh, cold, freezing air. He wanted to take off all his clothes, sleep naked as snow blew in. The room darkened as evening fell. He hadn't turned the light on. He needed a drink. An unopened bottle of whiskey called to him from his desk drawer. Next time Sebastien slept, he'd answer. He wished he had a phonograph. And some records. Jazz records. And some classical. The symphony intrigued him. He'd never been. Maybe that was something they could do, together, when Sebastien got better, when this hell was finished with them.

After minutes of stillness, Ben resumed rocking him. He rubbed his neck, his shoulders. He massaged the knots in his upper back and, with playful fingers, scratched his scalp.

Sebastien was so ravaged, it was as if Ben held in his lap a piece of raw, limp flesh.

"Think about something pleasant. Something you can look forward to. Come on. We'll make a game of it."

"You first," Sebastien said, coiled in his tight ball.

"I'm looking forward to you and me getting a place together. A place where I can write and you can paint. Something with lots of space and light."

"I would like that." Sebastien's voice strained through the pain. "And I want to finish my portrait of you. I want that very much. I miss my paintings."

"They're here. Some of them."

He climbed off the bed, retrieved the rescued canvasses, and showed them to Sebastien one by one. Eight paintings, all he'd been able to save.

Later, after another injection eased the latest wave of cramps, Sebastien said, "Wait. My paintings. Why are they here?"

"I . . . I missed you so much, I brought a few home. To be near a piece of you. Go to sleep. I love you."

"I love you."

By day four, the vomiting stopped. The shivers and cramps abated. Sebastien was no longer drenched in sweat. Color returned to his cheeks. His appetite returned, too, and with it, his desire to paint.

"You gotta tell him," Glo said. She had brought more soup while Sebastien napped.

"Not yet. He's still too weak."

"He's gonna take it hard no matter what. Sugar, he's sick, but he ain't no invalid. He'll resent you treating him like one."

A letter arrived from an American literary journal that once published one of his poems. They had rejected every poem he'd submitted since, were likely rejecting him now, so he stuffed the envelope in his pocket and headed to work, reluctantly, the first time he'd left Sebastien alone.

"Go, *mon chaton*. We will need the money now more than ever."

They had agreed to get an apartment together.

"There must be lots of room for my paintings."

It was late when Ben remembered the letter. He opened it during a break and was surprised to find another sealed envelope inside it. The sealed envelope had a Harlem return address for Ruby Tate, a friend of Angeline's.

> *Dear Ben,*
> *I hope this letter reaches you. I sent it to a publication that published some of your work and asked that it be forwarded to you.*
> *It is with the utmost sorrow that I inform you that Angeline has passed away. She died in the aftermath of childbirth.*

*As you know, I was quite close to Angeline. I daresay I was her best friend. After you left, she explained the untenable circumstances in which you left her.*

*I know she told you that she was not pregnant. In fact, she was.*

*She lied because you made it clear that you did not want to be with her. I know about the abominable way you treated her after she informed you of her pregnancy. Angeline was terrified that, if you stayed, you would treat the child in the same manner.*

*She gave you your freedom so that she and the child could have theirs.*

*It was a difficult pregnancy and a difficult birth. She died shortly after. We held a simple, yet lovely funeral, attended by a few of her friends and coworkers.*

*My husband and I are raising her child as our own. We named her Katherine. Angeline did not choose a name. I trust that she would approve of the one we have chosen.*

*In light of the way you have chosen to live your life, I am sure you agree that Katherine's upbringing and well-being are better served if she is raised by my husband and myself. We, unfortunately, have been childless. Katherine fills a longing void. That said, after much consideration, I felt it was my responsibility to inform you of this situation. I thought you would want to know about Angeline. Please know that Katherine is safe, healthy, and will be well loved and provided for.*

*Yours sincerely,*
*Ruby Tate*

# 52

From Sacré-Cœur, Paris looked like a cemetery. Snow and fog deadened the lights of the cityscape and made tombstones of the buildings. A cold night. Too cold and too late to be up here.

Ben's grief sat on top of him, bore down. *Angeline, dead.* Inconceivable, like some mythical creature that rises from nowhere and stands in front of you: You don't believe in it, the possibility is absurd, but there the monster is. He hadn't recovered from losing his folks before getting slapped with the near loss of Sebastien. Now this. His old pastor in Dogwood (or was it one of those street corner preachers in Harlem?) once said that God never saddled a man with a bigger burden than he was capable of bearing. Ben now had a chance to test that—if his repudiation of God didn't disqualify him from that experiment.

But this grief was no experiment. Experiments could be modified, ended, walked away from.

Angeline. Dead. And a daughter—*my daughter!*—left in her wake.

"Katherine. Katherine. My child."

He kept saying it. To convince himself of its truth. Or to undo it. He was caught in an indeterminate realm, somewhere between nightmare and dream. The bludgeoning grief over Angeline was compounded by guilt. Once more his selfishness had struck down someone who loved him. And this time a baby was a casualty. But the grief and guilt were tempered by the fact of his daughter. He sequestered himself there. He had to. It was the only safe place for him. Without it, without *her*, he'd have no choice but to leap from this hill and end it.

Did little Katherine have her mother's prettiness? He hoped so. Would she inherit her brassy mouth? He smiled at the thought. Or perhaps she possessed Angeline's beauty, Ben's shyness and creativity, both parents' work ethic. Ben tried to picture her little eyes and mouth; her little toes. He imagined two versions of her: one without hair, one with. Why hadn't Ruby enclosed a photograph? He'd never liked that woman and told Angeline so. They used to fight about it. Ruby was always telling people what to do, as if she knew best. How dare she take his daughter and inform him as an afterthought. But he was grateful to her: A parentless child was a tragedy; a parentless colored child in America doubly so.

He looked up at the moon and recalled when he'd wanted to explore its other side. He'd done so and found its shadows. But on *this* side was Katherine, a little soul, a small piece of himself.

He went home, found Sebastien in his ratty opium den clothes. It was staggering to see him so raggedy-thin, his body not much more than skin dripping off meatless bones. The wild blotches under his eyes remained. The smell of decay and near-death enveloped him yet.

Sebastien clutched a half-drained bottle of whiskey. He sat on the extreme edge of the bed, as if it was a cliff he might leap from.

"I went to my room."

He swigged from the bottle. Whiskey splashed down his chin. He drew his arm across his face to wipe it and moved the bottle toward his mouth again, so hesitantly Ben was unsure if he would drink from it or throw it. Sebastien slammed it down on the nightstand, tossed himself onto the bed, rolled onto his stomach, and wept.

Ben wept, too. But his tears didn't fall for Sebastien. Not at first. They fell for Angeline, whom he'd abandoned. They fell for Katherine, whom he'd abandoned. They fell for his parents because he'd abandoned them, too. So much abandonment. He'd caused so much death and pain.

But here was Sebastien, a man he loved; a man he'd risked his life to rescue; a man he'd nursed through fits of vomit and defecation and terror; a man he'd protected. The one person with whom he'd been selfless. One person. *One*. In his twenty-three years on this earth.

Ben sat next to him, laid his head on Sebastien's back, felt the protruding bones, could tell that only a flimsy layer of fat separated Sebastien's skin from his insides. But the near-death smell seemed less strong now, a little less foreboding.

"You'll have to start over," Ben said. "And you can. Those paintings were your life. You still have those eight in the corner. A small piece of you, I know. But it's something."

# love

## 1928

# 53

He dreamed he was on an ocean liner.

He was sitting on the deck, in the sun. A baby girl wrapped in a pink blanket rested in his arms. Plump cheeks. Sweet, drooling mouth. She stared at him with a worshipful gaze. He rubbed his nose against hers and she laughed, so he did it again, kept doing it, till she wore herself out with joy.

The water was smooth, the air warm and perfect, he and the baby the ship's only passengers. It occurred to him that he didn't know where he was headed or from where he'd departed. Was he going somewhere, or leaving something behind?

Night fell, abruptly, as if a switch had been flipped. They were still on the deck. The baby had fallen asleep. He watched her by the light of the full moon. A moon on which he could find shadows, if he needed them. But the only thing in the world he needed was to hold this baby.

Clouds draped the April sky, fat and drooping with imminent rain. Ben arrived at work earlier than usual to execute a creative project: Monsieur Rameau had requested an inventory report and Ben needed to devise figures that disguised the amount of booze that he and Sebastien and Glo had mooched.

Someone knocked.

"Not open yet," Ben yelled.

Another knock.

"Not. Open."

And then persistent knocks.

"*Merde*."

He opened the door, ready to bombard the knocker with rudeness, but an old pal stood outside.

"Norman! Come in! How the hell are you? Let me fix you a drink." He poured him a whiskey. "Been a while, Norm. What's happening over at Chez LeRoi?"

"Not a damn thing. Chez LeRoi closed down."

Norman explained that the club's lifeblood dried up when Baby Back left, and it never flowed again.

"LeRoi tried some new talent—brought in a 'star' pianist. Even hired one of them *Chocolate Jubilee* chicks to sing—one of them 'fresh buds,' as you always called them. Nothing worked. Some weeks he couldn't pay us. And turns out he was in debt up to his high-falutin' eyeballs. From spending too much on all them white women, if you ask me. I wouldn't never let no chick bankrupt me." He knocked back the last gulp of whiskey. "We closed the doors for good last night."

They shared a moment of quiet to honor the club that, until recently, had been anything but.

"So now," Norman said, "I needs me a job. Anything here?"

"Sorry, Norm. Got all the help we need. But I'll give you another drink."

"Suits me. Anyway. How you doing? You still with your friend?"

"Yeah. Got us a place in rue Condorcet, couple blocks from the boardinghouse I was in."

"Heard he was sick for a spell," Norman said. "He all right now?"

Ben sometimes forgot how small Montmartre was, how easily gossip roved up and down its hilly streets.

"Sebastien's doing fine. Got a job waiting tables near Parc Monceau. He's painting—sold a couple of pieces last month. I'm writing. All the usual."

Norman swirled the whiskey around in his glass. "Happy?"

Ben hated that question. Its pedestrian stab at courtesy; its intrusiveness. Happiness, like misery, was a private matter. He didn't want to talk about it. He didn't know how.

"Life's hard," Ben said. "It's nice having someone. We help each other through it."

"So . . . you *are* happy?"

Ben topped off Norman's drink, lit a cigarette for himself.

It began out of focus and fuzzy. From the fuzz emerged an empty Harlem street. Then a row of brownstones faded in. People appeared, magically, droves of them, hurrying here and hurrying there. Then they cleared out, revealing a little girl, alone, sitting on the steps of a brownstone. Five or six years old and pretty as petals. A braided pigtail dangled on either side of her head. She hung her head and hugged herself as if there was no one else to hug her. She looked like the loneliest little girl in the world.

It ended the way it began as the pretty-as-petals little girl went fuzzy and faded out.

He woke from the dream and then couldn't get back to sleep. Sebastien lay in his arms. Ben rolled out from under him with the expertise of an old married man and went to the kitchen. He poured a glass of whiskey, lit some reefer, looked around the apartment. It had everything they'd wanted. Space, light. A living room large enough to carve out two separate yet integrated artistic zones.

*Happy?* Norman had asked. Defensively, Ben had been ticking off his reasons to be happy ever since: a job, published poems, Paris, Glo, an employed artist-lover starting to earn money from his art. And no calls from the shadows. Not a mumble. He did not need them. He did not want them. His love for Sebastien was a steel skin that deflected temptation. They were so close now. Lovers. Collaborators. Partners. Co-conspirators.

Sometimes Sebastien gave off heat. Physical heat, body heat, the heat of desire, yes, certainly. But also gauzier, prettier. A pastel heat. Balmy. Warm, pleasant wind whirring on the skin. Heat that delved deep through Ben's pores, laughed airily in his blood, sailed in his blood past imperfections and grief, past disappointment, to dock at a place of contentment.

Sebastien's near-death served as an essential element that aligned them. They didn't regret it, weren't ashamed of it, were proud to have survived it, and made no attempt to put it behind them. Instead they kept it humming in the foreground of their life.

They named it The Crisis. They referred to it openly and constantly. Sebastien might ask, "You know that café in the Latin Quarter? The one where the coffee is so rich because they have not rinsed the urns in a hundred years? When was the last time we went there, *mon chaton?*" Ben would answer, "Oh, we haven't been in a long time. Not since before The Crisis." Or Sebastien might hold his nose and say, "What on earth are you cooking, *mon chaton?* It stinks worse than I did during The Crisis." Even Glo got in on it. One night at Café Valentin, the two men were giddy and giggling after consuming a carafe of brandy. Glo clucked her tongue and said, "Lord have mercy. Y'all freeloading more booze than you did before The Crisis. And that's saying something."

The Crisis empowered them. To both it was a trophy, a shiny, tangible prize to clinch to their chests and admire, each proud of the achievements it represented: to Ben, his overdue selflessness; to Sebastien, corporeal proof that the poet loved him.

An exclusionary love. Each reserved himself strictly for the other, sexually and otherwise. They set themselves apart from everyone. Except for Glo, and Norman maybe, neither had any friends. They were very lonely. But it was a collective loneliness that they endured together, as a unit. They accepted it. It hurt at times, but it suited them; suited their solitary natures, the solitary requirements of their art. They cultivated it, molded their loneliness into their own intimate work of art. They would both have been lonely anyway, had each been on his own. It was better to be lonely together. It was easier. They exiled themselves, cut the world out of their lives, their lives out of the world. Couldn't help it. It was who they were. And exile allowed for exclusive, consummate, dangerous investment in each other. They wanted that. They loved that.

Castaways, they had set up camp on an island of contentment.

And yet, these dreams.

Maybe they had begun because he'd kept little Katherine to himself all these months, stashed away from Sebastien and from Glo, like a picture in a locket. Maybe she'd grown so large and lively that she had to fly out, and Ben's dreams were her pilot. They tortured him, but he was indebted to them: They granted him the only means of seeing his child. She wouldn't let go. Her pastel heat also laughed in his blood.

*Happy?* Norman had asked.

Another sip of whiskey. Another hard pull of reefer.

A pair of arms hugged him from behind.

"I am worried about you," Sebastien said, his night voice soft cotton in Ben's ear, his bare chest warm and a bit stubbly against Ben's naked back. He'd put on weight, was sturdier than before The Crisis. Though still slim and svelte, the nooks and crannies on his body were filling in. His meatier chest was good on Ben's back.

"You have not been sleeping well," Sebastien said. "You have not slept well in a while." He took the reefer, dragged on it, took a sip of Ben's whiskey. "Your parents' death is an awful wound. It will not heal quickly. Still, I worry."

They passed the reefer back and forth and finished it off. Sebastien took Ben's hand to lead him back to their bedroom.

"If you had other family," Sebastien said, "perhaps that would ease your pain."

The reefer put him to sleep, planted a new dream in his head. Not a full-grown dream, more like an impression:

A living room. Him and Ruby. Baby Katherine in Ruby's arms. Ruby handing her, giving her, to Ben.

The impression blacked out.

# 54

"Glo, you think Sebastien's strong?"

They were having coffee-gin at her place. His question seemed to stun her.

"Don't tell me he done got caught up in that opium mess again," she said.

"No! No."

"Oh. Well. Sebastien's a good man. Kind. Talented. And, sugar, I know he loves you."

"Ain't what I asked you," Ben said. "Kindness and talent and love ain't the same as strength." He looked at her, hard, and repeated his question through teeth he didn't mean to clench. "Do you think he's strong?"

She looked alarmed. As if an imposter had suddenly replaced her best friend. She didn't answer.

"Glo! This is important. Do you think . . . do you think he'd be all right without me?"

Her alarm faded, replaced with her authoritative no-nonsense. "What the fuck is this about? You been acting strange lately. Quiet, distant. You tell Glo what's going on. Right now, you hear?"

He did.

All she could say was, "Lord, Lord, Lord, Lord, Lord."

"Fatherhood was so far down on my list of wants," Ben said, "it might as well have been buried in a hundred-foot-deep grave. But I *am* a father. And I love her. I ain't never seen my little girl but, Glo, I love her. *My daughter.*"

"Lord, Lord, Lord, Lord, Lord."

When she stopped Lording, Glo, in low notes of warning and fear, said, "Benjy. You ain't thinking what I think you're thinking. Is you?"

Last night's dream-impression replayed in his head for the hundredth time, the images not washed out and no less fresh for all the replaying. "She's mine, Glo."

"No, sugar. She *ain't* yours. She belongs to Ruby Tate and her husband."

"Not if I go back and say I want her. They'd *have* to give her to me."

She got in his face, took him by his shoulders, and shook him. "You stupid, stupid, stupid man!" She spat the words so hard, his face was wet. "You think it's gonna be that easy? You think you'll just walk into Ruby Tate's house, say, 'I want my daughter,' and she'll hand her right on over? Hell, sugar, if you think that, you're worse than stupid. You're plain silly."

"It can happen. I got the law on my—"

"Did Angeline tell that woman about you? About *why* you left? Who you left her for?"

It sunk in all at once. And slapped down all his hopes. Ben threw himself on the sofa. He drank the last sip of his coffee, then refilled the cup to the rim with straight gin.

"And even *if* you was to go through with this cockamamie plan," Glo said, "and even *if* some miracle happened and you got Katherine—then what? Stay in the States? What about Sebastien? You gonna bring him over there, too, and the three of you, what, live together? Like a family? Or you bring Katherine to Paris and what? You and Sebastien raise her? Together?" She laughed. A scornful laugh with teeth. "I can see it now: a colored man and a white man living together and raising a child. Sugar, that's too modern, even for Paris. And sure as fuck too goddamn modern for America."

She dropped into a chair, breathing hard, exhausted.

They didn't speak. They didn't look at each other.

Ben was angry. At Glo for being unkind and right. At himself for letting dream-impressions govern him; for allowing a child thousands of miles distant, whom he'd never met, wrap him body, heart, and soul around her darling little finger.

He drank his gin. His lungs screamed for smoke, but he had neither cigarettes nor reefer with him. Glo might, but he refused to talk to her right now.

Katherine versus Sebastien. Ben loved them both, wanted them both. He'd agonized at the injustice of having to choose one at the expense of the other. Glo's unkind logic rendered the choosing moot.

But since little Katherine couldn't have her daddy, at least Sebastien would keep his lover.

He finished off the gin, got up to go, decided he wouldn't say good-bye to Glo.

"Didn't want to be harsh," she said. "But you know Glo: She gotta tell it like it is."

She tried to hug him. He wouldn't let her.

"All right, Benjy. You can be that way for now. Ain't the first time you got mad at Glo for telling the truth. I understand. Hurts when someone tells you something you don't want to hear. Hurts the one telling it, too. You go on home. You go home to your man, you hear?"

# 55

Petals

By Benjamin Marcus Charles

Scatter petals over a grave.
Watch them flicker on the air,
    weightless,
Before settling.
Angelic flecks of color
Adorning the loamy soil.

Or spread them amidst the plaits
Of your pretty-girl hair
Where they will glow in the dark
Of our separation like a beacon
That could lead me to you.

Would you love me?
Am I worthy of you?
Am I worthy?
Would you watch as my sins
Put me on trial
And the verdict bloodies me?

344 • *Joe Okonkwo*

You, my ultimate juror,
You alone could shatter or redeem me.

The petals in your hair
Will age, wilt, die,
As you wither into the mire of
    adulthood,
As these poems gray and wrinkle.

*I love you.*
I exhale,
And a breeze blows a petal from your
    hair.
*I dream you,*
And the moon weeps jazz.

# 56

He refilled Norman's drink. "Sure am gonna miss you, Norm. Montmartre won't be the same."

Norman was packing up and moving back to the States.

"Think you'll ever come back?" Ben said.

"Nah. Had a good run in France. No need to come back."

It was early and dead at Café Valentin. One of two quiet periods that would bookend the June night. Glo and company hadn't done their thing yet.

"Ever think about home?" Norman said.

A picture of Katherine leapt into his head. An imagined picture. *Damn that Ruby Tate for not sending a photograph.* "All the time, Norm. All the time."

"Think you'll ever go back?"

The picture lingered. Pigtail braids with ribbons. A pinafore (did colored girls wear pinafores?). A runny nose. Knees scraped during a playful fall. "Don't know."

"That's probably 'cause you don't . . . well . . . you ain't got people no more. If you had people you loved, you'd think about going back. You'd have to, right?"

It bothered him, not having a photograph, trying to assemble a whole picture of his baby from imagined parts. And her name irritated him. *Katherine* was fine—it was actually beautiful, had to give Ruby credit for that—but Tate?

Katherine Tate. Kathy Tate. Kate Tate.

He loathed the staccato chilliness of each version.

Glo had warned him to forget her; trash the dreams; live for Paris, poetry, and Sebastien.

He dreamed the other night that he heard Katherine crying. The dream contained no visual, just the sound, and he woke up. Call. And response.

While Norman drank and babbled on about his return home, Ben tried a different name variation.

*Katherine Charles.*

Now, *that* had the warmth of home, the youthful grace of a newborn poem.

Norman finished his drink, said his good-byes. Said he was sailing in a couple of days, probably wouldn't see Ben again before that. Probably wouldn't see Ben again ever.

The evening progressed as evenings at Café Valentin did. It got busy. Ben dashed about. Glo and company did their thing. Prostitutes. Dealers. After-midnight music. The place got slow, then slower, then closed. Ben said good-bye to Glo and went home.

Sebastien was still at work, wouldn't be home for a bit, but Ben didn't feel alone. Sebastien permeated the apartment. His paintings. His scent. The scent of his paints. All tangible. All things Ben could see, touch, smell, identify. They were real. They were immediate. Not imagined or fantasized or invented or wished for. He had them. They were his. Whenever he wanted them. He owned them.

*Katherine. Katherine Charles.*

She existed, but was not much more than fantasy. She lived and breathed, but was more theory than reality. Katherine was a small piece of him. A small piece of his folks and Emma Jane and Li'l Jerry. Having her would be like having them. And having them would be wondrous. He missed them. Katherine was his only and final chance at having his family again. She was part of him, and separate. Like the moon was formed from and separate from earth, but still within earth's line of thought.

He had considered writing Ruby and asking for a photograph. Would he be disappointed if the cheeks and lips and eyes in the picture didn't match the perfection in the dream-impressions?

No. He wouldn't be.

Katherine may have been the moon, out there, separate, but Sebastien was his mirror-hemisphere, here, on earth. Ben knew his terrain, his euphoric cliffs and devastating valleys; had swum in his sweet, cold streams and been trapped in his ruthless deserts. Sebastien's terrain was Ben's now, too. He put his lips to it, kissed its ground, tasted the soil. It was home.

Katherine pulled him. But so did Sebastien. He loved her. He loved Sebastien just as endlessly. But this was where the difference lived between his daughter and his lover: His lover loved him back. Could he give up a lover who loved him back for a daughter who didn't?

No. He couldn't.

He would always have the moon, whether it was full or half or quarter-sliced. It would always be up there, in his line of thought. He would always love it.

# 57

"It is a very beautiful night. The sky so black. The stars. The night is like . . . like . . . diamonds scattered across a black velvet dress."

"Oh. So poetic. I thought *I* was the poet here. You trying to take my job?"

"We can switch jobs, every now and then, *mon chaton.* Have you ever tried painting?"

"No. You wouldn't want me to. Not unless you want nothing but bad splotches on the canvas. That I can do. Have you ever tried writing poetry?"

"I think I just did. *Diamonds scattered across a black velvet dress. A good start, n'est pas?*"

"I hope it's just a start and not the end result. Diamonds scattered on a black dress? *Mon dieu . . .* It *is* a beautiful night, though."

*Silence. Stillness. Interrupted here and there by the chirp of a cricket. Then stillness again.*

"Why do you like it here so much, *mon chaton?* This is your favorite place, I think."

"*Oui. Il est.* I love it here. This view—doesn't it speak for itself? At heart I'll always be a kid from Dogwood, Georgia. To anybody in Dogwood, this would be the tip-top of the whole world. And guess who's here—little Ben Charles. No other Negro from Dogwood has ever been here or seen this. Likely they never will. But *I'm* sitting right here. And I'm ... I'm not going anywhere. ... What's your favorite place, Sebastien? I don't think you ever told me."

"My old room. It was rundown and decrepit. But it was the first thing in my life that was mine, that I earned and paid for, that wasn't handed to me."

"That makes sense. But I hope you like your new room a little better."

*Sebastien kisses Ben. Stillness. Chirping.*

"We should go somewhere. A vacation. You know what my first and only vacation was? The trip over here on the ocean liner. A whole week of nothing to do. I had never done that before. It didn't feel right."

"Where would you like to go?"

"England. Italy. Maybe Germany."

"I see. All of the countries that Baby Back visited during his tour."

"Goddamn it, Sebastien. I don't believe you. Still jealous, after everything."

"No. I am not jealous. I am realistic. You and that man—"

"There is no *me and that man*. There is only you and me. I can't believe ... It looks like we still have a lot of work to do."

"There will always be work to do, *mon chaton*. We are lovers and artists. The work never ends."

"No, it doesn't. And it's never perfect."

"And there is always something more that can be done."

"Always something that can be improved."

*Quiet. A slice of moon in the sky.*

"Sebastien?"

"Yes?"

"I still want to go on a vacation. It doesn't have to be those countries. It can be anywhere. I just want to go somewhere. I'm so curious."

"We will ... I'm sorry. For being jealous. I know that Baby Back is ... that you no longer love him. I know you love me. But sometimes ... lately ... it feels ... when we are together, you are not ...

present. You are not *with* me. You and Baby Back share a bond. So
I wondered . . ."

"Don't wonder. Don't."

*Quiet.*

"Where else would you like to visit, *mon chaton?*"

"Egypt, for the pyramids. Russia, to see what all this Bolshevik
stuff is about. Japan and China, because they're just so far away.
How about you?"

"You are going to kill me. Or accuse me of being a cliché Frenchman, like you did that first night at Café Valentin. I want to go to
Harlem."

"Ugh."

"Because I love jazz and Negroes, yes, I admit it. And I want to
see where you are from."

"I'm from Dogwood, Georgia."

"*D'accord.* Fine. Then I want to see it because you lived there. I
want to see the place that fills and influences so much of your poetry. Ahhhh. You are not protesting now. Since my desire to see
Harlem has to do with *you.*"

"Maybe we'll go one day. Maybe. I'd like you to see it. Yes. I've
seen Paris. It's only fair that you should see Harlem. And I could . . .
catch up with old acquaintances."

"Do you keep in touch with anyone there?"

*Ben looks over the city, up at the slice of moon.*

"No. Not really."

"Not with Angeline?"

"No."

"You are still angry at her."

"No. Not anymore."

*Quiet.*

"Are you starting a new painting?"

"*Oui.* But not yet. I am finishing up that commission. It should
be done in a day or two. Then I want to begin a new portrait of
you."

"I never . . . I never thanked you for the first one."

"Ben, you do not have to thank me."

"Yes, I do. It changed how I look at myself. How I see myself. Never thought I was much to look at till that portrait. Until you, I never thought I was much, period. So, *merci, mon cher.*"

*He kisses Sebastien.*

"And you? New poems?"

"Always."

*Quiet. The flickering lights. The sliced-up moon. Ben and Sebastien. Sitting on the portico of this church. The highest point in Paris. Holding hands. Ben's leg draped over Sebastien's. Sebastien's head making a bed of Ben's shoulder.*

*Quiet.*

"Oh. This new portrait of me. Nude?"

"Of course nude. Silly."

# ACKNOWLEDGMENTS

Special thanks to my workshop colleagues and professors at City College of New York, where I did my Creative Writing MFA and where much of this book was workshopped. Feedback, tough love, and support from certain folks were especially helpful: Professor Salar Abdoh, Professor Linsey Abrams, Brian Brennan, Scott Cerreta, Dan Cicala, Jonathan Gabay, John Gregory, Regina Jamison, Lisa Ko, Sharae Allen Martin, Ben Nadler, Jennifer Sabin, Jordan Schauer, Emily Vient, Anna Voisard, and Justin P. Williams. Particular thanks to Professor Keith Gandal for teaching me about the "micro level" and for telling me what I didn't want to hear, which made me a better writer.

Thanks to my agent, Malaga Baldi, and also to my editor, John Scognamiglio, for believing in this book.

Thanks to Mama and Iris for always believing in me and to David Eye for his friendship and support.

A number of books were instrumental in researching and being able to write about the Harlem Renaissance and Jazz Age Paris: *When Harlem Was in Vogue,* by David Levering Lewis; *Paris Noir: African-Americans in the City of Light,* by Tyler Stovall; *Negrophilia: Avant-Garde Paris and Black Culture in the 1920s,* by Petrine Archer-Straw; *The Harlem Renaissance: Hub of African-American Culture, 1920–1930,* by Steven Watson; *A History of Homosexuality in Europe, Volume I,* by Florence Tamagne; *The Big Sea,* by Langston Hughes; *Harlem in Montmartre,* by William A. Shack; *The Sway of the Grand Saloon: A Social History of the North Atlantic,* by John Malcolm Brinnin; *Bricktop,* by Bricktop and James Haskins; *Josephine: The Josephine Baker Story,* by Jean-Claude Baker and Chris Chase; *Jazz Cleopatra: Josephine Baker in Her Time,* by Phyllis Rose; *Underneath a Harlem Moon: The Harlem to Paris Years of Adelaide Hall,* by Iain Cameron Williams; and *The Portable Harlem Renaissance Reader,* edited by David Levering Lewis.

# JAZZ MOON

## Joe Okonkwo

## ABOUT THIS GUIDE

The suggested questions and playlist are
included to enhance your group's reading
of Joe Okonkwo's *Jazz Moon*.

# Discussion Questions

1. Ben engages in a number of intimate/romantic relationships over the course of the novel. Is there a common thread that runs through these relationships? Is there any kind of progression? How do his emotional needs and his perspectives on relationships change over time?

2. How do art/creativity influence or shape the events in the novel?

3. How is Ben's move from Dogwood to New York similar to his move from New York to Paris? How is it different?

4. How is nightlife in Paris different from nightlife in Harlem? How is it similar?

5. The racism that Ben encounters in France differs greatly from the racism he encounters in the United States. In what ways does French racism manifest itself?

6. What makes Harlem a good place to be? What makes it a not-so-good place to be?

7. What role does sex play in the story and how does it shape the story's events?

8. After the breakup with Baby Back, Ben spends a great deal of time in the "shadows." How does it hurt him? How does it help him?

9. What influence do women have on the events in this story?

10. In what ways does the voyage on the *Bonaparte* prepare Ben for Paris? How does the voyage shape his expectations of Paris and how does it affect his relationship with Baby Back?

11. What is the significance of color—racial and otherwise—in the novel?

# Jazzing the Moon:
## A Harlem Renaissance Playlist

**"I'm Just Wild About Harry"**
By Eubie Blake and Noble Sissle, from the musical
*Shuffle Along,* 1921

**"Charleston"**
By James P. Johnson, from the musical *Runnin' Wild,* 1923

**"Riverside Blues"**
By Thomas A. Dorsey and Richard M. Jones
Performed by Joe "King" Oliver's Creole Jazz Band, featuring
Louis Armstrong. Recorded 1923

**"St. Louis Blues"**
By W. C. Handy
Sung by Bessie Smith; Louis Armstrong: trumpet. Recorded 1925

**"Shake That Thing"**
Sung by Ethel Waters. Recorded 1925

**"Black Bottom Stomp"**
By Jelly Roll Morton
Performed by Jelly Roll Morton's Red Hot Peppers.
Recorded 1926

**"Creole Love Call"**
Written and performed by Duke Ellington and Adelaide Hall.
Recorded 1927

**"Empty Bed Blues"**
By J. C. Johnson
Sung by Bessie Smith. Recorded 1928

**"How Much Can I Stand?"**
Sung by Gladys Bentley. Recorded 1928

**"West End Blues"**
By Joe "King" Oliver
Performed by Louis Armstrong and His Hot Five. Recorded 1928

**"Gimme a Pigfoot"**
Music and lyrics by Wesley Wilson
Sung by Bessie Smith. Recorded 1933